PENGUIN
MURDER

Jeanne Cambrai was born in Sri Lanka. She did her schooling in Kodaikanal, India, and since the late forties has lived in England, Colombia and the United States working as a secretary, running a photography studio and writing. Her published books include *Mother and Child*, *Horses of the West*, *San Francisco after Dark*, and *It's a Sunny Day on the Moon*, a collection of short stories for which she won the 1998 Grataien Prize for Writing in English by a Sri Lankan. She lives in Kotadeniyawa, Sri Lanka.

Murder in the Pettah

Jeanne Cambrai

PENGUIN BOOKS

Penguin Books India (P) Ltd., 11 Community Centre, Panchsheel Park, New Delhi 110 017, India
Penguin Books Ltd., 80 Strand, London WC2R 0RL, UK
Penguin Group Inc., 375 Hudson Street, New York, NY 10014, USA
Penguin Books Australia Ltd., 250 Camberwell Road, Camberwell, Victoria 3124, Australia
Penguin Books Canada Ltd., 10 Alcorn Avenue, Suite 300, Toronto, Ontario, M4V 3B2, Canada
Penguin Books (NZ) Ltd., Cnr Rosedale & Airborne Roads, Albany, Auckland, New Zealand
Penguin Books (South Africa) (Pty) Ltd., 24 Sturdee Avenue, Rosebank 2196, South Africa

First published by Penguin Books India 2001

Copyright © Jeanne Cambrai 2001

All rights reserved

10 9 8 7 6 5 4 3 2

This is a work of fiction. Names, characters, places and incidents are either the product of the author's imagination or are used fictitiously, and any resemblance to any actual person, living or dead, events, or locales is entirely coincidental.

Typeset in Sabon by Mantra Virtual Services, New Delhi

Printed at Baba Barkha Nath Printers, New Delhi

This book is sold subject to the condition that it shall not, by way of trade or otherwise, be lent, resold, hired out, or otherwise circulated without the publisher's prior written consent in any form of binding or cover other than that in which it is published and without a similar condition including this condition being imposed on the subsequent purchaser and without limiting the rights under copyright reserved above, no part of this publication may be reproduced, stored in or introduced into a retrieval system, or transmitted in any form or by any means (electronic, mechanical, photocopying, recording or otherwise), without the prior written permission of both the copyright owner and the above-mentioned publisher of this book.

For
Sally and Arj
the wedding present I promised you before
Ushi, Sanjiv, Rhenu, Priya, Ayesha, Minu, Anushka,
Chloe and Amrit were born

Chapter I

A Body in the Pettah
Dorothy Bell was found dead in the Pettah.

The Pettah is one of the oldest sections of Colombo and no stranger to murder. Behind locked doors the wholesale gem trade does its business and all manner of other high-finance legal and illegal operations have been run for hundreds of years. It is said that you can buy anything you want there if you know which turn to take on which alley, and whose name to call outside which room on which floor. There is a bright front of shops on the narrow streets that become crammed with pedestrians and vehicles and slimy with litter by midmorning. Local residents only go to the Pettah when it is unavoidable, but guidebooks make it sound deliciously exotic. It has, after all, Hindu kovils, Buddhist pansalas, Catholic churches and Muslim mosques—all of great antiquity. It has the Dutch museum, the bus terminal, the train terminal and fireworks shops. No tourist leaves the country without having taken on the Pettah by foot, but only once and always during the day.

At night few venture into the Pettah, for then it becomes as friendly as a cemetery. It was inconceivable that Dorothy would voluntarily have gone there alone at night.

'Someone killed Dorothy Bell last night,' CV heard Maggie's voice say. They'd been at a party the previous night so seven was too early a wake-up call, he felt. Then, he was hit by the impact of what she'd said.

'Someone killed Dorothy?'

'Looks that way.'

Maggie wore no make-up, had dark rings under her eyes and was wrapped in a faded cotton dressing gown; the soles of her feet turned towards him were dirty. Her voice was as slack. 'Amily listens to the early Sinhala radio news. She'd heard us talking about Dorothy, so she came up and woke me with the news.' Amily was their aunt's cook.

'Our Dorothy is not murderable. It must be another Dorothy.'

'No. The news guy said Dorothy Bell.'

'How come the only comment I can think of is "Oh my God"?'

'That's the thing. She was found knifed in the Pettah. She wasn't at the Gallery last night because of that opening at the Mount. What was she doing in the Pettah?'

'It's crazy.'

Later what came to disturb CV about Dorothy's murder was that it did not seem Lankan in style. The country has a high murder rate and one of the highest suicide rates in the world, but its murders are invariably murders of passion. Dorothy's killing had not followed a fight of any kind, she had not been raped, she had not been beaten, she had one bruise that she could have got anywhere. She had she died from a single knife wound.

Because she was English and her death was not related to the war, it became front page news. Sri Lanka was in a civil war now well into its second decade, but the Colombo socialites who referred to themselves as *our crowd* were physically untouched by it. A few days earlier the Tamil Tigers had attacked a government outpost in the northeast and more than three hundred rebels had been killed. There were photos of soldiers weeping to see they had mowed down girls too young to have breasts and tousle-haired boys who looked like their own younger brothers. Children were abducted from homes in and around the war areas to fill out the depleted Tigers' ranks and take the early fire. Yet the images of these dead children had not stirred Colombo's socialites as Dorothy's death did. Their lazy twinkling eyes fronted minds now serenely anaesthetized against distant horrors. Dorothy had, however, been one of them. She who had seemed invulnerable would never dance for them, drink with them or whisper innocent mischief in their ears again. She could have been in the wrong place at the wrong time—if not, her assassin could be one of them.

The Bet
CV, a Sri Lankan Dutch Burgher by birth, was on the island at the time of Dorothy Bell's murder because of a bet. His college education had been in the States, where he used his computer skills working on contract. He would come into a company, reorganize a system or set one up, and then go elsewhere to deal with a new set of problems. His last job had been in Chicago, and it brought into his life a red-haired programmer named Della Marsh. Their affair turned sour when he realized he could never spend the rest of his life with her. It had not been easy to break up with Della without looking like 'a bastard who had used her just for sex', her words when she threw him out of her high-tech apartment. Nor would she let him forget she felt she had been dumped. So an initially happy work experience became a torture, and when it finally came to an end with a farewell office party to him, he felt such deep relief that he hugged Della, who responded by calling him a compulsive worker who was letting real life pass him by. He was somewhat drunk and replied, 'You curled your lip! I've always wanted to see a woman curl her lip. Do it again.' And he was guiltily pleased at the general laughter and her flush of rage.

But, to his surprise, an older woman he admired took her side. 'You men can woof and pant and wag your tails, but Della's dead right,' she scolded. 'Jobs are not the big picture. You lugheads who laughed will have to get in touch with your big pictures sooner or later if you don't want to go through your whole life feeling something is missing. You need to be inactive for the spiritual jolt to hit. No jolt, no Nirvana! And CV, you are never inactive.'

He replied, 'Bubble talk. It so happens I have a big picture which is to become financially independent quickly and then continue doing what I am now at a leisurely pace until, like the equipment I recommend be phased out, I too become obsolete'.

'And then?'

'And then I return to being a Lotus Eater. I come from Sri Lanka, the land of the Lotus Eaters, so I'm a natural. I'm not a compulsive worker. I just do things fast. I brush my teeth fast, put my shoes on fast, eat fast, work fast. You've only seen me on the job. Off it I'm a slug. My big picture is to end up a turtle on a Lankan east coast beach.'

To which Della had replied, 'I'll bet you $200 that you can't spend even six months in Sri Lanka not working.' The words *six months* caught his attention.

The previous evening his cousin Maggie had phoned from Australia to say she needed a break from the fashion world and asked if they could spend a few weeks together.

He had never heard her so agitated.

'Take a deep breath, Mag. What's really bugging you?' he asked.

'My age,' and she had begun to cry. 'I'm only thirty-three, and it's nothing but diet, exercise and looking at my skin through a magnifying glass. So I'm going to stay with Aunt Maud for six months in Sri Lanka because she says it's lovely being eighty-two, and I need to be around someone like her. Six months is as long as I can be away from the cameras at my age, my agent says. I'm still popular, but six months is the max. Until then I have magazine features coming up, so my face will be out there even if I'm not. It's now or never. You're Aunt Maud's favorite still, her darling boy. You know she'd love it if you came.'

'Of course I will—maybe for a week or two.'

Maggie had said 'six months in Sri Lanka', and Della now said 'six months in Sri Lanka'. He had been brought up to believe that when two people use the same words to you, God or one of his deputies is talking.

'The spiritual jolt is here,' he told Della, 'Two hundred bucks it is. I'm going to take six months off in Sri Lanka.' Other employees came in on the bet. The final toll was $1,200 against him.

He emailed Maggie, 'I'm on for six months too.'

She wrote back within the hour, 'I love you, CV.'

Della caught sight of her name on his computer screen and said, 'The Maggie vander Marten? She loves you?'

'Yeah, she's my cousin. I didn't tell you?'

'No, you did not, and you know you did not.'

And a week later , Della spent one last night with Maggie vander Marten's cousin and then drove him to O'Hare International Airport. His last sight of her was of a tired face with a glued-on smile under lustreless red hair. Behind an airport barrier, he thought, Della can look positively vulnerable. Having nothing particular to do in Lanka, however, palled fast. He had been unprepared, too, for the intellectual numbness of some of his old friends—he presumed from living in an endless war they couldn't see or feel. When he asked why they didn't volunteer to fight and end this war faster, they looked at him as if he was mad. The fact was, most Lankans had their war thrust on them, and fighting wars was not their style.

Dorothy

The media described Dorothy Bell as an unmarried twenty-three-year-old English woman with an out-of-date visa, as if that made her a suspicious person. It was not, however, uncommon for visitors to the island to ignore the dates on visas. The lapse and immigration would see no reason to extradite someone who was already extraditing herself. Dorothy would have had her excuse ready: she had become ill with malaria, filarial, dengue, encephalitis or dysentery. In the trauma, she would have explained, she had forgotten all about the deadline.

CV had met Dorothy—if their brief encounter could be called a meeting—at one of the first parties he and Maggie had been invited to. They had grabbed chairs in the garden where a small band was setting up. She was, as usual, quite comfortable with the stares and isolation her fame had brought her. Quite suddenly a young blonde who was passing turned and abruptly sat on CV's lap to inspect her smoothly tanned calf saying, 'Sorry. I'll be up in a sec.'

He decided not to reply, 'So will I,' and responded, 'My lap is your lap. Use it as long as you like.'

'American?' she had asked without turning.

'Yeah. Dutch Burgher and American.'

'I've got a mosquito bite!' she exclaimed, and she scratched at her leg with sensual pleasure. Her moving around was doing a lot for him too.

He later remembered Dorothy had not perched but plonked down firmly and pressed back against his stomach moving her rear end to get comfortable with the not unexpected result. Not a shy girl, definitely. Her very short dress had ridden up, and he was not sure whether it was her underwear pressed against him or her naked crotch. He began to wonder if this was her way of saying she'd like to make his acquaintance, but she answered that by leaving suddenly with a 'thanks' and without a backward glance. As he watched her depart, someone called, 'Dorothy!' and she turned. He could see she wore no bra over attractively firm breasts and that the stretch fabric of her brief dress was thin enough for her nipples to show through. He cursed himself for not having prolonged her stay. She was laughing as she leaned forward to hear what was being said, listened carefully and forward to hear what was being said, listened carefully and laughed again. While she did this, he thought she glanced his way.

Maggie had been rolling a joint when Dorothy Bell had placed her shapely backside against what, as a child, CV had been taught to call his front, and she glanced at it now and giggled. She said loudly, for the music had been rising in pitch, 'That's her boyfriend,' and pointed out Michael Blue, a Sri Lankan with long dark hair who was playing the drums with little talent. The other three men were having better success on electric guitars and an electric keyboard, but the amplified sound they were making together was horrible.

Michael Blue was dressed in shiny peacock-blue pants, a scarlet shirt and a large pawnshop-type chain with a pendant. His straight black hair was brushed away from his forehead and hung to his shoulders. He had the chiselled good looks of a Native American: a noble face with a straight nose, Mongolian lidless eyes and a wide shapely mouth. His eyes were on Dorothy. She came up beside him and spoke in his ear. He smiled, and his face softened. CV, aware of his own much bulkier body, receding hairline and generally unkempt appearance, promptly gave up on her. But he kept coming back to why she had sexually aroused him, a stranger, in full view of a man she loved—besides others who must have seen the encounter. If he had tried to keep her on his lap—what then? Thank God Maggie ferreted gossip so effortlessly, he thought, and thank God she had stopped him from making a fool of himself. But it had been a surprise to hear that the blonde and Michael Blue were a couple. CV had seen the guy before and had thought he was a homosexual for he had had his arm around another man's shoulder. It was not the first time he'd made snap judgments about hetero men, and he silently chastened himself for it. 'Michael is not only a musician,' Maggie shouted above music that had become deafening, 'but an artist.'

'I know,' he yelled back. 'There was an article about him in

Jeanne Cambrai

Asia Week or *Newsweek* some years ago.'

'I only read fashion magazines,' she screamed and grinned and reached over to ruffle his hair. 'Paul knows Michael. They were in kindergarten together.' Paul was her younger brother. 'Paul was here last year and said a rich English girl was in love with Michael. Paul said he liked her, but he called her a bit of a tart, so I knew that even before she tried to rape you.'

'*Tart* is a word men call women who have a lifestyle like their own. What would Paul say if someone called him a tart?'

'I'm so proud of you when you say things like that, CV,' yelled the much-married Maggie who had complained only yesterday that since her return she hadn't met anyone worth taking her knickers off for. Aunt Maud had heard her and said, 'I hope I heard wrong, Maggie dear.' Maggie had replied, 'I was discussing clothes—which is all we models do.

'Thank goodness,' Maud vander Marten had replied.

CV adored their aunt Maud. In fact just before Dorothy sat on his lap he had been wishing he had stayed home with his aunt, but now he was glad he had not. A nice little something called Dorothy Bell had happened to him and left him lonely for a girl of his own and he liked the sense of adventure he now felt. He looked around to see if there were any more women who would like to talk to him or perhaps sit on his lap, but the few languid beauties without escorts didn't seem his type. Maggie and CV had seen Dorothy two other times, both at night parties where Michael Blue was present. Once or twice CV thought he saw Dorothy looking at him. He liked to watch her surreptitiously, but she hadn't looked his way much. Once she had brushed against his arm, and he wanted to touch her. Now that she was dead he tried to recall her better, but the girl who had pressed her butt against his front had now retreated into a generic image of a fresh-faced blonde. She had definitely been better looking than the smiling picture in the newspaper that made her appear sawtoothed and certainly much better than the after-death shot with slack jaw and open staring light eyes. It was not an unhappy face in death, but he wished the picture had never been published.

The specifics of the tragedy, as they learned quickly, were that her killer had struck only once and pierced her heart. The knife must have been thrust by someone with a professional knowledge of human anatomy. On the night she died, she had dinner with Michael at the Harbour Room on the fourth floor of the Grand Oriental Hotel, known affectionately for generations as the GOH. Dorothy particularly enjoyed the spectacular view of the harbour, so they often ate there. As his van had been out of commission all month awaiting an axle from Singapore, they had arrived by three-wheeler. She then had an appointment at the Oberoi Hotel on the Galle Road, and he had to meet his friend Jimbo Rao at Rosemead Place. As a section of the Galle Road was closed at Temple Trees, the Prime Minister's residence, to save time they took different vehicles. It was not usual for Dorothy to travel alone by three-wheeler at night, but this was not the first time she had done so. No three-wheeler driver had come forward to confirm his story, although one said that a little before eleven that night he had seen Michael Blue standing on York Street in the fort but at the opposite end from the GOH, though Michael insisted they left the hotel at 10.30. 'I was going home,' the man was reported saying. 'I recognized Mr Blue and sounded my horn. He was looking at his feet and did not seem to hear me.' CV had never heard a three-wheeler driver speak English that well but didn't rule out that it was possible.

Michael told the police that he hadn't asked who Dorothy was going to see. He did not even know if she was meeting a man or a woman. It could have been a lead on an apartment in Kandy, which she talked about constantly as an alternative to the heat of Colombo. She had also said something like, 'From the Oberoi I'll get a taxi to the Mount. If I get a too late, I'll go home.' Home, to Dorothy, was Michael's—a house his mother had given him when he was eighteen.

'Dorothy could also have been going with a friend to one of the casinos,' Michael had told the police.

'You didn't ask her who she was going to see so late at night?'

'No,' he had replied, 'It was only her breakfast dates I keep track of.'

'Are you making a joke, Mr Blue?'

'Yes.'

Unconcern about where Dorothy was going, and with whom, was typical of Michael. He never wore a watch and was usually very unpunctual. There was no question, however, of his memory being accurate about when they left the GOH because the waiters in the restaurant said it was some time after ten. Their bill showed they had dined on biryani, vanilla ice cream and chocolate sauce and nuts. They drank beer.

'Michael is vague because he's stoned most of the time. He didn't have to be jealous over her because she was crazy about him,' a friend had told Maggie.

She added to CV, 'He's been on something every time I've seen him. He smokes grass and also opium and probably takes all kinds of other stuff. That crowd does it all.'

'Three weeks after our arrival, and *our crowd* is that crowd?'

'You don't miss a trick do you?'

Dorothy had been killed around midnight. Michael's friend Jimbo Rao told the police they were to have met at ten. At 10.35 when he was about to leave alone, Michael drove up in a three-wheeler, got on the back of the BMW, and they went directly to Mount Lavinia for the opening of a new nightclub called the Red Fox. Jimbo's security guard confirmed their departure time.

'If Mr Rao had not waited for you, how would you have got there, Mr Blue?'

'I would have grown wings and flown.'

'Is that a joke, sir?'

'Yes.'

Several people saw them arriving at the Red Fox. Jimbo left the BMW at the front door, and a bouncer confirmed they arrived at 11.10 and left the Red Fox on the bike at about two. Jimbo dropped Michael and then went to his own home. Both men therefore had airtight alibis, and so did their friends who had been at the Red Fox.

A man like Blue with drug contacts wouldn't find it difficult to hire someone to kill his girlfriend, of course. CV imagined the police had thought of the same thing.

Unexplained was the fact that the Pettah is a half-mile north of the GOH, and the Oberoi is a couple of miles directly south of it. If Dorothy had set out for the Oberoi, she had either changed her mind or someone had changed it for her.

The police had received a phone call from two soldiers at about 2.30 a.m. Their jeep had been making a routine security check of the Pettah's tiny side streets for Black Tigers, the suicide division of the Tigers, who sometimes hid there. The soldiers had turned down Second Cross Street and seen someone asleep on a step. Drunks, prostitutes and derelicts sometimes sleep where they can in the Pettah, but this woman was well dressed and had long blonde hair and fair skin. The solders discovered she was dead.

One English-language newspaper joyously proclaimed, 'Dead Angel found in the Pettah by Soldier', and quoted the driver of the jeep as having said, 'her golden skin was shining like the moon. I thought she was an angel who had fallen from God.'

Amily, Aunt Maud's cook, insisted that the Sinhala radio news story had quoted him more accurately: "In the moonlight we noticed her pure white skin. I stopped and we shone torches on her and could see she was a foreign woman of angelic beauty, modestly dressed from neck to toe. She had golden hair and light eyes and lay on her side as if asleep. We turned her then saw that her eyes were open and that she was dead.'

Dorothy had been wearing baggy white pants, a red blouse and leather sandals, the same outfit she had worn to dinner with Michael. The bloodied red shirt prevented the soldiers from seeing the knife wound at first. One explained on live TV, 'I did not like to touch her body as I am a good Christian boy.'

Aunt Maud said to CV, 'I think, darling boy, that man did think she was an angel.'

Eventually they realized there was much dried blood on the back of her blouse and, overcoming their reluctance to violate her, lifted her shirt and found the knife wound, 'If you don't take the knife out for some time, there'll be very little external bleeding,' a doctor said on television. He thought she must have been killed elsewhere, the knife removed, and later she was dumped on that step for there was no blood on the step.

The multicoloured shoulder bag she had with her at dinner had disappeared.

Speculation ran that the driver of the three-wheeler had robbed and killed her and then dumped her body. The soldiers also assured the police that there had been no bag or knife visible on any street they had driven on that night. At 3.15 the road had been swept, and neither man working the garbage truck on Second Cross Street admitted seeing a coloured fabric bag or knife. There were a few homeless souls sleeping in doorways that night because it had rained. When these regulars were rounded up the following night, however, none was alert enough to remember Thursday evening. The doctor on TV described the weapon that killed Dorothy as being a sharp, long, thin blade that had been thrust with great force, and he was skeptical about the taxi driver-killer theory, saying, 'What thug carries such a knife?' He continued, 'I wasn't there. I don't know what happened, but it looks as though Miss Bell was leaning over when she was stabbed and, if so, probably had no knowledge that she was to be attacked. She might have been about to pick something up from the ground. I personally cannot imagine all this happening in a three-wheeler.'

'What about more than one man attacking her?' The interviewer asked.

'Her knees were not bruised, but her trousers were dirty at the knee. Not road dirt—household dirt. She has a bruise on the side of her neck. She had a knife in the back. I have difficulty seeing this as a gang attack.'

'Did she die instantly from the knife?'

'She bled to death quite quickly.'

All this information was passed around Colombo. On the second day one newspaper said that Dorothy Bell's father was supposed to come to Colombo for a holiday and coincidentally had arrived the morning after she had been killed. Another said he had taken the next available flight to Colombo when he had been told of his daughter's death.

Chapter II

Monday

The Memorial Service

The Monday morning after Dorothy died, CV and Maggie attended her memorial service as there was to be no funeral until the undermanned Colombo police could tie up their investigation. The service was held in a private home off the Galle Road in Dehiwela.

They showed up at ten in Aunt Maud's MG Magnette to find the road to the ocean jammed with parked cars. CV had to leave the Magnette near the railway lines, which ran parallel to the main road. Beyond them was the ocean, grey and mean, for it had rained most of the previous day and night. Even now there was a high wind. They turned to walk back to where other mourners were also being blown out of their carefully combed hair. Naturally, Maggie looked wonderful with her long hair all over the place. CV knew he looked like a turtle trying to shake off wheat chaff.

The road in front of the house was jammed with traffic. A green Mercedes driven by a khaki-uniformed chauffeur was in the wrong lane and head-to-head with a Nissan van followed by seven other vehicles. A military officer in full regalia sat importantly at the back of the Mercedes, which two smaller vehicles had followed. As no car could move in any direction, three drivers were outside their vehicles trying to persuade the

Mercedes and the cars following it to back up.

As Maggie passed the Mercedes, she tapped on its window, which the officer promptly rolled down when he saw her. The air-conditioned cool momentarily enveloped them, and she said to his smiling face, 'It is so hard to have confidence in our military when you officers act like selfish pigs.'

She didn't wait to see how he reacted, and neither did CV. When they got through the gates he said, 'Sometimes you amaze me by doing the right thing.'

They found themselves in a small garden crammed with people. From what they could see of the interior of the airy bungalow it was even more crammed. A white man in a black suit was standing at the front door shaking the hand of each caller. He had silver-grey hair and a smooth elegance in his black jacket, black shirt, black pants and black shoes. Those who had formed themselves into some kind of line looked shabby in comparison—this man's clothes hadn't come off a rack or from a tailor at the end of the road.

Those not in the line had glasses in their hands and stood in groups in the shade of two jacaranda trees. Among them was Michael Blue also entirely in black but without the designer cut.

Waiters wearing white sarongs and black shirts carried trays of food and drink through the side doors.

Maggie led CV indoors stopping occasionally to chat with people they knew. CV merely smiled and said, 'Great to see you,' because he couldn't remember their names. Somehow, she managed to pick up bits of whispered information, and the moment they were in the house she told him that luckily they'd just missed the prayer service held by an Anglican minister who was Michael's mother's uncle-in-law, that Dorothy's father was the white-haired man in black and that the Palace Hotel had catered the event so he must be loaded.

'Do you think they'll have anything as lowly as an arrack and soda?' CV asked his cousin.

Jeanne Cambrai

'Looks as if you could ask for it by brand. Did you see that bar on the veranda? Stay here. I'll get it for you,' and she was away after more gossip, he hoped.

Even on this day of mourning, eyes were on her. She was taller than most of the crowd, which parted for her as if she was Moses, and she suddenly turned and waved. A long arm reached high and, as he waved back, her manicured fingers folded—all but the middle one. He responded in kind. In moments like that she became his ideal woman, and he saddened for as much they had tried they never fell in love.

The question of whether they should marry would not come up this time for he had been watching her get as bored with him as he was with her. Was it possible to love a woman who bored you? Probably not.

Why, he thought with some smugness, I must be the only male here who doesn't see Maggie as a fuckable object, which brought him to Dorothy Bell. She had been a fuckable object, no question. That half-minute on his lap had become an erotically important half-minute now she was dead. The second time he had seen her he had thought her grubby. The clothes she wore were a fraction unwashed for his taste, and she herself was, too. There had also been an anxiety about her expression both those times, he suddenly recalled—as if she was at the same time sure and unsure of herself. But that first time she had shown no anxiety at all; she had ground her rear against him as if it gave her a moment of pleasure to excite a man and leave without even glancing his way.

What if Dorothy's had been an anxiety well founded, he asked himself. What if she suspected she was in danger? If so, why had she momentarily trusted a man who carried a knife and was waiting to slip it between the two ribs he knew were directly behind her heart?

In Sri Lanka deaths are not hidden away. Many of those who attended this service had, like CV and Maggie, come to share Michael's mourning with no need to make an Irish wake of the event on their own behalf. The usual rush for the drinks was to quench thirst, he noticed, and many did not touch the alcohol that had been provided in such abundance. When he tried to hear what was being said around him he found people talking about Dorothy with caring, and, because most didn't know her, tying her death to other calamities by any available thread.

'Remember that foreign woman who was killed as she slept in the Havelock town area?'

'Yes, the gardener who did it only got a thousand rupees. He thought she had more under the bed. Another expat was attacked in De Fonseka Road. As she walked home, a man pulled the gold chain around her neck.'

'It happened right next to where Auntie Irene's car broke down . . .'

At one end of the room hundreds of tiny candles in terracotta pottery bowls had been placed on tables behind which a photograph of Dorothy had been framed in flowers and mounted on the wall. Flower petals were all over the tables. The huge waxy sui, a favourite flower for temple offerings, was in profusion. There were bouquets and wreaths.

The candles depressed CV because he had long given up ritualistic religion, but he went forward to light one anyway only to find Maggie at his side, this time with two glasses of arrack. Side by side they lit their candles, and he stayed a moment longer to look at Dorothy's photograph trying to compare this woman to the one he had seen alive. The paper woman stood before a turquoise ocean and pale blue sky. The flowered sarong secured at her waist billowed to one side. Her round breasts were barely covered by a different flowered fabric knotted between them. Her golden hair, like the sarong, was blowing in the wind. She had been laughing rather self-consciously at the camera as the shot was taken. This was a stranger.

'What do you think of the picture?' he asked Maggie.

'Bad,' she replied. 'But it's probably Michael's favourite because it doesn't look like her. Men are like that.'

'Did you like Dorothy?' He had not asked her that before.

'I did—but what did I know about her? I like vulgar women. At least they're honest.'

She stopped a passing waiter and replaced their empty glasses with full ones. 'Let's go out. It's stuffy in here, and I need a joint.'

'No, you don't,' he said. 'You only think you do.' As the remark could be heard by a man smoking a joint, he continued, 'Pot fouls the lungs and messes with your mind,' and added raising a hand, 'Isaiah 17:8.'

'What else does it say about pot in Isaiah?'

'I've never read Isaiah but wish I had.'

As they moved to the door, Maggie told him that Dorothy's father was English, and her German mother was now married to a Belgian orthopaedic surgeon. She had been too upset to come, 'Poor woman.'

Poor woman, indeed, that German mother to have lost a daughter in such a brutal way—what did it matter which way—to have lost a daughter, period.

Michael and many of Dorothy's friends were standing outside by a large concrete duck on a pedestal on the lawn. The others were sitting on a mat on the grass as if waiting for something to happen. There was a row of tall cannas in bloom behind the group, so it seemed that their heads had potted plants on them.

CV noticed how thin they all were—which made him feel, not for the first time in such company, that he was the only one running to seed young. His lungs, however, were unpolluted, he told himself. Theirs were rotting even if they didn't know it. Michael was particularly glamorous. His black outfit was Turkish in style, and he had another of those heavy pawn-shop chains round his neck—this one with a massive opaque orange stone in a silver setting. He wore cheap dark glasses and moved his body continuously as if trying to get free of his pain, which made his earring swing slowly. He put his joint to his lips as if he hated it. His other hand was around the neck of a beer bottle. CV could not see his eyes but he seemed to be looking their way—at Maggie, probably. For good measure CV waved, and the other man raised his beer in acknowledgement and almost smiled.

Maggie went up to kiss him on both cheeks. CV stood where he was and waited for her return. 'Poor man. Poor man,' she said sadly as she rejoined him and, reaching over, took and drained his glass.

Some of the women around Michael had red eyes—in particular one who had just joined him to whisper something in his ear. Maggie was reciting the names of Michael's retinue and identified the newcomer as Emma, Dorothy's best friend. Emma was blowing her nose with enormous energy on a tissue. She had a large box of them under her arm and passed it around as if it contained hors d'oeuvres. She now searched in vain for a dry spot on a tissue. Then she put it into the pocket of her dress and took another. Emma had the unmistakable look of a Burgher, which only other Burghers recognize. Her Burgherness was in her terrible carriage, her way of moving her shoulders, and in the way she moved her head and eyebrows and chewed her lip. He'd seen her before but without the red nose and swollen eyes and had observed even then she was not making much of some spectacular attributes. She had a cute nose and unusual colouring: green-gold eyes, very fair skin and dark, curly hair. She was slender, he had also previously observed, but extremely short, more than a foot below his own height; no modelling career possible for Emma. She looked appalling now in a coverall brown garment like a Tibetan sheep herder's—one side with a pocket bulging with discarded Kleenex. Her face was blotchy and her lips swollen. But even now, at her worst, she did not have the unwashed look of her late English friend. That was of course part of being a Burgher, his mind complimented. Emma was a girl who wouldn't stop to put on lipstick or comb her hair but would never miss a chance to sit under a tap.

'We Dutch Burghers must be related to ducks,' he said to Maggie. 'See a bucket of water, and in we go.'

She said, 'For God's sake, you're drunk already. Well, why not? I'll get drunk, too. Do you want another arrack and soda?'

'No, I'm not drunk. Alcohol dulls the mind as the prophet Hosea said. Yes, another would be nice—'

Dorothy's father was behaving impeccably, CV noted. He greeted every mourner with grace and detachment—making it clear that he did not wish to make friends but was grateful for each presence nonetheless. One had to marvel at his poise, whereas another man who'd lost his daughter might have gone to the bathroom and wept.

'Thank you so much for coming,' Bell said over and over again, smiling into each person's eyes and pressing each hand warmly. 'Yes, it is a tragedy. Her mother wishes she could have been here.' Then he turned to someone else and said it all over again.

Reginald Bell was probably over forty-five to have had a daughter of twenty-three, so his hair was prematurely white. Even so he looked much younger. His facial skin was smooth and evenly tanned and his nails manicured—no outdoor man here—but his were wide shoulders under the black jacket and narrow hips under the expensive baggy pants. The same garments on CV would have made him look like a whale. Bell was, in fact, much better looking than his daughter. Maybe she had fallen for Michael because he had attributes of her daddy: a similarly chiselled face and equally well-shaped mouth. There was something similar in their style. The arrogance perhaps.

By now Maggie was whispering that Bell was a self-made businessman of some kind, and that he had been bankrolling his daughter in her hippie-style existence in Sri Lanka for three years.

'Michael detests him,' she said.

She was right. You couldn't see Michael Blue's eyes behind his glasses but you could smell his loathing of his host. CV intercepted a moment when the two actually locked eyes and Bell smiled slightly. Michael's lips pressed together but he didn't turn away. The expression in Bell's light eyes then changed—though the smile didn't falter. Then he turned to press another hand, to listen intently to yet another rehearsed speech and to thank the guest for coming.

CV and Maggie joined that line and were now facing Bell so there was no more time for speculation. It was also too late to ditch their glasses as others in the line had somehow done.

'I didn't know Dorothy well but felt I had to come,' CV said moving his drink to his left hand.

'Good of you to come,' Dorothy's father told him, 'It's a tragedy. Her mother wishes she could be here.' Then his eyes moved to Maggie who was about his height, and he looked at the lovely face with the usual double-take.

She put her hand in his and promptly burst into tears and sent her glass in the other hand flying. CV caught it mid-air before it could do more than spill its contents over him. For a moment Bell's cool was shaken and he seemed about to embrace her but recovered quickly. 'I am touched that you care so deeply,' he murmured. 'Do you need a handkerchief?' He forgot to add, 'Her mother wishes she could be here.'

Before she had completed her nod, CV, who was also shocked by her tears, produced a blue handkerchief he had already used from his pants pocket and forced it into her fingers. As he led her away she sobbed, 'Poor man. Poor man,' but out of Bell's earshot, she put the blue handkerchief into her purse and said without a tremor, 'He has a touch of some regional accent. North country, I suppose. I like the Buckingham Palace style, though, don't you?'

'I hate you sometimes Maggie.' Even he, who thought he knew her soul, had not realized the tears had been an act.

'Shhh. He's attractive. He's very attractive.' She looked up at her cousin mischievously. 'And single. That's what I hear.'

'Fuck you.'

'Oh don't. Men flex their muscles and take out their cheque books. Women have to make their opportunities, too.'

'What about trust?'

'He doesn't have to trust me because I don't trust him. His daughter's dead, and he's going through the motions. I want him to give me silk coats and perfume, not trust me.'

'Some men *try* not to show their pain.'

'Drivel. Look at Michael and look at Mr B. One's suffering, the other isn't.'

'Perhaps, but perhaps not. Perhaps Michael is the actor, and Bell is waiting to get away some place where he can fall apart. Maybe the last thing he needs is to get involved with a gold-digger.'

She giggled, 'I've never been a gold-digger and you know it. I just think the man needs cheering up, and I'm the one to cheer him. I'll cheer him up on his yacht, if he has a yacht.'

'So now he's the mourning father? A minute ago he was a cold unfeeling son of a bitch.' But he couldn't shake her good mood.

She said, 'Shhh. I don't want the whole of Colombo to know I'm after him.'

'I hope he's leaving tomorrow.'

'He's not. I've checked. He's staying three more days.'

They were in the house now, and Bell's back was to them as he greeted the mourners who were at last thinning out. She suddenly darted away, and CV was relieved it was to speak to a woman who was standing directly behind Reginald Bell—not to Bell himself.

Maggie said to her in a piercing whisper, 'I've got a bit of a sniffle, Carole, but we've got to get together next week.'

The woman looked confused, as this was Maggie vander Marten claiming friendship. Maggie then began to apologize for not having phoned and said Aunt Maud's phone number clearly. 'Carole, please do try to remember it this time,' she said and repeated it.

Reginald Bell moved slightly to see who had spoken and Maggie only then turned back to CV and whispered, 'Let's go!'

They had to run because the woman she had spoken to had sprung to life, and to cement the unexpected friendship was speeding to their side.

By now he was laughing at Maggie's wickedness, and on the way to the car knew he was no less superficial. Dorothy Bell's death had become the most interesting thing to happen since he arrived in the country, and her memorial service was definitely the most entertaining get-together so far. If that was so, he had been more bored by this indolent lifestyle than he realized, and he wasn't sure how he was going to handle the next five months. He could hardly hope for another foreigner to be murdered just to keep him ticking.

But he was curious about the man Maggie planned to make her lover. When they got back to Aunt Maud's it was nearly lunch time, and he asked if he could use her phone to call the States—reminding her that he'd be reimbursing her for such calls. She said, 'Darling boy, I don't want your money, and if it's an emergency, call now. If not, wait till this evening. After ten the charges drop.'

'Thank you, Auntie. Smart thinking! As Chicago is eleven hours behind us, that would be much more sensible.' Della was always at work by nine.

It was the first night for a long time that they hadn't gone out, as Maggie wanted to be around when Bell phoned. A delighted Aunt Maud persuaded a friend to come over to play bridge. Old Mrs Foenander arrived at seven, and as both she and

Aunt Maud were hard of hearing, their eyesight and memory slipping, and Maggie and he barely knew the game, they had a good time. They played a few more hands after dinner, and CV walked Mrs Foenander home.

He got back at 10.15 and went to the dining room to call Della.

'Have you fallen yet?' she asked.

'If you're referring to our bet, no. If you're referring to the good life, yes.' He imagined her at her desk, mouthing to anyone near it that it was he on the line. 'I'm having a great time,' he lied.

'Then you're calling to say you miss me?' she asked with an artificial chuckle. Yeah, she had an audience.

'That and to ask you a favour.'

'I might have known. Shoot.' There was a pause while she told whoever was listening to get lost as it was a private call.

'Do you still have that friend in the CIA? The one you said can find out anything about anybody provided they've had a credit card or a parking ticket.'

'Helen Portcullis? Yeah, she's in there for life or ten more years, whichever comes first.'

He laughed. 'Del, there's a Reginald Bell here. B-E-L-L. I want to find out more about him. He's English. Moneyed. Daughter Dorothy was found murdered here a few days ago. His ex-wife and her mother is a German married to a Belgian orthopaedic surgeon. The daughter was twenty-three which puts him past forty. Guy is prematurely grey. Five-foot ten. Maybe 160 pounds.

'How's the beautiful Maggie vander Marten? Saw her face staring at me on a newsstand. One of those magazines.'

'As usual.'

'You want the info by fax? Email's too public.'

'I have no fax. Phone, but not too late at night—we're eleven hours ahead of you. My aunt answers the phone in her bedroom.

Don't disturb her,' and after asking after a few people at the office, hoping he'd included whoever had been listening, he said, 'Thanks a lot, honey.'

She said, 'I'm seeing someone else. I thought you should know.'

He wished her well and tried to keep down his pleasure at the news.

'His name is Homer.'

'Well done. He wrote a great book I haven't read.'

He hung up and went to the library to watch some Hindi television. A beautiful Indian girl with snapping hips and enormous kohl-ringed eyes sang, danced and leapt across a green hillside. Also singing, dancing, swinging hips and playing a guitar was an overweight man with a moustache, rolling eyes and wall-to-wall charm—judging from the kohl-eyes' reaction. Maggie joined him, and he said, 'Marvellous Indian women are not prejudiced against fat men.

'Indians know what sex is all about. The *Kama Sutra* is all about "don't ask her if it's the biggest one she's seen".'

'Are you sure it says that? I remember it being about only kissing her thighs on the first date.'

'Maybe there are two parts.'

He leapt off the sofa, rolled his eyes, flipped his hips, jumped up and down and did a few leaps across the rug playing an imaginary guitar in time to the music. 'We don't boast about it, Mag, but we Americans are actually as sensual as the Indians. It's only our moviemakers who go for waterfalls of saliva and pubic hair glimpses on the rug,' and he crashed on to the sofa.

She said, 'He hasn't phoned.'

'Give him a break. The man's mourning his daughter!'

'It's because I'm getting old,' she said and her lower lip shook like a child's.

'We both are. But I can promise you Reginald Bell has

interest in you. When I turned back there he was watching us.'
'Why doesn't he phone, then?'
'I don't know.'

Chapter III

Wednesday

A Phone Call from Della

Reginald Bell hadn't called Maggie by Wednesday. That morning, however, while CV was having an early breakfast alone, the phone rang. He answered it before Amily could get to it. The sound of a voice coming through such an unlikely instrument always brought a primaeval wail from her.

'I phoned you a half-hour back but got some kind of maniac,' Della's clipped voice told him.

'Did you hear this?' he reproduced Amily's cry. She turned to glare at him then stomped off.

Della said, 'Yes. Is it a cockatoo?'

'No, it is Amily. She's more or less normal except in her reaction to phones.'

'Is Emily a relative of yours?'

'Almost. And we say that *Amily* here. We also call fish *peesh*. Amily is the cook and is a great hand at pixing *peesh*.'

He imagined Della's long jaw tightening. She did not approve of household staff—her theory being that you shouldn't live in a home you can't look after yourself. She had never bought his explanation that if you didn't want to do your housework and someone else did, why not? Or that in an underdeveloped country you were being selfish by not hiring people who needed jobs.

She said, 'I'm calling from home. We think the office phones are bugged to keep our personal calls down. Want the dirt on Reginald Bell now?'

'Yes. But I've a question for you. How does Helen get away with passing classified info to her friends?'

'Apparently all high-security organizations are a bit of a joke these days. If high school kids can hack into classified systems, imagine what you and I could do? Helen says mindless loyalty is old hat because we know government officials don't give a shit about what's good for us, just what benefits them. If they have a secret that's not under wraps for national security, it's probably to save their own asses. Helen never leaks important stuff—but she feels she's as qualified as anyone to decide what's important and what isn't. Also, she says, if your pals are leaking, you have to or you'd look like a poor sport.'

He laughed aloud, 'And does Bell have a CIA file?'

'Yes, but not that current and no old parking tickets. Only crises are updated properly. The last Bell entry was made in December—which means he's not currently hot. You want me to read the whole report to you? It will take a while.'

'Nah. Just the highlights.'

'Well, I have everything from his then credit cards—eight; to his net worth—twelve million, give or take a mil; to his health—excellent. He broke an arm skiing once.

'He's an only child. Born in Cumberland, England. He's forty-nine. His father was a mining engineer, his mother a bookkeeper. He was twelve when his maternal grandpa dropped dead in a tour bus in Nairobi and left him enough to go to a public school in Somerset. The grandpa died after a safari, but he got to see the animals first, so the trip wasn't a complete bust. If you want names, places, dates, it's all here. He got good results in O and A. Orthopaedics and Algebra probably.'

'Ordinary Level and Advanced Level. They're exams.'

'You're right! I heard that somewhere. Your future gets

mapped out when you're ten or twelve. There are advantages to living in the great US of A, I can see—you either graduate or you drop out—your choice.'

'That's definitely a good thought.'

'Thank you. There was enough inheritance left over to finance Reginald's first deal: a down payment on an apartment building which he bought and sold while it was being built. He eased into the really big bucks by wheeling and dealing in the value of money. I must try that. You wait till the pound sterling is up and sell—then buy some other currency that's down. Reverse when that currency goes up. Concurrently he bought run-down properties, cleaned them up and sold them. He's more recently concentrated on precious stones. Took time off when he was thirty-one to get a degree in gemology. There's a long list of places he's been stone-hunting—Asia, Africa, South America. He always unloads on Europeans, Arabs or Japanese.'

'He doesn't buy from Sri Lanka?'

'I thought you'd never ask. He's made eight trips there in all. The first was thirty years ago, give or take a year, and the most recent last year. The reason a file was started on him was because he got into a deal with Jimmy Jonas, that southern congressman who had a heart attack on the campaign trail five years back. Fourteen years ago Bell sold a Brazilian emerald to Jonas, and it disappeared within hours. It was a fifty-three-carat stone for which Jonas paid $550,000. Where do congressman get that kind of cash? Ah, I see he got it from the sale of a building he owned. Jonas showed up in the middle of the night at a police station—whacked by a blunt instrument. I didn't know they used words like that outside old movies. I'm paraphrasing this. It goes on and on.'

'I only want the gist.'

Amily was at his elbow with a cup of tea. He nodded his thanks. She scowled. When she left, he pulled a chair to the phone table.

'What's that noise?'

'I'm slurping tea served to me by Amily on her knees—we keep the servants in their place here.'

She made a raspberry and continued to tell him about the missing emerald. He swallowed hurriedly when she stopped.

'Does it say where Bell got that emerald?'

'Bought it legit from a society woman who was selling some big and some little jewels privately. Mystery remains: Where is the emerald? My bet is that it is hidden in Jonas's yard under a rose bush.'

'I don't get the rose bush.'

'Well, that's where I keep my emeralds.' She was delighted with her little joke. He'd almost forgotten, because of their later tensions, what fun she could be.

'Shall I go on?'

'Yeah. And in case I forget to say it later, thank you for all this trouble you're going to, Del. Send me the phone bill as we're running on a bit.'

'When you lose our bet I'll add the charges. To continue: since the congressman fiasco, Bell has kept his nose squeaky clean—but he has never done business in the States again. Also, of recent years, his deals, his women, his everything have been more difficult to trace because, it says here, he probably suspects he's being bugged and is travelling and checking into hotels under different names, which you can't do without false identification.'

'I would, too, if I thought the CIA was noticing me,' he said.

'So would I. Now for his personal life: married Marie Meyerharnish, a German. Divorced. Joint custody but he brought up their three-year-old daughter Dorothy. Marie is not married to a Belgian but to a Dutch orthopaedist who lives in Belgium. Reginald has had the sex life of a rabbit. If you could see the list of women here, you'll know what I mean: he's even hopped on, or under, an English princess and a marchioness. A marchioness? I bet some programmer was just having fun.'

'It's a legitimate title.'

'Oh yeah? How many marchionesses can you name? Don't you want to know which English princess it was?'

'No,' he yelled to stop her. 'Della, who Bell fucks is of no interest to me.' There was something obscene about knowing the names of Bell's bed partners—particularly as one might soon be Maggie.

Della said, 'You're right, CV. That's why I've come to hate you—you're usually right. This report brought out the worst in me at once. I was licking my lips over the princess. Let me hasten along. Drinks but not stupidly. Not a single drunk-driving charge. He smokes cigarettes and cigars. The report also says, and I quote, "Not known to take drugs of any kind," and he doesn't deal them.

'Exercise, other than sex: he likes to work out at a gym and jog, et cetera.

'Presently owns only one home—a flat in Bayswater, London. When travelling prefers good hotels. Sometimes sends for a call girl. The CIA can't leave the sex out.'

It came to CV that the reason Bell hadn't got in touch with Maggie yet might be because he already had an arrangement with a woman through his hotel.

Della said, 'You should know he's not sexually kinky but is no missionary either. The source here is a woman, alias R, who was fed into his bed by the CIA to make a report. He turned down her offer of a twofer with a girlfriend, and she said he's definitely not bi. He said to R, and I quote, "No more suggestions, please. I'll tell you what I want when I want it." What he wanted eventually was two positions and a blow job.'

'Jesus, Della, spare me the details.'

He hadn't wanted to know this much about Reginald Bell. The CIA should have other things to do with his tax dollars than bug men's bedrooms and plant prostitutes. What if Maggie decided to marry the guy?

Della was laughing—cackling: 'You've changed—must be the heat out there.'

He emptied his cup and found he'd made a puddle on the saucer.

'I can hear you slurping again. Where are the pretty manners we observed here, boy? To continue, Reginald Bell's only child Dorothy Mary Bell would be twenty-three. No mention of her death, and there are only a few lines on her. She works for her father. Born in London. Edinburgh University dropout. Ran away from her daddy once when she was thirteen and was brought back the following day by a policeman who saw her crying on a park bench outside their flat. Doesn't mean a thing. I ran away from home when I was eleven because my mother had grounded me—but perhaps Dorothy caught her father playing B'rer Rabbit—could be traumatic for a thirteen-year-old. Is that enough from that section?'

'How do I know?'

'I'll sign off then. He seems a pretty ordinary rich guy, don't you think?'

'Bless you, Del. Would you hang on to it all for a while?'

'Sure will.' Then her voice rose, and she squeaked, 'Don't hang up! I can't believe I nearly forgot that I was keeping the best for last. How did his daughter die? Someone stuck a knife into her back?'

A pounding like he'd only heard about actually started in his ears at her words and left him breathless. He steadied and said slowly, 'As a matter of fact, yes. How did you happen to know that, if there's no mention of her death?'

She gave a groan, 'Jeez, I didn't. I was just trying to be a smart-ass. It says here that in five years four men known to Bell have been assassinated that way. The killer in each case was never found. The knife went clean through two ribs into the heart. Assailant therefore has knowledge of both knives and anatomy. No weapon found but maybe a stiletto was used—then there are some pathology and other reports. The bodies showed no other injuries except for one guy who had old and new bruises—he was a drunk, so the bruises were presumed to be unconnected to his death. By the way, a stiletto is a long thin knife.'

'I've heard of stilettos. I wonder if there's a connection.'

'Of course there's a connection. Five knife-in-the-back deaths and there's no connection? The murdered guys were Vince Belli in Italy and Charles Yarrow, Desmond Crewel and Cruz Iglesias in England. Yarrow and Iglesias were businessmen. Crewel was an odd-job man with a drinking habit, and Belli a student. But the CIA doesn't seem to have got excited about these deaths. I think they only get excited when someone wants them to get excited, or perhaps they killed those men—in which case they killed Bell's daughter, too. I'd better send this to you. Bell had an alibi each time, of course, or he wouldn't be running around Sri Lanka, would he? It's called a weak alibi, but that's not enough to electrocute a man. His alibi was that he was asleep—and it seems that he probably was because people corroborated that he turned in when he said he did and the next morning took his wake-up call. There is absolutely no physical evidence that he did it. No motive. If his daughter's death makes his file soon, I'll get Helen to call.'

'Thanks, Del. Hope Homer is working out. Is he writing another book?'

'No. He's an industrial designer. He wants to marry me,' she said, without enthusiasm.

'I'll be right there, Aunt Maud,' he shouted, though his aunt had not called him, 'Got to go, Del. Thank you, honey, I'll keep in touch,' and he hung up hurriedly.

Chapter IV

Friday

Bentota Beach
When Reginald Bell still hadn't phoned by Wednesday evening, Maggie was so edgy that CV became concerned about her. It was not like her to take men's interest or lack of interest that seriously.

That afternoon she had caught him looking at himself in his long bedroom mirror. He had a towel around his waist and was staring morosely at his shape. She laughed, so he hit his stomach.

'All muscle,' he explained hopefully.

Muscle or not, he seemed better built for the sea than land. His was a body made to float. He blamed his shape on his Dutch ancestors, as he did his thinning nondescript brown hair. He realized he'd soon be bald like his father, grandfather and great-grandfather. Pot bellies and bald heads also occurred in the Sinhala race, but he could hardly blame his on the pretty Sinhala girl of sixteen who had eloped with his great-great- grandfather's father. She, her father, her mother and her eight siblings had all been slim and had had heads of thick black hair, according to her husband's diary.

He also blamed the Dutch for his face, which had the definition of a potato according to Della, hardly a cat to sheath her claws. She had also described it as 'formless,' adding, 'it lacks distinction.'

His was a pleasant face, he had told her, but it had no outstanding ugly features.

'Mummy once told me I had nice eyes,' he said to Maggie now and then remembered Della had described them as 'washed out'.

Maggie came and stood by him, unintentionally making him seem not just overweight but bulging. She put her arm around his shoulder. 'You have lovely eyes and a lovely smile,' she said sweetly. 'As long as you can smile, women will want you.'

'But women never mention my lovely eyes and lovely smile. All they talk about is my helpful nature. Actually, a cafeteria worker called Mrs Higgins did point out my shapely legs—but only once. See that thigh muscle? See the definition in the calf? The dimpled ankle? The ridged heel?'

'The twisted toes. The bumpy knees.'

'You never told me I had bumpy knees.'

'Lots of women like tall men, and you've got height. You don't even need great legs, though yours are not bad at all. Stand tall and smile, and women will surround you and bare their breasts.'

He kissed her cheek.

'We'll always be children, won't we?' she said to the mirror.

'We will,' he promised their reflection. He decided not to tell her about Reginald Bell's past, particularly about the princess, at least not yet.

Aunt Maud was at the door and said, 'Bread and butter and jaggery for tea.' Jaggery was the soft dark palm sugar they loved.

'We'll always be children, won't we, Aunt Maud?' he said.

She looked at him confused.

CV became frightened when Aunt Maud showed her age. He was not sure that he'd want to come back when she died. She was the last of that generation—the last reminder that there'd been a kinder time.

To relieve themselves from their only obsessive topic of

conversation, which was who killed Dorothy, they decided to take Aunt Maud to the beach on Friday and got a ride with friends who were going to Galle and would drop them off at Bentota. They settled in at the Bentota Splash—a particularly ugly hotel featuring heavy-handed murals and festooned balconies. The ocean however was the ocean, so they decided to find a hotel more to their taste the following day.

No sooner had they arrived than the woman running the hotel bookshop recognized Maggie and placed four copies of an Australian magazine displaying her face in the window. Before they were out of the lobby guests had begun to point at her, and CV heard the word *autograph*.

'I'd better go and hide now,' Maggie said in the manner of one used to hiding at a moment's notice. 'See you both down by the beach.'

CV found the manager who promised to get the magazines out of the window and led them to a secluded grove of mangroves where a pool attendant helped them set up. CV then went indoors to put on his swimsuit, and, when he rejoined Aunt Maud, he had beside him a shuffling tent made from two enormous yellow towels. Only two bare feet with painted toe-nails and a hand clutching a large bottle of sunscreen lotion revealed the woman inside. They had the pleasure of seeing their aunt who was lying under a large umbrella nearly laugh herself off her pallet.

'You're a great audience, Auntie,' CV told her.

'You're such rascals,' she replied.

He'd already lost the tightness he had felt in Colombo and decided he'd just needed sea air. He put on the mirrored sunglasses he had found on the hall table at Aunt Maud's, then lay on his back and distended his stomach to survey the sweat and hairs that covered it.

Maggie said, 'Dorothy Bell was ten years younger than I. She woke up, had breakfast and had plans for the next day, only somebody killed her before it came.' Even as she spoke she reached for a hand-rolled joint from the gold Benson and Hedges box where she also kept some white pills that pepped her up.

CV looked at his aunt, her eyes shut, holding the umbrella above her. Her long print dress lifted in the breeze showing her ankles. Eighty-two! On her it seemed right. Her skin had stretched across her face making it fragile, as did her thin grey hair tight in its small bun. There were age spots on those cheeks and her faded eyes had a permanent darkening below them. But where were the future Aunt Mauds? Who would be the eighty-year-old maiden aunts with unwrinkled minds, bright thoughts and clear lungs?

He said, 'Auntie? Why am I miserable?'

'Because you're bored, darling boy. All those things I taught you—like how to boil an egg, to knit and how to make holes in leather with a hot needle—I did that when you got bored because you became grumpy.'

He started to laugh. 'I've forgotten how to knit! Auntie, will you show me how to knit again?'

'I will. Tomorrow we'll get some needles and wool.'

'Aunt Maud, why didn't you come and see me when you were in Michigan last year? You went halfway round the world and didn't drop in. I haven't told you, but that hurt.'

'You were in Alaska, and Alaska seemed too cold for my bones. Besides, Dulcie said you shouldn't know I was in Michigan in case you lost your job by coming to see me. Your job is very well paid, Dulcie says.'

'It is, and I can't get fired. It's a benefit I insist on. I work on contract, and there's a clause that says if I want to take a few days off to see my favourite aunt in Michigan, I can.'

'If you need money, you must ask me,' she was saying. 'I can't take it with me, you know.'

'Auntie, if I need money, the bank will lend me enormous sums. That's how America works. Actually, I'll make $1,200 by being here. A girl at the office bet me that I couldn't do nothing for six months. She says I'm a work junkie.'

'Are you going to marry her?'

'No.'

'Good. She sounds like a fool. She'll bankrupt her husband.' She waved her open umbrella.

'Auntie, her part of the bet is only $200. She earns $65,000 a year, and she's only twenty-five.'

'Then marry her quickly before someone else does,' she gave a giggle.

Reginald Bell Makes an Offer

CV turned his head towards the hotel, and in the distance, as if in a mirage, he saw Reginald Bell floating towards them. Not a silver hair was out of place. He was actually not skimming the ground. If you looked carefully, you could see he was merely striding. CV sat up and said, 'Maggie, don't look now, but your number one guy is heading this way in tailored shorts, designer golf-shirt and blow-dried spray-and-hold hair.'

'Dorothy's father?'

'Well he's not hopping, but it's him—walking brisk.'

'Why would he hop?'

'Rabbits . . . never mind.'

'I told you he'd come,' she said and put her joint out in the sand beside her chair.

'You did.'

But when Reginald Bell reached them he ignored her. Instead he held out his hand to CV.

'Vander Marten?'

'There are actually three vander Martens here,' said CV shaking the proffered hand and moving so the other man could sit beside him. To his surprise he welcomed the new arrival—if not Bell himself—at least the sense of something happening. 'Under the pink and blue paisley umbrella is Miss Maud Agatha

Eve Claire vander Marten who is either asleep or pretending to be. At my feet lies Margaret Millicent vander Marten, an elongated woman who never goes anywhere except covered in sunscreen and two yellow towels. If you clap your hands, Mr Bell, a pallet such as ours will appear from the direction of the pool. Until then do share mine.'

Bell hesitated then sat down beside him and took out his Benson and Hedges. CV decided not to say, 'Maggie, you're soulmates. He even smokes the same cigs.' He supposed she'd noticed that Bell had not spoken to her yet.

'I am so glad to meet you again,' the Englishman said to him, 'You were at Dorothy's memorial service. I phoned your home this morning, but the individual who answered screamed. Fortunately, I was with a Sinhala-speaking friend who had better luck with her.'

'You got Amily, our answering machine. That scream means, "Please leave your name and number".'

'CV hasn't been drinking,' said Maggie who hadn't moved except to take a proffered cigarette from Bell's gold box. 'He's always like this.'

CV wondered why Bell was still in the island—he was supposed to have left two days ago. He also wondered why he had bothered to track down Maggie here when a phone call in Colombo the previous evening would have reached her and why, having done so, he was pretending disinterest.

The man exuded self-control. In fact, he was so much in control he did not even have to clap his hands for a pallet; one was brought to him with a tray of drinks and two tables, all carried by waiters in a row like a military detachment.

Bell began to play host. 'I've ordered four beers and four ginger beers to cover some eventualities. Would you prefer tea or whisky?' he asked them.

'Beer is fine for me,' CV said. 'Auntie would prefer a ginger beer—if and when she wakes.'

'Beer for me,' said Maggie, to whom Bell had still not spoken directly.

CV swivelled his eyes behind the mirrored glass without moving his head. The older man also wore dark glasses but CV could see his light eyes through the lenses and he was looking at Maggie. He then glanced at Aunt Maud who had fallen asleep.

Bell leaned over and carefully placed a cold beer on Maggie's stomach, then snatched it away quickly when she screamed and jack-knifed up.

'Sorry. Difficult to resist that very beautiful expanse of flesh,' he said. She took the glass from him and gave him her cover smile. Behind their sunglasses Maggie and Reginald Bell took stock. Professional charm was exchanged.

They're on, CV thought with irritation.

He sipped from his own glass and continued examining Bell. The Englishman was so correctly dressed for the beach he belonged on a poster. He was even wearing athletic shoes without socks. How could he have produced a daughter as wantonly uncontrived as Dorothy?

CV put down his glass on the sand and said, 'I think I'll go to sleep,' and wished the words had come out less surly.

Reginald Bell jumped in quickly, 'CV, I'd appreciate it if you could postpone that sleep for a few minutes.' He had not, however, invited familiarity with his own name. He continued, 'As I said, I had a difficult time finding you this morning.'

'How did you find us?'

'The woman at your aunt's house said you were with people called Bowling-Hammer. There were no Bowling-Hammers in the phone book, but the hotel manager said he'd heard the Canadian High Commissioner say the name, and his secretary gave me their mobile phone number. After that it was easy. They told me they'd left you at this hotel.'

Resourceful man, Reggie.

Bell continued, 'Your school friend Bundy recommended

you for a job I need done, CV. That's why I'm here.'

Maggie, bless her, did not throw her beer in his face.

'Who?'

'Mr Balasingham from the Casino Vegas. He said that if I said "Bundy sent me" you'd talk to me.'

'Oh, that Bundy!'

It was unlikely that there could be two Bundy Balasinghams.

Bell lay back on his pallet and kicked off his shoes. He was on his second cigarette and Maggie was also on another. They smoked quickly, but CV was not interested in their smoking habits. He was interested in the job, which he presumed was related to his work with computer systems. He wouldn't do it, of course, and he felt anger at Bundy for having thought that tossing a job his way would mend their friendship.

He had met Bundy in school, and later they had been fellow drinkers and for two weeks fellow coke-snorters. Bundy's father was Tamil and his mother Sinhala, the sort of mixed marriage that was becoming increasingly common on the island. There had been a time when such a coupling would have labelled Bundy as a child of 'bad blood'. The week before Dorothy Bell had been murdered, CV, Maggie and Bundy had driven up to Negombo. That afternoon he had found Bundy stealing from him, and their friendship had ended.

'Bundy is sure you're the man to help me.'

'Ah!' CV lay back and closed his eyes again. Then, because Bell did not speak, he said, 'Bundy is wrong. I cannot help you because I am on holiday and do not want to work. Even if I did, I couldn't help you because you have come through a man I don't respect.'

The older man sipped his beer and smoked his cigarette.

Maggie said, 'You're getting burnt, CV. Turn over. You're getting *cooked*.'

Lying on his stomach with her soft, strong fingers rubbing oil on to his shoulders, he knew she was only doing it to excite

Bell but that did not spoil his pleasure in the experience. Her fingers lingered on his shoulders, moved down his spine, touched the waistband of his shorts and then crossed his back. They went into the fissures made by his muscles. He wondered if porn actors felt as he did now—an erotic pleasure at being chosen as the instrument to stir another. At which moment Bell broke his silence. 'What I am asking has nothing whatever to do with Mr Balasingham. I would like to employ you to find out who killed my daughter.'

CV turned over abruptly and put out a hand to catch Maggie, who was nearly thrown on to the sand. He looked at Bell to see if he was joking and decided he was not.

'It must be a terrible situation for you, but of course my answer is still no.'

Bundy, he realized now, had really set him up, and he wondered why.

'You see,' continued Bell as if CV hadn't spoken, 'I was here when it happened. Let me tell you my story before you make up your mind.' He rose to fill their glasses.

'You may not have heard what actually happened the night Dot died because very little got into the papers accurately. I arrived at Bandaranayake airport on an early evening flight. I can't believe it was only seven days ago. We touched down just after six. Dot had insisted on meeting my plane, though I told her it was unnecessary. I waited for half an hour thinking she'd been delayed by traffic. When I realized she would not be coming, I took a taxi to the Palace Hotel where she'd booked a room for me. She wasn't at the Palace either. I still had no premonition that anything was going to prevent me seeing her again.

'There was no message for me at the reception desk, but they had my reservation, and I checked in. I began to wonder if Dot had taken ill. As time passed, I began to imagine her lying unconscious in her room unable to answer the phone, and as I was her father—my passport showed the same name—the manager took me up and opened her door with a passkey. She was not there.

'What struck us both was that her bed looked as if she had not been in the room all day—everything was apple pie. I had dinner and turned in early—about 10. I still had no feeling of anything amiss. I thought that she must have mistaken the day and that the following morning I would be seeing her. I woke at 6 o'clock on Saturday morning and waited until 7.30 to call her room not wanting to disturb her. No answer. I phoned the front desk; she had not picked up my message. I then became piqued because I hadn't come to Sri Lanka to sit around waiting. We had plans which had not included my spending even one day alone.

'I breakfasted and began to lose my irritation. I became worried. Dot was always punctual and considerate—and when a girl says, "See you tomorrow, Daddy," she means tomorrow, not next week. I went to the lobby intending to call the police—only to find the police were already there. That was when I heard my daughter had been murdered.'

'Horrible for you,' shuddered Maggie.

'Yes, and the way she had been knifed seemed so premeditated. I was told she had dined with Michael in the fort the night before and left him in a taxi and that was the last he had seen of her.'

'Why didn't you call him or one of her friends the previous evening?' CV asked.

'I had no phone numbers for her friends—except Michael—and I'll explain later why I did not call him. Remember I had no suspicion she was dead.'

'What do you think she was doing in the Pettah?' CV asked.

'Find that out for me because it is a mystery. I want to know who killed her and why.'

'Unlikely place—the Pettah! That is the oddest part of the whole affair. The Pettah!'

'Why? I hear that it's a district of low life and crime.'

'Not where I'd leave the body of a blonde kid I'd just killed. A foreign girl would stand out in the Pettah dead or alive. The guy who found Dorothy thought she might be an angel. Lying on a Pettah step she stood out like a giraffe in Alaska. Mr Bell, put yourself in her killer's place: You've killed a foreigner. Wouldn't you want to buy time? Wouldn't you put her body where it couldn't be found? Somewhere remote? The Pettah in daylight hours is as remote as Trafalgar Square. If you were already in the Pettah, you'd get her out of it because even if you hid her body there, she'd be discovered when the street guys arrived. Hundreds of nosy active people would soon be all over the place. The person who left her there must have wanted her discovered quickly. But why? Or did he have to get rid of her quickly? Perhaps he just left her and ran. But unless he was staggering around with her in his arms, I'd guess he just wanted her to be found quickly. Sorry, I'm not being deliberately insensitive—I just don't know how to talk about it any other way.'

Reginald Bell was staring at CV through his sunglasses. His hard, tanned face was without movement. CV was sitting up, his elbows on his knees.

'I'm sorry, Mr Bell,' he said.

Bell said softly, 'What if whoever did it was unaware she was dead? Even hoped she was not. He hadn't meant to kill her. She was unconscious. He can't take her to a hospital himself, so he leaves her where she will be discovered quickly.'

'Unlikely as hell. Why not take her to the gate of a hospital or call the police and run? From the fort, the Oberoi is in the direction of several hospitals—the Pettah is not.'

CV had forgotten his conversation with Della, and abruptly it kicked in. Four other times Bell had lost people he knew the same way. Was Bell looking for the killer because he thought he himself might be the next victim? He said, 'The single knife thrust must be unusual. Do you know anything about knives?'

Bell, who now had his head in his hands, said without lifting his head, 'This is not the first time a person I have known has been knifed. Two years ago someone I knew met the same fate. Of course, he was not . . . not my daughter.'

So Bell was willing to admit one death by knifing. Not all, but one. CV refilled his glass. Perhaps he'd misjudged Bell, who was just a father who could not leave until he knew the facts. The Englishman's smooth politeness might be a cover-up for his true emotions.

Maggie sprang into action to cover the silence and refilled her own glass and as an afterthought topped up Bell's.

'Why did Dorothy take a room at the Palace that evening?' she asked him as she slowly returned to her seat. 'She lived in Michael's house. It's no secret. They were lovers.'

Bell smiled tolerantly at her. 'I know about her life with Michael. But she's also had a room at the Palace for nearly two years. Her possessions are there: her toothbrush, her perfume and even her dirty clothes. Some of her laundry was picked up there two days before she died—it has been delivered.'

Clothes laundered at the Palace Hotel! When CV had last seen her, she had brushed against him unwashed, unpressed and smelling slightly of sweat.

'Did Michael know about her Palace life?' he asked.

'Of course. But he has refused to speak to me.'

'Why?' asked Maggie arranging herself attractively on her towel. One long leg was folded under her and the other bent so she could lean on her knee. CV had seen her in a magazine in exactly the same pose, only she'd been wearing a chiffon wrap of many colours, and, like now, two strands of hair fell across her eyes. He scowled at her. She gave him a wide smile and allowed her lips to tremble.

If Bell was intrigued with her dazzle, he showed no sign.

He said, 'I think Michael feels guilty. Only he could have stopped Dot from coming to the airport to meet me. If she had come, she'd be alive today.'

'Yes,' Maggie purred, 'I bet that's it.'

There was silence until CV spoke. 'And what have I to do with all this? I don't hang out with dopers—that is, I am not particularly in with Michael's crowd. I've never spoken to him. They're part of *our crowd* where I have some old friendships. I don't do grass. I don't do X. I don't even inhale nicotine. I'm here on a holiday. And finally, I am a computer man, not a detective. I barely know a knife from a gun and wouldn't use either to kill. I can't even kill an animal. Is Bundy connected with this murder? If he wants help, he's not going to get it from me, as he should know.' He lapsed into silence.

Bell said, 'Bundy told me that you were once instrumental in solving a crime in India. He said he liked you and you were good at that sort of thing. He described you as a true Dutch Burgher—honest, easygoing but tough. You speak both Sinhala and Tamil. When I first asked him to find me a man to look into Dot's murder, he suggested you. It surprises you?'

'It surprises me.'

It surprised him not just because he'd caught Bundy red-handed with his cash roll in hand, but also because Bundy knew the crime he'd been credited with solving in India he had not solved at all.

He said, 'As we have nothing better to do, would you like to hear about the crime I never solved in India?'

'Very much.'

Maggie's black eyes had a genuine sparkle at last. 'You've never told me about a crime in India. I never even knew you'd been to India!'

'I didn't want you to get jealous, Mag. I was a star for a week. A glossy magazine put me on its cover.'

It had happened in Delhi two years ago. On his way to London, suffering from a vicious hangover, he'd let a stranger—a Sikh at the airport—persuade him to carry a packet to London. The Sikh said it contained his father's ashes and was being sent to his ailing mother. The man had broken down saying this and offered CV $5,000. The tears seemed real, but the money did it. CV boarded the plane with the ashes. It was only minutes before take-off, when his head had cleared, that CV had realized he could be carrying a sophisticated bomb or drugs. He'd made a spectacular noise, forcing the captain to take him to the airport authorities where he handed in the packet and the $5,000. The packet had contained not ashes, not a bomb, not drugs, but millions of pounds worth of precious stones.

'TV reporters and cameras were brought in. I was interviewed and modestly denied any bravery and intelligence. I can be delightfully modest as you know, Mag. I was even given lunch in the First Class lounge. After lunch, photographers took pictures of me. I got to see what four million sterling of precious stones look like—impressively colourful but fewer than you would think. The gems and I got our portrait taken together. I held them too close to my face so it looked as if I had acne.'

'Who owned them?' Aunt Maud asked.

'You're awake, Auntie? They had been stolen from a jeweller in Calcutta. His watchman had been killed by the Sikh, who was actually not a Sikh but a Muslim called Abdul Fazil. So Fazil was wanted for murder, not just burglary.

'Sidelight! I mentioned that the store should have installed a better security system. A reporter and I got into that—how to set up a system to thwart the Fazils—stuff I'd read in *Popular Mechanics* about electronic surveillance. The guy wrote it all down and it got printed and a picture of me was displayed again.'

'I wouldn't,' said Maggie, 'trust a stranger with my four-million pound jewels.'

'Nor I,' said Aunt Maud. 'I'd swallow them.'

'Aunt Maud, that's a very dangerous thing to do—and the recovery will be nothing like as easy as it sounds.'

Bell was actually laughing. 'Actually, the recovery would be quite simple.'

'How is it done? With a sieve? Never mind,' CV continued, 'I'd better finish this. An Indian police officer—a really smart and funny guy—thought me a bit of a joke. It struck us both as pretty hilarious that when I am drunk I am willing, even eager, to be a smuggler. But sober I become an upright citizen.

'He invited me to his home, but I couldn't go. He told me that Abdul Fazil was an Iranian.'

'Did they catch Fazil?' asked Aunt Maud.

'They did—that day. He took a domestic flight to Madras which left minutes after he gave me the package. It was my describing him in detail that did him in. He was using another name and had ditched his turban, but I told the police he had a chipped right front tooth. He forgot to hide the tooth! An Indian Airlines plane to Madras had a passenger, apparently Indian, with a chipped right front tooth. When it landed, he was searched and found to be carrying a passport made out to Kirat Singh, the name he had given me.'

He stopped.

What he didn't tell them was that he had told Bundy the story and heard his friend repeat it to acquaintances jeering that only Clive vander Marten would be stupid enough to give back $5,000 nobody knew about. Bundy had always thought he was a bit of a fool, which had made him wonder why Bundy would recommend him to Bell. One reason could be that he wanted CV to fail—to demonstrate his foolishness; another was that Bundy, or Bell, did not want Dorothy's killer found. That could mean one or both of them knew who had done it. If his friend had merely wanted to reinstate their friendship, CV thought, he would have chosen a more typical Sri Lankan solution: he'd have had a third party come to him with an apology.

But he did not air his misgivings. He said, 'As you see, Mr Bell, I'm not in the crime business. I'm on holiday. Once I stupidly allowed someone to plant a fortune in precious stones on me. There were no dead bodies. No knives.'

Reginald Bell would not be put off. His gentle persistence actually reminded CV of the turbaned Fazil. 'So you've proved you're an honest man! I need one. I am looking for a Sri Lankan who thinks like a westerner, is young enough to move around the people who knew my daughter and old enough to make mature guesses. I ask you to help me find her killer and will pay you well, of course.'

'Why not Michael? He wants the answer, but I'm sure he can't afford to mount an investigation himself.'

'What if Michael killed her? If he didn't, his asking questions might put him in danger. You got yourself out of that mess in Delhi alive. You could have lost your life. If you had delivered the stones, why would Fazil leave you alive? His freedom was riding on his anonymity. By the way, I know something of gems. I heard of his arrest and knew of the case but did not know you were the man on the plane. I am delighted to hear the full story. Please help me.'

CV shook his head. 'You need someone who has a chance of success. I don't.'

'Your final answer is no then?'

'It is. But please have tea with us.'

'Thank you, but no,' Bell got to his feet slowly and a bit wearily. 'I have to go back to Colombo and find someone else for the job.'

CV rose to bid him goodbye without regrets. What he now knew was that Reginald Bell thought that the person who tried to find Dorothy's killer would be risking his life. To Bell and Bundy, CV vander Marten was as expendable as fish bait.

Maggie suddenly jumped up and ran after Bell calling his name.

CV Changes His Mind

If Maggie's edginess about losing her looks had left her so insecure that she was now running after men, literally, there was nothing CV could do. After he had settled back and closed his eyes, she returned. Her bare feet made no sound, but she must have stepped on a rock because he heard a short squawk followed by, 'Wake up! I want to talk to you.'

'Wake up Clive Benoit or Aunt Maud?' he asked not opening his eyes.

'The one with the big stomach.'

'Good, because he wanted to talk to you. Let Reginald go, Mag. He's not right for you.'

'Forget about him and me. I want to talk about you looking for the person who killed Dorothy. You can't say no to her father. What's happened to you?'

She sat down beside him and began stroking his chest with her palm.

He wondered how to get her to drop the subject.

'I can. I did,' he said finally. 'What's happened to me is that I know I'm being set up by Bundy. I suppose you've told Bell I'm going to do it? Well go tell him I'm not.'

Her fingers stopped moving, and he opened his eyes. She didn't move.

'This is nothing to do with Bundy,' she finally said quietly, 'This is to do with a man who's a stranger in a country where he doesn't speak the language. You have to try. I'll help. We're getting bored with all the nothingness. Doing something like this will wake us up. I know Michael and his crowd better than you do. I can ask questions. No one would think it funny because I'm a fellow inhaler, and I'm always asking questions.'

'I can help, too,' said Aunt Maud from under her umbrella, 'I play bridge with Michael's mother's friend Shantha. Old women are the confidantes of everyone.'

'Auntie, I'm not Mr Bell's last hope. I'm his first. If he was some poor bastard who'd mortgaged his home to come here to find his daughter's murderer, of course I'd help him. But this guy's T-shirts cost more than Amily's salary. He has other options besides the police who are short-handed. And what about losing my bet? The money was a joke, but to me it's also an important experiment in living.'

Maggie began to look at her face in a small mirror she carried in her purse, and he wanted to knock it out of her hand. She bared her teeth then wrinkled her nose at her reflection. He raged inwardly at her self-absorption even now when she was asking him to abandon his own.

She said to the mirror, 'If you don't want to go back to Della with your head hanging, you can always start the bet again.'

It was such a horrible thought that he smiled at her suddenly. She made a face at him and tossed her long hair. The gesture was provocative, brazen but pathetic—the gesture of a woman admitting all she had going for her was sex appeal. Maggie often used it in self-mockery. She lifted one of the beer bottles to see if it was empty and drank from it.

He said, 'And if CV will help, little Maggie will have a good excuse to keep Reggie around—right?'

She lifted her third finger at him behind the bottle so that their aunt couldn't see it. 'You're dead wrong. I am not sure now I even like the man. I just wanted to have somewhere nice to stay in London, and he owns a flat there.'

He raised his voice so his aunt could hear, 'I actually might have done it for you if you were crazy about the guy, but I don't like this new desperate you any more than you like the new selfish me. I don't like to see you adding his scalp to your already overloaded tomahawk just because you don't want to pay for a hotel room you can afford.' He knew he wouldn't get through if he stuck to that line. 'Be practical. An investigation will cost plenty because I don't like cutting corners when I work. I'll become that greedy vander Marten motherfucker who couldn't even deliver. Sorry, Aunt Maud.' His voice dropped to normal. 'There are thousands of three-wheelers in Colombo. Fifty thousand new ones next week, according to the *Island*. Why would one driver tell on another and give his profession a bad name? Now, Bundy is a crook and must know crooks. If he puts a wad of Bell's cash into the right hand and says, "Bring me the man who killed Dorothy Bell tomorrow," a killer will appear on his doorstep with a signed confession . . . end of investigation.'

'And some dumb fool who thinks he's signing on to be a cook in Saudi will be in jail for life, and you'll have helped to put him there.'

There was truth in that, and what about those other knifings? No three-wheeler driver did those. What if they were all the work of the CIA? Even with Helen and Della to tell him what they were up to, no way was he going to cross swords with that little crowd.

He said wearily, 'You want me to work for Bell, but I feel I'm being set up.'

'It would be against everything you and I believe in to refuse.'

'And I,' said Aunt Maud, 'Because all young people think about today is the easy way out.'

Her words were so unexpected that his anger was sucked from him. When he had rushed to her as a child to escape his father's wrath he had known that as long as she was there no one would dare touch him. She had always been in his corner yet had asked nothing of him before. Blood rushed to his face. He knew she had now changed everything because he would always give her what she wanted. It was she and only she, he later realized, who had turned him around.

He'd do it, but he wanted Aunt Maud to know why he had been so reluctant.

'Maggie, when you and I went swimming at that guest house in Negombo, Bundy got out of the pool and went to the changing rooms, and I followed. We'd shared a locker, and he'd kept the key. I'd forgotten my sunglasses—the ones I can't find. I walked in, and my money belt was open in his hands. I took my money out of his hand and counted it. He'd taken $900 and a travellers' check for $500.

'I said, "This is the end of our friendship, Bundy, I don't want to set eyes on you again." Bundy laughed. He said, "Don't be a fool, Clive. Where's your sense of humour?"'

'You should have told me. You just said he'd gone home. But why would he steal? He's a rich man. He owns a casino,' Maggie said.

'Maybe the murderer of Dorothy Bell is a rich man. Maybe her father is going through the motions of pretending interest in her killer—maybe he knows who killed her but doesn't want to point his own finger. Bundy doesn't think I can do damn—all but kick a football or swing a racket. In school I used to feel there was power in having other boys think I was a fool—even in college I played that game: *Let this old jock into your poker game. Shit, I lost forty today, may I play again tomorrow*? Tomorrow I'd skin them. Bundy expected me to end up cleaning shoes on a New York street. Now he wants me to make a fool of myself because looking for the guy who killed Dorothy will do it.'

She'd abandoned the mirror and was sitting on the edge of her chair with her elbows on her knees. She'd tied a handloom sarong around her waist, her long legs were bent, and for the first time in years, he saw she could be ungainly, even ugly, and he liked that. He leaned over and ruffled her hair, and she didn't pull away.

'Let's show Bundy he's wrong,' she said with that flat determination that had pulled her into the big time—that side of her that had lifted her above the other hungry go-getters in her trade. She almost hissed, 'Mr Bell is lucky that Bundy recommended you because this is something you can do. *Our crowd* is not overwhelmed with big thinkers. You may not come up with a murderer, but even if you make peace between Mr Bell and Michael it will be enough. What do you care what people think of you? You never have before.'

He said, 'So go call lover boy. I'm not doing it for you or Mr Bell. I'm doing it for Dorothy. She deserves some sort of an inquiry. And I'm doing it because Aunt Maud thinks she does.'

'I do,' said his aunt.

He said, 'I'm falling asleep out here, Mag. Tell Snowtop I'll meet him in the coffee shop. I'm going to take a shower and get the sand off.'

She was gone in a flash.

He asked, 'Aunt Maud, is Reginald Bell's manner natural for a father who's just lost his only child?'

His aunt moved from under her umbrella, closed it, then raised herself to a sitting position, swung her feet over the chair and started putting on her shoes.

'Want help with those, Auntie?' he asked.

'No, darling boy, I can manage. Mr Bell's not mourning like one of us, but he's English, and some of them don't have feelings like we do. In the old days when an Englishman fell in love with a girl working on his estate, he only loved her until there was a baby coming. Then he would send her away, her parents wouldn't take her, and she'd have nowhere to go. Those men never cared what happened to those girls they once told they loved. They never wondered about their children. Mr Bell loved Dorothy. She's dead. Maybe he's forgotten her.'

'Do you like him?'

'Not much, I'm afraid.'

'But you want me to help him.'

'Not him, Dorothy. I had a Mass said for her. She was twenty-three. Someone has cheated her of her old age. I like being old. She may have, too.'

'I was attracted to her. I didn't tell you that.'

'My poor boy!'

'I was both repelled and attracted. What I remember was that I couldn't stop looking at her. I loved her energy but was frightened to love her.' He had realized at last what Dorothy's hold on him had been. 'Will you be able to get to the coffee shop alone Aunt Maud, or shall I walk up with you?'

'Have your shower. I like walking alone. Do you think your friend Bundy stole your sunglasses?'

She could be right. He'd come back from Negombo without them.

As he showered he thought about Michael Blue and couldn't see the artist killing anyone—not for money, not for love, not even for honour. But OJ Simpson had also seemed a man who couldn't kill. And now, as Maggie had also come to realize, it was time to abandon sitting on the beach—physically and mentally. It just wasn't his style. Twelve hundred dollars had been well spent to learn that. Whether or not Bell agreed with his terms, he himself had to get back on the job before he'd lost the jive to keep up.

Bell, Maggie and Aunt Maud were in the coffee shop when he joined them.

'Thank you for not turning me down. Maggie's told me I've spoilt your holiday.'

He shrugged and then said to the waiter, 'Patties. Cucumber sandwiches. Love cake.'

'No love cake today, sir.'

'This country is going to the dogs. Chocolate cake then.'

'Yes sir. Cayuns, sir?'

'That will make up for everything.'

Maggie said, 'Cayuns for me, too.'

'Cayuns are fried, darling,' said Aunt Maud.

'Oh Aunt Maud, never say the word *fried* in front of a model. We break out in lumps. I have to have a cayun.'

A silence descended after the man had departed. CV wished

he could put on the opaque sunglasses and watch Bell surreptitiously. Eventually he said, 'There are hazards to this job, Mr Bell. You think it is too dangerous for Michael, so my price for taking a stab is ten thousand.' He wondered at the open relief on Bell's face, then realized the other man thought he meant rupees. CV liked that very much. He counted to three, 'Ten thousand pounds sterling.'

It was interesting to watch a rich man see a bargain slip away—the narrowing of the eyes, a tightening at the corner of the mouth.

He waited until they had smoothed out and decided to bring them back. 'For one week.'

Before Bell could speak, he continued, 'Out of which I will pay for all expenses except airfares or hotel accommodations. I can't imagine why I'd need those, but it could happen. I'll pay my assistants and we'll work all seven days, sixteen hours a day. At the end of one week the deal is off—win or lose. Next Friday at midnight or before, in which case there will be no rebate, I will deliver the murderer of your daughter to you if I can. I do not think I can, Mr Bell, if only because we're starting this investigation seven days after Dorothy died, but I'll do my damnedest. If you agree, I'll start immediately, that is today, which will be a freebie. I'll want your cheque for the whole sum today and will Federal Express it tomorrow to my bank so it arrives Monday. If the cheque bounces the deal is off.'

Bell had had time to prepare his own speech and delivered it with a smile, 'The deal is off anyway. I was prepared to offer you $5,000 a month—plus expenses against receipts. I'm interested how you came up with the ten thousand. Do you really think you're worth a pound a minute?'

So, he had facility with numbers!

CV replied, 'I didn't pick ten thousand out of the air. I'm a trilingual computer man with international connections. The figure would seem reasonable to me if Dorothy had been my daughter. I'm not a wealthy man, but I would actually put out a whole lot more than that to find the killer of my daughter. I'd mortgage my life to find who did it.'

As he had expected, Bell pretended to be thinking. He eventually said, 'The question is not how much I am prepared to pay or what I'm worth. I am not interested in your computer expertise. I am interested in whether your three languages and familiarity with Dorothy's crowd are worth a man who values his work time at half a million pounds a year. They are not.'

Maggie seemed to have stopped breathing. Aunt Maud started pouring the tea as if she wasn't listening. CV smiled at the waiter and took a patty from a proffered dish.

Bell finally broke the silence. 'I think you know you have me across a barrel. You're a shrewd man, and time isn't on my side. So I agree to your price. My cheque book is in the car. I want to be informed daily on your progress. I'm sorry we've started so late, but the police inspector assigned to the case insisted they'd have Dot's killer in a week. They had leads, he said. If they ever had, they have run out of them now, and there's a new CID man in charge. I don't think he's giving her murder any particular priority. May I give you all a lift to Colombo?'

'Thank you. My aunt can't find the keys to her car, so we were going to hire one to get back. But let's eat all this good food first. Perhaps the police will tell me what they've come up with so I won't have to go over areas they've covered. In the car you can fill me in about your daughter: her life, her friends, her enemies.'

The three Sri Lankans ate with enthusiasm, for the food was good, but they barely spoke. Bell ate a single sandwich, bit into a cayun and left it on his plate but apparently enjoyed the chocolate cake. All of them seemed to be lost in their own thoughts. Then CV became distracted when Maggie accepted a cigarette from Bell. Her hand touched his. When he took out his silver lighter, their hands touched again.

Maggie's cousin looked away and saw that behind him a

great seascape had developed for heavy clouds had moved in, and the sunlight came through them in shafts. Any other time he'd enjoy this scene, but now he was happy to leave it behind.

He turned back to her. She was standing, looking not at Bell but at her cigarette. His aunt was also on her feet and had a small smile on her lips. She caught his eye and blinked both of hers mischievously. She had never been able to wink. Bell seemed distracted. It struck CV that he could have misjudged the man and that he was going to back out of their deal. He could do that even after he wrote the cheque. All he had to do was stop payment on it. He himself would be disappointed if that happened, for he had now made a rough plan of how to proceed.

Bell said, 'Shall we go?'

'We mustn't forget our luggage, darling boy,' said Aunt Maud.

'Yeah and our bill. You going to change, Mag? Mr Bell, shall we meet you at the front door in fifteen minutes?'

The Englishman hesitated before saying, 'About fifteen minutes, then.' He brought on his patent-leather charm, 'I've never met a woman who could be ready in fifteen minutes, so this may be a first.' They watched him stride away as if he had something to do, and CV wondered what that could be.

He stopped to face the women: 'From this moment, I'm hiring you both because you got me into this. Mag, your job is to find out all you can about Dorothy through Michael's crowd and through her father. Get more than facts—get suspicions, reactions and ideas.' He led the way to the lobby, continuing, 'Aunt Maud, you don't have to work sixteen hours a day—three will be enough. Talk to anyone you can think of about Dorothy, Michael or those connected with them. Have your friends over for a gossip.'

'Bridge parties!' she said with obvious delight.

'Perfect! But I don't want your friends or Reggie Bell to know that either of you are working for me. We three'll have no secrets from each other, but no tongue slips outside.'

'You promised Mr Bell you'd tell him everything,' said his aunt.

'No, Auntie, he decided I would tell him everything. I did not agree. I don't dare to trust him. Right now the only people I trust are you two.'

Maggie said, 'God, I love you CV. It will be like *Our Gang*. They were a '30s group of kids who solved mysteries. You can get them on video.'

'The girl kids slept with the money men?'

'You want me to?'

'I want you not to.'

They had reached the lobby and, though her face was out of one shop window, it was now among the ebony elephants in another. The desk clerk had his gawk ready.

CV said into her ear, 'Maggo, don't ever sleep with any guy on my account.'

Aunt Maud's ears had been working, and she waved a finger at them, 'Tell Mr Bell, Maggie, I don't allow hanky-panky in my house.'

'Aunt Maud,' he said, 'would you buy me a small notebook and a pen from the bookshop? You're on an expense account now, so keep the receipt.'

She said, 'This is going to be exciting.'

'She's wonderful,' said Maggie as they watched her walk away from them. Then, 'See you in a sec. Head them off for me', and she ran for the elevator producing confusion in a beaming couple who were approaching them with a pen and paper. He wandered into their path so they had to detour. Maggie turned at the open elevator door, waved and disappeared.

The desk clerk said, 'Please sign here Mr vander Marten.'

The woman tourist said, 'You're a vander Marten, too?'

'Sorry, no. I'm vander Garten.'

He sat in the lobby thinking about the case. He had lost his sleepiness. When Maud joined him she gave him a small notebook with a blue fabric cover and a matching blue pen. 'Maggie's colour is pink and mine is red,' she explained.

'Auntie, you've set the right tone. We might not find the murderer, but we will at least look good with our designer accessories.'

She lowered her voice, 'Mr Bell is making two phone calls to Colombo and one to Singapore. Here are the numbers—it cost me Rs 500 to get them. Aren't we lucky that he had to book the calls through the desk? He's making them in one of the bedrooms. I probably gave the boy too much but didn't want to argue.'

He pocketed the piece of paper. 'Shhh, Detective vander Marten. Your quarry is approaching.'

When Bell reached them, Aunt Maud was still whispering loudly, 'Don't worry. If he gets engaged to Maggie, I'll shoot him. They'll never put me in jail. I'm too old.'

'Too old for what, Miss vander Marten?' asked Bell coming up behind her.

Aunt Maud's love of detective stories gave her the right answer. 'Too old to kill,' she said serenely, 'but not too old to want to.'

The Journey to Colombo

Bell was driving a white Toyota Camary, top of the line for a hired vehicle in Sri Lanka. He was withdrawn, distracted, but his manners had not changed, and he opened the back door of the Camary for the women. CV got into the front seat beside him.

At the hotel gate they were stopped by a guard who wanted the trunk and hood opened—a routine check for explosives. Maud said in Sinhala, 'I am old. Please do not delay me,' and the car was waved on. Within seconds they were heading north on the same road they had arrived on just a few hours earlier. It would take at least two hours to get to Colombo.

There was no small talk from Bell, so CV used the time to put his thoughts together. He considered the relationship between the Englishman and Maggie and decided she'd have to put it on hold during that week if only because she had helped force his own hand.

He moved on to Bell's change in mood. One of the phone calls must have upset him. He didn't seem like a man to sulk over having to part with a few thousand pounds nor, surely, could it be CV's one-week clause. At the end of the week they'd all have, at least, an expanded view of Dorothy's life. Bell could then hire someone cheaper to tie up the case or drop it. He might be wise not to try to vindicate her death, if she had been on the rim of the twilight world of illegal drugs and if that world produced her killer.

The Englishman's lack of emotion over Dorothy's death was problematic—what if it was not just English reserve? Lack of emotion was a sign of sociopathic behaviour. Helen's report had not mentioned such tendencies, but that did not mean they did not exist.

CV pulled back. He realized he was getting more curious about Dorothy's father than her murderer. He had to reverse that. He began to run through the facts and had a question immediately. Why had Reggie gone to Bundy for help in finding an investigator?

He said, 'Mr Bell, have you spoken to the British High Commissioner about Dorothy's murder?'

'Of course. He put me in touch with an attaché, Charles Wainwright, who went to see the Inspector General of Police and arranged that a Superintendent Senaratne be put on the case. Wainwright has promised to keep me informed after I return home. He's just turning wheels.'

'Wainwright didn't suggest that you hire someone to investigate the murder?'

'He advised me not to. He strongly recommended that I keep a low profile because of the political situation. "Deaths are easy to arrange in Sri Lanka, Mr Bell. We are very sympathetic but we'd be happier if you left the country".'

'Did you consider listening to him?'

'For at least a minute.' Bell did not smile, and his eyes did not leave the road.

'What made you choose Bundy as a confidant?'

'I would not call him a confidant. He knew Dorothy and came to me at the Palace to tell me how sorry he was to hear of the tragedy. I was touched that he took the trouble. We had dinner together.'

'And he produced my name.'

'He said he had a friend on holiday in Colombo. I then remembered you had signed the guest book at Dot's memorial service and had been Maggie's escort.'

They lapsed into silence again. Against the dark interior upholstery Bell was a photo negative with his white hair, tanned skin and light blue eyes that never left the road.

Had he decided on an investigation to show Mr Wainwright that Reginald Bell could not be easily dismissed? Hadn't CV himself done the same by charging too much? Rattle my cage, buddy, and you'll be sorry! A week. The local police and CID had got nowhere in the same time. Because Bell had balked at the ten thousand, he had added 'a week'. Foolish. He needed more time.

Well, he'd better get moving.

'Mr Bell,' he said, 'what exactly happened the night you arrived in Colombo? Start with what happened at Bandaranayake Airport.' He moved so his back was against the door and he could watch the Englishman speak.

Bell said curtly, 'I'll tell you the story again, but I don't want to keep repeating it. The police took my statement—they have it in their files. The plane landed around six. We were taken by bus to the airport building. I picked up my suitcase, put it on a cart and was waved through customs. In the arrival lounge there were a few men carrying placards. My name wasn't there. Dot wasn't there. I questioned an airport official who told me that my daughter might be waiting outside as you needed a pass to come in. I followed others down a walkway to where vehicles were stopping and new arrivals were being greeted. Dorothy was not there either. Touts offered me taxis—one man was persistent.'

His voice went through the recital as if he were reading. Even so, he was giving a detailed account. As he spoke the car had speeded up, and it was the only indication of any tension he might be feeling.

'It was possible Dot had been held up by traffic. I decided not to wait any longer and asked the persistent tout what it would cost to take me to the Palace Hotel in Colombo. He said Rs 1,200 and I agreed. I thought it was a bargain because last year the pound was Rs 80 and now it's Rs 95.

'Almost immediately a taxi pulled up, and I was driven to Colombo. I arrived at the hotel and checked in.'

'One minute. You waited for about thirty minutes outside the airport?'

'I waited twenty minutes there and less than ten minutes inside.'

'Could you identify the taxi?

'It was white and without a meter. I don't think I could identify it, the driver or the tout. It was not a smooth or noiseless ride. The driver revved the engine occasionally to keep it going.' The impatience was showing.

'The taxi needed to clear its throat?' CV tried to derail the recital.

Bell showed no amusement. He said, 'A perfect description.'

'Those two men, what about their age, their size, their faces, their clothing, their voices?'

'The tout seemed middle aged—the driver younger—both

thin, well dressed for those kinds of chaps—they wore shirts and dark trousers. Dark skin, black hair. Spoke a little English with a strong local accent. The taxi driver chattered incessantly—questioned where I was from and why I had come. I eventually told him to stop talking.' Bell at last seemed to be relaxing. CV was hoping for some clue to his personality and hearing what sounded like a recording wasn't going to produce it.

'Have the police found the tout or driver?'

'I suppose so. The hotel staff confirmed the time I checked in.'

'Which was?'

'About 8.30.'

Bell was making good time on the Galle Road which was not easy because local drivers had no rules. He had discovered that pedestrian crossings did not give right of way—they were for testing both motorists' and pedestrians' nerves. He took the Camary through the busier townships by driving around other vehicles as skilfully as a three-wheeler.

'You could be a professional driver, Mr Bell.'

'When I was a boy, I wanted to be.'

But suddenly they were overtaken by a bus on the right, and he had to pull back and move to the left because the larger vehicle was inches away. Immediately a beige three-wheeler swung into their path, and he narrowly missed it.

Before he could stop himself, CV said, 'An accident might keep you in this country longer than you want.'

'He ran into me.'

'And I am a witness. But do you want to tell that to a jury when the case comes up in five years?'

The Toyota was air-conditioned, which had kept the dust and diesel fumes outside. CV now rolled down his window as the three-wheeler was still alongside and pushing ahead. The driver displayed a wide array of yellow teeth and a red-saliva smile. His passenger was a middle-aged woman with terror in her gaping mouth and imploring eyes.

CV yelled at the driver. 'My friend has lost his daughter, and we are going to the cemetery. I see you are going there too.'

He rolled up the window.

Bell said, 'He's slowed down, what did you say?'

'I told him you'd lost your daughter.'

'I'll never understand these people. I suppose it's easier when you're one of them.'

'Much easier.' CV began to laugh realizing he was about to take enough money from Bell to put up with some patronization. He was surprised to see Bell begin smiling too. The tension in his face had eased and so did his driving.

CV continued, 'When you arrived at the hotel, Dorothy was about to have dinner with Michael. Did he know you were arriving that day?'

'I think so. On the phone she said, "Michael won't be at the airport with me. I wish you two got along better." I asked her why he was still antagonistic to me. She said "He's locked in, but he doesn't bear grudges. He'll get over it." I particularly remember the "locked in".'

'So you know him?'

'I told you I was here last year.'

'So you did. When the rupee was eighty to a pound. Which month?'

'February. I was on my way to Singapore and detoured here for three days. Dot and I went to see the ruins and those famous rock statues and paintings of the cultural triangle—Sigiriya, Polonnaruwa, Dambulla. We returned through Kandy.'

'You met Michael for the first time last February?' he asked. 'At that time, Dorothy and he were a couple. Maggie's brother is my source. He says they've been together for two years.'

'Dot told me in London she'd met a glorious man. I remember the *glorious*. Until Michael she had been secretive about her love life. If I asked questions, she'd get annoyed. So I was surprised when she began to talk about glorious Michael Blue. Unfortunately, from her accounts he seemed indisciplined in spite of some fame. I hoped she'd get over him but was curious, even eager, to meet him. He was the reason I came here early last year instead of asking Dorothy to meet me in Singapore. I was surprised that I liked the boy so much—he is intelligent and intellectually strong. He has a reputation as an artist, though I'm no connoisseur. I'm told famous people buy his work.' Bell chuckled and glanced at CV, 'I'm a better connoisseur of famous people than of artists. Famous people buy art mainly to impress other famous people. Michael's work therefore must be impressive.'

There was a rehearsed sound to all this, and CV tried to look fascinated.

Bell had not mentioned Michael's drug dependency—surely he must have found out about it and disapproved? Also, he would have found his daughter's boyfriend flamboyant, and he had not mentioned that. But it was not hard to notice that so far he had not talked with this much animation about his daughter.

CV tried to see them as a happy threesome but with difficulty. When they dined together, did Dorothy look the grubby party girl he remembered? Did Michael Blue wear satin tunics and chains? Maybe Bell had been less preppy, Michael less shiny, and Dorothy the angel in red and white the soldier had seen. Those white pants she had been wearing when she died had become off-white in his mind. He had imagined them stained at the knees and crumpled at the crotch—even the reverse. When Michael learned she was going to the airport to meet her father why had he talked her out of it—if he had? It didn't seem his style from what Maggie had said. Michael didn't care what Dorothy did.

Why had Dorothy and Michael had dinner together when she had insisted she'd be at the airport. She had even dawdled away another couple of hours—then departed for the Oberoi—only to end up dead in the Pettah.

Had she sent someone else to meet her father only they hadn't connected? She could have said to Emma van Eck, 'My father is coming in at 6.00. Would you meet the plane and take him to dinner at the Oberoi. I'll join you later.' Emma was single—so was Reggie. *They're both single so let's get Daddy and Emma together.*

The newspaper had described Dorothy and Michael entering the GOH. They had stopped in the lobby where Michael had played chopsticks on the grand piano—he'd knelt on the floor as there was no seat. She had laughed. Together they'd eaten from the buffet in the fourth-floor Harbour Room, had a couple of beers and left.

'Something is worrying you,' said Bell.

'Dorothy was reported to be relaxed at dinner. How could she have been relaxed when she had just stood up her father?'

'I've asked myself the same question.'

'Was Michael antagonistic to you when you met him here last year?'

'I had only one harsh word with him. I unwisely reminded him that Dorothy lived on my money. He got very angry and said she didn't need it. He isn't interested in money and that's foolish. You can't feel that way today. If you do you'll get left behind.'

CV wanted to ask, 'Just where will Michael get left behind?'

Bell continued, 'I think Dorothy fell in love with Michael because he was the perfect antidote to me. I am a businessman; he is an artist. I have rules. He has none. At my invitation he came to England the following month, and it was then that we really got off on the wrong foot. It had been my intention to introduce him to some younger hipper men in business and give him a taste of the kind of life I take for granted—something you Americans take for granted too. But we never got around to it. This time I was the innocent party. He started berating me for having neglected Dot. His accusation was nonsense, because even after Dot's mother stopped drinking she hadn't wanted to saddle her new marriage with the child. Marie's alcoholism drove me to divorce her. I took Dot and gave Marie visitation rights. I sent Dot's nanny along on those visits, and twice she brought the child home because Marie was reeling drunk when they arrived. Her mother married a doctor she met at the rehabilitation clinic, a fellow patient. They invited Dot to Belgium. He'd moved there after he'd killed a pedestrian in the Netherlands when he was driving drunk. He was lucky that the man was a heroin addict looking for a fix. It was thought he could have contributed to the accident. Dot never felt welcome at her mother's home, though she enjoyed her twin stepbrothers. I'm rambling. Did you want to know all this?'

'I don't know what I want yet, so don't leave anything out. What did Michael see as your neglect?' CV still wasn't getting a take on Dorothy.

'For example, he said I had rejected her when I sent her to a boarding school. Rubbish. She liked her boarding school at first. When she didn't, I took her out. Did you see that car? It nearly ran down a pedestrian. It shouldn't be difficult to have a few traffic policemen here and there.'

'There's a war on. Traffic police are a low priority.'

'Yes, the war! I didn't like my daughter living in a country with a civil war, but when I come here it's like *Grimm's Fairy Tales*—gruesome stories you don't really believe. You barely notice it.'

CV was surprised Bell had grasped that. He replied, 'Our generation has been brought up watching war movies. After two hours, we expect the war to be over. TV wars cut to the commercials every fifteen minutes. So we take commercial breaks from the war—only the commercial breaks have become the real show. Everyone is bored by the longer action because the plot barely changes. War has a lousy scriptwriter. Ah, but I digress. You said Dorothy liked her boarding school then didn't. What happened to make her change?'

He now knew that when Bell was irritated his eyebrows lifted fractionally in the outer corners and there was a flare to his nostrils. Both movements came fast and departed slowly. They were there now. Bell didn't want to talk about Dorothy's childhood.

'She changed. Women change their minds.'

'She was not a woman but a schoolgirl. Children like consistency.'

'Not Dot. She first liked the novelty. Then she was bored. Perhaps I should have found out more about what changed her mind about her school. I was engrossed in my work. I accepted that she didn't like the place and moved her to a private day school in London.'

Yet Michael had accused Bell of forcing her to go to the boarding school. Someone was lying.

'And eventually she left you to travel on her own. Why?'

The eyebrows and nostrils moved again, and Bell did not reply. Finally he said, 'Would you repeat that question?'

'Why did Dorothy begin to travel?'

'Yes! Because she had inherited my love of gems. I have made money buying and selling them. Before that my cash flow was a tenth of what it is today. I didn't have partners. She decided she was going to be the first. It was her idea to work for me, not mine. She'd dropped out of college in Scotland, and I suggested she start a business of her own. Something less . . . less . . . I think the word I want is *ruthless*. Less ruthless than mine.'

He thought Bell was going to say *dangerous*. Was his being in a ruthless and dangerous business the reason Bell was experiencing the fifth knifing of an associate?

'I gave in,' Dorothy's father continued. 'Her first job was as a scout for me. I thought she'd get bored but instead she got hooked. She went to Burma where there was a star ruby for which I had a buyer. I told her to negotiate the price.' He expanded, reliving the memory with obvious pleasure. 'Little Dot had been instructed to whittle the price down, instead she agreed to the asking price if certain other stones were included. It was an aggressive move for a newcomer. There was considerable profit because the small stones she selected were fine ones. I gave her a bonus. Later, she found me gems in other countries—some entirely on her own. All I needed to do was check the merchandise and pay the bill.'

'There are no restrictions on exporting or importing gems?'

'No. It's an exciting business, and it's open. There has been control in countries such as this in the past—not anymore.'

CV longed to know him if he had stolen the Brazilian emerald from Congressman Jonas but asked instead, 'Do you think someone in the gem business may have killed Dorothy?'

Her father glanced at him. He eventually replied, 'Anything is possible.' He bit his lip, then said, 'But I don't believe it. If someone in my trade killed her, she would have disappeared. You yourself said that in the Pettah she stood out like a giraffe in Alaska. She had a boyfriend here with local connections as well as a visiting father with sufficient cash to shake a few trees.

'Our trade depends on trust. You trust others to make money for you. Dorothy was respected for her integrity.' He added, 'She was my child. My girl.'

There was at last the passion that had been missing. Did Reginald Bell know his daughter had been killed by someone in their trade—by someone who always used a stiletto as a trademark? Did he blame himself? Was he throwing CV as bait to a killer to catch him—not wanting by his earlier admission to use Michael as that bait?

He said gently, 'We're nearly in Colombo, so let's tie it up. Last year you were in England with Michael. And he was lecturing you on being a lousy father. What then?'

Bell began speaking fast as he swung the car through the much heavier traffic: 'Dorothy was on a trip to Hong Kong and Thailand when Michael arrived. Our relationship began to deteriorate. Two weeks later she came home, and for a day we were happy together. Then we were fighting ceaselessly. Eventually I suggested it was time for Michael's holiday to end. Remember, I was picking up the bills and had paid for his ticket. Dot and Michael left for Sri Lanka the next day. I felt my relationship with my daughter did not have to be dependent on her boyfriend's temper tantrums. I expected us to resume our usual relationship—both the personal and the business side. But she phoned and ended our partnership saying she had decided to go it alone. She softened the blow by saying that, if I wished, I would still be her chief client—she'd offer me first refusal of all important gems. I didn't like it, but I also didn't like her playing such a dangerous game without me to protect her. So I agreed.'

He'd said *dangerous* at last.

'She never would have had the steel to go it herself and I'm not speaking as a father whose nose has been put out. Dorothy was never entirely confident of her own judgements—she always wanted me to check the stones and the figures and have the final say. Nor did I feel that Michael could replace me in her life in that way. I thought I'd give her head and see what happened. A mistake, for now her death has happened.'

The man had pulled surprises.

'Why didn't she tell her friends she lived at the Palace?'

'Because she loved leading two lives. She was an actress. When she was tired of being one person, she switched. She'd go to Singapore, work out a deal and then go bumming in the nightclubs that same night with sailors—pretending she didn't have money for a drink. She told me once she saw a wealthy Chinese at a nightclub from whom she had bought a stone that morning. He'd tried to get her into bed with him—most men did. She used her femininity but never mixed sex and business. They all learned that. The Chinese didn't recognize her and didn't give her a second glance. She was no longer his type!

'She had two wardrobes. You have my permission to visit her room—now mine. It was paid for so I've moved in. Her clothes are still hanging there. She could be an elegant woman. When she was with Michael she was—careless.'

CV suddenly recalled her careless warm body on his knees and the touch of her careless golden hair.

'Only Michael and you knew about her two lives?'

'She might also have told Emma van Eck—one of your community. Emma too won't talk to me.'

'Perhaps she'll talk to me. What drugs did Dorothy take?'

'She was not interested. She hadn't inherited her mother's addicts' gene.'

Few parents knew what their children were up to. His own, CV knew, had never known that he was smoking grass so never knew when he had stopped. He'd had a bad acid trip, and his mother thought he was getting flu.

'Perhaps Dorothy led two lives in other ways. With Michael, she spoke of her father as a monster who had neglected her as a child. With gem merchants, you became a successful entrepreneur she admired and was loyal to.'

'I have come to the same conclusion. I've never heard a whisper in the business that she's been disloyal.'

'For me it's all speculation. I have no conclusion,' CV replied. 'Did Dorothy correspond with you?'

'By fax and email—to confirm prices and so on. On personal matters we'd phone.'

'What personal matters?'

Bell's smile reached his eyes now. 'Happy Birthday, Daddy. Happy Birthday, Dot.'

'I asked for that. So you sent business messages by email, which is as private as sending a TV ad?'

'We used a code.'

'Mr Bell, please get me all Dorothy's fax and email messages. Any notes you've made on her phone calls too. Any exchanges between you during the past three years. They can be faxed or sent Federal Express to me. Perhaps Dorothy mentioned someone you've since forgotten. Perhaps she spoke of a concern that seemed absurd at the time.'

Bell didn't like it but replied, 'You'll have them Monday. It's Friday morning on London, but my secretary is off this week. Some matters I'll have to keep confidential to protect my clients. You have a fax number?'

'I'll have one by Monday. If I can't find a private machine, I'll use the little post office on Havelock Road. Contact me by phone. I'll be there waiting to prevent others from reading them.'

They were in Dehiwela. Nearly home. CV turned to the back seat expecting to find the two women asleep. Not so. They had been listening intently. Aunt Maud seemed sad. Maggie detached. He sat back and wondered what he had not covered.

'If you've finished, there is something I have to ask you,' Bell said, 'Something unrelated to my daughter.'

'Ask away,' said CV, expecting to have to produce his own credentials for the cheque hadn't been written yet.

'You and Maggie go everywhere together. Are you lovers? Those I have asked say not.'

'They say right.'

It was hard at this stage to know who was setting a trap and who was walking into it.

'Then you have no objection to my asking her to dinner this evening?'

'I don't vet her appointments,' he tried to keep the edge from his voice.

'I'm not suggesting you're her keeper, but you and I are now working together. That must be our prime interest. You still have no objection?'

'Why should I?' Then he thought of something he had not got to. 'But before you and Maggie set the date, one last question about Dorothy, Mr Bell. I'll need the name of every person, young or old, in whatever walk of life, who you recall your daughter mentioning.'

He wrote down the names in his new blue notebook as Bell reeled them off. It appeared Dorothy's father never forgot a name and easily spelled out ones like Weerasooriya and Coomaraswamy without missing a letter. He started the list with Michael and Emma. CV recognized only some of the names. There were nineteen in all. He turned and said to Maggie, 'Were you listening?'

'I tuned out when you were arranging my social life. How many thousands of pounds did you ask for lending me for dinner?'

Both men grinned, Bell wider than CV who said, 'The list, rattle-brain. You know those people?'

'Some.' CV glanced in the mirror and saw her staring back. She winked. He wasn't sure what that meant.

Maggie Learns More about Reginald Bell

Maud vander Martern's home had been named Bliss by her grandfather after his mother Oblissful Eden van Cuylemberg, who had been named after a Protestant hymn. In the half light of dusk it seemed larger than it was, and one didn't notice the yellowed walls and cracked woodwork. All one saw was an obviously old two-storey structure surrounded by tropical foliage. There were no ponds or garden sculptures around Bliss, just plants and more plants, and one could easily imagine gentle jungle creatures watching from behind the trees.

Reginald Bell was visibly impressed and got out of his car to stare.

'But this is a remarkable building!' he said to CV, who was immediately irritated by the *but*.

'We all have to live somewhere,' he replied. Maggie scowled at him.

'Mr Bell, why don't you come in and have a drink?' he said to make amends. 'My aunt would like that.'

'Not this time, I must get back to the hotel.'

CV waited to receive Bell's cheque and then excused himself. Aunt Maud was seated in the dining room already dialling one of her friends. He detoured to give her a hug, went up to his bedroom and stretched on the bed to think about what he should do next.

Maggie had stayed to talk with Bell. She came up a minute later and yelled, 'Bingo! Dinner date', and went singing to the shower. When she entered CV's room minutes later, she was drying her hair. He said harshly, 'There are some things I haven't told you about Mr Reginald Bell. Want them now or later?'

She sat down beside him, and he turned on to his side and said, 'Sorry, Mag, didn't mean to yell. By the time the week is over you'll have stopped talking to me.'

'Never.'

She listened grave-eyed while he told her what Della had found out about Dorothy's father, ending, 'So, one, we know the man might be a thief. Two, Dorothy is the fifth person known to him who has been killed this way within five years. Three, he's what Della calls a rabbit—does it a lot, perhaps indiscriminately, and sometimes pays for it. Four, he's been coming here for about thirty years, since he was eighteen. He didn't tell us most of this, you'll recall.'

She eventually said slowly, 'None of it is so bad really. It's good to know about the sex though because he could have picked up AIDS, so I'll be careful if it ever comes to that—which it probably will. But we all have little sins in our pasts.'

'Mags, we're talking five first-degree murders. And grand theft is not petty larceny. Tread more carefully than is your habit,

Mag, because murder is murder. Don't tell this guy anything you'll regret later. If he asks you to wear red, wear blue. If he wants to you hang from a chandelier, get under the bed. Listen to him. Ask him questions. If he drops names, go into the john and write them down on the toilet paper.'

'Yes, boss. You have plans for this evening?'

'Yeah. But not with a fuckable object.'

'Wish I could find one for you. Meanwhile, tread carefully yourself.'

No sooner had she gone than Aunt Maud came and sat on his bed on the same spot Maggie had vacated. She told him she was proud of him. 'But I've been praying that I haven't got you into trouble,' she said. 'So, I want you to know you can give the money back and get out now.'

'No, it's wrong that someone should get away with murder,' he said and told her about the four other deaths. 'You notice everything, Auntie. In the car, wasn't Mr Bell too cool?'

'Yes, I think so,' she began to rub his legs. 'Do you remember I did this when you were little?'

'Of course. What do you think about, Aunt Maud? When you're alone in bed trying to sleep?'

'I think about the past. There's no point in thinking about the present, and I don't want to worry about the future. When we were young, we'd go to dances at the Galle Face or one of the other hotels, wear our prettiest frocks and dance and fall in love—sometimes till three in the morning, and if I was lucky, I'd be dancing with a nice boy. When I got home, I'd fall into bed and dream about my cheek on that boy's shoulder.'

'Would you have been attracted to a boy like me, Aunt Maud?'

'Oh yes,' said his aunt. 'I always liked boys with mischief in them.'

'Even the mischievous boys who were fat and thirty-three?'

'You're not fat, darling boy. You're sturdy. We played

sardines and were packed into a small space and a naughty, sturdy boy like you once held my hand, but I couldn't see whose hand I was holding. I was in love with that sturdy boy I couldn't see, just because he held my hand, and when we all came out, I ran to the house, so I never did find out which boy it was.'

'Perhaps it was Arthur.'

Arthur was her fiancé who died in an accident. She had never loved another man.

'Perhaps it was,' she giggled.

He laughed, 'I would love to play sardines and grab the hand of a girl who couldn't see me, but that's called sexual harassment today.'

'We never talked about sex then, and we didn't even think about it much as we knew we shouldn't till we married. I only thought about holding hands and kissing.'

'Even Aunt Rosalind, who was caught with the gardener, only thought about holding hands and kissing?'

'Rosalind was always different.'

'I think Dorothy Bell might have been different too.'

'It has crossed my mind, dear, but we mustn't judge her yet.'

The Palace Hotel

After Sri Lanka had freed itself from British colonialism, in spite of all hopes, there had been no happily ever after. British domination and racism had been replaced by Sinhalese domination and racism. The country had rapidly descended into fiscal chaos as many Tamils and Burghers left to become citizens of other countries where they had prospered. Maud vander Marten had watched this change come about and never moaned about it. When others looked back on the good old days in their island paradise, she pointed out they had indeed been good old days for the rich. At least now the doors had been opened for some of the poor to better themselves. There was that improvement.

But, because doors had opened for the poor, Maud herself

had lost out. Household help, which had once been plentiful, was now swallowed up by the tourist hotels and factories. Maud felt lucky to have Amily who was an excellent cook, honest and hardworking, and the old lady ignored her authoritarian manner that so irritated Maggie and delighted CV. Maud's other live-in employee was an old and imposing chauffeur, Joseph. He was her friend and chief confidant in the long months when she had no family living with her. At the time CV started looking for Dorothy Bell's killer, Joseph had returned to his upcountry family village to attend a pirith, a ceremony of mourning, for a nephew killed in the war. Two weeks later he would have to attend another pirith for a different nephew. For thousands like Joseph there would be no restful holidays for years to come.

'Tomorrow, darling boy,' Aunt Maud said to her nephew, 'Joseph will be back and the car will be yours. You could drive yourself this evening but I still can't find the car keys.'

Amily, who loved it when menservants fell short, had even searched Joseph's room and come back shaking her head happily, 'No key. No key.'

'Does Joseph always go off without telling you where the keys are, Amily?'

'That's how it is.'

'Then let's put a hook in the kitchen. When he comes in—even if he is going out again in half an hour—take the car keys from him and hang them there.'

Amily grinned with savage pleasure at the thought of enforcing this rule. She said to his aunt, 'You see what good things the small master has learned abroad? Our people are useless!'

The small master who weighed over 200 pounds asked, 'Come and visit me in America, Amily?'

She waddled giggling towards the kitchen.

He timed his arrival at the Palace Hotel so Bell would be readying himself for dinner. He was to call for Maggie at 8.30. Exact times suddenly seemed important, and CV checked his watch as he walked in; it was seventeen minutes before eight. He used a house phone to call Bell's room.

'Yes?' came the now familiar voice on the first ring.

'It's your private eye. I'm in the foyer and would like to come up.'

While Bell thought of a response, CV watched six dancers twirling barefooted on an inlaid black marble circle.

Bell's voice was back without warmth: 'CV? Are you still there?'

'That is so.'

'It's inconvenient to see you just now.'

'I realize that, but I'll need a letter of authorization from you to look into Dorothy's murder.'

Again there was no immediate answer, and he thought he heard the buzz of a hair dryer.

'A week is not very long, Mr Bell,' CV persisted when the noise stopped.

Bell replied curtly, 'All right, but hurry. I'm on the fourth floor, room 411.'

When he stepped out of the elevator, the first door number he saw was 411. A door to the left of the elevator had no number. He opened it and found it led to the stairs. So it had been possible to visit Dorothy without anyone being aware of it. A guest could call her from the lobby or an outside line, take the elevator to the third floor and walk up. He could then wait behind the closed door for her to come out and tell him that the coast was clear. He could leave the same way—make sure there was no one in the corridor, go by the stairs to another floor and take the elevator down.

He heard a sound behind him, turned and found Bell standing in the doorway of room 411. He was looking spiffy in a grey suit and pink silk shirt open at the neck. His silver hair was brushed back, which made him look closer to his age than the more casual style at the beach, it also made him look more interesting.

'I asked you to hurry,' he greeted CV.

'Checking for bloodstains on the rug.'

'If you had phoned before coming, I would have asked you to bring Maggie with you. Now I'm afraid there is no time to offer you a drink.'

CV had left her blow-drying her hair into separate glittering black strands. 'I suggested that, but she said she hadn't planned being delivered to you with a card on her chest like a wreath.'

Bell liked that.

CV had not expected Dorothy's room to be so large. There were two double beds, and it had none of the cramped feeling of many hotel rooms. The curtains were not drawn, and behind the French windows there was a balcony with two blue chairs and a small round table. Indoors there were two more chairs, bedside tables, table lamps and a long narrow slab along one wall under which there were drawers and a small refrigerator. He had entered through a passageway flanked by a long closet opposite the door to the bathroom.

He said to Bell, 'Did the police make a guess as to whether she could have been killed here?'

'The officer in charge said he was ruling it out. There was no trace of blood, and the room, as I told you, did not appear to have been entered that day. He thought it unlikely that someone would have moved her if the job had been done here. It is difficult to take a corpse out of a hotel.' He did not seem to be talking about his daughter but some stranger.

'Difficult but not impossible. Wait till the coast is clear, put her in the elevator, get out at the basement and play it by ear from there. If the murderer is one of the staff or a guest at the hotel, it would be easier, and he'd want to move the body somewhere else to take suspicion off him.'

'Sometimes these corridors are empty. At other times there are people all over the place, and you have to wait for the lift coming up,' Bell responded.

CV thought about it. From this hotel the Pettah seemed as good a place as any to dump a body. If the murderer was a Lankan, had help and got her corpse downstairs and into a car, he might have decided to put it in a place as remote from the hotel as possible. It had been a night of showers. The Pettah was about a mile away and was guaranteed to be badly lit and almost free of traffic.

He looked around.

Bell was a tidy man but not meticulous. Some of his belongings were on the long table—a stack of papers, glasses, suntan lotion and bottles. A grey shirt was hanging across the back of one chair. On the floor were leather slippers. CV opened the French windows, and warm air rushed in so he stepped outside and pulled the door shut behind him. There was a spectacular view of the Galle Face Green, that once-famous grassy esplanade that ran along the sea-front about a half mile south from the fort. It was now sneered at as the 'Galle Face Brown'.

This was where Dorothy had probably stood or sat before she went indoors and transformed herself into that other Dorothy—the one her father was proud of—the girl who could hold her own among experienced gem merchants all over the world. Bell had said she was an actress. Whatever role she had been playing, Dorothy Bell had not deserved to die for it.

He turned and re-entered the bedroom. Bell was in a chair smiling to himself and when their eyes met he said, 'Maggie seems a bit spoilt.' So he had not been thinking of his daughter!

'Well, she's a bit beautiful. But even before she made a living off her looks, she preferred to be treated like a lady.'

'I had better apologize for my remark. Beautiful women make me feel I'm in a war.'

'If it's war you want, we have a real one going,' CV wanted to say but knew he was gaining nothing by being touchy. He locked the French doors behind him. 'What I came for was to get authorization from you to allow me to nose around. A note on one of your cards will be enough. Also, you said that Dorothy's clothes are still here. I'd like to see them.'

'Now?'

'Why not? I'm here now.'

'Then do so, but hurry.'

CV had no intention of hurrying or of telling Bell that Maggie would not be waiting impatiently. He had told her he would telephone before her date left the hotel.

Bell opened the closet. 'Her clothes are in here. Mine are on the left, hers on the right. Until I moved in there were no signs of a man having been here. I have put Dot's other possessions in those two suitcases on the right under the frocks. Do you want to look at them, too?' There was sarcasm in his voice.

'Yes.'

The way the closet was built, every time Bell opened its door he would have to look at his dead daughter's clothes. Would he himself have left them there? CV thought not.

He wasn't sure what he should look for but was jolted knowing these were outfits she had once worn: the physical evidence of her double life. The first dress he lifted out on its hanger was a floor-length black-and-white printed sheath with thin shoulder straps. Then there was a light grey silk also with very thin straps. The next was high necked—yellow and white. The most elaborate was lamé—silver, green and gold. The most simple outfits were two short-skirted sleeveless dresses with matching tailored jackets. He counted the coat hangers— twenty-five. On some hangers one garment was placed over another and others covered with garment bags. He wished Maggie was here with her experienced eye to tell him if there was some significance to these particular clothes.

He lifted one of the large suitcases, placed it on the bed and found it unlocked. Bell was now standing with his arms folded, watching him. Inside the suitcase was the kind of underwear men wished women would wear—fabrics so sheer that they looked as if they would fall apart if touched. But there were also grubby cotton panties, bras with ragged straps and a slip torn at the hem. There were long and short pants and several shirts. Then he saw a blue handkerchief and realized it was exactly like one of his own monogrammed handkerchiefs which Aunt Maud had given him after he arrived—the colour had been a joke between them; she had asked him what he wanted and he had replied, 'No more white handkerchiefs, please. I have a hundred.' So she had given him blue. He had one of those blue handkerchiefs on him now. The one in the suitcase was folded, and he half-opened it so Bell could not see what he was looking for. His almost-invisible monogram was on an inside corner. He decided to be frank.

'My handkerchief,' he said to Bell showing him the monogram and producing the other from his pants' pocket, 'I wonder where she got it?'

It jolted the man. 'Your handkerchief? You must have given it to her.'

'No. I only knew her by sight.'

Then CV knew. The evening Dorothy had sat on his lap she must have taken it from him. That was why she had sat there and why she had not looked back as she left. She had been having fun and had left with her trophy—which meant she had intended seeing him again.

He smiled.

'You remember?' asked Bell who was staring at him.

'I didn't give her the handkerchief, but I think I remember how she got it.' He wanted to place it against his face and smell her on it but put it into his breast pocket instead. He gave Bell a quick glance to see how he was reacting. He seemed to have lost interest.

The other suitcase was a little smaller and a lot heavier. It had boxes and bags of make-up and perfume, exercise equipment with springs and pulleys and also her books—a few novels. Her father could have tossed them into these cases—there had been no effort to sort or pack. CV imagined the police had gone through them item by item and wondered if he could get their list and see if it included his handkerchief. Somewhere in these suitcases Dorothy could have left a clue to whom she was meeting that night.

'No knives!' he said lightly.

'No knives,' Bell agreed with a wry smile. 'Actually, nothing but what you'd expect any young woman to own—there's even a diaphragm.'

CV had seen that—it was in a dark blue metal box. Della had one just like it.

'I'll come down with you,' said Bell, moving towards the door. 'I had wanted to impress Maggie by being on time, but I'll be late. I think I had better tell you that I am not pressing any unwelcome attentions on the lady. I was aware of the little performance she put on at my daughter's memorial service so that I could have her phone number.'

'She's whimsical that way,' CV replied, careful this time to show no hostility. 'She prefers to help herself at a buffet rather than wait for someone to hand her a plate. Why didn't you phone that evening?'

'I'm not sure. I was fascinated with her, and she knew it. But I don't like to be controlled by women. Also, my daughter's death had upset me, so I kept putting it off. I'm not going to be much fun tonight anyway.'

In the elevator looking at the smooth hard face, CV realized that he had underestimated Bell—he was more than a rabbit with a head for business. The man was very sure of himself and knew exactly what made people tick. If a romance was in store for Bell and Maggie, it would be harder on her than on him. Under her glossy exterior she was gentle and often lost; under Bell's he suspected there was pure granite.

CV refused the Englishman's offer of a ride back to Maud's saying he wanted to speak to the hotel staff. Then he dropped his ace, 'I told Maggie I'd phone her when you left the hotel so she wouldn't be kept waiting.'

Bell's eyebrows rose in the corners. After CV made that call, he went to the front desk and asked for the manager.

LL Perera

A Sri Lankan in wire-rimmed eyeglasses introduced himself as LL Perera.

'I'm sorry, sir, our manager Mr Guneratne is not coming in this evening. I hope I can help you.' LL Perera had the implacable patience of a man used to dealing with people, particularly difficult people.

CV handed him Bell's card.

Perera's face was familiar, and it dawned on him where they'd met before. It had been on the plane from Dubai to Colombo. They had sat side by side and discussed the Tamil war's disastrous effect on tourism.

Now CV reminded him of that discussion, and he seemed amused.

'As I saw you today I remembered that flight and wondered if you did. Come! We'll be more private in my office,' and he returned Reginald Bell's card to CV. 'I will help you any way I can to resolve Dorothy Bell's murder. The police have taken our statements. Inspector de Silva was in charge of the case, but it has been taken over by Superintendent Senaratne of the CID.'

'How does the police hierarchy work?'

'Inspector de Silva was the OIC—officer in charge—in the Pettah, and so the murder came under his jurisdiction. Then, because of Mr Bell's being an Englishman and the possibility of an international fracas, the superintendent was called in to head a wider investigation. Senaratne is a fairly young man with a reputation for solving unusual cases. He's from a well-known Colombo family and has a degree in law. He left me a card which is how I happen to know about the law degree.' Perera laughed aloud, 'I can see you wondering why such a man should take a police job.' He added mischievously, 'But it happens all the time, doesn't it? It is only us poor fellows with inferiority complexes who have to try to put money in our pockets for our old age before it is too late.'

It was hard not to like the man.

Perera's office was air-conditioned, and it was a relief to settle down and talk with someone this frank. He ordered an arrack and soda for CV and a ginger beer for himself—he didn't drink on the job, he said, 'Because I might smack a face one day if I did. Ours is a stressful business.'

'I suppose I shouldn't drink on the job either,' said CV, 'but I'm modelling my performance on movie detectives. They always drink. I'm holding the line at smoking, however. I've sworn off.'

'Then drink something stronger. Arrack is so low in alcohol—please do have a whisky and soda.'

'I actually prefer arrack.'

Perera was frank about Dorothy. 'Miss Bell had a permanent room here,' he told CV. 'She was a delightful young lady. The staff liked her because she was cheerful and generous. I've become very interested in this case myself. It has not had any bad effect on our bookings, but I'd like to see it solved. The staff won't stop gossiping until it is.'

'I want to know about her companions.'

'There I can't help you. Miss Bell was usually alone. Occasionally, when she was dining, someone would join her or she'd get up and visit another table—people she obviously knew. But after the meal, all the waiters agree, she did not leave with anyone. She excused herself from anyone she was with and left the room alone. A few of the bachelors on the staff therefore fantasized about her as if she was a princess who was looking for the right frog—it was innocent and such thoughts were admitted after she died rather than before.'

'And you, Mr Perera?'

'No,' his eyes danced, 'I didn't fantasize about her that way. And please don't ask me why.'

'I won't then,' CV said. 'Each time I met her she appeared to be of modest means. I was not expecting to hear she lived here.'

'After she died one of the waiters said he had seen her at one of those beach cabanas at Hikadua and she looked like a beach girl. He asked someone who she was and that person said, "Dorothy Bell". In this hotel Miss Bell impressed us as being wealthy. She never looked for ways to save a little here and there—did not look at the prices—if you know what I mean. She dressed well—in the evening, superbly. Her clothes were the kind women go to Paris and London for. We see a lot of expensive saris on our local women and other Asians dress up, but rarely do the white tourists who come to enjoy a tropical holiday; they dress simply—even inappropriately so. I didn't know Miss Bell was engaged to Michael Blue. We had an exhibition of his paintings here for several days last year. I never saw her at it.'

'Where did she go when she was dressed up? It seems strange to me that a young woman would dress expensively to go out alone at night in Colombo—there'd have to be a place she was going to and have an escort. I'm told by my cousin Maggie vander Marten that women dress to create a certain impression—that is, they are considering their impact on others. Dorothy must have had a social life other than Michael's.'

'You are a cousin of Maggie vander Marten? Some men are very lucky! Now there's a woman! I have a photograph of her in my bedroom. If I were to marry, I suppose, I'd have to get rid of it.' He grinned. 'I know what you thought when I told you I was not interested in Miss Bell, but I am an admirer of women not men. I don't like to speak unkindly of the dead, but we have hundreds of local girls much more beautiful than she was. Your cousin is another case altogether. The ultimate exotic woman. I heard she was in Colombo, but she has never visited this hotel. She has more world-wide fame than anyone else in Sri Lanka—more than our cricketers and even the President. Please ask her to come to dinner—compliments of the house.'

'When she's on holiday she keeps away from places where she'll be accosted by strangers and written about.'

'I promise no one will approach her. We have private dining rooms. Of course, I myself may ask for her autograph, but no one else I promise.'

'Then you're on. Now about Miss Bell . . .'

'She always left the hotel alone, the doormen say. She always returned alone and not always very late. She would come to the front desk or phone from her room when she was going out, and we'd get a taxi. If she had a companion, I didn't see him or her—except for last year when her father was here. They left the hotel together. They returned together.'

'Did they act affectionately towards each other?'

'I saw no hugging, no kissing. But I saw and heard no quarrels either.'

'What do you think of her father?'

'All our guests are superlative people.'

CV laughed and took another sip of his arrack. 'And as far as anyone knows, Dorothy always slept here alone?'

Perera hesitated. 'None of my staff has seen anyone enter her room or her enter anyone else's. But the maids have told the police that a man—who knows if it was the same man—sometimes slept with her at night.'

'Because he left semen on the sheets?'

Mr Perera nodded. 'And sometimes there'd be no cigarette butts in the ashtrays when she was here; other times there were many, and sometimes the room smelled of marijuana.'

'You're suggesting multiple partners. Perhaps my search would be over if those sheets had never been washed and the ashtrays not emptied.'

'Our sheets are changed daily, so they had been changed that morning. When Miss Bell didn't use the room, of course, they weren't changed.'

'Did she sleep here on a schedule?'

'No. The laundry and restaurant bills show she was here about half of every month, but there was no pattern, and sometimes it was less than a week. Our monthly guests do not always expect the bed linen changed every day, but Miss Bell insisted on it. She'd complain if her room wasn't done to her satisfaction. She was never impolite, just came down and told us when she wasn't happy.'

'You have a list of those complaints?'

'No. But I can tell you most of them. Bathroom towels or sheets unchanged. Her room service order wrong. Once a cockroach got into the room,' he grinned. 'Can't stop them flying in through open windows, but it rarely happens on the fourth floor. The night before she died she'd had a boyfriend. There had been quite a tussle—a fight.'

'Was that a common occurrence?'

'Apparently not. Her room could be a bit of a mess, but this was the worst. You must understand that none of us were following her movements closely. But the staff would notice a blonde girl more than, say, a middle-aged couple. Her bedroom activities had once previously torn a sheet. Sometimes there was blood and that is not unusual for a young woman, but it is unusual for a guest to make a very big mess overnight when alone. The last night the bedclothes were bloodstained, and on the floor liquor had been spilled, a glass was under the bed, and a lamp had been smashed—it had been pulled from the wall and the bulb was also broken.'

'That's not love! That's war. If she had not died the following night, you would have billed her for the damage?'

'I would have spoken to her privately about it. Knowing

Miss Bell, she would have volunteered to pay for it, and I'd have refused to take the money—as a gesture of goodwill. If she had not volunteered, I'd have put it on her next bill.'

'That's nice thinking. When she called for room service, was it always for one?'

'I don't know. She had snacks rather than meals in her room. There are enough glasses there for guests—there are soft drinks, liquor, chocolates and so on in the refrigerator. Miss Bell loved caviar. She'd call room service regularly for coffee, caviar and toast. I can show you the bills.'

'Yes, I'd like to see them. When can you have them for me?'

'In five minutes.'

Perera paused, and when he spoke again, he'd changed the train of his thoughts. 'May I have that card from Mr Bell? I'm going to make a copy of it for our records. If you do come again, I know you'll understand that this is a hotel and our guests must come first. You may not always be able to question one of our staff at the time you would like.' He went out of the room and returned almost at once saying, 'As soon as Nihal's free he'll bring you a printout. I'm afraid I have only the last month's bills on the computer here, and we don't network directly with our head office except during their working hours. On Monday I can get you the older records. What do you need?'

'Three or four months should do it. I'm trying to get a sense of how she spent her day. What was her schedule?'

'When she was out the previous evening all dressed up and came in late, she usually had a late breakfast at about ten or eleven. If she was not out late, she left early the next morning—if she breakfasted it was elsewhere.'

'Did she drink much?'

'I never saw her drunk and she didn't sit at the bar. She kept a few bottles in her room—her own Bacardi, a Black Label, a vodka, a gin. When she dined here she always had a red house wine with her dinner and sometimes, but not always, beer at lunch.'

'And Michael Blue was never here?'

'He has been here but not with her. Everyone knows him in Colombo—the newspapers publish articles on him. You don't forget his face if you've seen it. From what our staff has told the police, Mr Blue dropped in during the evening with friends. They'd have a few beers. He was occasionally seen alone in the lobby during the day. Perhaps he was waiting for Miss Bell.'

The front desk clerk Nihal came in with a long paper printout and asked if CV wanted it cut.

'No. That'll be fine.' He glanced at it and found that the more recent entries included Dorothy's father's and did not point that out to Perera. He rolled up the paper, flattened it and put it in his pocket. He described to Perera how easy it would be to have got in and out of Dorothy's room without being seen. 'Is there a way out by the basement?'

'There is, and let me answer your next question before you ask it. In a business like this where tipping is usual you could use that door exclusively. If you put twenty-rupee bill into the right hand and the police asked later if anyone used that door, the answer would be, "No" because our staff are forbidden to let guests leave by the basement. They'd be fired for breaking that rule.'

'And the police did ask?'

'Yes. No one has admitted seeing anyone take that door,' he shrugged. 'Of course I've seen people use it. I get annoyed when the staff is lax because there is a definite security risk in having a door used without any check.'

'Does Dorothy's father have visitors of the opposite sex?'

Perera hesitated just long enough for CV to have his answer that belied his response, 'Not that I know.'

CV smiled. 'I'll rephrase the question. Would the hotel staff find a call girl for a guest if one was requested?'

Perera hesitated again. 'It is not our hotel policy to do so, but we are not policemen,' he said at last. 'If it was brought to my attention that a prostitute was using the Palace, I would stop her and would dismiss an employee caught soliciting a guest. But I do not consider myself a moral watchdog. Whew! I think I handled that question well.'

They smiled at each other. CV wasn't sure what to ask next but was reluctant to close the interview as long as he had Perera willing to talk.

'Mr Perera, do you feel that the police have been following up sufficiently on this case?'

'I ask myself that. We cooperated with them fully and yet did not welcome them running around here asking questions about a murdered guest. I am happy they have not been back. But if she had been my child, I would feel that not sufficient effort has been made. There is also the fact that we have become a country where certain politicians are known to be behind murders. They eat in our dining rooms. Black Tigers have put bombs in hotel bathrooms. I have become shockproof. Imagine what the police are like.'

On his way out, CV took the elevator to the basement and found a labyrinth of wide walkways along which huge metal doors were bolted and locked across storage facilities. There were dim overhead lights. He went towards the west face of the building and found an unbolted door and guessed it opened towards the parking lot. As he let himself out, he saw an attractive woman in an identical sari to those worn by the hotel staff coming towards him, and she called to him to hold the door open. She slipped past hurriedly, thanking him, and went inside without a backward glance. As it snapped shut behind her, a guard materialized beside him.

'Sorry, sir, you must not use this door.'

CV put a twenty-rupee bill in the man's hand.

'Goodnight, sir,' he smiled.

'Goodnight.'

Bundula Balasingham

'Good luck, sir,' said a young saried woman in the air-conditioned foyer of Casino Vegas.

'Good luck, sir,' said a man in a navy blue suit who opened the door.

'Thank you. I'm here to see Mr Balasingham. My name is vander Marten. He's expecting me.'

One of the phone numbers Aunt Maud had bribed off the desk clerk had been this casino's. Before leaving Bliss that evening, he had first tried the Singapore number and got a Chinese who had said something either in unintelligible English or his own language.

'Mr Reginald Bell calling from Sri Lanka,' CV had opened in his best British accent and was cut off immediately.

He tried again and this time said, 'Please stay on the line as I have a call from Mr Reginald Bell.'

Again he was cut off.

The third time, the line was busy. Later, it was still busy.

He had also tried the first of the two Colombo numbers and had no trouble connecting. A cheerful male voice said, 'Casino Vegas!'

'Bundy in?' he asked.

'Mr Balasingham will be here about eight, sir.'

'Please tell him that Clive vander Marten will be at the casino at ten this evening to speak to him.'

After that he'd tried the other Colombo number and got a busy tone. He looked in the phone directory and found his suspicion was right—that number was the Palace Hotel. He dialled it again and tried his British accent on a man who said, 'The Palace Hotel.'

'This is Reginald Bell, room 411, did you get the message I left?' he tried to sustain the English.

'Please be on line,' he was told, and after a brief wait, 'We have no message, sir. Nihal says he told you there was a call from London, but he doesn't remember that you left a message.'

'Sorry—I've slipped up. Would you give me the London number again?'

'There was no number. Someone asked that you call Isaac, sir.'

'Isaac! Thank you.'

He phoned Singapore again and got through: 'Isaac?'

The receiver was put down.

While he was waiting for Bundy, he watched a blackjack table where the dealer gave himself five cards adding up to exactly twenty-one, followed that with a blackjack and then two kings. Two women sighed as their money disappeared. The four men who had also lost remained impassive. The dealer then went bust, and everyone smiled.

The Vegas was underground and large enough for four blackjack tables, four baccarat, two roulette and a platform where two talented but obviously tired singers were keeping to a beat. It was a cheerful little place with a well-dressed amiable clientele for the most part. There were also some grouchy locals and sweaty white male tourists who looked as if they'd wandered in off a cargo vessel. Among the well dressed were East Asians who were spending a lot of money. No slot machines here—all the slots in the island had been destroyed a few years back on President Premadasa's orders.

'Mr Balasingham would like you to come this way, sir.'

'Thank you. What is your name?'

'David, sir.'

'Thank you, David. We've spoken on the phone, I believe.'

'Yes, when you called to make an appointment with Mr Balasingham, sir.'

CV ambled after David towards a door behind which he had already seen Bundy at a desk. Bundy's usual expression was a smile. Now as he saw CV approach, his smile did not waver.

Murder in the Pettah

Even as a boy Bundy had smiled too much. It had given him an air of being soft. He had smiled through sports triumphs and failures as well as failed and passed tests. He had crashed his first motorbike with exactly the same expression of joy as when he saw something delicious to eat or was discovered stealing by CV. But now, as he was seated in a dark suit in the casino he owned, his smile was at last appropriate. It made him a relaxed figure of authority.

As CV entered Bundy rose and held his hand out. CV didn't want to take it but did so because they were being watched from outside.

The air-conditioned office was windowless and glass walled. It was empty of filing cabinets, computers and other office accoutrements. There was a bookcase without books but with a black metal vase containing a single purple orchid and a sprig of asparagus fern. The heavy desk was otherwise bare except for three phones: red, dark green and white. There was not even a notepad or pencil beside them.

CV knew Bundy looked older than he did, although they were the same age. Now, as they measured each other, there was something else about him that CV had not noticed before—it was a twist in that ever-smiling mouth. He wasn't sure if the twist showed cruelty or pain.

A waiter entered with a tray on which there were two whiskys and two dishes of hot cashew nuts. Together the old friends sat back on their chairs and attended to this peace offering.

Bundy finally said, 'Shall I rise and take your shot like a man or would you like me to beg for mercy?'

CV had run through variations of the opening of this conversation and was glad not to have to take the initiative. He sipped his drink and made a face—he had been expecting arrack.

'Let me get you something else,' Bundy said quickly, 'I

thought you'd like Black Label.'

'Everyone likes Black Label—I was expecting arrack. This is fine.'

Bundy picked up his own drink. He said, 'Clive, we're not children to quarrel over small things any more. I realize you are angry with me but can we put that behind us?'

CV didn't reply.

'Mr Bell told me you're going to try to find who killed Dorothy. He also told me you were a hard-headed son of a bitch. I take it that you put the price up.' Bundy smiled wider and showed his silver fillings.

'Let's go back to square one,' CV stopped him. 'I've lost my ability to laugh off criminal behaviour in my friends. I think you'd better say your piece on that before talking about the Bell affair.'

Bundy must have had a bell with which to summon the waiter for again one appeared and took CV's whisky away. Bundy said, 'Replace it with arrack.'

'Forget the fucking whisky. I came to talk to you, not to try out your bar.'

The waiter practically ran from the room.

CV started on the cashew nuts. His silence forced Bundy to speak, and he did so carefully.

'Reginald Bell was leaving Sri Lanka yesterday. He cancelled his flight because he didn't want to go without making some effort at finding out who killed his daughter. I recommended you because I owe you a favour. I was hoping you had put our disagreement behind us. What do you want? My blood?'

'No. I want the truth.' He actually didn't really know what he wanted, so he decided to tackle what had been eating at him most. 'You tried to steal from me. The way you and I have been brought up, we don't steal. I would never have spoken to you again if not for this Bell affair. To please my aunt, I've got stuck in it.'

He'd kept his voice down and realized he was doing that to protect Bundy.

The other man managed to smile and look stricken at the same time and replied, 'When you found me taking your money, it was the first time I had been caught by a friend. I was ashamed. My family know I do it, of course, but no one brings it up. If I take something from my sister or my mother, they take it back. Of course you know the name for my sickness. I'm a kleptomaniac. I stole from you in school. I stole from you on your last trip here. I stole three hundred dollars from you at a party. But I only steal from people I know and care about...' He was moving his glass in his hands compulsively. He said harshly, 'You shouldn't get angry with me, Clive, you should pity me.'

'I suppose you've tried psychotherapy.'

'No. How can I? This country is so small. Word would get around. Even if it did, only the poor pay for their indiscretions. Us—never. We can get away with murder.' He smiled even wider. 'Murder! Back to Dorothy Bell's murder! You're going to look for Dorothy Bell's murderer?'

How neatly he had dropped the kleptomania and turned to Dorothy. CV got him back on track.

'Where does your stealing leave us Bundy? I'm protecting you, and I don't like it. Out there men and women who work for you are being watched by others, who are being watched by others, and they're all being watched by you. Let them pocket a hundred rupees, and you'd show them the door. Yet, you're a thief.' He stood up and looked out at the busy casino. Those employees who had been trying to guess what was going on quickly averted their eyes. The gamblers had not taken their eyes off their own games.

He sat down again.

Bundy said softly, 'I steal money, and sometimes I steal things—but I'm fortunate that my illness lets me take only from those who have it to lose. At times I feel I have to have something—it is mine. An hour later I would be incapable of feeling that way. I don't steal what is irreplaceable. And now that you know my trouble, you can come to my home and say to my wife, "Bundy stole money or a watch or another possession from me. May I have it back?" She will return it to you.'

CV sipped at his arrack, and they sat there, two grown men twisting glasses in uneasy confrontation. Again a waiter entered at exactly the right moment.

'Bring Mr vander Marten another arrack.'

'Yes sir.'

When he was gone, Bundy said, 'I actually don't drink much these days, Clive. My heart is playing up,'

'Oh shit, Bundy, don't do this to me! What are you and Reginald Bell up to?'

'What do you mean? Bell asked me to find him a private investigator, and I found him the best I knew. I know at least forty fellows who could put on some kind of show, but only you will make a real try. You're Mr Incorruptible. Remember in school when we wanted to break in and change the test marks, and you wouldn't let us? You even hit Ronnie. You said something like, "What's the point of coming to school if we're going to give ourselves the marks we want? We'll never know how we're measuring up." That was funny to me, because you were never measuring up.'

CV started to laugh because he had hit Ronnie not to prevent him changing the marks but to prevent the others from knowing how well he himself had done in those tests. He had been so protective of his role as fool that he'd have been damned if he was going to let them take that away from him.

'Clive, you don't have to be a genius for a job like this. He's not expecting a lot. Just run up and down the field, and if the ball comes close, kick it. He was prepared to pay you five thousand dollars but says you got more.'

'Did he?'

'Come on. Between us old friends. What did you get out of him?'

'Ten thousand pounds a week.'

Bundy laughed in disbelief.

CV said, 'Bundy, do you have an alibi for the time Dorothy Bell was murdered—that's between 11 p.m. and 2 a.m. Thursday of last week?'

If his dark skin had allowed it Bundy would have paled. It didn't prevent him from choking. He spluttered and took a handkerchief from his breast pocket and coughed into it. When he could speak, he said, 'Are you accusing me of murder?'

'If Bell knows you, you're involved. I'm asking everyone involved for an alibi.'

'I was playing poker here. You can check with the staff.'

'David?'

'We call him David—it's easier for the clientele. His real name is Dravi Pushpakumara.'

'Please call Dravi now, and tell him that you have given me permission to question the staff who were here that evening, even if that includes him. Mr Bell wants me to explore every avenue and turn over every stone.'

'You're still a joker, Clive.'

Dravi Pushpakumara's expression did not change when Bundy told him that CV would be investigating the death of Dorothy Bell and that any questions he was asked were to be answered.

'It will be a pleasure, sir. Please call me whenever you need me. If I am not in the casino I will leave a telephone number and get back to you in half an hour.'

'Thank you, Dravi,' he tried to make his own smile as warm but suspected it was the smirk Maggie hated. It came to CV that he should be very nice to Bundy and Dravi because men like this probably had the connections to put him under ground.

'Send us more cashews,' called Bundy at his manager's back. Then, 'He's a bloody fool but the gamblers like him.' He leaned back on his chair with a smoothness of expression a lot like Dravi's. 'You know, Clive, your credit is good here. If you want to gamble, you can cash an American cheque, put it on your credit card or just ask for the cash and pay later. Meals are always on the house. If you come between meals, order short eats. Drinks are always free.'

'Returning to your alibi, Bundy. What time did you start poker that evening?'

'I don't remember. Probably about nine.'

'Probably? Question two. How do you happen to know Bell?'

'His daughter was interested in gemstones, and I had a friend with a sapphire—cornflower blue and a little under seventy carats. I told her about it. She told Mr Bell. Two days after she died, he called to ask about it.'

Why hadn't Bell told him about this?

'So you knew Dorothy?'

'You could say that.'

'You could say that! What the hell do you mean? Did you or did you not know her?'

'Let me tell you what I know about Dorothy Bell because you'll hear it from the staff anyway.'

But the story was not what CV had been expecting, and it was his first real breakthrough as to why Dorothy Bell could have been a candidate for murder.

For the last year and a half Dorothy had been coming to the Casino Vegas—sometimes several evenings a week, at other times less often, and occasionally they had not seen her at all for more than a month. When she came it was with an Arab and sometimes several Arabs. Rarely did non-Arab friends accompany them—and never Sri Lankans. The only regulars were her boyfriend Mahmoud Mahmoud and Mohideen his bodyguard. Both men caused a stir when they came for they wore their national dress—the *thule*. With the white cloth and the black band on their heads it was like Lawrence of Arabia when they were here. Bundy said, 'Their party always arrived late in the evening and left after two or three hours—well after midnight.

'Having Dorothy here was like having a film star with us. Her clothes and her jewellery were incredible and people stared. They asked who she was. She asked us not to give out her name, and I respected that.' Bundy had some knowledge of Sri Lankan precious stones, and according to him, one ruby and diamond necklace she wore was worth a lot. 'At least a million dollars if all the stones were as genuine as they looked! The setting was superb and she had a matching bracelet. It's so unusual to see women wear spectacular jewellery here.'

Dorothy never clung to the men—she didn't touch them—not even to take an arm—but it was clear that Mahmoud considered her his property. He would order her around, 'Get me a drink,' or 'Go and see which numbers are coming up at the roulette table.' He once struck her when she spilled her drink on a baccarat table.

'He hit her?'

'Slapped her face. I didn't see it, but Dravi told me. She was angry, and he thought she was going to walk out, but then she apologized for her clumsiness. Dravi went up to Mr Mahmoud and said that we do not allow violence in the casino.'

Mahmoud had replied without taking his eyes from the table, 'Did I touch you, Dorothy?'

Her cheek was scarlet, but she replied, 'No. Why?'

'But Dravi had made the point,' Bundy explained, 'and it

never happened again. I'd have to close down if it was known I allowed women to be slapped around here.'

The first time Dorothy and Mahmoud had come to Casino Vegas he had lost over two lakhs at roulette, about $4,000. Dorothy had watched the play. When he moved to baccarat, she whispered in his ear and drifted from his side towards the ladies toilet that is out of sight of the tables. But she didn't go in. She called a passing waiter and asked if she could speak to the owner privately.

Bundy explained, 'It was sheer luck I was here that evening. I often wonder what would have happened if I had not been. Would she have just looked for another casino?

'There was something about her,' he continued, obviously unaware that CV had seen Dorothy alive. 'She didn't look like an Arab's whore but like one of those rich society girls. I am trying to give you an image of what she was like. She was very sure of herself.'

Bundy had taken her to a room out of sight of the main gambling hall, and she explained she had a business proposition but they would have to talk fast: 'Mahmoud thinks I'm in the loo. I've told one of your men to call me if he gets edgy. I hope he'll remember.'

'He will if I tell him to,' replied Bundy and went out to give Dravi the message.

'When I returned, I found her looking through the desk drawers.'

'A woman after your own heart.'

'Don't be like that, Clive.'

It was then she made her proposition.

'Mahmoud has bottomless pockets,' she had told Bundy coolly, and it was a word CV would hear again in connection with the man. 'He likes an honest casino. He plays a lot and we both know gamblers like him lose steadily. The losses don't upset him. He does all his playing at one casino in each city—he has a favourite in Monte Carlo, London, Atlantic City and Las Vegas. I heard your casino is honest, and I've been watching. It is.' She then looked Bundy straight in the eye, 'We can come here or go somewhere else. He's left the choice to me. The place I settle on will pay me ten per cent of his losses. Are you interested?'

Dorothy's blonde hair that evening was pulled back into a French knot. She was wearing a black and white sheath, with very narrow straps. When Bundy described the dress, CV realized he had seen it hanging in Bell's wardrobe.

'She looked such a lady,' Bundy said and abruptly his smile was gone. 'Now I see she was just a millionaire's tart. I asked her, "What if he wins—do you give me ten per cent?"'

'"No," she had replied coolly, 'Do we have a deal?"'

'Did she gamble herself?' CV interrupted Bundy's story.

'Only on his money. But she stayed at the minimum bets which are Rs 200, except at roulette where the minimum is twenty.'

'And you agreed to her ten per cent?' CV asked.

'I agreed. Once a week she would come into my office and pick up her envelope. I never cheated her. She knew that.'

'How much did she earn that way?'

'I can't tell you that. I have partners.' Bundy actually looked sheepish. 'But it was a lot—a lot—less of course when he was on a winning streak. He was not a stupid gambler and the most he dropped was $80,000. The next night he won back about $10,000. Remember they didn't come every evening and sometimes would miss a week. There was also that long absence—I presumed they were away or had gone somewhere else.'

'What does Mahmoud look like?'

'An Arab is an Arab is an Arab, as the song goes—but his eyes are a little lighter than one expects with that skin—curly hair, long nose, neat beard with a path in the middle, thick eyebrows. About five feet nine. Middle aged. A regular sheikh. Sometimes he wore a *thule*, at other times trousers and shirt, occasionally a suit. He has a long nail on one index finger.'

'Other women?'

'Sometimes, but I never saw a Sri Lankan—man or woman—with them. If you want to know whether he came along with other foreign tarts when she was alive—no.'

'And since her death?'

'He has not been here.'

'Bundy, did you ever see Dorothy except here at night and all dressed up?'

'I may have. When I saw the papers, I realized she looked different during the day. In those pictures—she looked like a girl.'

CV was not sure what this new revelation about an Arab in Dorothy's life meant except that if Mahmoud had found out she was taking that ten per cent, he may have killed her. The suspects had just multiplied to include Bundy and his entourage and Mahmoud with his. He finally asked, 'Bell knows about Mahmoud?'

'Not from me,' Bundy said quickly.

'Come on!'

'Not from me.' CV got the feeling he was hearing the truth. 'It has never come up. Bell knows his daughter visited my casino but, when he came here, I didn't say, "You must be the father of that materialistic little tart."'

CV snapped, 'If a man made that deal, you'd call him a good businessman. Dorothy makes it, and she's a tart? What you told me was that she asked for a ten per cent share of a client's losses. Do you have proof she was selling her body too?'

'He would never have hit her here if he hadn't done it before. He would never have done it before if he wasn't paying her to take it. That one would have slept with a gorilla if he'd paid her.

Her father is a gentleman. She was a disgrace to him and to her country.'

Strong words coming from a self-confessed thief. But it seemed that Bundy was ambivalent towards Dorothy and her lifestyle. One moment he'd speak of her with salivating admiration and denounce her as a tramp the next. CV suspected he'd made a play for Dorothy and that she had turned him down. Perhaps he had offered her money for sex? It must have hurt that she'd take both from Mahmoud but not from him, a Lankan man.

His friend said, 'I'm sorry about taking your money, Clive. I really am. However, I might as well warn you not to leave money lying around near me again. To make up, let me help you find Dorothy's killer. What will you need? Someone to work for you? I'll get you a good man.'

'No.' He wasn't going to let Bundy plant a spy on him. But there were things he needed. 'Tell me where I can rent a mobile phone right away. Even two of them or three.'

'A car?' asked Bundy.

'No. But I could use a computer with an Internet connection. I want to be able to receive and send emails and faxes. What I need is the usual office set-up—to rent it.'

'And someone to operate it?'

'I have someone,' he lied.

Bundy sat back and put his fingertips together. A waiter had brought in another arrack while they were talking, but CV hadn't touched it. Now Bundy reached for it and took a sip. CV spent the time looking through the cashew nuts, selecting one here and one there as he tried to put what he'd heard into perspective.

Finally the other man reached for the red phone, then thought better of it and replaced it. He said, 'I have an office. You'll find everything you need there: phones, computer, fax machine, copier. It would be perfect for you.'

'I have only one week!'

'You still don't trust my word?' His broad smile showed his fillings again. 'Clive, you'll have an office tomorrow.' He took out a business card and pushed it across the table. 'Those are the numbers where you can get in touch with me. You'll have what you want, and it will cost you nothing.'

'We'll talk about that later—I'd prefer to pay,' but he wedged the card in his notebook and looked at his watch. It was past eleven.

'And so to gambling?' he said. 'Your blackjack dealers were having a run of luck, I'm hoping it will have run out.'

'Dravi will give you five thousand rupees to get started. On the house. Shall I tell the restaurant you'll have dinner here?'

'Please.'

CV went to the blackjack table, and Dravi brought him five Rs 1,000 chips which he converted into hundreds. The dealer's lucky streak had indeed run out, and after playing through two shoes, CV was two thousand up. He went to the roulette table and put chips on eight and thirty-three. Eight was because there was no eighty-two and that was Aunt Maud's age. Thirty-three for Maggie and himself. He played for twenty minutes during which eight won twice. That was as lucky as a man deserved to get.

The dinner was fine, but he scarcely tasted the biryani or the shrimps or the lamb. He kept thinking about Dorothy Bell and Mahmoud and wondered if he or his bodyguard had an alibi for that terrible Thursday night. The presence of them in her life provided Michael Blue too with a motive: jealousy. The presence of Michael in her life provided Mahmoud with one.

Why had Reginald Bell not mentioned the seventy-carat sapphire? He had, in fact, mentioned damn all. Who, CV wondered, had bought Dorothy those clothes from Paris—her father, her wealthy lover or herself? What had happened to the jewellery she wore when she went out at night with Mahmoud? If she had been going to meet him at the Oberoi, wasn't a red shirt and white pants somewhat underdressed for a woman who showed up at the Vegas in diamonds? Why had Dorothy been leading yet another life?

He asked a waiter for a phone and the number of the Oberoi Hotel. Dravi delivered both to his table.

'No,' said the switchboard operator. 'We have no Mr Mahmoud registered here, sir. No Mr Mohideen. No Mr or Miss Bell. Have you tried the Intercontinental, the Hilton, the Palace or the Galadari?'

When he returned the phone to Dravi, he had discovered Mahmoud was currently registered at the Palace in a suite with two bedrooms. The Intercontinental, the Hilton, the Galadari, the Galle Face and every other large Colombo hotel denied that either Dorothy or her father had been their guests.

CV decided enough was enough and went over to say goodbye to Dravi before cashing in his chips.

'You've done well this evening, sir.'

'Beginner's luck. A happy gambler always returns.'

'I hope so, sir.'

CV returned the Rs 5,000 he had been given, though Dravi did not seem to expect him to.

The Pettah

Outside the air was warm. It had started to rain.

'Take me to Second Cross Street,' he said to the three-wheeler driver

'In the Pettah, sir?'

'Right.' He switched to Sinhala and explained that he wanted to see where that English girl had been killed.

The man replied, 'Someone said she was an angel but no angel would be lying in the Pettah in the middle of the night. Very bad girl, sir.'

'Is that right?'

On the way they were stopped at a military check-point by a soldier in a waterproof camouflage cape who asked their destination.

'The Pettah?' he repeated. 'Why would a tourist want to go to the Pettah at night?'

CV leaned over and said in Sinhala, 'I came here for a holiday and can't go back to America without looking at the Pettah. I want to see where that English girl was killed.'

They were flagged on.

Second Cross Street was almost deserted, and he asked the three-wheeler driver to slow down. Nothing had prepared him for the volume of litter around them. The street could have been hit by a hurricane. Enormous piles of wet and dirty plastic bags and every other kind of debris were everywhere as if a warehouse had been blown apart.

He said to the driver, 'How do we find where the English girl was lying?'

'Don't worry,' said the man, 'I know the place,' and he pulled into a puddle before a shop with a metal grating protecting its entire face. CV got out in the rain to look at the step closely, then down the street in both directions—it was empty. He looked up. Not one window was open anywhere.

'Better to get home as not a good place and also getting wet,' yelled the driver.

'Right.' But he insisted that they drive through the Pettah's other major streets. Here and there a body wrapped like a cocoon lay in a protected doorway. One man lay on his back with his legs propped high against the jamb. A fat woman was almost concealed in a plastic wrap. Rats were ignoring the rain and foraging in some discarded food once wrapped in newspaper. A few dogs were curled in doorways like the homeless. In all, they passed only four vehicles, all moving.

He wondered if Bundy could have hated Dorothy enough to

kill her because surely only a Sri Lankan could have thought of coming to the Pettah in the middle of the night to leave a body on a step. He didn't like the thought of Bundy having turned himself into a creature of the night, nor that his own memory of the Pettah as mysterious and romantic had been now replaced by this sordid slimy killers' hang-out.

Conversation with Maggie

He got back to Aunt Maud's after one. The rain had stopped. The house was in darkness and her very old security guard in his khaki uniform was sitting on a chair in his shed just inside the gate. His eyes were closed.

'I'm back, Security,' CV shouted.

'Good evening, sir,' trembled the man getting on to his feet too fast and nearly falling. He stumbled to the gate and pulled the heavy bolt. He then crept around the three-wheeler and wrote the registration number down in the book he carried. Michael Blue had taken a three-wheeler to Jimbo Rao's on the night of Dorothy's murder and Jimbo's security guard had confirmed that. If he had written down the registration plate number it would have enabled the police to find the three-wheeler driver.

CV decided he'd have to go to Jimbo's himself to check it out.

In his room he turned on the overhead fan, stripped, put on a sarong and lay on the bed thinking about Dorothy's double life. He heard the front door open and went out to find it was Maggie. She minced up the stairs and without greeting him led the way into his room and lay down. She didn't bother to pull down her blue mid-thigh dress which slipped up revealing her g-string. Then as an afterthought she modestly placed her scarlet clutch purse across her body to hide it. She let her scarlet shoes with tiny straps and monster heels dig into the sheet. Her hair still stood on end but her make-up was so immaculate she looked like a discarded doll.

CV took the other end of the bed facing her. She threw a pillow at him, and he put it behind his head. He unbuckled her shoes, dropped them on the floor and began to stroke her calves.

'Tell me you hate him. I need good news.'

'He's taking me to Kandy tomorrow morning. At six—that's five hours from now. Bad evening. I took him to three bars and that was before dinner. He didn't want to talk about her—he wanted to talk about me. I'll do better tomorrow. I'm going to stop playing an innocent and come across like a hooker.'

'In Kandy? In the presence of Buddha's tooth?'

'You can't have it both ways. Mata Hari didn't get her secrets out of generals by playing Scrabble with them. Men have a need to tell you about their lives in bed.'

He laughed but withdrew his hand from her leg imagining Bell's hand on it. 'No way am I going to take responsibility for you and Bell fucking. If he's not going to confide out of bed, forget it.'

'Oh, don't be silly. I know you think I'm a bimbo, but I can keep my private life separate from business. I've been doing it for years and years. I'm going on the Kandy trip because he's going to see a jeweller who is someone Dorothy knew too. Please go on rubbing my legs. You can't believe how I missed you this evening.'

'Sometimes I love you.'

He told her about Dorothy's wardrobe and finding his handkerchief. He showed it to her, and they sniffed it.

'You're disgusting, like a dog,' she said. 'I'm only looking for the odour of the weed. At least I'm being a detective. I know what you're smelling it for. Admit it.'

'No, you're wrong. I'm trying to identify her laundry soap. If it smells of Lux, Michael killed her. If it's Lifebuoy, it was her Arab friend.'

'She had an Arab friend?'

'I'll get to him.'

She said, 'You better. As for her clothes, I can't go through them with Reggie in the same room. Get him out of there, and I'll do a search. What will I be looking for anyway? More stolen hankies?'

'I don't know. Her jewellery. Bundy says what she wore cost mega bucks. Reggie didn't mention any. He also didn't mention an insurance policy or a will. Her ID stuff wasn't in the suitcase, no passport or return ticket to England. I suppose they were in her missing purse or he's put them away. I'd prefer to confront him with the truth rather than rely on him for a story. What else should she have had? If she had my handkerchief, there should have been other men's.'

'You poor fool. She didn't have to have a fetish. She just had a crush on you.'

'I wish. But you have one of mine, and you don't have a crush on me.'

'You're right.'

'So that doesn't get us anywhere. Mag, try and get back early tomorrow. We had seven and a half days to find out who killed her. Now we have only seven.'

'Of course I'll hurry. But remember I'm not driving the car, and no way am I going to take a bus back looking the way I do. Don't you want to hear about my evening? He can dance. He likes good food. He kisses well. I bet he is a good f.'

'I'm tired of him. I want to tell you about my own evening.'

She began to laugh and worked that up into hysterical giggles, and finally he joined her laughter. He was acting like a jealous lover. 'Shhh,' they said to each other, 'Shhh. You'll wake Aunt Maud.'

There was a vacuum flask of iced water on the bedside table, and she reached to pour herself a glass. He drank his from the lid. 'That's good,' she said. 'After you left here I went to see Emma van Eck. Did you know she lives on the other side of the Galle Road in a concrete dump? God, she hates me.'

'Why would she hate you?'

'Because she knows how superficial I am. She knows how much time it takes to look like me when I could spend that time mopping floors in a hospital or feeding starving babies. She makes me hate myself because she hates me so much. I had to go there in a three-wheeler and was dressed like this because Reggie was coming. She was dressed in a faded sarong.'

'So Emma prefers recycled clothes.'

'It's not how I look. It's because of the hours it takes to look how I look. The dieting. The creams. The watching for the lines to remove them before they can appear. The having to go with what's new. The exercising. It's a full-time superficial job, and she despises it. I could see it in her eyes. Thank God she's not hypocritical enough to pretend otherwise.'

He said, 'You do all that to keep looking this way?'

'Of course I do. That's why it takes me hours to get ready. I do it more and more now I'm getting old. I fuck men who'll help my career,' she began to sob. 'I had an abortion because the baby would have been born during the season. And that stupid little virgin Emma fucking van Eck looks at me from her more beautiful and fucking younger face and despises me because she hasn't even been tempted to sell out. She'd never have killed her baby because it was inconvenient.'

She had told him on the phone from Sydney that she was cracking up. Now he held her close and understood it could be true. He said, 'Shhh, Shhh,' and to bring her to more rational thoughts, 'What did Emma tell you about Dorothy and Michael? You didn't go there to get her assessment of your career. What did she actually say?'

She pulled away but reached forward and placed his arms around her again so she was sitting within their circle. Her dress was rolled back almost to her waist. The make-up had now smeared so her eyes were a mess. But she still looked beautiful. Poor mixed-up butterfly who envied the toads. He was angry with holier-than-thou Emma van Eck.

Still sniffing, Maggie told him, 'Emma says they all killed Dorothy. She did too. Do you have a tissue?' He gave her the blue handkerchief Dorothy had taken from him, and she blew her nose into it noisily, wiped her eyes and saw the mascara had run. Her face twisted again, and her eyes flooded. He took the handkerchief and dabbed at them.

'Did she talk about the Arab Mahmoud?' he asked.

'An Arab like a horse? Or a man? Neither! Not one time did she mention an Arab. She said that Dorothy—Dor—had been broken by her family and friends. She supposed she should be glad that Dor died quickly without pain, but Emma wants to put the person who did it on to a hook and leave him in the sun.

'As she hated me, I tried to make her like you so she wouldn't go silent on us. I'm afraid I told her that Reggie had hired you—and that made her laugh what is called the mirthless laugh. I told her that you didn't want to help Reggie—I told her I had persuaded you to take the job. I told her I was going out with Reggie. I knew you said it was all to be a secret, but I would have told her anything to get her to like me. I told her you have kept me sane, and I'd fucked up your holiday by making you do this job that you hate. I told her we'd both liked Dorothy. And you know what Emma van Eck said? She said Dorothy had asked around about you. She said you were the most attractive man she'd seen in ages.'

CV felt happy. 'Do all women lie to each other?'

'Oh, you're such a fool. Most women hate pretty men. I've told you that before.'

'Reggie Bell seems to be doing all right.'

'It's his money, not his face. Of course, he has a good body too. It's his being in control. The nicest men lose out because they don't have self-confidence.'

'We'll have to have a long talk about that one day. So, Emma said nothing about an Arab in Dorothy's life?'

'You keep talking about an Arab. No nothing.'

'Emma is jealous of you and feels guilty about Dorothy dying. Reggie has the hots for you, postponed the big play and is taking you to Kandy in four and a half hours. Anything else?'

'Yes, I haven't been dieting and haven't put on an ounce. I must be naturally thin.'

'Good news. How about anything else about Dorothy?'

'No. Tell me about the Arab.'

'Are you up to it? I worry about you.'

'Tell me.'

He told her. When he'd finished she said, 'Reggie is not expecting this kind of action from you. You're not even on the payroll yet, and you've searched her room, talked to the hotel staff, know about the semen on the sheets, found out she had an Arab john and that Reggie came here to see a sapphire. You've also been to the scene of the crime.'

The self-flagellation was gone.

'All blind alleys,' he said. 'Now listen carefully because I want your input on my list of suspects. First, there is Mahmoud. If he did it, Mohideen his bodyguard was probably there or killed her himself. There are also Bundy, Michael, Jimbo, Emma and, not least, Reggie Bell.'

She said, 'I guess Mahmoud or Bundy because both have been abroad and could have met the other victims, or the CIA or the Mob, in which case there'll be no justice, but it would be nice to know which. You don't kill your daughter, which rules out Reggie. Emma's about as dangerous as a cotton ball. Michael wouldn't be cold-shouldering Reggie if he'd done it. He'd be trying to look innocent.'

'I don't rule Reggie out, yet.'

'I do. I should sleep. Where's my alarm clock?' He had borrowed it from her. Last year he had sent it to her for her birthday—a teddy bear with a stomach that lifted to reveal the time. She told him it reminded her of him. It was on the bureau.

Maggie took it in her hand and said, 'My teddy alarm is the only lover who never lets me down. I'm falling apart. Don't try to deny it. I know I am.'

He walked to the door with his arm around her and kissed her cheek. 'What you've got isn't fatal. I suspect the Supreme One thinks you've lived that life too long. It's just that you don't know how to get out.'

'So how do I get out?'

'Cut the wires, dig a tunnel, hide in a laundry basket. But don't try to swim ashore, the current's too treacherous—and don't stick knives in those who stand in your way.'

She hugged him, 'Love you, CV.'

'Love you, Mag.'

Chapter V

Saturday

Bundy
Maggie had disappeared, Aunt Maud told him, shaking him awake. 'She's gone to Kandy with Reggie Bell,' CV told her.

'Oh no!'

'Remember, Auntie, she's taller than he is. She's looked after herself all these years. She's taken a course in karate.'

'Karate!' she was obviously relieved. 'Maggie can kick the top of the door, but I can only reach the chair seat. I'm having a bridge party this morning, and I'm making a scrapbook about Dorothy. Shantha is bringing her old newspapers and we're going to look for the stories about her and cut them out. Amily is helping, so we'll have the Sinhala accounts too.'

'Don't forget to put them into chronological order. Also include the bylines.'

'What is that?'

'Byline is the reporter's name.'

'Byline! I love being a detective.'

'When you get a computer you can investigate crimes all over the world. Let's spend some of Bell's money on a phone for this room.'

'I have another phone somewhere. Do we need the-Man to connect it?'

'This is a situation where I can be the-Man.'

'Amily is making you kiributh for breakfast.'

'She won't talk about our investigation to her friends, will she?'

'Amily? She's so secretive she won't tell me what she's making for lunch.'

He shaved, phoned Bundy and caught him at home. They made an appointment to meet at the casino at nine. Then he phoned Della.

'Did I wake you?' he asked. 'It's tomorrow morning here, and the birds are calling to their mates though it's too hot for sex or making nests.'

'Glad you called. I just can't get all those knifings off my mind.' She shouted to someone else, 'It's my old boyfriend.'

'Reginald Bell is paying me to look into his daughter's death, so you've won your bet.'

She gave a hoot. 'Am I a judge of you or am I? And I get reimbursed for the phone calls too?'

'You do and a sari as an extra thanks for your snooping.'

'You always were a generous man. Remember the colour of my hair when you choose.' She dropped her voice and whispered dramatically, 'Homer is jealous of you.' One of her complaints about CV had been that he never got jealous. 'Why doesn't Reggie hire a real PI, I wonder!'

'That million-dollar question has been worrying me too. Meanwhile, no one has a motive. Everyone has an alibi. I'll just shake a few trees.'

'You'll shake the murderer's head right on to a platter. You're compulsive. You worked on this till ten last night, I bet.'

'One-thirty, because I've agreed to only one week. You're wrong Della—it will be an empty platter.'

'I'll bet the two hundred bucks I just won that it won't.'

When he hung up he called the Palace and left a message for Bell. 'Lunch tomorrow. I'll be at the hotel at one.'

At breakfast Amily was surly. 'Lady says you're not eating my lunch. What's wrong with my food?'

'I had three helpings of kiributh but I just won't have time to come back.'

'Then I am making sandwiches in a box.'

'Not today, Amily.'

Shantha arrived within minutes. Behind her came a man carrying a huge stack of newspapers, and she stopped to say, 'When Dorothy Bell went to Sushila's to have her hair and nails done, she used the name Louise Lawrence. She was a natural blonde but her hair was brightened and pushed up with plaits and knots. No matter how much trouble Sushila took, the next time Dorothy came in her hair'd be a mess again.' Sushila was Shantha's daughter.

'Sushila is certain it was Dorothy?'

'Oh yes. Sometimes she saw her with Michael Blue.'

'Did she confront her?'

'No, Sushila thought she must have another boyfriend she dressed up for. Here is the best bit. One day when Sushila called Dorothy *Miss Lawrence*, she said, "Don't call me that again! My name is Dorothy Bell." What about that?'

'No explanation?'

'None, and after that she always booked in her own name.'

A three-wheeler had stopped at the gate. Maud peered at the driver. 'He looks an insolent creature,' she declared.

'I'm bigger than he is.'

He kissed her on both cheeks.

Bundy was outside the casino in a bright blue BMW 3201, a really beautiful automobile. He was wearing CV's sunglasses and smiling. They drove to Colpetty where, behind a private house, there was a building that reminded CV of Maggie's description of Emma's home: a concrete box. Bundy explained it was an office he rented but rarely used as he spent most of his time at the casino. CV hoped he showed none of the misgivings he felt. He'd learned two things about himself however: one, he no longer cared about Bundy's attempted theft of his money; two, he didn't want him to be a murderer.

'It's a rugged set-up, but there's Internet access,' Bundy said as they walked up the path. 'The computer's an IBM clone—a powerful bugger. I'm pleased you'll be using it, as it shouldn't be left idle in this humidity. I've moved my files to my home computer. The manuals are in the drawer.'

'I'm really grateful, Bund. I'll need your email address and fax and phone numbers here.'

'I'll write them down.'

They were still outside the building, and Bundy hesitated as if about to speak and then decided not to say whatever had been on his mind. CV took stock. The garden needed pruning except for the area close to the main house. A middle-aged woman watched them from the back steps. Bundy raised a hand in friendship, so CV did too. She waved her broom.

'Who owns that house?' he asked.

'It's rented by a Mrs Fonseka and her unmarried sister. That woman is their cook, Lakshmi. She'll bring you a cup of tea if you want one.'

He had taken a ring of keys from his pocket and opened the front door, which was fitted with a double-bolt lock. Inside, cold air enveloped them. CV took a quick survey. There were dust cloths over the three tables and a dull red light glowed from under one.

A large fax machine with an attached telephone was on the far left. Another cloth covered a printer and a third covered the photocopier. Bundy had produced exactly what CV needed— a utilitarian space with the essentials.

His friend now opened the cupboard near the windows. It held copy paper as well as floppy, CD and zip disks. One shelf held Maxwell House instant coffee, Lipton tea bags, powdered milk, cutlery, an electric kettle and other kitchen items.

'Help yourself,' Bundy told him.

'Thank you. I'll replace what I use.'

'Don't be silly. The phones are in the desk drawer. They'll need to be charged. Haven't been used for months. That door leads to the kitchen and the other one to the toilet.'

Bundy showed him which key fitted which drawer. In one there were identical mobile phones and two chargers and he put them into the plastic shopping bag lying folded in the same drawer. 'The phone numbers are taped to them.' He added, 'I know you're a computer man, but I could start it up for you if you like.'

CV said, 'It will save me the time of figuring things out for myself.'

Bundy pulled a chair to the table and the screen sprang to life at his touch. 'I don't know what I would have done without your help, Bund,' CV said.

He was startled by the response. 'You've forgiven me, then?'

'Forgiven? Oh sure. But try to get help. Of course, I'd like the sunglasses you're wearing back. They're good ones.'

The smiling mouth became slack. Bundy took the glasses off and stared at them as if he didn't know how they had got there.

'You took them from me in Negombo,' CV, now amused, reminded him.

'I'm sorry, Clive! I don't remember doing it.'

'No problem. They're only sunglasses.'

Bundy said carefully, 'When we were in school it was predictable that I would be running a casino one day. Remember the lotteries and card games I organized? But no one would have guessed that by the time we were thirty-three you'd be so successful.'

CV said, 'You're worried about me, aren't you? Don't worry. When I'm out on the tracks I'll look both ways.'

'You're out on the tracks now. It was a mistake to involve you.'

'Don't worry so much. How much travelling out of Lanka do you do?' he asked, hoping the question seemed innocuous.

'Not as much as I'd like. Once in two years. Why?'

'Had you met or even heard of Bell or Mahmoud before—other than in connection with Dorothy?'

'No. And you?'

'No. Did you know Charles Yarrow, Cruz Iglesias, Desmond Crewel, Vincent Belli?'

'A rock band?'

'You really haven't heard the names?'

'If I have, I've forgotten them. None rings a bell.'

Bundy picked up the bag of phones, and they returned to his car.

CV accepted a ride to Colpetty junction saying he'd walk to his next appointment from there and bade his friend goodbye. Then he went into the corner bookstore and watched through the window until the BMW slid away and turned south at the crossroads. He hurried out and took the first three-wheeler he saw going in the same direction. When he was sure there was no sign of being followed, they were near Bagatelle Road where Michael Blue lived.

He had no idea which was Blue's house, so he asked a slender middle-aged man if he knew the name. The response was 'Good morning, sir! I work for Blue Master.' The man pointed to the third gate from where they were standing, and approaching from the opposite direction was Michael himself. He was not wearing satin this time or even a neck chain, and his straight hair was tied back. He was in faded blue jeans and a yellow T-shirt and looked like any long-haired American college kid. You could put Michael down in a desert, on a mountain, in any country, on any street, and he would look at home. The world would always be Michael Blue's oyster.

Michael strode towards him. 'What a pleasant surprise.' He put an arm around CV's shoulders to guide him through the gate.

'Emma told me you're working for Reggie because a wicked princess Maggie-van has set you up. True or false?'

'Both,' CV replied. 'Maggie and my aunt think Dorothy's memory deserves better than it's got, and Maggie's about as wicked as a puppy.'

'Dazzling puppy!'

A small, haphazardly put together dog had begun to howl at the sound of Michael's voice and now was on her hind legs pawing at him.

'Don't jump. Don't jump, Sweetie,' he implored as he closed the gate behind them and pulled the bolt to secure it. 'She doesn't obey me.'

Sweetie changed her vertical leaps to a horizontal gallop around Michael. When he reached down she ran under his hand so he could rub her back. He said, 'If I'm out for five minutes she behaves as if I've abandoned her for weeks.'

CV also bent down to pet the animal and she rewarded him by licking his hand.

The garden was shaded by kottan and other shade trees and psychedelic red, pink and orange bougainvillea. The bungalow's veranda was lined with painted pots, some containing plants as tall as a man. The house, like its owner, had been built conventionally but somewhere along the line had become eccentric. Like the flower pots, the doors had been daubed as if Michael had wiped his brushes on them, but the effect was neither accidental nor crude.

They left their sandals on a step and followed Sweetie into a room that was the full width of the house. It could be entered by three sets of double doors, all wide open now and secured by sea shells as large as footballs. In one corner stereo equipment, CDs and sheet music were on the floor, and a man in a checked sarong and grey undershirt was asleep on his side among them. In the same corner there was a poster of Mick Jagger and David Bowie advertising *Dancing in the Street*.

This was obviously Michael's studio. Around the rest of the room there were paintings, easels, canvases, brooms and poles of different lengths propped against the walls. CV placed the bag of telephone equipment on the floor near the door, explaining, 'I've been lent two mobile phones. A private investigator has to have mobile phones. I also have a blue notebook and pen. What else do I need?'

Blue gave a looping laugh, 'Luck!' He took a charger out of the bag and plugged it into the stereo corner outlet, carefully stepping over the sleeping man to get to it. 'I don't know who this is,' he explained, prodding the man with his toe. 'Do you?'

'No. Do unconscious strangers often appear on your floor?'

'Oh yes. On yours?'

'I don't recall it happening.'

Michael tried the buttons on one phone, put it to his ear and said, 'Well, this one is ready to go. Let's telephone someone.'

'Bundy said they hadn't been used for months.'

'Bundy lied—it's a Lankan habit. Who is Bundy?'

'A friend, I think.'

The second phone was also alive, and Michael said, 'If you're new to these, leave them charging because otherwise they give out when its inconvenient.'

Michael was obviously enjoying himself and dialled a number. 'Hello, Mum. I'm testing CV's new telephone. Over and out. That's my mother,' he said to CV.

'I gathered.'

Michael was still grinning as he dialled on the second phone. 'Hello, Mum. This is CV's other phone. All right, but you must be nicer to your heir.'

CV had begun wandering around the studio. The artist did not join him. He was better known for his impressionistic style, but some of his work here was as meticulously executed as any Old Master. An easel supported an oil-in-progress of Sweetie. She gazed from the canvas with the grotesque adoration she had shown at the gate. Michael had come up behind him and his hand moved the canvas from the easel to the floor. Sweetie approached it slowly then growled. He laughed and replaced it on the easel. He then lowered another painting of her. In this one a swirl like a dust devil showed her in motion. She came up to it wagging her tail.

'She has taste,' he said proudly. 'Not always my taste, but she's discriminating.'

'Probably judges them by their smell.'

'I thought by their mood.'

There were a few large sculptures in the room including a terracotta of Sweetie, hindquarters high, head on the ground, nose touching a ball. The piece was small because she was small—it was life-size. Michael patted its raised rear end as he passed.

CV now stood before the picture he really wanted to gawk at. It was a four-by-five oil of Dorothy. She sat on a low stool in an off-white dress, her golden arms around her legs, her blonde hair tousled, her mind between thoughts. The fearless audacity of the face brought her back as nothing outside his imagination had done, and CV felt tears come to his eyes. He blinked them away and said to her lover, 'Dorothy left an impact on me which became sealed because before I had time to know her, she was dead. The photograph at the memorial service was unlike my memory of her.'

'It was of her father's whore. We mustn't complain. He was picking up the bill.'

Her father's whore!

'Maggie guessed wrong then. Her words were, "It's probably Michael's favourite because it doesn't look like her. Men are like that."'

'The words of a woman misused by men.'

'I wish I could deny it. But why would a father choose such a superficial portrait?'

'He didn't know her. Reggie doesn't know anyone. He makes them up and expects them to play the part he has written. What role has he given you?'

He didn't know whether to trust Michael but then realized that, with only one week, he had no choice.

'My role is the clown.'

'Then let me give you some advice about Reggie. He is, right now, convinced that you are his puppet. Let him continue to think that. He is a man who thinks we function because he gives us permission to do so. He must approve even the words he hears. When he's tired of your talk he'll expect you to stop.'

'He says you won't talk to him at all.'

'I've lived in his home. We rose in the morning at the time most convenient to him. No matter how hungry we were, we ate only when he was hungry. When he wanted a drink, everyone else was expected to drink. When he felt like going to bed, the lights in the flat were turned out. I would read at night. He'd come to my door, open it, look at me and leave. He did that three times in one night! I eventually went to sleep with the light on to annoy him. I avoid manipulative games but he trapped me into playing them. Eventually, it's give him your life or walk out, as I did, and as Dorothy did.'

'A megalomaniac?'

'Oh yes!'

'He says he likes you.'

'He has to like me to get what he wants from me.'

'And that is?'

Michael said wryly, 'My company. He wants me around.'

'Enough to have killed his daughter who was making that impossible?'

'I hope not, because then I'd have to kill him and I don't know how to kill. Let's go outside.'

Michael pushed some newspapers on to the floor off a long teakwood chair and carried it above his head outdoors to a shaded area under the trees. He lay down on the chair and swivelled its two long arms so he could hang his legs over them. Sweetie crept under him and spread there on her back with her legs and her mouth open, her tongue hanging out.

He called, 'Bring out the other *hansiputuwa*. It's cooler here. There's a breeze.'

CV cleared two cameras and several more newspapers off another old chair and carried it to where they could see each other as they talked. These were heavy chairs, yet Michael had lifted his easily. CV had observed that painters and sculptors have exceptional upper-body strength from lugging their work around. The artist Michael could easily have shoved a knife through a torso and carried the body to a car.

'Where did you find Sweetie?' he asked.

'On Duplication Road. She was a pup with a broken paw, so I took her to a vet. She's been attached to me ever since. When I went to England last year she wouldn't eat and had to be fed intravenously. Do you like my new painting of her?'

'You have to ask? When you're good you're very very good.'

Michael liked that. 'And when I'm not, I'm vulgar, slick and trivial. I was fifteen when Raul Cameron took three of my paintings to London for a critic to label me a genius. Genius is Stephen Hawking, not Michael Blue. Once you're an artist who sells they'll buy your underpants, your toothbrush, your toenail clippings. All you have to do is crap on a canvas and sign your name. I'm only twenty-five but I've read of others: "He paints in the style of Michael Blue". I have no style. I just try to do a good one. My Dorothy is good. If I don't do something stupid to the new Sweetie, I may have another good one. It is influenced by Andrew Wyeth's Helga lying naked on a bed. Sweetie is my Helga—exquisite yet coarse. She's my favourite model. But no one will write, "Blue has painted Sweetie in the style of Wyeth"—because I am that dreadful word *established*.'

'Dorothy was also a favourite model?'

'She never appealed to me that way until she died, and now I want to paint a hundred Dorothys. She was quite ordinary to look at and ordinary in her taste. She had a beautiful head but never had the courage to shave off her hair. Her feet were also very fine, but she wouldn't even decorate them with jewels. The portrait you were crying over is one of four I have made of her. But enough of my beloved! You've heard me play the drums. There's an art! What do you think of my drumming?'

A yellow flower floated down from one of the trees and landed on CV's shirt. He said slowly, 'I think you should call music your hobby, not your art.'

Michael Blue's laughter was fast and noisy. He sounded like a hyena and had to sit up and hold his stomach, for his whooping laughter threatened to choke him. At last he lay back again, looked into the golden tree above, scratched his head and yawned. 'She never leaves me. She is everywhere. I think I see her walking towards me. I turn because I've heard her voice.'

More yellow flowers were floating down on them and they began to reach out to catch them and gave themselves to the task in earnest until Michael broke the silence.

'Emma doesn't want to see you. I told her she's silly—we all want to know who killed Dor—we just don't want to do the poking around ourselves. I'm glad you'll make a stab at finding her killer. I don't even care who you're working for—just don't bring him near me.'

'You don't give him an inch do you?'

'I'd cut his throat if I knew how to get away with it.'

'Why?'

'Because I'd like him to be dead.'

'Yet he warms when he talks about you.'

Michael shuddered.

CV had presumed that except for the sleeper they were alone in the house, but now a fair-haired man joined them. He walked as if he was dancing, moving to music as Maggie sometimes did.

'Hello, Jeff,' said Michael, 'I wondered what had happened to you.'

Michael introduced the newcomer as 'Jeffrey Fournier, one of those French buggers here to provide our beggars with condominiums.' To Jeff he said gleefully, 'Remember you asked me who the man with Maggie was? You said it was the third time you'd seen that goddess with her ape?' Michael enjoyed the young man's embarrassment; he had gone scarlet.

'The first time Jeff saw you, CV, he called you a gorilla to Dorothy, and she said she'd like to swing in the jungle with you.' He grinned and cleared his throat noisily. 'She said to Jeff, "There goes the most exciting man in the island." Jeff thinks attractive men should have high cheekbones and was very put out.'

CV felt the colour creeping into his face.

'Michael is teasing us,' said Jeff plaintively. 'I didn't mean you were an ape like *that*.' He had a musically soft voice with a lisp that added to his exaggerated femininity, but his accented English was flawless. 'You see, Dor kept talking about you as if you were a god, and you are not a beauty, which of course you know, and Michael is so handsome, and she was in love with him. I just wondered what Maggie-van saw in you. I am so childish. You must forgive me.'

'I feel much better now you've explained,' said CV.

'Oh, you too are laughing at me!' pouted Jeffrey. 'I promise it was just in fun.'

He wrung his hands together. Michael guffawed.

'How about some lime juice for our guest, Jeffrey?' he said.

'Yes, yes, of course! And for lunch? We have no money. We have a tin of tuna, one of sardines, three of baked beans, one loaf of bread and about a thousand limes. One papaw.'

Murder in the Pettah

'Stop it!' Michael said good naturedly. 'Clive, may I borrow a couple of hundred?'

CV tossed his wallet to Jeffrey who fielded it easily with his left hand. 'Jeff, beer too. Get whatever you need, or shall I take you both out?'

'No, because you think we are going to steal from you,' Jeff declared. 'But it is not so. We borrow often but we always pay our debts.'

'It's not even my money,' CV insisted. 'It's Mr Bell's. There'll be no debt because we'll be eating off him.'

'How much is he paying you?' asked Michael.

'If his cheque doesn't bounce . . .'

'. . . and it won't,' said Michael.

'How do you know?'

'Because his cheques don't—it's a part of his style. If he gives you cash, on the other hand, hide it. It will be back in his pocket before nightfall. How much?'

CV broke the news slowly as he had to Bell, 'I'm getting ten thousand . . .'

'Ten thousand rupees? Well, fellow, you've been taken—he'd have given you more.'

'Not rupees—pounds sterling.'

'Really?'

'Yeah.'

'Well done!'

Then CV dropped his ace of trumps as he had to Bell: 'For one week.'

Michael Blue was delighted and applauded, 'Superb!' he said. 'So Dor was right about you. She said you'd be a good fuck and also good company because you were no fool. If you managed to squeeze £10,000 out of Reggie, you're no fool. How did you do it?'

'I now think I should have asked for more.'

'No. It is exactly enough to get his respect and not enough to be able to turn down without looking like Scrooge. I advise you to lock up the cash the moment you get it. Dor said he used to get her to take money out of guests' pockets when she was a child. It took me six months to stop her pilfering. For safety, don't carry a lot of cash.'

Bundy, Reggie, Dorothy—lives joined by thievery?

Jeffrey was slipping out of the front gate. He had left them to change his clothes, all without making a footfall. 'Who exactly is Jeffrey? Does he live with you?' CV asked.

'He's my lover—a silk screen artist. He's in love with me, as you must have noticed, and I may come to love him. These days he's holding me together because I miss Dor. Day and night I miss her. The loss of her has cut through to my bones. Sorrow is a vile disease.'

'Then you did love her?'

'I loved her! She was my—no she was not mine. She was me, and I was her. We seemed cut from the same soul. If it wasn't for Jeffrey I'd follow her to where she has gone, but as my mother says, it is wrong to make such decisions so soon after losing someone. You have to wait and see what God wants you to do. A decision like that should not be made hastily. Do you agree?'

He seemed to be speaking to himself and continued, 'Dorothy was cut from the same soul cloth. Around us we saw lovers knotted in a pain we didn't feel. My male lovers came to understand my feelings for Dorothy.'

'The men were not jealous?'

'Of course, at first they were. But eventually they saw that without my love for her, my love for them would have been less. Jeff would weep because I turned to her more often than to him. Now he understands. I loved him more and better when I had her than I can now.'

They were now covered with yellow flowers, but flies had found them and were buzzing around. The breeze was steady, so the usually stifling heat outdoors had not overwhelmed them, but the flies came through regardless. CV had not noticed that Michael had anticipated them and had brought two fans with him. One arced through the air, but he saw it too late and it fell on his face. It opened to reveal a woman in a kimono.

He said, 'Michael, if Jeffrey and Dorothy were both your lovers—over the same period of time—that makes him a suspect. Motive: jealousy. Is there anyone else I should add to my list?'

'Me,' the artist replied lightly. 'Motive: he always kills the thing he loves.' He swung his fan at a fly.

'But unless a dozen people are lying, you have an alibi. Of course, you could have got a third party to do it. Were you jealous of the Arab she was seeing?'

Michael merely smiled. 'The M&Ms at last! You've moved very fast. No, I was not jealous of Mahmoud.' He was playing with the yellow flowers now tumbling like rain everywhere. 'This tree blooms once a year and loses its flowers in two days. For three days we will have a golden carpet, then golden-brown, then brown. I want to die today and be wrapped in them.'

'Reggie Bell?' prompted CV refusing to be distracted. 'Does he have a motive?'

'Reggie, the saintly father who wants his daughter's killer found? Would you like a joint or pipe? Opium?'

'Why do you need it?' The question about Bell had remained unanswered he realized later.

'Why do I ride a motorcycle? Why does Jeff go to church?'

Michael began filling a long pipe and, as with the Japanese fans CV wondered why he hadn't noticed the pipe before.

CV said, 'Tell me about Emma van Eck.'

'Trust her.' He rose suddenly, went into the house followed by a scrambling Sweetie then returned almost immediately with a bottle of water, two glasses and one of the Celtels. He poured a glass of water for CV and one for himself. 'I don't know how Emma'll react to you.' He pressed six buttons on the phone and asked if Emma was there.

'Hello yourself, it's Michael,' he said after a long wait. 'No, nothing is wrong. How about you?'

He listened for a while and then said, 'Well, I don't want to spoil your afternoon but Clive vander Marten was here an hour ago and I gave him your address.'

He was sitting on the edge of his chair and stood to bring the phone to CV. He held it against his ear and put his finger across his lips. The rush of words from Emma van Eck told CV she was frightened that Dorothy was becoming the centre of an unpleasant investigation, and that she was angry with Reginald Bell, Maggie and him, in that order, for making her worried.

Michael took the phone back, listened again and said, 'Of course, I'm still here. I can't stop the man. He has a job to do and he's going to do it. He's going to be at your gate at about two-thirty. That's in an hour.'

From where he sat CV could hear her shouting.

Michael said, 'At least shake his hand. I promised him you'd see him. You don't have to talk much. Give him a cup of tea and throw him out.'

He put down the receiver.

'Come on,' he said. 'The sun is too much. Let's go in.'

Jeffrey was back. He handed CV his wallet and set about opening the beers, then unrolled a palm leaf mat in the studio and settled on it cross-legged.

'Jeff,' said Michael just when CV had his mouth to a bottle, 'CV has put us on his list of suspects.'

Jeff's composure crumbled, and he seemed about to weep.

CV said, 'If you have an alibi, I can eliminate you now.'

'I haven't,' Jeffrey moaned. 'I wasn't at the Red Fox with Michael. I was here working on my painting. It is my alibi, but it can't talk.' He showed CV the painting, which was of Michael—a larger-than-life head with glittering eyes and an oddly stern mouth. 'Michael wanted me to try oils. I was working on the drawing all evening, fell sleep and started again in the morning. Then the phone rang. Dorothy had been killed. I did not kill her.' He shuddered.

'Hard to believe this is a first oil.'

Blue said, 'You can see why I want to keep the idiot near me. How can I not?'

But Jeff was not to be mollified. Looking morose he began to roll a joint, 'You want one?'

CV shook his head. 'All that evening you stayed here and painted?'

'No. I worked on the drawings. At about ten I went to the beach to feel the air.'

'You didn't see anyone you knew?'

'Only people at the cadday.'

'So someone did see you!'

Jeff's face lit up as if he'd seen a vision. 'I have an alibi, Michael! I have one! They saw me.' Then he fell again into a depression, 'But who will remember? It is many days ago.'

CV said, 'It was the night she was killed. People hang around caddays to gossip. Someone saw you. Also ask if anyone saw Dorothy in those last days—except with you two.

'Of course I will,' said Jeff. 'Michael you must come so they will know what I am saying.'

Michael said, 'This is the first time I've heard of suspects being asked to arrange their own alibis. What's to prevent us bribing someone to say he saw Jeff?'

There was a groan from the mat. 'Did you have to say that?'

'I don't have time to suspect my suspects of lying. Did you see Dorothy that evening?' CV asked Jeff.

He nodded. 'About four o'clock the three of us had tea, and then she left. Michael told her he would be with her soon.'

'She say where she was going?'

'To the hotel—to change her clothes.'

'She came at four and left when?'

'About five or five-thirty. Michael went to join her about eight. I'm not sure.'

'What were you wearing that evening?' CV asked Michael.

'What was I wearing, Jeff?'

'Wasn't it black? Black shirt. Black trousers. Black Bata sandals.'

'And Dorothy?'

'Pink and white sarong,' said Jeff. 'One of those little short tops. You could see her breasts from the bottom side.'

'Silk?'

'Cotton.'

CV didn't ask if it was clean.

'And did you kill her?'

Now, at last, a smile. 'Dorothy? No. I loved her.'

'Who do you think did?'

Michael interrupted, 'A person who could kill like Mahmoud: "Off with her head!" Mo: "Yes, sir, leave her to me." That man at the Casino Vegas? Some jealous woman? Look for someone who can kill. Jeff can't.'

So Michael knew about Casino Vegas.

CV said, 'You think Bundy could kill?'

'Your telephone thief?'

'Who is the owner of the Vegas. Bundy had a sapphire for Dorothy to show her father. A seventy-carat sapphire.'

'Bundy Balasingham who owns the Vegas gave you the phones? That Bundy? He had a sapphire for Reggie? Did you know about Bundy's seventy-carat sapphire, Jeff?'

'No, only the ruby.'

'So now there's a ruby and a sapphire.'

'You say a ruby, and I say a sapphire,' Michael sang off-key, 'Poor Clive. You're trying to find who killed Dorothy and you haven't even heard about the ruby. Reggie didn't tell you about it? I don't think Dorothy ever mentioned a sapphire, but I sometimes forget what I hear.'

When you're stoned, CV wanted to say. 'Did you know about Dorothy's ten per cent deal with Bundy?'

'He must have done it. He'll save that ten per cent now.'

'No way. Mahmoud came to that casino only to please her and hasn't been there since. If Bundy killed her, it would be because the sapphire deal went wrong. I wish I knew what I was looking for,' he said slowly and wished he hadn't started on a second beer. He'd have to walk to Emma's and miss lunch to wake himself up. A seventy-carat cornflower-blue sapphire, a fifty-carat emerald in Bell's past that he nearly went to jail over and now a ruby. 'Was the ruby big?' he asked.

'A stone to kill for, she called it. Prophetic?'

'Where is this ruby to kill for?'

'Reggie came here to buy it. That's why he was here the day she died.'

'But he never mentioned it to me. Was she meeting someone about the stone when she left for the Oberoi?'

'I didn't ask.'

'Of course you asked. Why did she stand up her father at the airport that evening? She could dine with you any time.'

For the first time Michael Blue looked confused. He said slowly, 'Clive, she didn't stand him up.'

'You didn't know?'

'I'd have known.'

'He says she offered to be there—insisted. He's told the police that, too. Her father was at the airport wondering what had happened to her while she was dining with you at the GOH.'

Michael put his hand across his eyes and began to rub them. 'My head's not up to this.'

'Just say it one more time.'

'What? Yes, she knew he was coming. No, she was not going to meet him at the airport.' He enunciated each word clearly.

Before he collected his telephones and left, CV asked,

'Michael, are you hiding something?'

Michael put an arm around CV's shoulders for the second time. 'Many things,' he replied, 'because I gave my word to Dorothy that I'd never speak of her affairs.'

'Even now that she's dead?'

'Particularly now, Clive. To venerate her memory, but also because I don't want to die with a knife in my back. If you say to me, "Michael is this true?" If I know the answer I'll say *yes* or *no*. But I owe it to myself, to Jeffo, to my mother, to my friends, not to stand on the tracks and wait for the train to hit.'

CV had used the same metaphor with Bundy.

Back to square one, he thought as he strode down to the Galle Road. He, CV vander Marten had been chosen to stand on the tracks in front of the train. Did Bell, Bundy and Michael all know from which direction the train would be coming? But it wasn't quite back to square one. Bell was to buy a star ruby worth killing for. Jeff Fournier was a highly emotional and jealous man who currently had no alibi. He ran through his suspects: Michael, Mahmoud, Mo, Jeff, Emma, Bundy. Six! Reginald Bell: seven!

Emma van Eck

Maggie had described Emma van Eck's house as the most unattractive in Colombo and had not exaggerated. She lived in a concrete box between the Galle Road and the ocean. In the same compound there was an equally grim larger concrete box. The land on which they stood was a desert landscape—difficult to achieve in a country of equatorial heat and humidity. As if to make sure that not even grass could survive, an old man was scraping a bamboo-claw broom across the barren soil.

CV did not have to be inside the eight-foot high wall to see all this. He examined the property through a hole in the green metal door that served as the gate.

Emma's desert compound was surrounded by an oasis. The

surf rolled on to the beach beyond the railway lines to the west. Coconut palms laden with fruit grew everywhere. All other homes had a profusion of plants. Emma's home was therefore better to look out of than into.

Michael had told CV to reach over the gate, lift the bolt and let himself in. He did so and waited on the threshold of her open door, then cleared his throat and called, 'Miss van Eck!' No answer. He entered and saw her sitting on a stool with her back to him working on a laptop. A fan was on beside her and several pages had been blown on to the floor, which was partially covered by a threadbare reed mat.

There were four equally threadbare brown children sitting on a bench, and they gazed at him with such intensity that it was like entering a cave inhabited by wild animals. The eldest was a boy of about six, and there was a baby clinging to a girl. A toddler, naked except for a shirt that reached his navel, sat between them. CV smiled, which was a mistake. At once the two older children were on their feet and out of a side door, and the toddler fell off the bench on to his face, shrank from CV's helping hand, scrambled up and weeping loudly followed his siblings.

Emma had turned. She went to the window and shouted after them in Sinhala. 'Tell Mother to bring the tea. Are you Mr vander Marten? Michael told me to expect you. How kind of you to come.' She stuck out her hand.

He took it remembering Reginald Bell's identical words and gesture at the memorial service.

'Did I say something funny?' Emma asked.

'You forgot, "Her mother wishes she could be here."'

She bit her lip.

CV put his bag of telephones against the wall and said, 'Sorry I scared the kids.'

'Everything scares them except watching me type. I'm their television. Their father beats them, so they don't like men noticing them.'

'What future is there for kids like that?'

'There's always hope.'

Emma did not, he noticed, dress with more care at home than she did at parties, but today she was wearing a purple, pink and green sarong and a short loose blouse of a different green, the most attractive outfit he'd seen her in yet.

'I'm Clive, but most people call me CV,' he said. 'I have one week to find Dorothy Bell's murderer and everyone tells me you were her best friend.'

'And I suppose Michael told you I didn't want to see you.'

'No.' After all, Michael had merely let him listen in on her yelling.

'Oh dear,' she smiled at last, showing an overbite. 'Now you know. Did Maggie tell you what I said?'

'She said you detested her.'

'I don't. I don't detest her. I don't even know her. But I was very bad tempered when she came.'

'She said you think she's superficial.'

Her large amber eyes became mournful.

'Oh this is awful because I suppose I do. I didn't know she guessed. Is she?'

'Sure, on one level. It's not easy to be told morning, noon and night that all you've going for you is your looks. Puts pressure on her to preserve them because what if that's all she has? But Maggie's not superficial within—she's frightened.'

'You make me sound the superficial one.'

They were still standing facing each other, and he towered over her. He held his hand out, 'Let's start again. Good afternoon, Emma. So kind of you to see me.'

She put her hand in his, 'Good afternoon, Clive. So good of you to have come. Her mother wishes she could be here. Please sit down. Tea will be served any minute.'

He smiled at her and held her hand as long as possible because he liked its small size and coolness. Then he dropped it because she had started to blush. The happy moment was broken by a young woman with her hair in a konday and a green dress stretched tight across her pregnant stomach. She came bearing a tray with two mugs and a plate of store-bought cookies. She carried her swollen body easily and smiled at him warmly showing a mouthful of broken and missing front teeth. When her mouth was closed she was pretty.

'Thank you Renuka.' Emma handed one mug to him and put her own on her makeshift desk.

'Is she really the mother of all those children?' he asked. 'She looks sixteen.'

'She's nearly twenty-five. I'm twenty-eight and I haven't even had an affair yet. Makes you think.'

It did.

She continued talking as she put the cookies beside him and began to gather her papers from the floor. 'When she's my age she'll probably have two or three more children. She has a baby every year, and her husband drinks. They work for my landlady, Mrs Soong, who's Chinese and a doctor. Renuka's husband stays away a lot, thank goodness. He is HIV positive. Renuka lost two babies, and she isn't HIV positive yet. There's also a Dr Hoong who is Soong's husband.'

Emma stopped and frowned. She put down her cup and began moving restlessly around the room. He sat on the bench vacated by the children and watched her until she stopped her pacing and returned to her stool.

'You mustn't buy clothes for the children, Soong says,' she read his mind and spoke too loud and then softened her voice as if its volume had surprised her. 'They must learn to cope with their lot. We should do things that have a longer lasting effect—lift social injustices.'

'And meanwhile the kids are paupers and other children look down on them. Dr Soong is wrong. We'll get Maggie on to their outfits. She's very sensitive about the right clothes.'

'I don't know,' Emma literally wrung her hands as she sat hunched and unhappy on her stool. 'I don't know. They shouldn't look too smart.'

He wondered if he should say, 'It's all right, Emma,' because he didn't know if it was.

She raised her chin and smiled determinedly.

'I hear you're writing a book,' he said to fill the silence.

'Yes. I don't know why. It's full of stupid anger at injustice. It's useless—like what you're doing is useless. You're trying to solve a crime that can't be solved. I'm writing a book that won't be read. Maggie is in love with a man who destroyed his daughter's hopes. How useless people like us are. Even Michael doesn't paint the victims of war any more—he paints his dog.'

CV said gently, 'You've been crying a lot. Is that why you're shaking? Or is it because I want to talk to you about Dorothy?'

She turned away. 'I can't stop crying. She made my life such fun.' When she turned back he saw her fawn's eyes had flooded.

'I specialize in providing a shoulder for people to cry on.'

She looked at his shoulder and began to weep in earnest, leaning forward and sobbing into her hands. He went to her, knelt on the torn matting, took her hands from her face and put her arms around his neck. Then he sat back on the floor Indian fashion and held her in his lap as if she were a baby. She wept convulsively pulling away occasionally then clinging to him and starting again. 'I hate the impermanence of everything. You'll go away too,' she sobbed noisily against his neck. 'Everyone goes away. Everyone.'

Beyond her he saw the four children in the doorway observing them gravely.

'Shhh, shhh. I'm not going anywhere,' he said into her untidy curls. 'Dorothy deserves to have her death mourned. I didn't know her, but I too wish she wasn't gone.'

'She was my friend,' sobbed Emma.

'I know.'

Eventually she took the border of her sarong up to wipe her nose. Once again, all he had to offer a weeping woman was a crumpled monogrammed blue handkerchief. She accepted it gratefully.

'Do you make much money from writing?' he said, with the start of an idea.

'Nothing. Mummy sends me £200 a month.'

'It's not enough.'

'Actually, it is. One hundred for rent and meals. It's cheap, but I'm the only person who understands why Mrs Soong hates plants and loves concrete. Garden plants mean disease to her. Plants need water and mosquitoes breed in water and rats make their homes in soft houses—but they can't dig into concrete. I hate my ugly house but I'm grateful for the low rent. I take the bus. I eat packets from the caddays. I don't need many clothes, and every now and then someone gives me something like this sarong, which was my birthday present from Dorothy. It's top of the line—look at it. It was very expensive. Daddy gave me the computer and printer and sends me ink cartridges. Paper is a big cost,' She had again got lost in her whirl of words and stopped abruptly.

He was angry at having been amused at her awful clothing—of Dr Soong's lack of landscaping—of so much. He heard his voice, 'I need someone to work for me this week—someone like you who is computer-savvy. The wage is $500—that's about £300, with a bonus if we succeed. But it will be a full-time job to coordinate the information we get, send the faxes, make the phone calls. There are only three of us working now. Not enough. Will you do it?'

'I need the money, but I want to do it, too. I can't work for you unless you tell me who the others working with you are.'

Jeanne Cambrai

'And I can't tell you unless you join us. There's no time for personal likes and dislikes. If you come on board, it will be as a member of a group who are trying to find out everything about Dorothy, something which will lead us to her killer. We can't have people on the outside knowing who is working for me. I still have to know if you had a motive to kill your friend and an alibi, but my gut reaction is that you had nothing to do with her murder.'

'I didn't. I was at the Red Fox that night because she said she was coming. When she didn't come, I went home at two.'

'And Michael was there? Michael and Jimbo?'

'They came after me. I asked Michael where Dorothy was and he said she'd got caught up. He was so happy that evening. He danced with me, so I know. He'd never have been happy if he knew anything had happened to her.'

'And Jeff?'

'I didn't see him. You can't think Jeff killed her?'

'Who do you think did? What about Mahmoud?'

'Do you know about him? He'd do it in a blink and so would that pig Mo, but Mahmoud didn't have a reason.'

'He hit her at a casino.'

'Oh no! She didn't tell me.'

CV noticed she had brightened at the thought of being able to make a little money, so he continued, 'So you're hired. Expenses are on me but you have to keep track. No more buses. Take taxis. No cadday food. There's no time to waste on stomach upsets. We have an office—a computer with Internet, email, fax and a photocopier. You'll be working there. The bag I brought has my phones. Do you have a phone?'

'Soong lets me use hers. I pay for my calls so I don't make many.' She was twisting her empty mug in her hands again.

'There are two phones in that bag. I'll keep one with me. You'll hang on to the other. They're on radio frequency so someone may be listening in. We'll have to talk in code. Yes?'

She gave him a smile, 'You know it's yes. Dorothy would want me to. Who are the others?'

'Maggie—she's trying to find out what Bell knows. There's something fishy there.'

'Then she's not one of his women? I was so wrong. But he'll be too smart for her—for anyone—because he's much more than fishy. You'll see. And the other one?'

'Our Aunt Maud.'

'Maud vander Marten? But she's very old. She kisses me and tells me my mother was a very fine girl.'

'Auntie's wiser than all of us put together, and she's pumping gossip out of the geriatric set.'

'Did they know Dorothy?'

'Yes, and that she used the name Louise Lawrence when she didn't want anyone to know who she was.'

She got up, went to the window and said with her back to him, 'I didn't know she was calling herself Louise Lawrence. How sad.'

'It will be cooler outside. The sky has clouded over. Let's finish this talk on the beach.'

As they walked, he told her about the beautician who got Dorothy looking spiffy for Mahmoud and Aunt Maud's scrapbook of newspaper cuttings.

'I have some snaps for the scrapbook,' she said. 'Some letters too.'

'Dorothy's? Who wrote her letters?'

'I haven't looked.'

The surf pounded on to the beach, broke against their legs and soaked them almost to the waist, then swept the sand from under their feet as it pulled back. They tried to ignore it as he told her about the men who'd died like Dorothy.

Emma said, 'Dor couldn't have known, or she'd have told me. But she had a knife, you know.'

She had a knife? He took Emma's hand. 'Where is it—her

knife? What did it look like?'

'Michael hasn't seen it since she died. He wondered if it had been used to kill her. It was quite long and thin. I saw it in her hotel room in a drawer, and I said, "What a lovely knife." She said, "It's a beauty, isn't it? But be careful because it is very sharp and I've lost the sheath." I told Michael she couldn't have been stabbed by it because she'd never take it out in the evening.'

'When she travelled, did she take it with her?'

'She may have. We'd go upcountry or down south for the weekend but I never saw it among her things. In the hotel room it was in a drawer but not hidden. It was with her pens and writing paper.'

'Did you go to her room in the Palace often?'

'Only twice. After I found out about her life there, I didn't go in case I ran into Mahmoud.'

'Those two times, you went alone?'

'No, with Dor in a taxi.'

'You entered by the lobby?'

'Yes, why?'

'The hotel staff say she never had visitors.'

'I wasn't a visitor who asked for her. She needed something from her room. We went up, got it and went down. The taxi waited for us.'

This meant the hotel staff's observations couldn't be relied on.

They turned and started walking back,

He said, 'Emma, no matter how much we trust someone, we don't tell them everything. Dorothy might have thought she confided her life to you but something could have slipped her mind. You must speak with every friend she had. Get them to remember incidents, names, places. Write them down. I wish I knew what she told Michael, but he's taken a vow of silence. Bell has given me a list of names. I want you to go through all nineteen and list any who might have had a motive and add others he may have missed. Talk to them and get their alibis. Maggie's going to ask questions too.'

'I'm very tired, and there's a party this evening. I'd better sleep if I'm going to start asking questions.'

'Emma, I only have a week.'

He suddenly became frightened. What if he let this chief source of information out of his sight and returned to find her dead too? You don't think like that unless someone you know has been murdered. He didn't want Emma to die without telling him what she knew . . . What was he thinking? He didn't want Emma to die. Period.

Emma said, 'Would you like to come to the party this evening?'

'I suppose I should. But be warned I'm a bore at parties—I don't do drugs—don't drink enough to be fun.'

'I don't either,' her amber eyes became mischievous. 'I fake my drugs. I'll show you how to do it. You hold a joint to your lips and pretend to draw on it.' She was enjoying herself now and demonstrated. 'See, those people think I'm smoking, and I don't even have anything in my hand. I carry my own powders and pills to parties. My cocaine is made from icing sugar and milk powder. My uppers and downers are little homoeopathic pills. So is my Ecstasy. You can put a drop of anything you like on any homoeopathic pill and it will be absorbed. Eucalyptus oil, Drambuie, vanilla! Dor and I'd go into a corner and pretend to be puffing away. Nobody notices—they're in their own space.'

He said, 'Wish you could get Maggie off that stuff.'

'If what you say about her is true, then it mightn't be wise. It may be what's holding her together.'

Oh, God. What if she was right?

He said, 'I need to stretch out so I'm going to run. I'd like your company.' Emma lacked competitive spirit and long legs, so she was easy to impress. When they returned, she was complimentary. 'You'd never think someone built like you would be able to run that fast.'

Maud vander Marten

His Aunt Maud had taken her afternoon nap and was sitting upright against a stack of pillows. He sat next to her in a small teak armchair with the cane seat tilted back.

She said, 'It's always sticky before the rain. Let's have a cup of tea.'

'Could we make that a cold drink, Auntie?'

'We could. There is homemade ginger beer, or would you like something stronger?'

'Both.'

He went downstairs with a sense of returning to a normal life, and when he came back with the tray, he found his aunt ready to tell him about her day. 'I was hoping I'd discover the murderer but there was nothing much in all those cuttings, only a few contradictions. You probably don't need to hear about them.'

'Tell me.'

'The newspapers are careless and copy each other's mistakes. Dorothy died wearing a T-shirt, they said, but it looks like a silk blouse in the pictures. T-shirts don't have collars. Her trousers are called slacks, which are tailored trousers. Hers are silky pleated trousers gathered at the ankle. In the car lights the white and red silk would have glowed.'

He said, 'That's important, Auntie. Dorothy was going to see someone she had dressed up for. She didn't dress up for Michael. It looks as if he is telling the truth about her going to the Oberoi.'

The iced ginger beer didn't cool him, and he was sweating heavily though the overhead fan was on. It provided a hot whirlwind, and mosquitoes hiding under the bed came out to bite his bare feet. CV took off his shirt and turned on the floor fan, and immediately sheets of paper, envelopes and playing cards were lifted from the tables and tossed around the room so he had to pick them up as he talked.

He told her that Emma would be on their team. 'I don't know why I trust her, Auntie, probably because she's so miserable. She's cried so much over Dorothy her face may be permanently swollen.'

'Swollen faces always go back. A woman didn't kill Dorothy, so you're right to trust Emma.'

'Lizzie Borden took an axe and gave her father forty whacks. Then, when she was done, she gave her mother forty-one. Lizzie swung her axe as efficiently as a woodman.'

'Lizzie didn't kill her parents. An axe would have been too messy because she'd be the one to clean up afterwards. In those days women used poison.'

'Let's get back to our crime. Tell me about Michael's parents.'

'His mother Frances owns the Life of the Party on Thurston Road. She sells bits and pieces. When she was twenty, she told Shantha she was pregnant and that she was going to bring up her baby alone. The baby's father lived abroad. He wanted to marry her, but she didn't want to leave and he didn't want to live in Sri Lanka. So he gave her money to get her business started. She never told anyone who he was. I think he was a ne'er-do-well.'

'I've always wanted to use that word, Auntie.'

'You're cheeky. Shantha says a Swiss boy was in love with Frances and she thinks he was Michael's father. But when Michael said to Shantha, "Was a Swiss artist my father?" all she could reply was, "I don't know."'

'Michael could be Swiss,' said CV. 'His face seems carved out of the Alps.'

'But he's an artist too. The Swiss aren't artists.'

'There must be one or two. I must see Frances. Do you know if she liked Dorothy?'

'I don't visit her because Shantha says she calls me a

holier-than-thou-Hattie. Be careful. When Michael was born she had her tubes tied and it made her worse.'

'Gossip or fact?'

'Both. Shantha gossiped it to me but she heard about the tubes from a nurse, so it's fact. Frances has a new boyfriend now, an Australian.'

'Another lover with no name?'

'This one has a name. John Smith.'

'At least he's not John Doe.'

'Was John Doe a bad man?'

'He's everyman.'

She liked that. 'From what I hear Frances has gone from one John Doe to another. I also want to tell you about Emma van Eck. Shantha says she'll never get a husband because she doesn't have two rupees to rub together and is uncompromising. Her parents are fine people but haven't done well abroad the way most Sri Lankans have because everyone owes them money. They're socialists but fine people.'

He said, 'No Burgher finds another Burgher less than a fine person.'

He took her red notebook and wrote his mobile phone numbers in it. 'Aunt Maud, when someone is crazy enough to kill once, he might do it again. Be careful, it's the fifth killing not the first.' He kissed her and headed for the door but turned back to ask, 'Will Joseph be available this evening?'

'Yes and all this week. Where are you going?'

'On a sleuthing date with Emma.'

'Remember, her family are fine people.'

'It won't be out of my mind for a minute.'

The Rain Came

The rain came at 7.33 p.m. when he was on his way to Emma's. First thunder rumbled a lot, and then lightning began to slice the sky. Within minutes the city was reduced to delighted helplessness in a show of humbling celestial power. Debilitating heat evaporated leaving a warm, wet night.

Joseph had pulled to the left at the first thunderbolt so they were already at snail's pace as the road became a river. Their headlights provided a few feet of visibility; the overhead street lights almost none. Those drivers who had not cut their speed sufficiently had already run off the road or into each other.

The road beside Emma's sliding gate was a raging river. She was waiting outside the gate, a shadow under a broken yellow umbrella. CV shouted, 'Swim for it!'

She closed the umbrella and, crouching low splashed her way to them, handed him a waterproof backpack, climbed in and shook out her wet head, drenching him. She apologized and somehow managed to cover him with more water. Her high-waisted pale-blue dress was soaked, and she continued to apologize as she slipped on the wet sandals she had tied outside the backpack. 'I didn't want you to come and get me at the house because then we'd both be wet,' she told him. 'Umbrellas aren't much good as the rain's coming sideways.'

'If you tell me where you keep your clothes I'll go in and get you something dry. Then we'll go back to Aunt Maud's and change.' He had to yell because of the nonstop thunder.

She shook her head which sprayed him further and yelled back, 'Everyone at the party will be wet. What does it matter if I am?'

She foraged in her backpack, produced a comb and flattened her wet curls.

'Is this better?' she asked, showing him a wet face and hair plastered to her scalp like a bathing cap. 'Why are you laughing?'

'From pleasure. We're going to the Casino Vegas for a minute—to dry you off in the air conditioning and give you pneumonia. Then we'll go back to the house and you can borrow something of Maggie's.'

Emma wailed, 'I can't go to the casino in case Mahmoud is

there. I'll stay in the car and lie on the floor so he won't see me. Also, I'm too wet for a casino.'

'No way, your clothing is somewhat curious, but you do have that face. With that face you can go to a fashion show in a gunny sack. Mahmoud won't be there. Comes in late and leaves after midnight. Gambling men are men of habit. He hasn't been there since Dorothy died, anyway.'

Dravi greeted them effusively but only CV with previous recognition. He acted as if it was quite normal for a woman to come to the casino mid-evening in a dress so wet that her long white underwear with black spots could be seen through it. Emma held her head up and marched through the room ignoring the puddles of water and footprints in her wake. It was an abortive trip, for there were no greetings or smiles of recognition for her, which was why CV had wanted her with him. Anyone who knew Emma might know Dorothy. He asked for Bundy who greeted them with smile in place, and on hearing her name told Emma he was sorry to hear she had lost her friend. He had obviously never met her before. He had Dravi bring her a towel and insisted they have a brandy in his office, where he turned the air conditioning down. He had always shown hostility when talking of Dorothy but showed none to Emma.

'Dor called Bundy Balasingham a slime ball,' she told CV when they were back in the car sitting on a cotton rug Joseph had found in the trunk. 'I'm surprised he's one of your friends. He asked what her price was and said if she took it from Mahmoud why not from him? She knew all these terrible people.' She suddenly relaxed. 'It's funny really—that casino was part of her life. She'd be there with all that money being thrown around, and I'd be with Renuka and her four children having a much better time.'

'Recognize anyone there?'

'No,' she said, 'but don't worry. If I meet Bundy Balasingham again, I'll be nice to him because he is a friend of yours.'

'You're very charming, Emma.'

'Don't be silly. I'm going to ask Maggie to give me charm lessons, actually.'

He put an arm around her and kissed her cheek. 'Did I tell you I kiss on first dates?'

She yelled, 'Don't do that! You'll get wet.'

'I am wet. On the second date, I propose.'

Her smile showed again. 'If you did, you'd be married by now.'

'No one will marry me because I'm fat.'

'You're not fat. You're just not thin.'

Emma pulled a large plastic envelope from her wet bag. 'I didn't forget Dor's letters and photos,' she said. 'See, they aren't even wet. I also brought my computer; it's in the other plastic bag. She sometimes wrote letters on it but didn't save much. There's a folder called Dorothy, and it has a few files.'

'Have you read them?'

'No. I couldn't.'

He put the backpack on the front seat beside Joseph.

Jimbo's family home was in Rosmead Place. There was already a large crowd indoors and cars were parked bumper to bumper on both sides of the road outside. Above the rain, loudspeakers thundered rock music. The trees were decked in thousands of tiny lights that the rain had turned into a fairyland with the wind helping by whipping the branches to send the lights spinning.

Houseboys under enormous striped umbrellas stood at the gate to escort the guests into the house on a bridge of wooden pallets. To Emma's disappointment, when she got inside she was the only one soaked to the skin.

'I don't know how people do it,' she complained to CV. 'Do you?'

'Raincoats.' He took her hand and told her that she was a high-fashion advertisement for a new look—polka-dotted long-johns under see-through wet cotton. Only then did she realize that her clothes had been transparent all along, and she tried to hide behind him.

'You can see my knickers! And everyone saw them in the casino, too. Why didn't you tell me?'

'Because they are magnificent knickers.'

'They are things that Dorothy was throwing out. Matching bra, too. Can you see? When I wear them I can stand on my head and not show my bum,' she shouted.

'You'll have to demonstrate,' he shouted back.

They began to look for Michael, but a straw-haired American girl came up and greeted Emma saying, 'If I can't find somewhere to crash this evening, is it okay if I sleep at your place, Em? Who's the big guy?'

'Of course. We'll give you a lift there. Is that all right, Clive?' She introduced the American as Julia Ware.

'Sure.'

'You're American too!' accused Julia.

'Yeah, but also a Dutch Burgher.'

'I miss home, so perhaps we could talk one day?'

'Any time.'

A darker blonde named Kathy said, 'Emma, do your Chinese doctors do acupuncture? I pulled a muscle in my knee.'

'They do everything but antibiotics or pain killers.'

While Emma was talking to Kathy, CV sighted Michael with two bearded Arabs in their national dress. One was middle aged with a long hooked nose, coal-black bristling eyebrows and a carefully trimmed curling black beard. The other was like an Aladdin cartoon genie, huge with the round features on a too-small face. His eyes had a way of darting around rapidly. He spotted Emma, and without taking his eyes from her, bent forward to whisper in the other's ear. That man looked up, saw her and said something to Michael. They began to make their way towards her. Michael saw CV, waved but turned in the other direction.

CV had no doubt that the older man was Mahmoud and was glad they would meet at last. Emma however, had sighted the Arabs too. Her hand was still in CV's and he closed his fingers on it instinctively as she panicked and tried to drag herself free. Unable to do so she began to pull him towards the door.

'Hold on,' he told her, turning her so she was forced to face him.

'That's Mahmoud,' she screamed and again tried to pull away. 'Clive, I have to go home now. Stay. It's a great party, but I have to go.'

He had his back to the approaching men who had to move slowly through the guests to avoid knocking into glasses and cigarettes.

'If you don't want to talk to them you don't have to, and I'll tell that to Mr Mahmoud.'

'He won't listen. I'll be able to get a three-wheeler at the corner. I'm going home.'

'You're not alone, Emma. I'm here.'

She used his body to hide from Mahmoud and wasn't listening. 'Please, Clive, I want to go home!'

He felt a touch on his shoulder and saw from the corner of his eye that it was Mo trying to get his attention, so he did not turn. He followed Emma into the rain and down the driveway of wooden pallets and they were quickly on the road. Looking back now he saw Mo take an umbrella from someone's hand and hold it above Mahmoud.

'There's Joseph,' Emma began yelling. 'There's Joseph!'

Their chauffeur had been endlessly cruising to find a parking place. They ran to the Magnette and were on their way before Mahmoud and Mo had reached the gate.

Once again the back seat was drenched.

Emma started apologizing. 'I hate him. I'm really sorry. I'm so sorry. Now I won't be able to ask questions for you. I'm so sorry.'

He replied, 'Take a lot of deep breaths.'

'What has happened to small missie?' asked the old man in Sinhala.

'Someone frightened her.'

She replied in the same language, 'He's a very bad man called Mahmoud, Joseph. Very bad. He's from Saudi.'

'Ah!' said Joseph, as if that explained it all.

She was shivering and rubbing her wrist.

'I'm afraid I hurt you,' CV said.

'Just a little. But you were right. It would have been awful if I had run. I'm glad I left with dignity.'

But when she spoke again it was not about Mahmoud. They'd pulled up on Galle Face Green where the storm spread before them like theatre. She said, 'I'm so sorry, Clive. Now I've lost you a whole evening. Go back to Jimbo's, I'll wait with Joseph until Mahmoud leaves. He never stays long. Then I'll go inside and ask lots and lots of questions. Oh, Clive, I'm so sorry. I can't undo it but you don't have to pay me, I'll work for you anyway. Will that be all right?'

He said in exasperation, 'For God's sake, forget about the money. Do you mind Joseph hearing why you were frightened?

'I suppose not.' She took a deep breath then spoke fast, 'Mahmoud met Dor last year. He got her into his hotel room pretending he wanted her advice on jewellery he was buying and then he and Mo raped her. After that she became his—*mistress* isn't the right word. She became available to him—a sex prisoner, kind of.'

'Honey, she was no sex prisoner. They went to the Casino Vegas frequently and she made money there out of him.'

'I know. That part I'll have to tell you about later.'

'All right, forget Dorothy. You think he's going to rape you too?'

"I think that now he's lost her he wants me to replace her. He never calls me Emma, he calls me Beauty. It makes me sick. After Dor died he phoned me. I told Renuka and Soong to tell him I was out if he phoned again, but he phoned again five times, and when I was walking down Duplication Road his car came up and he asked if I wanted a lift. I said no. Eventually I went into a shop to hide, but he stayed parked outside. So I came out and went up and said I knew about him and Dorothy and didn't want to speak to him again for the rest of my life. He said, ever so coolly, that Dorothy had been going to introduce me to him. He laughed at me. I told him I knew he killed Dorothy. He laughed even more. Mo was sitting there behind the wheel of the car grinning like a goat. I was shouting at them through the window, and they just laughed like they knew they were going to win. You saw what happened—they came right at me again.'

CV absorbed what she had said as best he could, and what annoyed him was that his presence with Emma had not stopped the Arabs. 'If he killed Dorothy, we're dealing with a murderer and a rapist. You were right to leave.' He reached for the phone.

When Amily gave her screech it was a very welcome sound. Then Aunt Maud was saying, 'Darling boy! Are you all right? Amily says it's an emergency.'

'Aunt Maud, Emma and I have had an upset, but it's not the car, and no one is hurt. How's the dinner situation if we come home now?'

'Where are you?'

'Galle Face Green.'

'Come at once. Amily was going to make me soup and a sandwich. Is Joseph there? He can pick up dinner for us at Jade Gardens.'

He passed the telephone to the front seat and heard Joseph say, 'Very well, missie ... Very well, missie ... Very well, missie.'

He told them in English, 'Lady telephone Jade Gardens Chinese for takeout. She say you go Galle Face Hotel not sit under fan, no ice for stiff drink. I go pick up dinner taking half or one hour. I take you and Chinese food to home.'

Emma could still smile, it seemed.

Reginald Bell and His Daughter Dorothy

The Galle Face Hotel is a relic of the past that has not lent itself to modernization. It is a reminder, however, that the British once ruled the island with a Victorian taste for large over small, comfort over style, and good manners no matter what.

The new Sri Lankan owners of the Galle Face Hotel had only somewhat kept its colonial atmosphere intact, but all that was left of the British now was the solid construction and massive furniture.

CV and Emma entered the hotel on its famous red carpet and white marble floor. At his request, they were shown to the dining room veranda, which was drenched. The surf was not fifty yards away.

'Better to go inside, sir,' said the waiter hopefully.

'I'll come to the bar for our drinks so you don't have to walk through the water.'

But the old man would have none of it and hurried off for their whiskys.

Emma said, 'What I hate about England is that if you get soaked, next thing you're an icicle and that night you're dead if you couldn't thaw out in the bath. Here wet is lovely—it cools you and next thing you're dry. This is actually my favourite Colombo hotel but I can't afford it.'

He said, 'Well, Miss van Eck, it's tell time. Mr Mahmoud and Dorothy are the topic.'

She sighed, 'It's a horrible story. If I started when Dorothy met Mahmoud you'd never understand. It was so wrong for her to have to die when she'd survived all that. I'm only telling you about her life because I don't want to think one day I should have spoken up when I had the chance.'

'That's the introduction. Now the story.'

She began to shift uncomfortably. Good! He didn't want a smooth telling; he wanted a sense of what had been going on under the surface.

He said, 'Only six more days—only six more days.'

She looked at him. 'It was Dorothy's father's fault.'

'Emma, no more explanations!'

'Shall I start from the beginning?'

'Start where you want.'

So she told it all, and sometimes her eyes filled with tears. At other times her voice shook with rage.

Dorothy's earliest memories had been of living with her father in London in a roomy terrace in Bayswater. Kitchen and utility rooms were in the basement; living, dining and guest rooms on the ground floor; Bell's apartment was above that; Dorothy, her nanny and a live-in maid shared the highest level. A handyman came in twice a week to help with the chores. Her mother was separated from Bell, and Dorothy had a vague recollection of hearing her parents quarrelling and of trying to get away from the sound by crawling under her bed. The woman Dorothy remembered best was a nanny, Louise Lawrence, who came to look after her during the divorce and stayed eight years. She became the only real mother-figure Dorothy would know.

'Louise Lawrence! That's the name Dorothy used at the hairdressers,' CV said.

'That was why I was jolted when you said her name. I never knew that Dor called herself Louise.'

Once a month Louise drove Dorothy to spend a weekend with her mother. Marie Bell was an alcoholic and always seemed sober when they arrived but began to break down during the visit. Dorothy was glad that Louise took her home immediately when her mother's good humour became glitteringly unreal and maudlin.

Reggie travelled a lot, so saw little of his daughter. He left her to Louise. If she went home to Hertfordshire she took the child with her. She taught Dorothy to read before she attended kindergarten, helped choose her elementary school and built her up to believe she could be a success at anything. She took her to the zoo, to museums, to shows and the movies. Dorothy often asked her why she hadn't married and heard, 'I tried it but it didn't work. One day I'll try again, but don't worry, he'll have to like you too.' The child therefore thought Louise would never leave her.

Then one afternoon, when she was eleven, their house maid came to pick Dorothy up from school and she never saw Louise again. She got only one explanation from her father: 'Louise left us without giving notice.'

CV said, 'Did Dorothy think Bell fired her?'

'Yes. He had bruises on his cheek and forehead when she got home. She thought they must have had a fight. Later, when she tried to live with her Mum, Marie told her that Bell had slapped Louise and she had grabbed a table lamp and hit him with it.'

'What did they fight about?'

'Dorothy. Louise phoned Marie after the fight and said she was worried about Dorothy. She found Reggie's collection of nude photos of Dorothy in a painted metal box. Louise said, "It seems so sick. All nudes." She confronted Mr Bell and eventually called him a pervert. He hit her. She hit him. He then threatened to destroy her and her parents if she spoke of the pictures to anyone. Marie told her not to take the threat lightly but to go to the police. She herself refused to help saying he was no longer her business.'

'But Dorothy was.'

'She was a terrible mother.'

It was at this point that CV began to wonder if Dorothy had made the story up. Bell was a cold fish but hardly seemed the type who slugged nannies and then threatened them. Of course, CV had never met a voyeur or a man who slugged nannies. Della had described Reggie as a man who was sexually compulsive, but there had been no mention of physical violence. There was also the fact that Bell had rejected one call girl's suggestion of a threesome.

'What about Dorothy's grandparents?' he asked. 'They must have played some part in her life?'

Bell's parents had visited him so rarely that Dorothy only knew them as a couple who patted her on the head and gave her chocolates. Grandmother told Dorothy that she had pretty hair and she never forgot that. Grandfather taught her to ride a horse and to play hopscotch and chess. They lived in the north country but she was never taken to see them there. Her maternal grandmother had died in an accident about the time she was born. Her maternal grandfather had emigrated to Canada, from where he sent cards and presents but never came to visit. Both of her parents were only children. There were no distant uncles or aunts or cousins that she knew of.

After Louise disappeared, Dorothy was only aware that her life had changed for the worse. She could not understand Louise not saying goodbye to her; there were no letters and no phone calls. She once accused her father of lying when he said he didn't know where Louise was, and he sent her to her room. She began to pretend that Louise had gone away on holiday and that she'd save up things to tell her when she returned and listed them in a diary. Dorothy became moody and lonely.

The following Christmas her father called her into his office as he had a card for her from her Canadian grandfather. At some point when she had her back to him, she realized she could see his reflection in the mirror on the wall. She began to watch him opening his mail. One envelope made him frown and he threw it into the trash basket. That evening he went out to dinner and she went into his office, looked in the trash and found the envelope. now torn into small pieces. No other papers in the trash had been torn. She took the basket to her bedroom, emptied it on to her bed and returned it to his office knowing he'd think the maid had emptied it. Then she locked her bedroom door and tried to put the torn pieces together.

'That's strange behaviour for a kid of eleven.'

'It isn't really. Children live in a world of make-believe. I was always looking through my parents' drawers and making up stories about what I found. Mummy told me she once found condoms on my doll's legs. I thought they were dolls' stockings.'

Dorothy's diary became two diaries when she discovered her father was aware of things she'd written—things he couldn't have known if he wasn't reading her diary. To trap him she wrote that she wanted a tiny yellow radio like Sonny's in school, and next week he came home with one for her. He spoilt her with gifts and also loved to hug and kiss her, but that seemed natural in a father. She kept one diary for him in a drawer under her clothes and used it to write what happened every day and mentioned things she wanted. The diary with her true inner thoughts she kept in a pocket of a blazer. 'Oh dear, I'm going off track, aren't I?' said Emma wringing her hands.

'You were telling me about the letter in the trash.'

'Oh, yes.'

Dorothy sorted the scraps of paper, stuck them together with transparent tape and came up with a letter, a Christmas card and two envelopes—one which must have been sent inside the other as it had no stamp and was addressed with the words 'For Dorothy'. The larger envelope was addressed to her father and had been mailed. The letter started 'Dear Mr Bell' and was signed 'Louise Lawrence'. It asked that he give Dorothy the card and if he had given her the other cards she had sent since she had received no acknowledgement of them. The card had a nativity scene and a letter written to her on the inside and back.

Emma said, 'Dorothy memorized the words on the Christmas card and repeated them to me more than once.

Something like, "Darling Dotty, Miss you a lot and hope you remember me a little bit. Have a lovely Christmas. Daddy has my address, so I hope you will write." It had a story about a stray dog she had found and taken home and the letter ended, "Love, Louise". It had been a relief knowing Louise had not stopped caring for her, but it was also the beginning of her distrust of her father. She now knew he lied to her.'

CV began to think Dorothy's story might be true after all. The fact that the nanny had included the anecdote about a dog turned him around. Until then it seemed a story any fanciful little girl could have made up: the ideal nanny, the wicked father, the cold mother. But a nanny writing to a previous charge would have included more than good wishes—the little anecdote. Also a Christmas card would have had just enough space for that short letter to Dorothy.

The child hadn't known where to hide her find and eventually taped the letters inside the dust cover of *Anne of Green Gables,* the least likely book she thought her father would take into his hands. She took that book with her whenever she travelled and often reread the card.

'There's an *Anne of Green Gables* in a suitcase at the Palace with her other books. It is the only children's book there,' he told Emma.

'Do you think he'd give it to me? Would you ask? I can't, because I'm not talking to him.'

'I'll ask and he'll probably agree. He was more interested in her diaphragm than her books.' And so was he, CV realized. 'If he doesn't agree, I'll steal it for you.'

'You will? Promise?'

'Sure.'

'Clive, you said she had a diaphragm? I suppose she never got around to throwing it away. You see, Dorothy couldn't have children, so she didn't need one. I begged her not to get sterilized but she said that you have to make sacrifices in life and that would be hers.'

'What a crazy thing for a young girl to do. Why?'

'Michael and she decided not to have children.'

'Jesus!'

'Yes.'

The waiter was replenishing their drinks and the rain had stopped. Minutes before water had been pouring out of the sky, but now the stars were out.

Emma had had to raise her voice above the noise of the storm but dropped it now.

CV said, 'You were saying Dorothy now knew Louise had not abandoned her.'

There was no return address on the envelopes, Emma explained, and Dorothy thought the omission of the address could have been to trick Reggie into opening them. The outer envelope showed it had been mailed in Watford, Hertfordshire. Her father's address book had no Lawrence in Hertfordshire and no one in Watford. She snooped every way she could to find some mention of Louise. If he mentioned a phone number she'd memorize it and call it later. The following Christmas she looked in his trash basket every day for weeks but found no other letters from Louise. The next year she did the same thing, then gave up.

Dorothy bought a large ceramic piggy bank and secretly called it Louise. She told her father she was saving to buy herself a car one day, and when he gave her money, she'd slip a pound or two into the pig and eventually began to feel guilty if she didn't. She put in larger denomination notes. She'd steal from him or his guests. When she was eighteen, she broke the pig because she couldn't get even one more coin inside and found she'd collected over £2,000. She put the money in a savings account in her name and Louise's. She wrote a will and left her estate to Louise. She'd changed that will after she met Michael.

'Michael is in her newest will, and also, I think I am,' Emma shuddered. 'She said, "And a little something for you."'

'Dorothy has a will? I forgot that. Of course, she must have left a will! Where is it?'

'I don't know. She made a new one after she came back from England last year. The lawyer who drew it up must have a copy.'

'If he did, why didn't he contact the police? Maybe lawyers don't have to. Did she mention the lawyer's name?'

'She called him Ivor.'

'No last name?'

'She didn't use surnames much.'

'Any insurance policies?'

'I don't know.'

He was drinking too fast. Her second straight Scotch was untouched and he was about to help himself to it, then changed his mind, called the waiter and asked for black coffee. Emma wouldn't join him.

'Are you too tired to continue?'

She shook her head. 'When I get home this evening I want to be able to sleep.'

'Go on about Dorothy.'

Bell had not replaced Louise because Dorothy at eleven no longer needed a nanny. He began to see more of her. She knew nothing about the nude collection until later, but she did remember before and after Louise left he took a lot of pictures of her in her bath and would make her tumble and pose naked for the camera when they were alone. Then suddenly he put her in a boarding school when she was twelve. There was little warning. One day he said, 'Next week you'll be going to Raburn.' This all-girl school was in Northumberland and had a reputation for scholarship. She hated it because most of the girls seemed to know each other well. Their families went skiing together in the winter and sailing in the summer. She knew her father took part in those sports with his friends and now resented that he had never taken her with him. For the first time she felt how much she had been missing out.

At school she'd lost the freedom she had had at home—hated having to eat meals at exactly the same time, wanted to be able to read into the night. She ran away often. She'd take a train to London and show up at the flat hoping her father wouldn't be there. A sympathetic maid would spoil her. She'd have breakfast in bed, and they'd play cards together, watch TV, go shopping and to the theatre. Bell's staff rarely stayed long, but they were the only friends she had at that time. When they left, Dorothy thought they just moved to more exciting or better-paid jobs. Louise had been in her thirties when she left, Dorothy guessed. Some of these maids were middle-aged, and all were kind.

Her father would be angry when he learned she'd run away. The headmistress would call him and he'd have to return to England. Dorothy began to steal cash from him about this time. With increasing paranoia she hid the piggy bank—eventually in a large copper urn on a high ledge in a hallway. Then, frightened that someone would find it there, she split the stomach of a huge teddy bear her Canadian grandfather had sent her, removed most of the stuffing, put the pig inside and closed it with a Velcro strip.

CV interrupted Emma's story.

'Michael told me Reggie taught her to steal.'

'It was a game between them. Careless guests wouldn't notice the missing notes or, if they did, blamed themselves for miscounting. But now she was stealing things he never knew about.'

'Did she steal from you?'

'At first, but she always gave me much more than she stole. Mr Bell stole an emerald once and nearly went to jail. He told her she must never touch anything that belonged to a client because even though no one could prove he took the emerald, it was like starting all over again because some dealers were reluctant to trust him. She said that when you are in business, you must give your client back even five rupees if he overpays. I think from what I've read that she was stealing love. When she knew we loved her she didn't steal any more.'

Bundy stole only from friends. Was he, too, seeking love?

'You stayed friends knowing she, who had so much, was stealing from you who had so little?'

'She was so much more important than the things she took.'

'She stole my handkerchief.'

'Then she wanted your love too. The moment she saw you she liked you. She said her father had cut her off from men like you. Were you attracted to her like she was to you?'

'I guess I was.'

Emma frowned. 'Was she the love of your life?'

He liked the frown. 'I'm afraid she also repelled me.'

'I loved and hated a man like that once.'

'And?'

'And I got over it.'

'That's good news.'

She buried her face in her glass, gulped, then hurried on.

Dorothy began to give Louise the pig ten per cent of what she stole and only later discovered that she was tithing. 'When our friends talked about their religions,' Emma said, 'Dor would say, "I used to tithe," and she'd look at me.'

Eventually Raburn refused to take Dorothy back as a rash of copycat thefts and runaways was seriously upsetting its discipline. The headmistress told Bell in front of Dorothy that she had become incorrigible: 'In a few years your daughter will be a serious delinquent if she doesn't get help. She needs a psychiatrist, not a school for normal children.'

Emma began to laugh. 'She'd often mimic that headmistress.'

Meanwhile, Dorothy's mother had decided to get help for her drinking problem. When she left the clinic she married a fellow patient who wanted Dorothy to live with them. Bell refused. But after she was expelled he let Dorothy go to them. Almost immediately she was caught stealing from her mother's purse. She promised never to do it again because she wanted to stay with her small twin stepbrothers Carlo and Mark, the only siblings she'd had. But her mother said, 'It isn't just Carl who doesn't want you. It's me, too. You remind me of an unhappy time in my life.'

'Dorothy said she wanted to kill herself that day,' Emma said. 'And when so much worse happened later, she felt she should have, but then she wouldn't have met Michael.'

'I hope this story is going to get somewhere or I might kill myself too,' said CV.

'You don't understand. It was torture for her.'

'I know. And what I said was in particularly bad taste. Go on.'

Thirteen-year-old Dorothy could pass for eighteen and knew it. She put on high heels, frizzed her hair and returned to London. When her passport was checked, the immigration official barely glanced at it—didn't look to see if she was a minor. She had nowhere else to go but to Bayswater and went fearfully. To her surprise, this time Reggie was pleased and amused to see her looking so grown up. He laughed at her stories of her mother and stepfather, took her to dinner in the West End and shopping the next day.

'He bought her a new wardrobe then brought her home and raped her,' Emma paused to let that sink in. She was glaring at the ocean and her hair was curling as it dried, and it gave her a cherubic look—albeit an angry cherub.

The words had been shoved at him so casually that he needed a moment for them to sink in. Eventually he said, 'Dorothy told you that when she was thirteen her father brought her home from a shopping trip and raped her? If that's true, what is the guy doing out of jail?'

Emma frowned, 'I want to finish telling you all this.'

'Sorry, honey. I didn't know he stole the emerald, but I knew he had been a suspect when it disappeared. People he knows have a habit of getting knifed to death. He's a compulsive womanizer. Now you say he's a paedophile and an incestuous rapist. If it's true, why wasn't that in his CIA dossier?'

Finally she murmured, 'You don't believe any of it do you?'

CV felt frustrated and angry. 'Don't cut me off like that. I have to question. There are conflicting views of Dorothy. She's a saint; she's a tart; she's a one-man woman; she's a thief; she's an actress. Now she's been raped by her father.' He rose and walked to the edge of the veranda, looking out at the end of the storm, but that did nothing to help. He returned to his chair and said, 'I can't believe a father would rape his daughter but fathers do. Of course they do. Please go on.'

She was curled sideways on her chair. Her eyes were in a shadow and her lips tight. She continued as if he had not interrupted. 'Dorothy was in her bedroom trying on a new yellow frock. Mr Bell came in, locked the door behind him, and told her that he loved her and they could give each other great happiness.'

A minute ago his daughter had adored him. Now he was putting his tongue in her mouth and his hand between her legs. She began to fight. She bit his lip and tried to kick him, but he tore her new dress off her, and, as efficiently as he did everything else, he tied her to the bed with her new stockings, pulled down her panties and raped her. Then he sat beside her stroking her body, telling her how beautiful she was and that he loved her and eventually he turned her over and raped her another way, all the time talking about what he was doing, explaining it as if he was talking to himself.

There were tears behind Emma's voice as she spoke, but none fell. CV reached forward to take her hand, but she picked up her glass and moved it away.

'Go on,' he said quietly, 'I'm sorry about my boorishness. Just say it.'

Afterwards Dorothy's father had taken her into his arms, all the while telling her that he loved her and she would come to find such things as he had done a source of pleasure. She stayed curled into a tight ball her arms around her knees. She went into the bathroom eventually, had a shower to wash the blood off and all the time wished she'd killed herself the previous day instead of coming home.

When she came out of the bathroom, her father was gone. Their maid had looked at Dorothy with shock as she came downstairs. Then Dorothy saw the blood trickling down her legs again and said, 'Daddy fucked me.' The woman helped her to bed and put an ice pack between her thighs.

That night, before her father returned, Dorothy ran away again but now had nowhere to go. She first phoned her mother in Holland and again said she was sorry she'd been so difficult and would like to live with them and would never steal again, but she was told that they were glad she had left.

Marie had said, 'Even your face depresses me. Carl thinks you'll corrupt the twins. You don't have a home here again, Dot. I'm sorry.'

Dorothy had then told her mother what her father had done to her. Marie had replied, 'He is not my responsibility now. Louise Lawrence told me about all those pictures he has of you. When you were a baby, I used to tell him he was in love with you, not me. I'm going to give you the same advice I gave Louise. Report him now. Somebody must do it—but not me.'

That was when Dorothy realized she had become her father's obsession. He later told her he had not taken her with him on trips because he didn't want to share her. She became frightened. She didn't want strangers to know what had happened to her. She didn't want to be put into a foster home. That, to her now terrified imagination, might be worse.

She spent the night shivering in the park, and the next morning a policeman told her he would have to take her into custody if she didn't have a home.

CV told Emma, 'Her being out on that bench is in the CIA file.'

'But you don't believe the rest do you?'

'I didn't say that. I said one fact has been corroborated. Dorothy has been murdered, and she didn't do that to herself. I don't want to be sidetracked by what didn't happen.'

'When you doubt her, I can't stand it.'

'Would you prefer me not to say so?'

'Yes.'

When Dorothy came home she learned Bell had gone to Paris but had left a phone number where he could be reached.

That was when she realized that she could never have a life like other teenage girls. Louise had told her she could succeed at anything. She would succeed at bringing herself up. She would be her own mother.

She phoned Reggie and asked if she could go to a London day school. She wanted to take her A-levels and go to college. He spoke tenderly and told her that he adored her and would make her happy any way she wanted. When he hung up, she went to his bedroom and smashed his mirror with a hammer. She took his favourite box, which had a lid embossed with precious stones, and sold it. She took his favourite jackets and other clothes and gave them to the Salvation Army.

When he returned to London, as she had expected, she became his mistress. She tried to avoid him and developed friends to have somewhere else to go when he was home. She signed up for organized tours and camping trips—anything to avoid his bed. She knew he had other women and longed for him to fall in love with one of them. He never did.

He often promised that he would not molest her again: 'Just this one time, because it's the last,' he'd beg and then turn into a crazed creature. He'd remove any lock she'd put on her bedroom door.

Emma said, 'Dorothy would sometimes cry for no reason, and I'd put my arms around her. She was remembering those days. She once came to Michael's crying and saying, "I saw a girl today who reminded me of me."

'It wasn't a romance for her father. It was having someone he could be cruel to. He knew shops that sold things made to hurt where it doesn't show. One time, Charlie, their handyman, came into her room when her father was hurting Dor and beat Mr Bell up. Reggie paid him £5,000 in front of her and told him that if he wanted to see his son again, he must never speak about what had happened. He said to Dorothy, "Everybody has a price." She guessed her father had made Louise choose between her own family's safety and Dorothy's and given her money to stay away.'

Charlie came to see Dorothy one day after her father left the house. He begged her to leave. She said, 'I'm only fourteen. I have nowhere to go. My mother doesn't want me.'

Emma blew her nose again. 'People don't believe children. You didn't believe it had happened to Dorothy.'

'I guess I didn't.' But did he now?

She continued sadly, 'Dor became an expert on how to survive. She said, "It's easier if you don't struggle. Rape isn't such a terrible thing anyway—it's only your body. Daddy'd be saying, 'Is that good?' And I'd be praying that one day I'd meet a nice boy who'd understand. My prayers were answered. Michael doesn't even care that I got pregnant twice and had abortions. I went to a family planning clinic and said I was seventeen, but I was fourteen. I always wanted children, but I've killed two of mine." Then on top of that she had herself sterilized.'

Emma had become Dorothy as she spoke. He saw the two of them: friends standing together defiantly accepting the injustices of the world but determined to survive.

'She wouldn't let Michael go with her to India where she had it done. She didn't want him to suffer that too. It was a secret. But now I've told you.'

He remembered how Dorothy's body had felt against his and that he had not wanted her to leave him. She had not been a bird of paradise, as he thought, but a damaged sparrow, and he felt humbled.

'This is a terrible story, Em.'

'I want to finish it.'

Dorothy learned to trade sex for what she wanted from her father. But when she went to college and he came to visit her there, she always had friends in her apartment. She took them with her to his hotel so he could not be alone with her. He told her he knew what she was doing but that sooner or later she'd come back to him. She knew she would not. She left college before graduating because she had got excited about precious stones one holiday and saw that through them she could become financially independent. That was what brought her to Sri Lanka, where she met Michael.

On one trip home, Bell had told her he would give her anything she wanted in return for a night with him. She had replied, 'Give me Louise.' A few days later he told her he had tried to find Louise only to learn she had died in a road accident the year before. Reggie gave Dorothy the phone number of a Hertfordshire newspaper that had published the story. She called the editor who read the account to her. Louise had been living with her parents and one morning went out to buy bread. Half an hour later her mother had had a phone call from the police saying her daughter had been killed in a hit-and-run accident. The car was a stolen vehicle and was found that evening. The driver was never caught.

Bell begged Dorothy to ask him for something else. She said, 'I have everything else.'

At some point she accepted Bell's offer of £5,000 a month to help him in his gem business. That was why she could live at the Palace.

'Five thousand again,' said CV.

'You mean Charlie the handyman got five thousand?'

'And he offered me $5,000 to take this case. He thinks in five thousands. I should have asked five for an advance, five for expenses, five on completion. He'd have paid it. That's it?'

'You don't want to hear about Mahmoud?'

'I don't. No, I do.'

'Do you mind if we walk now the rain has stopped? It's been a horrible evening, but I'm feeling better,' she said.

'Good Scotch will do that to you.'

'So will confession. I'm glad you know because Michael doesn't talk about it.'

They went down the steps towards the sea. Charcoal grey clouds were moving fast so the storm would resume soon. She took his hand. 'Do you mind?'

'I think I can stand it.'

'I don't usually like touching men because they get ideas.'

'I'm above all that.'

She gave a soft laugh. 'Is it because you're funny that people trust you?'

'Maggie says it's my beautiful toes.' He threaded his fingers through hers. 'I do this not through lust but in case you bolt.'

She didn't pull away. 'Where was I?' Her voice trembled slightly.

'Mahmoud.'

'But I didn't reach him yet. Dorothy lived at the Palace to impress the gem people. She said the rich only trust other rich, but that she was the exception. She was rich and trusted only Michael and me. She never trusted Mahmoud except once, and then suddenly it was too late.'

At that moment a message came that Joseph was outside, and immediately the rain started again.

On the way to Aunt Maud's he did not hold her hand. Instead he said, 'Emma, listen carefully to what I'm going to say. No tears. No anger.'

'I'm listening.'

'Dorothy was your friend, not mine.'

She moved away and turned to face him. 'I don't want to hear anything against her.'

'I understand that. But I can't put this thing together unless I keep an open mind. So think about the possibility that Dorothy's double personality ran deeper than you imagined. Go into your memory. Is it possible that you saw only one side of her, as did Michael? She obviously was a very complex girl. On every detail imagine where she could have lied, and if she did, where could the truth be?'

She had turned to look through the window.

'Emma,' he said, 'there is no time. In a week all efforts to find her murderer might be dropped. If Dorothy didn't lie, you'll know it because she could not have lied. If she did, you won't love her less. But only the truth will lead us to her killer.' He watched a tear roll down her cheek unchecked. He turned away. He didn't want to soften his words.

She said fiercely, 'I wish you had known her. You'd have understood.'

'I know that. I almost loved her. But is it better to love a real woman or a fairy tale she made up?'

Dorothy and Mahmoud

When Emma came downstairs in Maud's kimono and embroidered slippers, his throat tightened. So recently Dorothy had taken over his fantasies and replaced his nostalgia for Della's robust bedroom laugher. Now as he watched this other girl on the stairs, she had slid down as a child and tried not to trip on the trailing kimono. Della, Dorothy and other lovers seemed to have been a rehearsal for what he now felt.

Emma bunched the kimono higher and waddled across the polished red floor to the sofa and climbed into one corner of it.

She noticed he was staring and became uncomfortable.

'Aunt Maud, do we have time before dinner for Emma to finish the story of Dorothy and Mahmoud?' he asked.

'Yes, but I may doze off.' She closed her eyes and began breathing deeply.

Emma put her hand up to her mouth to hide her smile, then said, 'Clive. Is Clive okay? I don't like to call you CV.'

'I'd prefer darling boy.'

'Darling Clive.'

'Don't flirt with me, ma'am. Tell me how Dorothy met Mahmoud.'

Dorothy had first seen the two Arabs at the hotel one morning having breakfast. Mahmoud had come to the table where she sat alone and asked her to join him. She had replied, 'I'm waiting for someone.'

'No you're not. The waiter says you always eat alone.'

'I like doing so,' she had replied.

He gave her his card. She told Emma she had liked his manners, his looks, his mouth. She liked to watch it move when he talked.

CV realized suddenly that Emma was looking at his own mouth and put his glass up to it to cover its nondescript shape.

She continued, 'She'd say what was on her mind when she met a new person. She came right out and said "Jeff's hangs way down his thigh."' Emma stopped abruptly and glanced at Aunt Maud. 'Why did I tell you what Dor said about Jeff?' Emma whispered.

'Because it came to mind.'

'I'm so embarrassed.'

Two days later, Dorothy found two enormous boxes of chocolates and two large bouquets of flowers in her room. A note from Mahmoud was with each. Emma wrinkled her forehead, 'One said something like, "I've always preferred to eat with a friend, and for that reason I approached you." Another said, "Do you like champagne?"'

Dorothy wrote a note saying thank you, but she had a boyfriend. Emma said, 'She wasn't attracted to Mahmoud like she was to you. Even so, they began lunching together when Michael was working. Mahmoud told her he was interested in precious stones. One evening she went to his suite to see some jewellery he'd bought for his wife. Mo opened the door to her knock and locked it behind her. When she protested, her mouth was taped, and they raped her.

'She called it déjà vu. You see why I'm frightened they'd do the same to me. She said it was weird because Mo took off her frock carefully, and when he tied her to the bed the scarves were rolled around small towels so she didn't get hurt. Afterwards he untied her, and they watched her dress.'

'My poor child,' Mahmoud had said, 'it was the only way I could get through to you. Why are you angry? This is a game you're familiar with. You're not hurt.'

Dorothy had replied with every insulting word she knew.

'I propose an agreement with you,' he said. 'You will be available when I want you, and I will pay you very handsomely. I won't give you gifts. Buy your own trinkets.'

She had suddenly realized this man could help rid herself of her father permanently. She agreed, but her terms were that they must not be seen together at the hotel, no physical abuse, no sex with other men she might meet in Colombo, no risking AIDS. Mahmoud agreed. Dorothy had never told Emma the exact amount Mahmoud gave her, except that it was a lot.

A woman who on her own admission drove a hard bargain with her body!

One day, Mahmoud had suggested that Dorothy's boyfriend join them. Michael knew what she was doing and had been less shocked than cynical at the Arab's proposition.

'Her point and Michael's was that they needed money and Mahmoud had it. It was only sex. It was like life. Each person approaches it through different eyes. They could pretend there was no audience and they were at home alone.'

'You need money, yet you turn from Mahmoud.'

'I know it is wrong, but to her it was getting even.'

When Dorothy found she was making much less than she had hoped, she decided to take a cut from his gambling losses.

CV said, 'She told you Mahmoud agreed there'd be no physical abuse. Bundy says if a man hits a woman in public, and Mahmoud did, he'd hit her in private.'

'Sometimes he did. She said that after he hit her, she'd get money presents—large money presents as an apology.'

'And Michael shrugged that off too? Does he still see Mahmoud?'

'Of course not. I think that's why Mahmoud started coming after me. Four days ago Mo was on the main road near my house. Soong told him to leave.'

'And you waited for me today on the same road? That was stupid. You let Maggie in. She didn't call.'

'Because I recognized her.'

'You can't live there anymore.'

'I'll never get another house so cheap. Besides there are the children. If their father shows up I have to be there to protect Renuka now that she's getting near her time.'

Aunt Maud yawned and woke. 'It must be time for dinner.' She got to her feet and took CV's arm saying to Emma, 'Excuse me, dear. I have some letters for my nephew.' In her small library, she whispered, 'Darling boy, we'd better get Emma in here with us.' Not waiting for a reply, she led him to the dining room.

Ali Sharif

He lost Emma sometime after the pudding and before the brandy. CV turned to find her sitting upright in the corner of the sofa fast asleep. He lifted her into a more comfortable position with her feet up, and she frowned at his touch. She asked without opening her eyes, 'Is it time to go home?'

'Not yet.'

Amily tut-tutted like a nanny around the exhausted girl glaring at CV as if he had caused her state and went upstairs to ready the guest room.

'I'm glad you're here today,' he told his aunt. 'When I hear stories about child abuse I usually go out and get drunk.'

'And hurt yourself?'

'I think that's the point. I wish I knew these people better.'

'I think I'll go to bed now because my prayers are going to take a long time tonight.'

'I'm frightened for Emma,' he said almost to himself as he helped his aunt up the stairs. 'If Dorothy was killed to keep her silent, Emma and Michael could be next in line. He is aware of the danger, but Emma's idea of protecting herself would be to hide when she sees a gun.

'Dorothy knew her father, Mahmoud and Mo were rapists. She knew her father stole an emerald years ago and knew Bundy would pay for sex. Do you think she was blackmailing one of them?'

Maud sat on her bed and he took her slippers off. Before he could answer, she said, 'The guest room is ready for Emma.'

'I'll carry her up later. For now I want to drink brandy and think about our criminal.'

But as he sat at Emma's feet, he thought about her instead. He wondered if he could kiss her without waking her and at that moment heard the front door open and he rose to hug Maggie when she joined them. She pulled free when she saw Emma.

'Sometimes you surprise me,' she told him. 'Her presence here is one big surprise.'

'For me too. How was your day?' he asked.

'Awful and strange. And yours?'

'The same. Tried to get Michael to talk—not much luck but we have a new suspect in his lover Jeffrey. Tried to persuade

Emma to talk and she over-talked—leaving me with thousands of pieces that may not even belong to our puzzle. She's going to be on our team—man the phones, computer. You want a drink, Mag?'

'No.' She sat on Aunt Maud's chair and stuck her legs out. 'I deserve a halo, not a drink.'

'He's a very bad man, Maggo.'

'You mean Reggie?'

'Who else?'

'Maybe, but I have a new suspect. His name is Leyland Ali Sharif.'

'Tell me.'

Something was obviously bothering her because she kept moving around, but he knew better than to question. She never liked to be pushed. He handed her his own glass. 'Drink, because when I tell you about my day, you'll wish you were drunk.'

'Bad!'

'Worse.'

She nodded towards Emma, 'Go ahead and kiss her—you were going to, when I came in.'

'I desisted because when she unloaded her agonies, I noticed the villains were all men.'

Maggie said, 'Get me another brandy. I drank this one too fast.'

'Coming up. You want to sleep, or talk all night—in which case I'll need coffee.'

'Talk all night. I'll put the kettle on. By the way, I've spoilt everything.'

He lit candles and turned off the lights before he joined her in the kitchen. 'Take it from the top, Mag.'

'It's a two-part. One is Dorothy's murder, the other is my own sad story.'

'I'd like to hear both.'

'They mesh.'

'So be it. You woke at dawn—then what?'

'Woke. Dressed. Looked out of the window. Reggie in white rental car. Breakfast at a resthouse. Decision not to visit the elephant sanctuary. Queens Hotel in Kandy is decaying but Reggie books a bedroom for the afternoon. Cut to street with gem shops. Nice door. Posh room. Four chairs. One table. And,' she took two mugs out of the cabinet and slammed them on the counter, 'the door opened and a man came in, took one look at me and broke up. Laughed!'

'Santa Claus!'

'Don't joke. He wasn't even embarrassed. I was Donald Duck to him. "My name is Ali Sharif," he said, and cracked up again.'

'You hadn't met before?'

'No. I'd have remembered. Even Reggie was taken aback by the ho ho ho. I was there for him to display to Mr Sharif.' She took out a cigarette, lit it and said fiercely with it between her teeth, 'Don't ever laugh at anyone, CV, because God keeps a list and will stick it to you. I got it for laughing at those small people at the circus when I was ten. I never knew what it feels like when someone laughs as if you're a basset hound.'

Sharif had held his hand out. She placed hers in it and he continued holding it so she pulled away. 'He deliberately set that up to make me feel that I'm too scared to let a good-looking guy hold my hand, for God's sake.'

'Good looking! A clue.'

She managed a smile. 'Average face, hair, nose, eyes, mouth, lips, beard. I'm lying. Above average: cheekbones, dark hair, longish nose, bloody wonderful eyes, shoulders, hands. Which was why it was destructive that he found me a joke—not that I didn't probably look a clown—no sleep last night.'

'His job?'

'Don't laugh, CV. He's a jewellery designer.' Maggie didn't wear jewellery.

'Am I allowed a smile?'

'No.'

'Sharif had then said, "A wonderful surprise, Miss vander Marten." And I replied, "Likewise, I'm sure."'

CV said, 'I've lit candles. This story needed candles.'

Padmani's Blood

Reggie and Ali had begun to talk to each other, which put Maggie on hold. She learned only then that Bell had come about a star ruby, which they referred to as Padmani's Blood, and that it had something to do with Dorothy. Maggie knew this could be important to the investigation, but at the same time felt she was being manipulated by the men, if only because she couldn't walk out. Sharif, sensing her unease, included her in the conversation. Reggie, on the other hand, excluded her.

When she told this to CV, he said, 'Michael says that Reggie is a control freak who gives his permission for others to talk.'

'He does. That was it.'

She had said, 'Will someone tell me about Padmani's Blood and what it has to do with Dorothy?'

Ali replied, 'It's a historical and mysterious star ruby. Dorothy had arranged for Mr Bell to buy it but it's disappeared.'

'I don't think Maggie is interested,' snapped Bell.

Before she could find a stinging response, Sharif said, 'But she says she is.' He then asked her, 'Would you like to hear Padmani's story?'

She replied, 'I don't wear jewellery but stories about famous stones like the Great Mogul and the Hope Diamond have made me feel they're alive—like people.'

'Padmani's Blood and the Great Mogul have a lot in common—a habit of disappearing,' said Sharif. 'But unlike the Great Mogul diamond which was never found, Dorothy discovered where Padmani had been hiding just before she died.'

Maggie said, 'Reggie, why didn't you tell CV this?'

'Because I wanted to find out what Mr Sharif knew first.'

She decided not to say, 'Bullshit.'

Ali looked from one to the other and said, 'Come, Mr Bell, I have many other gems to show you. Please make yourself at home Miss vander Marten.'

As they talked and Emma slept, Maggie had placed a silver candlestick on the floor beside her, and she now lit a cigarette from its flame. 'And off they went leaving me sitting in a room full of nothing,' she said sourly. 'I was at the door about to leave when Ali returned.'

He said, 'My brother Kaz will take care of Mr Bell. May I join you on your walk?'

She now chuckled at the memory. 'He'd used the bombast to swipe Reggie's Maggie trophy from under his nose, and was he pleased with himself! Even so, I decided not to ask him why he thought me such a joke. He'd still look at me and snigger.'

'You must have had spinach on your teeth.'

'I checked. I didn't.'

Sharif bought her an umbrella from a sidewalk vendor insisting the sun was too hot for her. He'd chosen pink, red and white although she was wearing blue and made her look at her reflection in a shop window, saying, 'Don't you like the combination?'

She said, 'That's not the point. I'm on to you. You're up to something.'

'I'd hold the umbrella above your head, but it looks so nice when you hold it.'

'And you're deaf too?' But then she had to be frank. 'Ali, I have to know about Padmani's Blood. Reggie has hired my cousin CV to find Dorothy's killer and he didn't tell him about this stone. Is it valuable enough for someone to have caused her death?'

'It is. It's worth at least $10,000,000 wholesale. Star rubies are rarer than rubies and this one's colour is pigeon's blood. I don't think he's told the police about it, either.'

'He hasn't.'

He took her arm and they crossed the street. 'Who is CV?'

'So I told him about you,' Maggie said. 'We went to the temple and sat in the shade. And then he told me about Padmani's Blood.'

Dorothy saw a drawing of a Kandian king holding Padmani's Blood and went to Ali to ask if it was a myth. He had replied, 'The stories around it are, but a stone by that name exists.' She said, 'I want to buy it.' He was amused but liked her spunk and said he'd ask around, but he didn't want to be involved.

'Why?' CV asked.

'Because it has a curse. He's not superstitious, but if he touched the stone, every time something went wrong in his family someone would say, "Padmani's Blood has spilled again."'

CV said, 'This must be the ruby Michael and Jeffrey told me about. Go on.'

Ali called Padmani's legend a King Arthur story: 'It is like one person insisting there was no King Arthur and another finding Excalibur in a lake the next day.'

A Kandian king had received an enormous uncut Burmese star ruby as part of his first wife's dowry. Her father warned him not to cut the stone, because it had been found in an abandoned well into which a tyrannical landowner had tossed any servants who irritated him. One of his heirs found the stone among the human bones, showed it to a fortune-teller who declared that it had once been a star sapphire but had turned red—become a ruby—because it had seen so much blood. It would destroy anyone who took a blade to it.

When the king's brother died from a snake bite, he took his sister-in-law Padmani into his household as a second wife, as was the custom. He promptly fell in love with her and foolishly gave her the star ruby because she asked for it. Without telling him, she had it cut and polished by a master and, it was found to weigh 992 carats. It was also the rarest colour, pigeon's blood, and the star was of perfect symmetry.' A stone like that becomes historic, Ali explained. 'But this one became a legend because three months after she had the stone cut, Padmani bled to death in childbirth. After that it was called Padmani's Blood.

'Twenty or thirty stories tell of its vengeance. In each, someone falls in love with the stone, acquires it and bleeds to death.'

'By the time Ali had completed his story we were standing in front of the Temple of the Tooth. There we were with Buddhist monks in orange robes, the lake, three elephants! I didn't want to go back to the shop, but Ali's brother Kaz had taken Reggie off his hands as a favour, and he had promised to return as quickly as possible. Also, Ali felt that sneaking away with me hadn't been playing very fair to Reggie.'

'You're playing butting horns,' she had replied. 'What CV calls power games.'

'Do you play butting horns?'

'Do I! Thank you for the Padmani story. I wish beautiful things weren't hidden away. They should be put where everyone can look at them. You said Dorothy found it and Reggie was going to buy it. Where is it now?'

'She died, and he says it has disappeared.'

'Someone stole it?'

'His words were, "I have lost contact with it."'

As they walked back, Ali had told Maggie, 'When Dorothy came to me I suggested she run ads to say she was interested in the history of Padmani's Blood. Eventually she found it and arranged for her father to buy it. Then three days before her death she phoned to thank me for my help, and I suggested she offer the stone to Sri Lanka and that a lottery be run to reimburse her for it. She said, "Don't confuse me."'

'And?'

'Leyland Ali Sharif then took me back and handed me over to Reggie Bell,' Maggie said.

CV yawned, went into the kitchen, refilled their mugs and washed his face under the tap to freshen up. When he returned she was taking the petals of the flowers in a vase and filling a brass bowl with them.

'Can you disconnect from the guy and consider if Sharif could be our killer?'

Without hesitation she replied, 'I don't know how to.'

'Okay, what else was said? Try to repeat it word for word.'

'When we got back, Ali said, "Would you like to see my etchings?"'

His etchings were two old prints showing Padmani's Blood. One was of a wedding with a Kandian king in full regalia that made a man's waist seem sixty inches and his chest thirty. The king was seated on a throne with an elaborately dressed young woman standing beside him. Courtiers with banners lined up behind them. In the king's hand was a red globe the size of a cricket ball. The other print showed a woman with kohl-rimmed eyes and a Mona Lisa smugness to her smile. In one hand she was holding Padmani's Blood poised on the tips of her fingers. The star was visible and threw light in all directions. In the other hand she grasped a large erect penis that was dripping blood. In the background her poor castrated king stood among weeping women. Above the whole was a black bird its beak open and an infant in its claws.

'Aristocratic sadomasochist porn!' Maggie commented.

A door opened and Reggie and a man who resembled Ali now joined them. Kaz Sharif shook Maggie's hand warmly.

'How unbelievably wonderful you look,' he said frankly.

'So do you,' she had replied with a smile.

Bell said to Maggie, 'Sorry I had to leave you alone. What

have you been doing with yourself?'

She did not reply.

'What about lunch?' he asked the men.

'A previous engagement, I am afraid,' Ali replied.

'And,' Maggie told CV, 'he turned and walked out leaving Kaz to get rid of us.'

On the way to the hotel Reggie had called Ali an arrogant swine.

She continued sourly, 'After lunch we did it. You won't believe what Reggie pulled afterwards. He told me to go shopping because he wanted to have tea with Sharif alone and when I was around the conversation got diverted. After he left I went down to the hotel shops and bought lots of silver and brass and antiques, an ivory statue, a lovely pot, and I put it all on his bill. I had it delivered to Ali Sharif with a note from Reggie saying, "Please give it to the needy." Then I went back to the room and slept.'

'Oh Maggie!'

'I know. What have I come to? He has dyed hair and a surgically lifted face. I didn't tell you about that, did I? While he was convulsing I looked at his hairline and eyes. No question, the little scars are there. Also behind the neck.'

'His hair is dyed?'

'It's greying, but there is a darkness at the scalp. I haven't even heard your exciting day yet, but I'm not that sleepy because I slept in the car.'

'You think Reggie is going to be difficult now you've charged all that stuff to him?'

'Not him. I thought of that as I did it. He has to collect on his outlay. Buying that stuff is going to keep him around—you'll see.'

'This Sharif is not married, is he?'

'He isn't. I asked, and he replied "I have no family," and, "My daughter died when she was a year old." He did not say what had happened to that daughter's mother. But then he smiled at me. "I should have said, "I have no wives." We Muslims may have more than one. What do you think about such an arrangement?"'

'I think it's just male bullshit to victmize women,' Maggie had replied.

'I thought it victimized the men.'

'Well, I've been married three times, and two at a time would have been worse,' she said.

'You married for love?'

'No, are you supposed to?'

He laughed. 'Why did you marry then?'

'Loneliness. Despair. I had given up on finding my knight.'

CV took much less time to tell her about his day, prefacing his remarks with, 'I'll give you the gist. The details can come later.' Then he carried Emma upstairs and placed her on the guest room bed with a pillow under her head and a sheet covering her to the waist.

Together he and Maggie stood looking down at the girl who, even deep in sleep, showed puffiness around her eyes.

'Go on. Do it,' she said.

'I can't take advantage of a defenceless woman.'

'She's dreaming of her prince. You have to kiss her so she can live happily ever after.'

He leaned down, placed a hand on either side of her pillow and lowered his lips on to Emma's. They did not kiss him back. 'Let's get out of here because the predator in me is suggesting an attack on this unresponsive female.'

Maggie took his hand, and they went out closing the door behind them softly. She whispered, 'I'm ever so glad you're here.'

Chapter VI

Sunday

The Morning After
CV woke tired but showered, shaved and was at the breakfast table before eight. His aunt was in the kitchen. Maggie and Emma were still asleep.

He saw Emma's plastic bag on a chair and removed the package of photos and letters, took the computer from its wrappings and plugged it into the dining room wall outlet.

He was disappointed to find most of Dorothy's letters were in fact notes or invitations from friends. She had kept no envelopes. There was a pencil drawing of Michael's face scowling and a single line scrawled under it: 'Get over here. I miss you.' It was unsigned and undated.

There were also four half-page letters from her father which started 'Dear Dot'. One was on hotel stationary, the others on lined sheets. The only return address in all cases was the name of the city from which he had written, and all were dated the previous year. One would have been written just after Michael and Dorothy had returned to Sri Lanka. In it Bell implored his daughter to 'think more and react less. You must be more open to me.'

The last and longest letter was dated December 28 from Geneva: 'You have not returned my calls. If you don't want to talk, leave a message on my machine. I must know your plans. I am going to Singapore and Colombo early next year. Try to have it for me to look at. If it's the genuine article I'll buy it on the spot.'

Like the other letters this one too was signed 'Your loving Father'.

'It' could have referred to Padmani's Blood. Bell had not asked how Dorothy had spent Christmas nor sent her good wishes for the new year. Of course other communications—faxes, emails and phone calls—could have passed between them.

Aunt Maud came in while CV was studying the letters and began looking through the snapshots using the magnifying glass she no longer tried to read without. 'Which one is Dorothy?' she asked and passed him a group shot of eight young people on the beach. He pointed her out, and Maud continued examining the pictures but made no comment. He looked at them and found few surprises. Most were of Michael and Dorothy's friends, including Emma. There was a picture of Michael seated in a long chair with Sweetie on his lap. There was none of Jeffrey and none of her father.

The most interesting and largest picture was of Dorothy with Mahmoud and three other Arabs in their national dress. They were at a dining table, and she wore the grey silk that he had seen hanging in Bell's closet. CV studied the picture closely. Her hair was elaborately braided and crowned by a gold clasp. She wore a sensational diamond choker with shining pendants, a diamond bracelet and drop earrings. The girl in this picture and the girl he remembered barely resembled each other.

Maggie had wandered in still wearing short pajamas and was now standing behind him yawning. She said, 'You can see why I don't like jewellery.'

She took the chair beside him and began to peel a boiled egg getting the soft yoke all over her hands, then went to the kitchen and came back drying her fingers on a towel. 'Aunt Maud, Amily is impossible. She said I have the manners of a dog.'

Her aunt replied, 'What did you say dear?'

Maggie did not repeat the complaint but continued to CV, 'Jewellery is a penal uniform. A collar of rubies is what the owner grabs if he wants to control the dog. Necklaces remind men and women who's the boss.'

'I've never seen a man grab a woman by her necklace to control her.'

'The grabbing is figurative.'

'I'd forgotten your philosophical morning bent.'

'Listen to me, empty head! Fashion should not be a prettified medieval restraint. Clothing should clothe. It should not be a symbol of bullying.'

He put the picture down, lifted the cover off one of the dishes and helped himself to a slice of pineapple. He said, 'Auntie, do you like Maggie yelling like this?'

'Yes, darling boy.'

'Wrong reply.'

'Cattle, pigs and bears have nose rings so they can be dragged around. In dungeon pictures, the prisoners are shackled by the neck, by the wrist, by the ankle. Metal bands are made to squeeze a man to death. The man who wears a crown is squeezed by it. Reggie and Dorothy were into jewels because jewels symbolize control. They didn't buy stones because they loved the pretty round things. They did it to make money off others' weaknesses. Reggie doesn't wear jewellery. He doesn't like being controlled. Find out who owned the jewellery Dorothy is wearing in that picture, and you'll know who was jerking her leash. I don't think the jewellery was hers. When she was with Michael, she never wore any.'

'You got all that from a photo of a girl in a grey dress and some jewellery?'

'I got much more. That jewellery,' she continued earnestly—now on her third boiled egg, 'is real, because you don't drape yourself in stuff that looks like that if it isn't. She was wearing it only because it was worth a bloody fortune. Those diamonds are not good-looking on her—sapphires would have been better with that colouring.

'Dorothy,' Maggie said with the picture with Mahmoud still in her hand, 'has been spoken of as intelligent by Emma, Michael, Reggie and Ali, so she knew this kind of outfit made her invisible. I bet everyone who saw that jewellery on her said, "Wow! I wonder what it cost?" as if she wasn't there. That's how she could live in her two worlds.' She sighed. 'I'm so hungry, but I suppose I'd better not eat another egg. I'll have a slice of papaw—that big one. Shove it here.' He'd never seen her eat so much at one time, and this chatter wasn't like her. He could hardly avoid noticing that she had started ranting against jewellery the day after she had met Sharif. CV had never seen her helplessly in love and wondered if what had seemed impossible could be happening.

'I thought that's the nearest I've seen her look beautiful,' he said.

'Oh yeah?' she looked at their aunt. 'If you saw her in that get up, would you want to f— her? You wouldn't see her, and you know it. I think to be powerful Dorothy found she had to hide. At first she must have hated discovering that she could only get her way by disappearing behind good clothes, but jewel thieves have to look expensive. She was visible to Michael no matter what, so she cut her father's chains.' She pointed to the picture with Mahmoud and threw at CV the one of Dorothy standing dishevelled with her friends on the beach.

He took the pictures from her. Maggie was right. That other Dorothy he had desired so suddenly was in the picture with her friends. He wouldn't have crossed the room for the one with Mahmoud.

'And now?' he asked his cousin. 'Mahmoud wants Emma to make herself invisible?'

'Not necessarily. Emma will never disappear. She could

sleep in a gutter, and she'd still be Emma to herself and to us. Dorothy must have felt she belonged in the gutter till she met Michael. Wouldn't you if your father was Reggie Bell? I spent an afternoon in bed with him, and I became invisible. I wanted to prove I could handle him, and I couldn't . . .' She glanced at her aunt and began to drink her coffee angrily, slurping it as if she hated it too. 'Couldn't sleep thinking about that pig and all the other pigs like him.'

'You're so bright, Mag,' CV said getting up, for it was time to work. 'You understand people better than anyone. I wish to God you could get into a job that uses your mind.'

'You want me to become a teacher so I can amuse little kids by making faces?' she started buttering a piece of toast.

'I guess I do.'

'I know why I'm eating like this,' she said. 'It's knowing that all those years I haven't had to diet. I'll be ill later, but it will be worth it.' She stood up and patted her stomach. 'Just look at that little paunch. Isn't it beautiful?'

After breakfast he said to her, 'I need Sharif's phone number. I think I'll drive up to Kandy this afternoon and see him. He knew Dorothy and might be more objective than the others.'

'And I suppose you want me to stay here and hold Reggie's hand?'

'Stay with Emma. Talk to her. She may be the one who has the key we need.'

Sharif had two phone numbers. CV tried his home first. Maggie pretended to be interested in her cup of coffee as they spoke.

CV introduced himself and then said, 'I'd like to speak to you some time today about Dorothy Bell.'

'Oh yes. I hear you're handling the case.'

'And it's turning out to be complicated. I'd like your insights and suggestions. I have a luncheon appointment but could drive up to Kandy this afternoon if you're free.'

Jeanne Cambrai

Sharif spoke American English.

'I'm afraid you'll miss me because I'm leaving for Colombo in a few minutes. Perhaps Maggie, you and your aunt will dine with your new suspect this evening.'

'You're still only a tentative suspect. Dinner will be great. Aunt Maud prefers to make last-minute decisions for dinner because she tires. Maggie—hold on,' he said to her with his hand over the mouthpiece, 'You want to have dinner with Sharif?'

She managed to scowl and smile at the same time.

He tried to keep the amusement out of his voice. 'Maggie is on too. Why don't you come here for dinner. It's hell for Mag when she gets recognized in public places.'

'Then let's have dinner at my home. Is there anything in particular you want to know?'

'Your motive for killing Dorothy and your alibi.'

Sharif said, 'My motive is that she spilled beer on my Maggie vander Marten poster. My alibi is that I was cuddling my Maggie vander Marten doll when the crime took place.'

'Don't speak so loud. She's sitting quite close to me. If you can think of any clue Dorothy gave you—names, places—please write them down. I don't know what I'm looking for.'

When he hung up, Maggie said smugly, 'Yesterday evening Reggie said in the most off-hand way, "See you tomorrow". Do you think I have to phone and say I'm busy?'

'You don't, but I'll mention it during lunch.'

They turned because Emma had come into the room. She clutched the kimono around her and stood staring from the doorway as if she wasn't expecting them to be there. Then she said, 'Good morning. I don't remember going to bed last night.'

Maggie said, 'Good morning. CV kissed you to make you wake up, but you were no princess. He had to carry you upstairs. Don't worry, I was there to save your honour.'

The girl looked confused. She said, 'I'd better go home now.'

'Breakfast first. Then I'll drive you over.'

'And me? What will I do? asked Maggie.

'Explore every avenue and turn every stone. Unrelated to Dorothy's death, Mag, there are four kids at Emma's who need outfitting. Dr Soong does not approve of socially correct garments for paupers. What do you think?'

She said, 'Denim has no class. Cotton has no class, nor does leather on the feet.'

'You see?' he said to Emma. 'When it comes to clothes, she's it. Ask her to tell you her theory on Dorothy from one glance at that photo in the grey dress. Did she own the diamonds she was wearing?'

She stood there still blinking sleepily. 'No. I don't know where she got them. They weren't hers.'

Maggie hooted.

He looked at his watch. 'It's nine already? We need a way to get into Bell's hotel room and look through Dorothy's things when he's not there. Perera will give us a key.'

'I'll do it while you're at lunch with him.'

'Too dangerous—we're eating in the hotel. Tomorrow should be okay.'

'Jeffrey,' said Emma, 'is good at things like that.'

'Take him with you, Mag.'

He had actually forgotten Aunt Maud who was listening to their conversation. She said, 'I know how to break into hotel rooms—it's in detective books. You can use a credit card to open the lock or go in when the maid is cleaning the room. Or you can go in with Mr Bell and then fix the lock when you're coming out.'

'Auntie!'

'But it's against the law,' said Aunt Maud.

'So is murder,' he reminded her.

The Explosion

CV told Emma his aunt wanted her to stay with them at Bliss.

'Humour her for a few days!'

She said to Maggie, whose sarong she was wearing, 'I'm going to need my printer.'

'I'll send Joseph for it,' Maggie promised.

'I'll go with him and get some clothes.'

She seemed to be, at least temporarily, free of the terrors that had overwhelmed her the previous evening.

CV planned to introduce Emma to Bundy's office after returning from Soong's, so he went along too. But a block away from the house they saw a huge crowd at the entrance to the lane. Joseph could barely keep the car moving because people were all over the road. He told them it must be some political gathering, in which case it would be better for them not to go further. 'You are staying in the car—I am finding out what's going on.'

He was back in about five minutes and hissed through the window, 'Miss Emma please to lying on the floor. Hurry up. Hurry up.'

She dropped down. 'What's wrong?' she asked.

CV kept his hand on her head and also asked, 'Yes. What's wrong?'

'Bomb in Miss Emma's house, sir.'

'A bomb? The Tigers?'

'I think. Last night Miss Emma is dead.'

'Oh no,' said Emma's voice from near CV's knee.

'Shhh,' he said. 'The police are there?'

'Many, sir.' Joseph was back in the driver's seat.

The crowd hurried by them, but few glanced into the car, which had its windows up now. CV wound down one and leaned out. He saw the police trying to get the people to disperse.

Joseph told them the Black Tigers were suspected, but a passing woman said a thief had gone into the building, attacked the woman who lived there, stolen her money and then set a bomb. The two Chinese doctors had been woken by the explosion and called the police. The bomb had been too small to bring down the whole building.

'At least the doctors are all right,' said Emma's voice from the floor. 'It must have been Renuka who was killed. I'll have to look after her children. I have to go there and get them.'

'I'll go. You both head home,' CV said.

'Soong must think I'm dead. Tell her I'm alive, Clive.'

'If they'll let me speak to her,' he said. 'What about that American girl who wanted to spend the night with you?'

'Julia? Please go quickly, Clive. Please, God, let it not be Julia or Renuka. Perhaps no one was there at all.'

'When you get home, tell everyone they mustn't let on that you're alive.' But he didn't open the door yet. 'Now listen carefully. Phone your parents so they'll know you're all right, but tell them not to confide in friends yet because they'll be putting you in danger. Stay out of sight. Don't let anyone see you go from the car to the house.'

'What about Michael? We have to tell him.'

'Right! He may not have heard yet. Can you trust the Chinese doctors?'

'Absolutely. I bet Renuka's husband did it. She must have run into my house to hide.'

He watched the Magnette pull away, then walked casually to the lane and asked a man in the crowd what had happened. 'It's the second murder of a foreign girl,' he was told. A woman broke in angrily, 'First one in the Pettah, now one here. What is happening to us?'

'You are sure it was a *foreign* girl?'

'That's what they are saying.'

The green gate with the rust holes was closed, and two policemen were standing outside. CV explained to them that Dr Soong was his doctor and he had to speak with her urgently on a matter of his health. One man went inside, and CV tried to look through the rust holes, but the other signed him away. Then the gate was opened, and Dr Soong stepped outside. She looked at him without expression.

He willed her to understand and looking into her eyes said sternly, 'Dr Soong, I am Emma's friend Clive vander Marten, whom you treated last week. I have dislocated my shoulder again.'

Soong did not change expression. She said loudly, 'Come inside, sir. I cannot discuss your body in front of other people.'

Inside the wall about a dozen onlookers, mostly uniformed police, were standing around Emma's house. The side nearest the road showed some damage, and the windows and door had been blown out. The policemen were standing around a man who was not in uniform but seemed to be in charge. He turned and watched Soong lead CV away from the buildings to where a wall provided some shade. CV could see Renuka and the children huddled together, and then Dr Hoong approached. Both doctors were of short stature, calm, impassive and trim. The narrow eyes were anxious and, in Hoong's case, stricken.

'Renuka will tell you I am Emma's friend,' CV said. 'Emma is alive.'

A policeman from near the house was approaching them, and Dr Hoong waited and addressed him in English. 'This man is our patient. Because one person has died, we cannot neglect others who need help.'

The policeman looked annoyed, and CV quickly repeated what the doctor had said in Sinhala.

'Who are you?' the policeman asked rudely.

'I do not answer questions just because you ask them,' he snapped back. The man continued to glower but hurried away. They watched him give the message to his boss, who had not taken his eyes off them. He turned away. Apparently, they were to be left alone. Then Renuka saw CV and tried to join them. She was intercepted by a policeman and returned to where she had been standing.

'Emma is alive,' repeated CV trying to speak so his voice wouldn't carry. The doctors nodded gravely. 'Yesterday evening she fell asleep at our house after dinner. Are they sure someone was in her house?'

'A woman's body has been removed.'

'It may be her American friend Julia Ware. Last night Emma told Julia she could sleep here. Emma sends her affectionate thoughts to you through me.'

Hoong's eyes showed no concern for a dead woman he did not know. The tension had fallen from his wife also.

'Tell Emma we are very happy. Very happy. Tell her.'

'I will. What else do you know?'

'Superintendent Senaratne says someone stole from the house,' said Soong, pressing her eyebrows together in a stern frown. 'Emma's computer was stolen.'

'It is at my aunt's house. We were coming to get the printer.' He then tore a sheet from his notebook and started writing. 'This is where she is and our phone number.'

'I have not seen you before,' said Soong.

He told them he was looking for Dorothy's killer for her father. 'Please try and remember every person and every incident that can help me.'

'Dorothy! Nothing but troubles!' But Hoong did not sound harsh or critical. 'These two deaths are connected. It is better for Emma not to show her face.'

'I agree.'

They walked him to the gate. The man who had been giving orders came up briskly and blocked their way.

'Your name?' he asked CV.

'Clive—that is CV vander Marten.'

'Your business here?'

Soong replied quickly. 'He has come for medicine for his shoulder. He was Emma's friend.'

'I am Superintendent Theodore Senaratne from CID, in

charge of this case and that of Dorothy Bell's. Can you shed any light on why someone would have wanted to kill Emma van Eck?'

'No,' CV said. He had not taken his own advice to the Hoongs, he realized, and had forgotten to look suitably distraught. He thought it better not to correct that now and hoped the Superintendent would dismiss him as a callous American.

'You were a friend of Dorothy Bell's too?' asked Senaratne looking at his intently.

'I barely knew both girls.'

'You sound American. You are on holiday here?'

'I'm a Lankan Burgher, but my family has become American—and yes, I am on holiday here.'

The other man almost smiled. 'You must be related to Maud vander Marten who is the last of that family in the country. I hear Maggie vander Marten is in Colombo. She was a friend of my wife, Nora, before we married.'

'Maggie's hoping to get together with all her old friends.'

'I want to talk to you again, Mr vander Marten. Where can I find you?'

CV said smoothly, 'I'll give you Aunt Maud's phone number. She will always know where to reach me.'

He bade Soong and Dr Hoong goodbye, nodded to Senaratne, and set off to the top of the lane. Before he reached it and was still in sight of the gate he turned. The superintendent was watching him. He waved and received a raised hand in acknowledgement.

Regrouping

Maggie was at the gate waiting. 'What are you up to?'

'How's Emma?'

'Scared. Who would want to kill Emma? Her parents want her to fly to England immediately, and she won't go. She got to them minutes after someone from here told them she was dead.

She kept screaming, "It wasn't a joke! Someone else got killed instead of me! It was a mistake!" What's going on?'

He put an arm around her to still the trembling and said with more confidence than he felt, 'They don't know Emma's alive. We can't conceal that from the police for very long. The question now is who the victim was.'

He hugged his aunt, who was at the door. Inside Emma was seated bolt upright in a high-back chair with her hands on her lap.

'Hi,' he said. 'Everything's under control again. Renuka and the kids are fine. Soong and husband send their love and are overjoyed you're okay.'

She made no movement.

'How can we help?' he asked, taking her hand.

She said, 'Mummy and Daddy are angry with me.'

'Auntie will talk to them. They've had a shock. Come upstairs, Em. I have to talk to you.' He caught Maggie's eye and shook his head, which she correctly interpreted as, 'Don't follow us'.

Emma followed him listlessly holding on to the railing like an old woman. He led the way to his bedroom, closed the door and asked her to sit down. She did so in the same dreamlike way.

He pulled a chair opposite hers and said as firmly as he could, 'You've had a bad shock. Lots of people react with anger or numbness when they get scared. But this is too serious for us to sit back. After Friday you can have six breakdowns, honey, and I'll see you through them all. But now I need you.'

She frowned. 'I wish I was dead. I don't know what to do.'

'I'll tell you what to do. Do you have a book to write things down?'

She said, 'Somewhere.'

'Use my blue notebook and pen for now. Sit at the desk and write what I tell you.'

To his relief she moved there, opened the book and poised the pen on it.

He took the pen and wrote *Della* and a row of numbers on the top of the sheet.

'That's the phone and fax address of Della Marsh who lives in Chicago.' He wrote another line. 'That's Della's office phone which her boss bugs.' He went on writing and explaining. 'Della is at the office eight to five Chicago time. It's 11.30 yesterday evening there now. Call or fax her any time day or night. She knows Dorothy was murdered. She's a computer nerd, so keep it cool. No emotional outbursts.'

'I don't want to call her.'

'You have to. I don't want to do any of this, but I have to. I won't have the time to phone Della myself, and Maggie is too famous to put her name on line. Aunt Maud is forgetful and tires. Make the phone calls only on Auntie's phone. There's a jack in this room, and Amily knows where a spare phone is stashed. Maggie can rewire anything if it's not a simple plug-in. The mobile phones are out for now as I don't want your voice on them. Keep out of sight. You mustn't even go downstairs until we say it's okay.'

The colour was coming back to her face. She said, 'I think I'll phone Mummy and blast her because after all it's me who nearly died.'

'Now you're talking. What about a cup of coffee?'

'Oh yes.'

He went out and yelled down the stairs, 'Amily! Two cups of coffee.'

Maggie yelled back, 'Amily's praying for us at her temple. I'll get them.'

Emma asked, 'What do I tell Della?'

'Tell her what's happened. Read her a list of every person connected to Dorothy's death, close to you, to Michael, to all of us. Don't forget Aunt Maud's friends who knew Dorothy or

Louise Lawrence. I also want Della to find out if Reggie's CIA file has been updated yet.'

'The CIA?'

'Don't say the word, just his *file*.'

'It's a lot to ask of her.'

'She'll love it. Maggie will help,' he said.

'Yes, she will,' said Maggie from the door. 'Lucky for you both, I just made a pot of coffee.' She shoved his clothes off a chair, used it as a table for the tray and then handed out the cups.

'I have to go. Tell her what we need, Emma. Then take a shower and make yourself at home upstairs because it may be a long stay.' He pressed Maggie's shoulder hard and hoped she understood that meant 'Help her'.

Theodore Senaratne

Superintendent Theodore Senaratne was a short, wiry dark man with huge, deep-set black eyes and unruly black hair. He would have looked like a cross between an Aberdeen terrier and a Scottie if his legs had been shorter. He had the disposition of a bulldog and had been put on Dorothy Bell's case of after the British High Commission had called for more police action. Teddy had suspected that her killer would never be found, and he had been reluctant to give her murder precedence over those of his own people. He had been selected for the Bell murder, however, for the frequency with which he had seemed to let go of a crime only to produce, months or even years later, an airtight case against the wrongdoer. In the case of Dorothy Bell, Teddy expected no revelations from the men in the street who often helped find criminals. He suspected the local people were not going to stick their necks out for a rich foreigner.

So, from the first, Dorothy Bell's murder hadn't interested Teddy Senaratne much. He had presumed it to be drug related for the Michael Blue crowd were hardly abstemious. He knew about rich spoilt socialites because he had been born one of them and had come to the conclusion that they were a good-hearted lot. If they wanted to kill each other off he actually had little objection because, other than providing jobs for those less endowed, he saw them as part of the liabilities of Sri Lanka rather than the assets.

Teddy had therefore done little more than go through the motions of trying to find Dorothy Bell's killer.

But the pipe-bomb killing of Emma van Eck shocked him into realizing he had misjudged the first crime badly. There was something going on that had taken the lives of two women, and if he didn't find out what, two could easily become three, four or five. He became angry with the killer for the guilt he felt.

Teddy was to tell CV much of this story later, and how, while he had been looking at the scene of the second crime, he had become aware of the arrival of Clive vander Marten, whom he recognized. He did not believe that he had come to the Chinese doctors to obtain medication because he looked around the compound as if trying to memorize everything he saw and seemed in perfect health. After he left, there'd been whispering between the servant girl Renuka and Dr Soong. Teddy suspected someone had sent CV there to check out the situation.

Teddy had therefore traced the phone number CV had given him, and as soon as he could get away, he had driven to Maud vander Marten's home where he learned from a hanger-on at the gate that her nephew was there. He entered the drawing room to find the three vander Martens looking guilty of something, if not murder.

The superintendent had not seen his wife's friend Maggie up close before and, as was his way on first acquaintances, he studied her closely. She was even taller than he expected and wore a very small pair of shorts. He liked the way the corners of her mouth were turned up and could see she was an extremely desirable creature. Maud vander Marten he knew only by sight also. Her keen dark eyes examined him with interest from her very old face, and it was her hand he took first.

'Sit down young man and have a drink,' said Maud.

'No thank you, Miss vander Marten. Your nephew came to the Hoongs' this morning to find out what had happened to Miss van Eck. I want to know why he didn't ask me.'

'Ahhh,' said CV and Maggie together.

CV said, 'Superintendent, I think you had better sit down and have at least a soft drink. Then, I'd like to talk to you one on one because everyone here knows what I know and won't want to hear it again.'

So Teddy sat down.

CV then explained briefly that Bell had hired him to find Dorothy's killer. He described the previous evening and how Emma happened to be out of her home. 'We think the girl who was killed may be Julia Ware.'

Teddy thought about that. He then said, 'And you want the fact that Emma is alive to be kept a secret. The problem, of course, is that the real victim must be identified and her family informed. Emma's parents are flying here to arrange a burial. They must also know the truth immediately.'

'Emma has phoned them.'

'May I speak with her? I will have to see her for myself.'

'She's doing some work to take her mind off the shock she's had,' Maggie said.

'Later then. How did Julia Ware get into the house? The doctor said that Miss van Eck locks her door before leaving. The gate was also locked.'

'Almost locked. You just reach over and lift the catch,' CV told him. 'I've done it myself. Julia knew Emma leaves her door key in a crack on the windowsill.'

'Even if the intruder came in by the gate, it is unlikely he would have left that way after throwing the bomb. It's more likely he climbed over the broken wall that overlooks the railway lines to escape detection,' the policeman told them.

'Can you tell us what exactly happened?'

'The motive seemed robbery as the computer was missing. But now I don't know. At some point the assailant threw a small pipe bomb into the bedroom and must have run like hell because he got away completely. The girl inside is so burnt she is almost unrecognizable. Because Miss van Eck is fair skinned and small sections of skin can be seen, we presumed it was her. The dead woman was lying on her back in bed and must have been asleep, drunk or under the influence of something because there are no signs of a struggle. That's what it looks like now. After the autopsy we'll know more.'

'Doesn't it have to be premeditated if the intruder brought a bomb with him? A bomb seems like overkill. Were there knife wounds? Bullet wounds?'

'I have to wait for the autopsy. Bombs have been used to kill as well as to frighten—to make a statement. If someone knew Miss van Eck was with you, it could have been a warning to either of you. You're right, a bomb is a very deliberate premeditated weapon. Who carries a bomb? Black Tigers. Guerrillas. Lonely madmen.'

Aunt Maud said, 'I think I'll go upstairs and pray for their souls.'

Maggie called Amily to see that their aunt reached her room safely for she looked tired. 'What now?' she then asked Teddy. 'We can't just sit and wait for someone to come after Emma again.'

'He may have killed the woman he wanted to kill. How well did Miss Ware know Dorothy Bell?'

'We'll have to ask Emma,' CV said. 'Shall I get her?'

But the doorbell rang.

Teddy moved to the window. 'Michael Blue has been very protective of Emma van Eck. In fact, he told me last week that she should have police protection—that he could look after her himself but she was unaware of the danger she might be in as

Dorothy's friend. Let him in.'

Michael had been weeping. CV, however, did not take him to the drawing room first but to the library. Michael said, 'I came to tell you, but obviously you've heard. I don't know which way to turn now.'

CV said, 'Good news—it wasn't Emma. Emma was here.'

Michael took the information in slowly. 'Who?' he asked at last.

'Emma told Julia Ware she could spend the night,' said Maggie from the door. 'It could be her.'

'Julia? Who'd kill Julia?'

'Or Emma? Or Dorothy?'

'Come, the others are wondering what you're talking about.'

In the drawing room Michael dropped on to the sofa and buried his face in Maggie's hair. Only then CV realized how stoned he was. He wondered if Teddy knew it too—and that they were wondering if they could light a joint with a policeman in the room.

Emma had slipped in. CV's attention had been on Michael when she sat down beside him. 'As they all know I'm not dead, do I have to sit upstairs any more?' Her face was red and puffy.

CV put his arm around her and said to Teddy, 'You want proof? Here it is.' To her he said, 'This is the officer in charge of the case.'

Teddy took her hand. 'I am so glad you are all right, Miss van Eck.' As if he were asking for a ginger beer, he continued, 'I wonder if you would be willing to identify the body today.'

'Yes, of course,' she said earnestly to CV's astonishment. 'Because I must call her mother if it's Julia.' She whispered in CV's ear, 'I've given the list of people to Della. She asked me if I was sleeping with you, and I said none of her business. She said it was.' As her voice had risen during this confidence, the others heard it too.

He said, 'Della likes to keep an eye on me.'

She whispered loudly, 'She wants to marry you, and I said I'd pass it on.' In a normal voice she added, 'I'm pulling myself together.'

CV said to Teddy, 'I'm having lunch with Reggie at one. Why don't you join us? I'd like your fix on him. It's twelve now. We can sit down somewhere first, and I'll tell you what we know.'

'May I borrow Joseph, Auntie?' he asked at the front door.

'He's ready to help.'

CV said to the old man, 'I'm going with Superintendent Senaratne to the Palace Hotel. Drive to the Pettah, and talk about Dorothy Bell to everyone in Second Cross Street.'

'Yes sir,' said Joseph, eyeing the policeman nervously.

'Ask who saw what the night she was killed. Who knows about that bomb last night. They may not know another foreign girl has been killed. Then go down to Bagatelle Road to Michael's house. There are caddays near there. Ask about Michael and his friend Jeffrey, a Frenchman with yellow hair who says he walked to the beach the night Dorothy was killed. See if anyone remembers that.'

Joseph fingered his moustache. 'And then?'

'Between two and two-thirty I'll look for you in the parking lot of the Palace Hotel.'

'You've a knack for investigation—and organization,' said Teddy as they drove towards the fort. 'Help me and I'll help you.'

'Do I get to see your files on Dorothy Bell in exchange?'

'Under the table. I don't want the whole department to know that I'll cave in to every demand from an expat.'

'What I tell you is also under the table. In my concern that Maggie was getting interested in Mr Bell, I ran a check on him.'

CV and Teddy Talk

CV did not recognize the two men at the front desk at the Palace

Hotel, so he did not stop there. He led the way to the coffee shop and they chose a table where they could not be seen from the front door.

For almost an hour he told the policeman what he had learned about Dorothy and her associates but included only facts he felt were directly related to her death. He included what Emma had told him about Dorothy being raped by her father.

What Teddy was most interested in was that there had been four other deaths known to Reginald Bell in which a stiletto thrust had been used to kill the victims.

'I should have looked into Bell myself. I am not happy with the way I took things for granted,' he exclaimed half angrily. 'And Della, who wants to marry you, is going to find out more about the four murdered men?'

'I also want to use her to check a butler Charles who was an eyewitness, and a nanny called Louise Lawrence who is dead.'

'What I don't see is how Della in Chicago will be able to get information about a man's crimes in England unless she has access to police files.'

'The Internet is wide open,' CV said as casually as he could. 'Kids in high school break into confidential files and don't mind sharing the knowledge. The world is a see-through bubble.'

'Nice comparison,' said Teddy, adding ruefully, 'but depressing that in a day you, a civilian, by brushing aside the rules, have uncovered more than we have in a week.'

'Are you sure you're a policeman?'

A smile played on Senaratne's face. 'I'll need someone like you around.'

'But a civilian is still hampered in a way you're not. Can you find out if Dorothy and Emma have done something to cause an organization such as the CIA to snuff them?' He pushed on. 'The attempted attack on Emma seems so ferocious to me—though the two deaths must be connected.'

'I can ask, but I have to play by rules. If the body is Julia

Ware's, then the American ambassador will have to be told, and I'll have to persuade him to delay a public announcement. The longer the murderer doesn't know he killed the wrong woman, the longer Emma is safe. It isn't so easy to hide a white woman here.'

CV said, 'Maggie is a master of disguise. She spends her life dressing up. What about changing Emma's appearance?'

Teddy surprised him by taking the suggestion without argument.

'Can you do it?' CV asked Maggie on the policeman's mobile phone.

'Of course.'

'How is she?'

'She and Della have been calling back and forth.'

He said to Teddy, 'You think we'll get our man?'

'We'll get him. With a little help from the public, we can get anyone. If it is a foreigner, he might walk free. That's what embassies are for, to whisk their nationals out of foreign countries before they seriously embarrass their governments.'

So Senaratne thought the killer might not be a Lankan.

Lunch with Bell

On their way up to the restaurant they had a word with Assistant Manager Perera who was on duty. Teddy admonished him to speak to no one about the case, not even Mr Bell or the hotel manager Mr Guneratne. Perera observed wryly that he wished he could help them more actively but he was an employee and not an independent agent. He sounded eager to have the mystery cleared up. One of his clerks then asked Teddy to take a phone call at an in-house phone across the lobby. The policeman returned to tell them that the caller had hung up without speaking. His absence had given Perera enough time to say to CV, 'Mr Bell has been pumping me to see what you're up to. I am being cautious in my responses.'

'Thank you.'

Senaratne gave Perera permission to let CV, or anyone he authorized, enter Bell's room even when he was not there. Perera replied that Bell had already authorized the investigation without restrictions.

'I hear a friend of Miss Bell was killed last night. Are the two deaths related?'

'We are not sure,' said Teddy. 'Did Emma van Eck come to the hotel with Dorothy Bell?'

'She may have.'

'If you hear her name, please let Mr vander Marten or me know in what context.'

'I will, sir.' Perera then said to CV, 'I told you on Friday our guests have to come first. The staff will be informed to put your needs first now because of Superintendent Senaratne's orders.'

'You have a Mr Mahmoud staying at the hotel. Keep an eye on his comings and goings for me, will you? Also his bodyguard.'

'Mr Mahmoud? He has something to do with these murders?'

'I wish I knew.'

In the elevator Teddy said, 'Perera obviously trusts you more than he trusts me.' CV told Teddy that Perera had invented the phone call and the response was, 'He plays games, then.'

They joined Bell in the Western Trail dining room on the top floor where a spectacular buffet was arranged. The Englishman did not seem surprised to see Teddy.

'I am so glad you could join us for lunch, Superintendent Senaratne,' he said. 'I thought you had dropped the inquiry.'

Teddy shrugged, began waving across the room to other people, frowned at Bell as if he couldn't remember who he was, then said heartily, 'Mr vander Marten has been persistent on your behalf. Why you did not tell him or me you were here to purchase Padmani's Blood?'

CV tried not to smile.

'You know of the stone?' Bell replied.

'Its reputation is part of our lore.'

'I did not tell you because I thought it would become a red herring. Let's go to the buffet. We can talk while we eat.'

Teddy was the first out of his seat and the last to return. Bell was again trying to control the conversation, but he was doing it with the wrong man for, the moment he returned, Teddy got back on the subject of Padmani's Blood.

'Mr Bell, what price did you agree to pay for Padmani's Blood?'

'I can't divulge that.'

'Were there others buying it with you?' asked Teddy, helping himself from a dish of chutney.

'I am afraid I cannot tell you that either.'

'Can't or won't?'

'In this case there's no difference. Superintendent Senaratne, when large sums are involved in a private purchase, it is up to all the principals to decide whether their affairs should be made public.'

'Even when the daughter of one may have been murdered by an interested party?'

'Let me explain.' Bell put down his fork. 'There were three people involved, the seller, the buyer and the middleman, and any of these could have had partners, although only one person handled the exchange. I was a willing buyer. That lets me out. The seller already had the stone. That lets him out. She, the middleman, didn't kill herself. That lets her out.'

'Great logic!' CV applauded.

'But, Mr Bell, the stone has disappeared.' Teddy waved his fork. 'How?'

'The stone is irrelevant. It's a red herring in finding the murderer. I know she didn't have it. I don't have it. I would still like to know who does.'

Bell now turned to CV, asking what he had found.

'Michael won't talk about Dorothy's affairs. He's bound by a vow of silence, but I hear you are here to buy yet another precious stone, a seventy-carat sapphire, which has begun to sound like a grain of dust next to Padmani. No sale?'

'Balasingham? No sale.'

Teddy said, 'A seventy-carat sapphire is also a stone someone might kill for. It would be a lot easier to get rid of.' He was eating as if he hadn't seen food for months, and he often appeared not to be listening. He looked at CV blankly as if about to ask him a question, then turned to Reggie. 'Did you know your daughter had been sterilized, Mr Bell?'

The eyebrows and nostrils moved very slightly. After a moment the reply was, 'That's hard to believe. She always spoke of having a family.'

'The autopsy report confirmed it. It was done in India last year.'

Bell sat brooding. It seemed this information was a shock. And well it might be. Dorothy had cut off his chance of having grandchildren.

'Why would she do that to herself, Mr Bell?' Teddy asked. 'A lovely young woman who always wanted children and had a boyfriend she wanted to marry? She'd had at least one abortion the autopsy showed—not an early abortion, which would have been difficult to detect, but at least one later into the pregnancy.'

Bell had been enjoying prawns in garlic butter but now pushed the plate away. He drank from his beer, and when he spoke, it was carefully.

'I have no answer for you, Senaratne. Dot did not consult or confide in me about her abortions or any other surgery.'

'You knew of her relationship with Mr Mahmoud?' continued Teddy, pushing his plate away too and ordering a cup of coffee from a hovering waiter.

'Yes,' Bell's blue eyes were ice. 'I have not publicized the fact that my daughter was a prostitute. It is not a matter a father would publicize. How long have you known?'

'I did not know until Clive told me this morning,' said Senaratne. 'It has made both Mahmoud and his attendant suspects. I feel you obstructed justice by not speaking of it before.'

Surprisingly, Bell now relaxed. 'Mr Mahmoud approached me in the lobby the day after Dorothy's death and questioned me about what had happened. He was very upset—his sorrow seemed genuine. He told me he had been her lover for some months but did not want his wife to know of the association, so would I look among Dorothy's belongings and destroy any evidence of their relationship. I had no intention of revealing the relationship, of course, but I did look. Dorothy had a notebook—your policemen did not realize it was in code. She and I used code to communicate on the gems—our private language. In the book I found evidence that Mahmoud was giving her money—she made a note of the amounts thinking these were gem sales. I confronted him. He hedged then and admitted he had paid her for sex.'

He took a pen from his pocket, and Teddy offered a sheet from a very small notebook. Bell wrote: 'MM(M)SAAR(F)'. He said, 'Those six letters were followed by a lower case code giving exact amounts. Below that was the date. If Mahmoud had not approached me, I would only have known she'd had business transactions with a man whose initials were MM and who came from a country that had two words in its title. One started SA the other AR. Now I read it—MM: Mahmoud Mahmoud. (M): Male. SA: Saudi. AR: Arabia. And finally (F) a new one on me. Knowing Dorothy, I guessed, F: Fuck. The first time her price was $1,000. It rose.'

How could the man talk about his daughter this way?

Bell could and continued, 'Dot never hesitated to have sex with a man if she felt like it—both before Michael and afterwards—but this was the first time I knew that it was also a business. We had had arguments about her promiscuity. But this relevation shocked me.'

CV couldn't resist saying, 'A man who objects to a woman taking money for sex must be one who hasn't given money for sex.'

To his surprise, Bell laughed aloud. 'There's a difference between a woman who asks for money to make a living and a woman who has other options.'

'Is there?' Teddy had been silent and continued tightly. 'Women prostitute themselves to survive. The sex itself is as unimportant as typing. If your daughter was having sex for money, she was doing it because she felt she had to.'

'That's nonsense,' said Dorothy's father. 'Dot did not have to. She had a boyfriend. She had a father who provided for her so lavishly she did not have to work at all. She was not compulsive in that way—in any way. Help yourself to one of the puddings?'

Only Teddy took him up on the offer and departed for that section of the buffet. Eventually, CV asked, 'And in the book you found? What else had she written?'

'It was an account book. She was making a better living than I thought. But there were no other names with Fs.'

'May I look at it?' He did not recall such a book among her effects.

'I destroyed it. As the police showed little interest, there was no purpose in keeping it.'

CV wrote in his own notebook: MM Mahmoud Mahmoud, SA Saudi, AR Arabia, (F) Fuck.

Teddy had returned and heard the end of the exchange. His large eyes were blank. He said, 'I recall no such notebook among her effects. If Dorothy was killed by this Arab, you might have destroyed the only evidence we had of a relationship between them.'

'Did you ask him any more about their relationship after you realized she was taking his money?' CV didn't like the look on Teddy's face, but there were still questions to be asked.

'I told him I had destroyed the only evidence. He saw my anger at him and said, "If Dorothy didn't want to see me, she didn't have to, Mr Bell."'

'Did you mention Mahmoud to Bundy?' asked CV.

'Of course not.'

Senaratne said, 'I should be going.'

On the way to their cars Teddy said, 'Mr Bell's sorry he's started this investigation. He's trying to confuse us. There was no notebook in her effects. What are you going to do if he calls the investigation off?'

'Continue it.'

'Is there anything else I should know? You didn't tell me Emma had visited the Palace.'

'I didn't mean to withhold that. I'm hoping to get her to put it all together chronologically. You can read our stuff and catch up.'

Teddy extracted a promise from CV that he would bring Emma to the morgue at three.

Hooded Men

CV slipped into the passenger seat next to Joseph and said, 'We must go back to the house, pick up Emma Missie and take her to the police station. Did you have any luck?'

He did not expect the reply he got. 'At both places I go, everyone is telling to me.'

'Is that right? Tell me what happened in Sinhala,' Deciphering Joseph's English was always a strain.

'I parked the car on Olcott Mawatha,' the chauffeur said loudly as if he was delivering a public address. 'Then I walked on Second Cross Street, smoked a cigarette and talked to this one and that. As I am old, they were not suspicious of my interest in the murder of the English Missie and had much interest in it themselves. Tourists come to see where she was found.'

'And?'

'Two men put her there.'

'Someone saw men putting Dorothy in the Pettah? Who?'

'Mr Solomon. He works at night after dinner. He was looking through a small hole in the door before going on the road. He thought the men came to steal his tyres. He was thinking about calling the police.'

'And he knew these men?'

'No. Their heads were in bags.'

'What kind of bags?'

'Cloth bags with holes. They looked at his car. They went to their car he thought for tools to remove his tyres. The thin one then carried something on to the step behind Mr Solomon's car. It was the dead yellow-haired lady. After they left, Mr Solomon got into his car and drove away.'

'And never told the police?'

'No point. He does not know the men. He did not know the woman.'

'And doesn't want to make himself a target.'

'That's always true.'

'What about their car? Could he identify that?'

'He saw.'

'Will he speak to me?'

'Sir, I do not know this man except that he is a Muslim and has a good reputation. The men who spoke to me are fellows who do nothing. Today his shop is closed. Tomorrow perhaps you can visit Mr Solomon, but do not tell him I was there.'

CV sat back thinking how easily Joseph had broken through barriers the police could not.

'Joseph, I'm going to have to put you on the payroll.'

'Sir?'

'Pay you a salary while you work for me.'

'I am only doing my job for Maud Lady, and she will look after me.'

'We all need extra cash, Joseph.'

The old man brought the car on to Havelock Road, looked at CV with amusement and shook his head.

'About Mr Jeffrey. Shall I tell you now?' he said still laughing.

'There's more? Yes, of course.'

'Only one cadday was open on Bagatelle Road because it is Sunday. The *mudhalali* is a Muslim. He says Mr Jeffrey had a cup of tea there on the night Dorothy Missie was killed. Mr Jeffrey has already asked if anyone remembered him. Three men remember. The *mudhalali* remembers her also because she was always laughing. She'd come with Mr Blue and buy cigarettes for everyone. He likes Mr Blue more than Jeffrey, who complains when he finds a hair in his rice packet. He is always complaining.'

'Did he mention what else Jeff complains about?'

'About the heat and the chilli in the curries.'

'Did he say what time Jeffrey was there?'

'Mr Jeffrey said, "The beautiful moon. Look at the moon." After the *mudhalali* heard about the murder, he thought perhaps Mr Jeffrey had killed Dorothy Missie from jealousy of Michael Master. So he looked at the sky the next evening and the moon was over the same coconut tree at 10.40. She died after eleven, so he knew Mr Jeffrey didn't kill her because he was in no hurry that evening and went off towards the beach.'

'He says he visited the cadday on his way back?'

'They can't remember. But before he went to the beach, he said, "Look at the beautiful moon".'

If Jeff was the murderer, then it had to be a very carefully planned crime. It was possible he did not go to the beach but drove to meet Dorothy at the Oberoi, killed her and then dumped her in the Pettah.

They had been sitting in the driveway, and Maggie came out

to ask why they didn't come in.

'First real progress in this case, thanks to Joseph,' he told her.

'Well come inside and tell us about it,' she said taking his arm. 'We have a visitor.'

The Chinese Girl

In the front drawing room there was a girl sitting on the sofa talking to his aunt who was working on her scrapbook. From what he could see, the newcomer was a pleasant-looking kid with blunt-cut shining black hair and slanting eyes. He presumed she was a relative of the Chinese doctors. He greeted them all quickly from the door because he didn't want to get into socializing, pushed Maggie who was behind him back into the hallway and said, 'I've got to take Emma to identify the body. Can you get rid of that young woman?'

Without waiting for a response, he ran upstairs, but Emma wasn't there so he came down again, put his head into the front room and said, 'Aunt Maud, I'd like to speak to you.'

She came outside with her scissors in one hand.

'Where's Emma? If she's gone out, I'll kill her. She won't have to wait for a bomb to do it.'

Maggie called out, 'She's in here.' So he went back into the front room. Then he heard their laughter, knew something was up and realized he'd been had. The Chinese girl had an overbite when she smiled.

'We did it,' said Maggie triumphantly. 'If she's fooled you, she'll fool anyone.'

He said, 'If you all hadn't started giggling, I'd still be fooled.'

'Maggie did it,' said Emma. 'Even I can't recognize me.'

'But you've got to work on your smile,' scolded Maggie. 'Lips together—don't show your teeth.'

Emma's eyes were darker now, and it had taken very little make-up to give her more Asian blood. Her eyebrows were thin pencilled lines. The biggest change was in the way she carried herself—she seemed to have grown four inches, if you counted her high-heeled sandals. Although she had never looked her twenty-eight years, she had now become a teenager in white jeans rolled at the ankles and a matching blouse knotted above the waist.

'I've been practising with a book on my head,' she told him in high-pitched and rather loud clipped English exactly like Dr Soong's. 'Maggie says disguise is in the body—you have to give a different impression. Maggie's wig cost £800 and was made in Paris by a master. Four months' income for a wig! The contact lenses are clear in the middle, so I'm not seeing everything brown—you can get them without a prescription. I don't even feel them except sometimes.'

He wanted to hug her for finding something to be happy about even when things were going so wrong.

She bubbled on, 'Amily and Maggie got everything in Nugegoda—except the wig and contacts. Usually I never can find anything in those shops. And look at my fingers.' She extended manicured hands. Her toes were painted the same opaque pink.

He said, 'Senaratne wants to get the identification over with today. I'm afraid I came back to take you to the morgue—you did offer.'

She said, 'I don't mind because I've seen dead bodies before. When I was going to be a nurse, I worked in an accident ward. I know what to expect.'

It was time for her to slow down, he knew, so he sat down, drank coffee and told them what Joseph had discovered. 'This is the first information we have on the actual crime—all the rest has been speculation and looking for motives.'

Maggie said, 'Are you going to tell Teddy about the two men?'

'Not until I hear what Solomon has to say.'

'I'll tackle Nora about Teddy—how much we can tell him before he has to blast it across the networks.'

His aunt was sitting at the table listlessly moving stacks of clippings. Now she said, 'Thank goodness I have something to keep busy with. I've never had to deal with murder before. When will it end? I know . . . let's say a prayer,' and she made them stand in a circle, hold hands and say a prayer for the two dead girls. At times like this, a call to prayer seemed unexpectedly appropriate.

'Amen,' he said. 'I hate to ask you to hang around, Mag, but use your noggin, won't you? Don't go out again on your own.'

She said, 'I'm worried about you too.'

She hugged him and he held her.

'Ready?' he asked Emma.

The Body

Outside a building with a hedge and two hibiscus bushes a policeman stood. He came forward to open the car door.

Teddy was in an office. When they entered, he stared, though Maggie had phoned to warn him. Finally he said, 'Good Lord,' and moved his eyebrows up and down. Then, with his eyes full of delight, he told Emma, 'Just when the job begins to depress me, something like this comes along to cheer the old heart. Maggie has performed a miracle. Nora says there's nothing she can't do when she puts her mind to it.'

Emma said in her Chinese accent, 'I'll tell her you said that. She's a bit low because everyone is getting killed.'

'Not everyone is. Not by any means,' he assured her.

He led them through stark corridors with orderlies who showed interest but did not stop and stare. A closed door led to where the body was on a gurney under a sheet. He did not introduce them to the woman attendant wearing a mask, and she left as they arrived. Senaratne uncovered the head and gestured Emma to it.

CV had not known what to expect—certainly not this blackened, unrecognizable, hairless human form with sightless bluish eyes and hanging mouth. Emma stared at it stonily and said, 'I'm not sure. It could be Julia, but lots of girls have blue eyes. I'm sorry, I thought I would recognize her, but I don't.'

The entire sheet was now removed. The dead woman was naked except for very small pieces of brown fabric adhering to her skin. Emma went to the feet and touched one of the toes which still had unburnt skin on it.

'Yes, it's her. These are Julia's toes,' she announced.

'You're positive?' asked Teddy. 'You recognize her from the toes?'

'I painted her toenails once, and her second toe was longer than the big one, and Soong said it showed she'd dominate her husband. But that's not all, the left middle toe doesn't have a nail. It was removed last month because she got an infection under it. She had to go to hospital, and a doctor took the nail off. It was very painful afterwards.'

'Which hospital?'

'Durdans.'

'Which doctor?'

'Dr Williams.'

'Thank you,' said Senaratne. 'You have been very helpful. Any other way you could identify her from what is left? We'll get Julia's dental records. Do you know her dentist?'

'The Peace Corps recommended someone. They do look like her teeth, but I'm not sure. Except for the toes, I can't actually say it is her, but it all sort of looks like Julia.'

She, who wept so easily, was dry eyed. As they went back to the office she said, 'I wish I'd seen Dor's body. It makes it easier when you see for yourself that the soul of your friend has left, and you can't do anything about it.'

'Mr Bell wanted his daughter cremated,' Teddy told her. 'But I've vetoed that for now. It won't be pleasant, but you can see her corpse too, if you wish.'

'I suppose I don't really. It's been too long.'

CV had said nothing because his stomach was still heaving. Teddy noticed his pallor and suggested he go outside for some fresh air. Emma joined him on the veranda and said softly, 'Don't feel bad. It takes time to get used to death.'

'I could have saved her.'

Teddy joined them. 'All right?'

The nausea was still there, but he said, 'Better. I think I'll go to the airport now. It, at least, will be open on Sunday. Any reason Emma shouldn't come? Joseph is driving.'

'No. Just don't take her anywhere else without telling me. First let's get the Wares on the phone. I hate this part of the job most.'

'No doubt it's Julia?'

'No. Dr Soong also recognized the toes and mentioned the nail being removed. Dr Soong is certain it is her—her build.'

Emma broke the news to Julia's parents.

Teddy had already prepared them. He had said there had been an accident and that Julia might be one of the victims but he'd appreciate it if they would not make that public yet. He dialled their American number now and handed Emma the phone.

She explained simply to Mrs Ware what had happened. She ended, 'I am so sorry—and I know that isn't enough. She knew it was okay to use my house. Someone is trying to kill me.' She listened intently for a few minutes and then began to cry. At last she sobbed. 'I don't like to ask this, but Superintendent Senaratne thinks it might help if the person who did it doesn't know yet he got the wrong person . . . Yes, I will be careful, and I'll call every day to keep in touch. Thank you so much. No I won't cry any more. You've been so kind.'

She finally turned the phone to Teddy who gave Mrs Ware his official version of the attack. For the first time CV learned that Julia had definitely been unconscious from a blow struck above her right ear and so had not struggled. The pipe bomb had covered any clues that the killer might have left. 'Julia did not suffer,' Teddy told her parents. 'Though that won't make you miss her less. It was as if she died in her sleep.' He put down the phone and said, 'Now that's the way a lady should behave.'

'I wish my parents had taken it like that,' Emma said. 'You should have heard Mum screaming at me. After Auntie spoke to her she said sorry.'

'She screamed at me too,' said Teddy grinning at her. 'She screamed at me in Sinhala and Tamil too—hasn't forgotten a word of any of them.'

Emma was wiping her nose on another of CV's blue handkerchiefs. 'She's a terrible screamer. I am going to be like Mrs Ware. She says Julia had a short lifeline and expected to die young. I'm not to blame myself because God decides who dies when. She says that she is lucky to have had Julia as long as she did.'

Teddy told her, 'You hear these stories about Americans being difficult and self-centred, but then you run into people like the Wares. But Emma—we have to have a new name for you.'

'I'm Nellie Soong. Maggie has a Chinese friend in Australia called Nellie who is very short like me, and she's made me up to look like her. I hate this make-up, but it's a lot better than being dead.'

'Well, Nellie,' he said. 'Time to move.'

Before they left, Teddy gave CV a thick manila envelope, explaining quietly it contained copies of the reports made on both killings. He asked that he not open it until he was alone because it would be easier if no one here knew he had it. He also gave him a letter confirming that he was working with the police and should be afforded the same privileges. Then he said, 'In return for this I must ask you to tell me immediately what you find out. There is talk of bringing in someone from Scotland

Yard to help us, but I've explained to the IGP that Mr Bell has hired a Sri Lankan-American who has got further in one day than we did in nearly two weeks, and he's agreed to wait till the end of the week to see what we both come up with.

'This week this case will be my priority,' he continued. 'When you phone you'll be put through to me at once, but not as fast as Nora is put through, so send me messages through her. Nellie, thank you for coming. I've seen a lot of deaths in my job and, like Mrs Ware, I believe we are at the mercy of our fate. But now we know what we're up against, so we won't allow someone else to decide the time of yours. Don't even walk into a room alone from now on. If the doorbell rings, hide.'

She nodded, but her mind was obviously elsewhere and so was CV's.

On the way to the airport he looked through the folder and read Bell's account to the police. The story did not differ from the one he already had—scarcely by a word. The other report also held no surprises but added details.

Teddy's letter gave them quick entrance into the airport. The arrival lounge was a large rectangular room with two banks, an unattended snack bar and a few information booths. They went from booth to booth asking the same question: Had anyone seen a good-looking, white-haired, middle-aged Englishman arrive at 6 p.m. about a week ago. They thought they had not, but CV left them with a phone number to call if their memory kicked in.

They had left Joseph outside to find the tout and the taxi-driver whom Bell had talked about. He came up crestfallen to tell them that no one remembered them. The porters seemed to suffer from a numbness on the job, but with no intent to deceive. When Joseph offered to pay for information, there was considerable consternation that they could not earn it.

'On the plus side,' he told Joseph as they headed for the car, 'this is the first time we've come up with a big zero.'

Tea at the Senaratnes

They were barely out of sight of the airport when his mobile phone rang.

'Where are you now?' Teddy asked.

'Heading home.'

'Nora wants to talk to you.'

'You beast,' were Nora's first words to him after eight years. 'You never told me Maggie and you were back.'

'You never told me you'd married a police hack. I hear there's a baby, lucky you.'

'We're happy.'

Nora and he had once held hands, kissed and spent a few days wondering if they loved each other. That was a long time ago.

'I think you know you married a great guy.'

'I've always been attracted to men who look weird.'

'Thank you so much.'

He remembered that chuckle. She said, 'Can you come to tea now?'

'Thirty minutes should bring us to your doorstep if I knew where that doorstep was.'

She said, 'Joseph knows.'

'You know our Joseph?'

'He's our cook's uncle.'

'We'll be there.'

He looked at his watch. They'd been at the airport forty minutes, and it was now just after five. He turned to tell Emma they'd be going to tea with the Senaratnes and found her asleep, chin resting on her chest. He toppled her towards him so she could sleep against his shoulder.

The Senaratnes lived in a three-apartment complex with his mother and father above them and her sister and brother-in-law below. Emma was barely awake, so CV offered to carry her upstairs, but she insisted on shuffling up on her own.

Murder in the Pettah

Nora was at the top of the stairs with Teddy behind her, and CV enveloped her in his arms and told her that she had married the wrong man. Childbirth had had little effect on her physically, but this was not the girl he had known but a sophisticated woman.

CV told them a man had seen Dorothy's body placed in the Pettah that night and repeated Joseph's story. 'Tomorrow I'll try to talk to the witness.'

Teddy said, 'Go without telephoning. Let him get a sense that you're a true Lankan. You'll have better luck. What else do you know that you haven't told me?'

CV accepted a cup of tea from Nora. 'Emma has a background on Dorothy that you should know. But I want to make a trade with you.' He cut himself a slice of cake. 'She needs protection, and it's going to slow me down to keep her with me all day. My aunt lives alone with Amily. The security guard looks ready for the grave. Maggie too can't keep a twenty-four-hour watch on Emma. Can you provide someone out of uniform but experienced who can stay with her?'

'Of course. Day or night. I was going to suggest that.'

Emma said sleepily, 'Thank you, Teddy.'

At that moment CV's phone rang. It was Reginald Bell on the line. 'Did you know that Emma van Eck was killed last night?'

CV thought quickly. 'The police want that kept under wraps until there is official identification.'

'You and that CID man sat at my table and never said a word. Is he paying you, or am I?'

'You are, but I didn't want to antagonize him. What are your plans for 8 a.m. tomorrow? Breakfast at the hotel?'

'Fine.' Bell calmed down.

'A question: Did Dorothy leave a will?'

'There may have been one in England at her bank.'

'You're not sure?'

'She had one. If not, her mother and I will be her heirs.'

After Bell had hung up, CV said, 'I don't like that man. Sorry, Emma honey, it's time to move again.'

Teddy Senaratne moved fast. When they got back to Bliss a tall young man in an open-necked checked shirt and navy-blue short pants opened the front door and introduced himself in English as Sergeant Steven de Mel. He and two other police officers, he told CV, would work in shifts to protect them all—particularly Emma. He lifted his shirt to show he had an automatic held under his arm in a body holster.

'I'll see no one comes near her, sir,' he said cheerfully as if he was longing to be able to prove that.

'Steven, drop that *sir*, would you?'

'Yes, sir.'

Emma had entered Bliss like a sleepwalker and wandered off up the stairs with Amily ahead and Officer Steven behind. CV and Maggie followed, trying not to giggle at the procession. Amily's anger showed from every pore at having to put up with a male intruder. Emma's make-up was awry, and she could hardly lift one foot after the other. Steven's eyes darted around as if expecting an assassin behind the newels.

He allowed no one to enter Emma's bedroom until he checked that it was ready for his charge, and then, while Maggie helped her into the bed, explored the rest of the first floor opening and closing windows and gazing through them with powerful binoculars. CV had to remind himself that this man was trained to search for political assassins, and after what had happened on Soong's property, it was no time to shrug off danger.

Emma was already asleep, so they left her in Steven's care. He placed a chair outside her open doorway then looked out of the window through his binoculars.

Dinner with Ali

Downstairs CV found a message from Ali Sharif saying he would pick them up at eight. 'What a charming man,' said Aunt Maud. 'He invited me to dinner too. I refused because I would be worried about Emma, but I didn't tell him that. Will Emma's bodyguard be sitting at the table with us?'

'It would be the democratic thing to do.'

'Well, I'll try and explain that to Amily.'

Steven said from the doorway in English, 'Madam, I will not have dinner with you as I will be on duty. A little rice on a plate upstairs will be enough. Tomorrow I can bring my night meal from my home.'

'Oh, I think we can do better than that,' she beamed. 'Please don't take notice of my cook—she worries about men.'

Maud had taken advantage of their absence to sleep. She told CV, 'And you should do the same thing—you can't get through the day during the hot season without a nap.'

Maggie came in to ask, 'What should I wear to dinner? I want to correct any bad impression I've made.'

'Cover your thighs and your breasts and try not say *fuck*,' he advised. She woke him at a quarter to eight, and he dressed hurriedly.

Ali Sharif drove a Mercedes 280, which meant that they did not hear his arrival. He was also punctual, and Maggie's description was accurate. He was relaxed in the manner of those who are sure of their welcome, and the laughter that had so irritated her was in his eyes.

'Thank God,' said CV looking at Ali's slacks and shirt. 'I take it we're not wearing coats.'

'Thank Allah. I kept one in the car in case you dressed up. I heard about the attack on Dorothy's friend on the way down. Who did it?'

CV decided on caution. 'She was killed as she slept, and then a pipe bomb was tossed into the room, and the bed caught fire, burning her beyond recognition.'

'How is Maggie taking it?'

She came down the stairs quickly and said, 'She's a wreck.'

Ali took rather than shook the hand she offered him. He released it slowly.

She had taken CV's advice and wore a simple knee-length white cotton knit with a round neck. Her arms were bare and the texture of the dress emphasized the smoothness of her brown skin. She was wearing silver sandals, and they were the only glitter about her. As usual, she wore no jewellery and her long dark hair was in a loose bun. She said, 'Auntie has the drinks out in the front drawing room. She's dying to meet Ali because of his voice.' She added slyly, 'In fact, the moment I heard him speak I became allergic to Reggie.'

'When I saw you were with him, I became allergic to him myself,' said Ali.

CV was taken aback. She had come from Kandy in anger over this man, and now she was flirting with him happily.

But, by the time they got on their way, Maggie had become silent and stayed that way. They drove almost without conversation to his home—a two-storey building in what was an unusually large garden for Colombo. Two Dobermans came up, and Maggie got down to put her arms around the animals saying to them, 'Ferocious creatures. I bet you're as dangerous as kittens.'

'They are selectively protective,' Ali told her.

Maggie's silence promptly disappeared, and she started chattering about dogs.

The house was an old one that had been renovated. Ali pointed out how he had gutted the building, and where there had been walls there were none now. 'It was a rabbit warren of small rooms because my mother kept putting up walls. There were eight of us, and she wanted each child to have his or her own space. Now we have five bedrooms upstairs, and all this space downstairs.'

'You don't work at home then?'

'I do. I'll show you my high-security rooms.'

'Maggie tells me that you helped Dorothy find Padmani's Blood.'

'I am unhappy I did it. The stone belongs to Lanka—but I didn't make a move to get it when I could have. It was she who went after it. She was very persuasive when she wanted something.'

'Men will promise you anything on the way to bed,' said Maggie to CV.

Ali put an arm around her shoulders. 'Because we are the more romantic sex.'

'I wish.'

'This dinner has to be more than a social visit,' CV broke in. 'Because now there has been the attack on Emma, and the existence of Padmani makes you a suspect. We have to go into all that.'

'Don't waste your time on me—I didn't kill Dorothy or her friend. When we disagreed about the stone, it was without hard words. I was in Kandy when both the deaths took place. Of course we Muslims are known to give our family alibis even if we haven't seen someone in years.'

'Would you?' asked Maggie.

'Give a member of my family an alibi? Wouldn't you?' he replied.

'I have a Puritan streak. If the sin was murder, I might refuse.'

Maggie was drinking red wine, which seemed to amuse her host though he made no comment. Finally she came right out and asked him why he was laughing at her again, and he said, 'If I tell you, you'll be out of that door and on your way home.'

'What if I promise to sit on her to prevent her leaving? We

cousins do get a few perks like that. Will you tell us then?' CV asked.

'My father told me to offer a woman wine. If she chooses red, her heart is warm; if she chooses white, forget her—the warmth will never be there.'

Maggie said, 'You are drinking red wine too. What does that mean?'

He replied, 'Come. I have something to show you. You will understand my choice of red wine then.'

They took their glasses with them and followed him through a door that had to be opened with two keys. Inside there was a showroom with a few shelves of unmounted gems displayed on stands. He said, 'Don't waste time here. I want to show you my workroom.'

CV did hang back, though, because on one shelf there was a ruby that seemed to be floating. Closer inspection revealed it was balancing on a glass wand. He turned to join the others but was still outside the door when he heard Maggie say, 'You were sleeping with Dorothy, weren't you?'

Ali replied, 'And you with her father. Do you want to hear the words he used when he told me?'

'You two were gossiping about me?'

'Life can be awkward, but I think he won't mention your name in front of me again.'

CV entered and found this rectangular room displayed jewellery of all kinds, most very simply mounted. He said, 'I suppose it's all genuine.'

Ali replied, 'All the metals are gold and platinum. We in the gem trade use no other metals. But those big green and blue stones are bottle glasses. I am no longer a purist. I have been breaking our tradition—as with the piece I am going to show you.'

There was one more door to be unlocked and flush against the opposite wall. They went in to a larger room and were confronted with a life-size cardboard Maggie. She seemed amused at their surprise—her eyes were soft and gleaming. She was wearing a white ankle-length sheath and from a slit to her left thigh one bare leg emerged. On that foot was a deep blue sandal with two straps and a high heel. Only her hair was not smooth and sculpted. It was shorter than she wore it now and ruffled. One hand was in her hair and the other stretched out at her side. CV knew the picture. He had torn it from *Elle* where it had first appeared. It was one of his favourites.

'It's me,' Maggie said.

'It's my girl.' Ali then showed them books of sections of the same picture. In some there was only the torso, or her arms, her face, a foot. And on each there were sketches of necklaces, earrings, bracelets, anklets. He said, 'Five years ago I saw that picture and decided to design jewellery for that woman. I needed a dream girl, for that was the time I lost both my child and my wife. This skinny brown creature became my child and my wife. I didn't even bother to find out her name when I had the picture copied. Very soon afterwards I saw other photographs of her and found out she was one of us—a Sri Lankan called Maggie vander Marten. So, Maggie, I've lived with your face, your arms, your body for years. I probably know your image as well as you do yourself. When you walked into our office in Kandy, there you were—my girl—only not my girl. Now you were real, but you were with another man.'

She said sadly, 'Oh, it's such a compliment, but you don't understand. I'd better just blurt it out. I'm without jewellery in that picture because I don't wear jewellery, that is, I only wear it professionally. I persuaded Calidan to try the shot without jewellery and then it became a poster because there I was—white dress, blue shoes—that's all. I know jewels are your whole life, but I don't wear them. Do I, CV?'

'You don't.'

Ali said, 'I've noticed that. Why?'

She said unhappily, 'Because they're a symbol of women being chained.'

'And you're frightened of men's chains?'

'It's not fear really—it's the knowing you have to watch your ass all the time.'

'Won't you wear this?' He went to a cabinet and took out a tray from which he lifted a mass of links and small transparent stores of many colours, and he said, 'Stand still for a minute.' He placed the elaborate fabric of chains across her, and it became an over-blouse of glittering jewels. 'This is the prototype—I got the idea from those wooden elephants encrusted with semiprecious stones. I've used the same stones here—for fun. I thought chains would be fun.'

He pushed Maggie to a longer mirror set into the wall and said, 'So now you are in chains. The undergarment should be almost invisible, I think, like a nylon stocking.'

She looked at her image. 'It's very beautiful. I'd love to model it. It's superb. We must show this somewhere.'

'You can do what you like with it—it's yours. I want you to have it.'

CV wondered if they remembered he was there but didn't want to miss the exchange. He'd seen her push necklaces and bracelets away. Could she push this? She could and did.

'I can't. You don't understand.' She turned to Ali anxiously. 'All this is frightening. You've got me all over the place. You don't even know me. But I'm not a little girl any more trying to please someone I like only to wish I hadn't. I don't own any jewellery. None. I'd love to wear this piece some time—perhaps you would lend it to me if I need to make a splash—but I can't own it.' She looked as if she was about to weep.

Ali said, 'Wear it to dinner then.'

'Oh yes. Of course, I will. What do you think, CV?' She was suddenly happy. 'Is this super? Look, it covers my back too—it's not just a Hollywood front.'

During dinner, CV said, 'Tell me about Dorothy, Ali. She's the one who holds the key to why she died.'

'I wish I had something to tell. I think her killer hates women.'

CV had left his mobile phone in the living room. Before he could reply he heard it ring and went to answer it.

The caller was Bell. 'Where are you now?' he asked.

'I'm having dinner.'

'I drove down to Miss vander Marten's but there's a policeman outside. He wouldn't let me in. What the hell is going on?'

'Senaratne's orders.' He returned to the drawing room signalling the others not to speak and took his place at the table again. 'Maggie and I are not at my aunt's. We were invited to dinner by one of her friends who knew Dorothy, so I'm on the job. I can't give you the name yet.'

'I'd like to speak to you this evening,' said the English voice.

'Tomorrow morning will be more convenient. We said eight but midmorning would be best because I have several things to do tonight and some others early tomorrow.'

After he had put down the phone, he said, 'I try not to tell a lie because next moment I'm drowning in them, but how do you tell the truth to that man?'

After dinner the men had a few minutes together when Maggie was freshening up.

CV asked, 'Was Maggie right about Dorothy and you?'

'She was, but there was nothing long term there for either of us. She was not as simple as she seemed. I've seen terror in her face, great sorrow, anger. That was why I call her a friend rather than an acquaintance. I don't think she allowed many people to see that side of her. She didn't like to stay overnight, but she once fell asleep in my bed and began crying in her sleep. I went to comfort her, and she screamed, then calmed down and said, "It's only you. I had a bad dream." After that there was friendship. I'd ask "How are you?" and mean it. She might say, "Not so good." I sensed Dorothy was playing a game very intensely to shut out her reality.'

Maggie came in and said, 'I have to give you back your beautiful jewellery. CV's investigation ends on Friday. Will you come to dinner after that?'

He did not reply but touched her cheek. He then unhooked the clasps that held the chain vest in place and placed it on the table.

At Bliss the policeman on guard let the Mercedes through the gate with barely a glance. Before he got out of the car, CV said to Ali, 'Have you heard of Bundy Balasingham?'

'I know him quite well.'

That was a surprise.

'You trust him?'

'I like him,' he had to turn his head to talk to CV who was in the back seat. 'Trust is too broad. In fact, I put Dorothy in touch with him—not in connection with Padmani. I thought he might know of other gems of the quality she was looking for. Bundy knows people in every field. Obviously, if I thought he would cheat her, I wouldn't have recommended him. Were they connected?'

CV said, 'The trouble with this case is just when you think you have a lock on someone it becomes unlocked. Are you telling me she knew Bundy before she took Mahmoud to the casino?'

'I don't know. Who is Mahmoud?'

'Mahmoud Mahmoud. You don't know of him?'

'It's a familiar name, but I have never met him. It's a Muslim name. He's not from around here?'

'He's from Saudi.'

'Involved with these crimes?'

'I don't know. Dorothy was seeing him. As for Bundy—he's a kleptomaniac—that's obviously not something he wants known. I went to school with him. Now he seems to be the only person who knows everyone connected with Dorothy's other life. I think he's working with Mr Bell but am not sure in what capacity.'

'You are suspicious because you object to Bundy's working with Bell, but you're doing that too,' said the other man sharply. 'Tell you what, I'll try and find out something about Mahmoud Mahmoud and Bundy too. We're a big family, and someone may have heard of what they're up to.'

'I'm hoping to have lunch with Mahmoud tomorrow—or at least to see him.'

'You do the frontal attack. I'll dismantle him from the rear. Now will you get out of the car so I can kiss this woman goodnight? If she slaps my face, I don't want there to be a witness.'

Night Calls

The phone rang while Maggie was still wandering around downstairs. She beat him to it.

She joined him a minute later in the kitchen over the kettle. 'Just Ali calling from his car.' She grinned smugly. 'Wanted to thank me for not slapping his face. What am I going to do?'

'Go to bed. Until we've tied up Dorothy, we've no time for our personal feelings.'

She said, 'I hate personal feelings.'

'I have difficulty with them, too.'

'Is it because we're so smart?'

'No, it's because we're so stupid.'

He went up with her to do a body count. Maud and Emma were asleep in their rooms. Steven was on his chair outside Emma's reading a newspaper.

CV picked up the phone and dialled. Bundy answered on the fifth ring. 'It's you? I heard that Dorothy's friend was killed. Why didn't you let me know? Any idea who did it?'

'No. The police are on to it.'

'I called you, and a policeman answered. Why do you have a policeman in the house?'

'Because I'm investigating a murder—thought you'd heard. Surprisingly, the CID is interested.'

'You're hand in glove with the police?'

'I can hardly leave them out of it. For God's sake, Bundy, what's the big fuss?'

'I think you should drop this investigation before there are more tragedies.'

'I don't think I should. Initially, I was doing it out of curiosity. Now I'm angry.'

There was silence then. 'Clive, think about what I said. Two deaths can become three or four and one of those could be yours. How are my phones working out?'

'As they're on radio frequencies, I'm taking it easy on them.'

'No one knows you have them except me, and why would I want to intercept your calls?'

'Why indeed?' CV wanted to reply. What he did say was, 'You're right, of course. The fact is I've been legging it. Eye-to-eye talk brings bigger rewards than the phone.'

Bundy continued, 'And the computer and fax?'

'Had a busy day over the Emma crisis. She was going to help me by working on the computer. I'm breaking in another girl tomorrow. The fax and email are already much needed and I'm grateful. Met someone who knows you—Ali Sharif.'

Again silence.

Eventually Bundy replied, 'I haven't seen him for years. Is he involved?'

'He's a suspect because he was a friend of Dorothy's.'

'Does her father know about the friendship?'

'Yes. Ali also told me that he likes you.'

Again a pause before speaking. 'Thank him. You hear a

name like that from your past and wish you'd kept in closer touch.'

'Can I trust him?'

Bundy did not make the kind of flip rejoinder CV was expecting but replied with intensity. 'Ali's more than trustworthy. He goes out of his way to help. That was why I'm surprised he considers himself a friend of Dorothy Bell, who only thought of herself. He's started a school for Muslim refugee children from Jaffna. When he was married, I saw something of him. It was a tragic affair, but he coped magnificently. He's been abroad a lot. I don't know what he does there, but he always was a high-minded type.'

CV said, 'And you, Bundy? Anything you've learned that will be of help to me?'

'I told Mr Bell that he should pay you off because he's endangering your life—that's between you and me. He said the decision would have to be yours. I'm trying to protect you, Clive. Listen to me—a bomb means that someone is taking risks.'

But he hadn't answered the question.

CV continued, 'If I'm in danger, so are you. Look out for yourself, too, Bundy.'

'I never know when you're joking.'

'Two murders have killed my sense of humour.'

The coffee and the conversation had fired his mind. He dialled Della prepared to leave a message on her machine, but she answered on the second ring.

'Thank God it's you,' she said. 'I'm completely obsessed with Dorothy Bell because it's been like dropping rocks in a pool. The circles won't stop widening. She's got my mind one hundred per cent, so I'm taking sick leave. I have a doctor friend who's going to say I'm overstressed. Homer says he's leaving if I do this, and I don't care.'

She'd been checking the names Emma had given her on the

Internet by using the 'rule of four'. She was talking about the theory that if a person you were looking for had a phone you could find him if you knew his town in four phone calls or less. Call the person most likely to help, he/she phones the most likely person to help, and after four calls, bingo, you have the person you want on the line.

'If the person has no phone, I bet we can do it through the Internet.'

'I've got to try that. Who's called in?' he asked.

'Some jokers—some not. Every Hispanic in the world knows or has heard of a Cruz and/or Iglesias, but none who died of the knife. Do you have fax or email yet?'

He gave her both numbers but told her he'd need about twelve hours to check them out. 'The computer has a network connection, and I suspect every movement on it is registered elsewhere.'

'And what are you doing about it?'

'Any ideas?'

'It's more your field than mine. I have a nice surprise for you. Remember Charles Yarrow the businessman who got knifed? I've found the Reginald Bell connection.

'Yarrow ran a manpower service in London—one of those places that provide household help. He'd find you someone to paint your house, dig up your petunias or dust your wall art. His agency was sold after his death. His son Peter Yarrow is working on railway timetables out of Belfast. That's in Northern Ireland.'

'I know where Belfast is, Del.'

'But do you know Oceano?'

'As a matter of fact I do. It's on the Pacific coast near Pismo Beach—Clam Capital of the World. So what about Oceano?'

'Just testing. My God, you're educated. I'm also glad you're paying for this call, not me. To continue about Charles Yarrow—Peter says his dad worked as a butler for Reginald Bell and caught him fucking his little daughter and beat him up. One of Bell's pearly whites was knocked out of his head by Yarrow, who stepped on it on the way out and stuck it in a flower pot, so there must be a plastic replacement there now. I asked for some proof that Peter wasn't putting me on, and he said, "Ask the incestuous paedophile how he lost his right front incisor." Bell was the person Yarrow Senior hated most in the world. When he got drunk, he'd say he wished he'd killed him because he felt guilty as hell about having left Dorothy with the monster. Apparently Bell told Charles that he would have Peter offed if the police got a complaint about the incest. Charles frequented a particular London pub, and three years ago he was found stabbed in a mews, that's English for an alley. Bell was in London when it happened, and the police checked on him because Peter asked them to. Bell's live-in cook said that she would have heard him leaving the house, but she didn't, so he couldn't have done it.'

'Being asleep when someone he knows is getting murdered must be his favourite alibi.'

'You're so cynical. Where would you be while someone in the next street was being murdered at 2 p.m.? Asleep! When Charles died, Peter told the police what he had said about Bell—the rape. But Bell impressed the police as innocent, and they dismissed Charles Yarrow's story because he was a disgruntled alcoholic ex-employee.'

'They didn't ask Dorothy if she was raped?'

'Peter says he never heard any more about it.'

'Looks like Dorothy told Emma the truth. She even had the butler's name right.'

'And that's not all. Peter says Charles knew Desmond Crewel who had died the same way and in the same locale two months earlier. Desmond was a three-day binge-drunk who'd go to jail then go on the wagon awhile. A Scotland Yard detective, name of Peesbeer—I swear I didn't make that name up—

mentioned to Peter Yarrow after his father's death that Crewel too had been knifed. Peter found a pub regular who had known Crewel who had worked for Yarrow so knew about Reginald Bell and his little daughter. He'd say he wanted to go over and rip the guy apart and hang his balls on a tree. I think that must be a common English torture because, when I asked Peter, he said he'd heard the expression before only the word used was *testicles*. Detective Peesbeer found no evidence that Bell had ever met Crewel—so much for Scotland Yard. Looks like they've fallen apart since Sherlock Holmes died.'

'Holmes is a fictional character, Del.'

'Really? Do you know that *iglesias* means churches in Spanish?'

'As a matter of fact, I do.'

'You know Spanish?'

'Spent one summer in Mexico. Della, keep to the point.'

'Sorry. Iglesias died in England also, some place called Bournemouth—don't tell me you've heard of it. Among the calls about Cruz Iglesias I got an email from a Maria Perez who had a *tio* called Cruz Iglesias. *Tio* is uncle in Spanish, as I suppose you know already. She says Tio Cruz Iglesias mentioned a Mr Bell to her, but it could have been a Mr Ball, Bill or Bull. There definitely were a B and two Ls in his name. Maria's accent is Español all the way. Tio Cruz was crazy once about a woman with green eyes, and Reginald Bell, Bull or Ball did wrong by her.'

'How wrong?'

'I'm a nice Methodist girl. I don't say words like bestiality, ass, snake and whip. We're only allowed to say leather, chains and thorns—because they're in the Bible. The acts were nonconsensual, and she had to be hospitalized. Cruz was later knifed and thrown off a train near Bournemouth and found by the tracks by two Eagle Boy Scouts, i.e., Navajo Trackers, with a British accent. Peter has agreed to be my authority on curious English behaviour.'

'We have Eagle Scouts in America, Del.'

'No kidding? I'll tell Peter. Maria had no idea that the police had questioned Bell about Tio's killing. Think he threatened to bring a complaint against Bell about Green Eyes?'

'Maybe. Problem is Bell doesn't look like a man who travels by train.'

'What does a man who travels by train look like?'

'Like a man who travels by bus. Bell is a limo-man. Image is all. He must have taken buses and trains as a kid, but I don't think he'd do it today.'

'The bad news is I've had no word on Vincent Belli. He was killed in Milan, which is in Italy, which I suppose you know. He could have been a relative of Bell's. Bell and Belli—get it? It says in the document that Belli's name used to be Horatio Belladonna.'

'There's a deadly plant by that name—nightshade family—beautiful flowers. See if you can come up with anything on Horatio Belladonna. You're terrific, Del.'

'Is it true you're not fucking your telephone operator Emma?'

'Ask the Internet.'

'She says you're not. I love her Princess Di accent. For someone who could easily be dead, she's been cool. Only chokes when she speaks of her friends. She's invited me to come and visit, which is more than you have.'

'When you see the burnt concrete box she lives in, you may want to reconsider.'

'She's going to find me a guesthouse nearby. What's that noise?'

'We have a policeman called Steven who guards Emma. He's patrolling the house—presently he's testing the windows in my room.'

'I've spoken to Steven. When he calls me Miss Della, I have impure thoughts.'

'You? Never!'

'He says he has dreams of women with blue eyes but doesn't have any blue-eyed women friends. I don't want to miss out if Steven is available. What does he look like?'

'Tall. All legs and arms like a cricket. Nice smile. Black hair. Shy.'

'Wow. Your life sounds so exciting compared to dull old Chicago. Oh yes, I have some stuff on Leyland Ali Sharif, aka Ali. He used to play cricket. I tried to watch it once when I was visiting England with a tour—obviously an acquired taste. Sharif also played polo, sport of kings and mega-buck costly. A Desireé Johnson saw my long list, which now includes his name. She emailed to ask what happened to him. Tell him she's eager for a reply. I have her phone, fax and email. She has monogrammed blue suitcases and will travel.'

'Did Desireé Johnson volunteer the info on her suitcases?'

'No. I asked if it was true that the wealthy had monogrammed suitcases, and she told me about hers and where to get mine done. You should only monogram leather—monogrammed plastic isn't cool.'

'Good night, Del. Sweet dreams to you.'

'Good afternoon, CV. Have a cuppa tea on me.'

After she hung up he sat there a while trying to digest what he had heard. The information on Charles Yarrow had been the most disturbing, because he and Crewel seemed men who could have driven a man with fear of exposure and homicidal tendencies to murder. The incest story had seemed far-fetched, but here was evidence that Dorothy had not made it up. He saw how easily men like himself who had never thought of a daughter as a possible sexual partner could be persuaded that the girl might have lied.

This was the first time that a clear-cut motive for Bell to kill anyone had surfaced. It didn't take much imagination to guess that a drunk like Crewel might have tried to blackmail him after Yarrow had told him what he had seen. Speculation! *It's all speculation, your Honour.* It was time for another cup of coffee.

First, he dialled the Singapore number Bell had called from Bentota. A disembodied voice told him in English that it had been disconnected.

CV went downstairs and poured a half cup of coffee, returned and settled on his bed to reread the papers he had accumulated. He started with Dorothy and Reggie's hotel bills and could find nothing incriminating, though there were interesting details. On the evening before she died, at 11 p.m., room service had brought her two plates of cheese toast. So she'd had company. The following day she'd had neither breakfast nor lunch at the hotel. At 7.35 p.m. she had asked for Rs 20,000 ($350) cash at the desk—the amount had been charged to her bill. Apparently, that was how she obtained cash, and the record showed she paid her monthly bills with a Visa card. If she had paid cash for dinner at the Taprobane, she still should have had over $300 with her in rupees when she died. All-night grocery stores in the States were burgled for less—this was Sri Lanka where there was no minimum wage. So there was a new motive now: cash.

In the medical report he found no speculation about how she got a bruise on the back of ear. He made a note to discuss that with Senaratne. He then reread her letters, looked at the snapshots and again came up blank. Emma's computer was plugged in on the table. He had been twice interrupted when about to read the 'Dorothy' folder. He found it on the desk top and opened it.

'A cup of coffee, sir?' Steven was in the doorway, a vacuum flask in hand.

'No, thank you, Steven. Della would like your home phone number.'

The policeman looked embarrassed. 'Did you tell her I am a poor boy, sir?'

'Steven, she didn't ask for your net worth, she asked for

your phone number.'

When he left, CV opened up a file named 'Will' and found:

Michael. Trust.
Louise. Trust
Emma's projects? Salary?
Frances?
Carlo and Mark.

There was also a list of names with figures next to them but no note of whether the amounts were rupees, pounds or dollars. One was Renuka—1,000.

A second file was named 'Bank' and not unexpectedly consisted of a list of bank accounts: four in England and one in Sri Lanka. One in England had security deposit box number 8131.

In the third file named 'Documents,' Dorothy listed her credit cards, two insurance policies (but not what they insured), her passport and the addresses of those to contact if any items on the list got lost. She had also made a list of the contents of her security deposit box: birth certificate, parents' marriage certificate, parents' divorce papers, insurance policies and important letters. There was no mention of a will. Most interesting was the name of a mortgage company: Bromley Building Society with information on a deed of sale. It looked as if Dorothy Bell had been buying or had bought a house or other property in Kent.

CV wanted to phone Senaratne, but it was 1.35 a.m. Of course, if he waited till daylight, Teddy might have left the house on other commitments. He made the call.

Teddy picked up the phone on the first ring. 'Who is it?'

'Someone who is wondering if you ever sleep?'

'Just came in. Nora's grandmother is fading again. We took her to hospital.'

'Tell Nora I'm hoping Grandma pulls through.' He then told the policeman about Dorothy's files on Emma's computer and also the Charles Yarrow, Desmond Crewel and Cruz Iglesias connection with Bell. He ended telling him that the name Horatio Belladonna was the birth name of Vincent Belli.

'This is quite a haul. Can you get me a printout of Dorothy's files tonight?'

'No printer here,' CV said. 'I'll copy them by hand and leave the list with your man Steven.'

'I'll send someone for them early in the morning,' said Steven's boss yawning noisily.

'Stop that now. You've started me yawning. Oh yes, what about that bruise behind Dorothy's ear? Did that happen before or after her death?' CV yawned again, sat up and began to move his feet to keep himself awake.

'The knife killed her and was probably left in her body, which not only hastened her death but minimized the external show of blood. Dr Mendis thinks she could have been unconscious before the stabbing either from a blow not heavy enough to kill or by striking her head as she fell.' He too yawned once more. 'He didn't commit himself, and I'm afraid I let it go. I think it doesn't matter much.'

CV wasn't so sure. Was it a coincidence that both Dorothy and Julia had been killed after being struck? Was this murderer someone who didn't want his victim to feel pain?

He said, 'Am I reading more into the Crewel/Yarrow deaths than is there?'

'What you're reading is there, but there may be another explanation. Why kill? Men are constantly accused of sexually abusing their offspring nowadays, and many of these young women have turned out to be either deranged or spiteful. A few accusations stick, but what would Dorothy have to gain being a witness to her father's ruin now that she was in business with him? Without her testimony the charges would be dropped.

Now she has died. Why should we think she was going to tell the world about Daddy at last? Does Emma say that Dorothy was going to publicize what happened?'

'No. Dorothy didn't confide her father's abuse to anyone but Emma and Michael.'

'And Michael Blue is hardly the man to bring something like that to court.'

Before falling asleep CV thought about Teddy's words and wondered what they were both missing. 'Come on Dorothy,' he found himself demanding. 'Help us.'

Chapter VII

Monday

The Microphone

CV was back in Bliss before Maggie woke. Another police officer had taken over from Steven at 3 a.m. At seven Teddy had sent someone to pick up Dorothy's lists and deliver two mobile phones and a note that read, 'These GSMs are digital. No listeners. T.S.'

The new policeman Upul was a skinny fellow with enormous eyes like an alien from *Close Encounters*.

Maud and Emma joined them. 'Why is a man hiding behind the kitchen door, darling boy?'

'Teddy's policeman wants to keep his place, Auntie.'

'Oh dear. You left at six, where have you been?'

He had gone to Bundy's office and arrived to find a man leaving it. 'I wondered if he was going to attack me because he looked as shocked as I was,' he told them.

CV had asked what he was doing there, and he replied that it was his job to clean the building once a week. He then departed on a motorcycle that seemed oddly inappropriate for a cleaner, the lowest paid of all household staff.

'I went in and looked around. Everything seemed fine. By then there was a light in the big house, and I found Lakshmi making tea.'

She had offered him a cup and, without prompting, told him

that the man had been there the previous evening also and had asked her if CV had used the office that day.

'He asked for me by name?'

'He asked about a large white man from abroad.' The term in Sinhala was one usually used as an insult. 'I told him you were a Lankan and to talk of you with respect,' Lakshmi said virtuously.

'Who is he?'

'He has never been on our property before yesterday. He had a key, so I couldn't stop him. This morning there were lights behind the curtain but I was too frightened to go there. Then he came out and you arrived at the same minute.'

'He told me he was the cleaner. Perhaps Mr Balasingham sent him.'

'That one? He's a mechanic. Yesterday he was going in and out, in and out with wires and tools. The man who cleans is a Tamil. He comes on Thursdays.'

CV thanked her, drained his tea and hurried back into the office. He pulled the dust sheets off the equipment and tried to recall every piece as it had been. Almost immediately he noticed a trace of what seemed like sawdust on the floor. It was streaked as if a broom had been used to sweep it away. The first time he had entered the room, he had particularly noticed how dustless the dark floor had been. He examined the coir bristles of the broom in the utility room and saw similar dust. Not wanting to waste time, he got the computer started and deleted most of the files in it.

He then opened a new document, named it 'Hello' and typed, 'Hello User 1. After we've found the killer, would you like to marry me? Your devoted admirer, User 2.'

He found there were two printers connected to the machine that were set to print simultaneously. Only the printer Sphinx was in the room, which meant someone else was getting printouts on a machine called Gloria. He sent a note to be printed only on Gloria, 'Hi. This is CV. Hope you're having a nice day, Gloria.' When he was sure it had gone on its way, he turned Gloria off. Then he sent the same message to be printed on Sphinx only, and the machine in the room leapt to life and spat out the single line on a white sheet.

He shut down the computer and unplugged the power cable.

At the back of the machine there was a mess of cables and some belonged to the fax machine with its built-in phone. Others led to a box in the wall. He sorted them out and replaced only the computer and fax connections to the main electrical power supply. He then restarted the computer.

He sent an email to Della: 'Hello, redhead. Are you ready for Sri Lanka?' Then he sent the same message by fax adding: 'Email message also en route.' And he sat down planning to wait ten minutes. In exactly three the fax responded, 'Hi. This is Della glad to hear we're communicating—I'll look for the email message.' Two minutes later came an email, 'We're in business, buddy.'

He replied, 'Bingo. Don't send unless you know there is someone here to receive. Ask and expect the first words in response to include a comment on the weather— specifically the heat. If none, try later. Emma will be here in an hour or two. Gotta go. CV.'

Outside the building he found a barely visible rectangular groove in the outer wall. He tapped that section and was not surprised to find it hollow. Using a knife, he pried into the groove and a drawer the size of a small shoebox slid out. There was no back to this drawer so that the cables from the office could enter it. The contraption had been clumsily tooled. Three cables entered it and continued upwards into the wall. He pulled them free and placed them on the ground beside him. The box also contained a few loose computer wires, electrical connections and plugs, which he left there.

He remembered seeing mastic in the supplies cupboard and used it on the inner rim of the hole using a plastic spoon to spread it thickly on the box edges as well. He then replaced the box and wiped off the ooze. It now looked pretty much as he had found it, but to remove it would not be easy.

Looking for the source of the sawdust was next, and that was not difficult for there were only a few items in the room made of wood. He inspected the chairs and tables, and then the desk on which the computer sat. It was an unattractive old piece with a two-inch decorative moulding along the front edge. He opened the top drawer and found computer manuals, but when he ran his finger along the edge he was rewarded with a few grains of sawdust.

'Someone sawed the drawer?' Emma interrupted CV.

'To have enough room to hide a tape recorder at the back of it—to record what was being said in the room.'

He told them a voice-activated Panasonic recorder had been secured where the drawer could not hit it and a mike secured out of sight behind the front moulding. CV now placed that recorder on the dining table and removed the cassette inside. 'The tape hasn't advanced because I never said a word in the room. When I found the recorder, I turned it off.'

He then set about making fast the doors and windows. It was a simple matter to nail the windows shut. As there was an air conditioner, there would be no need to open them. The door took a while. He removed the existing lock and replaced it with the identical unit Joseph had found for him but that needed a different key.

Before leaving the office, CV went to say goodbye to Lakshmi. He gave her a hundred-rupee note and asked if she would phone him immediately if anyone entered the building again.

'That man did bad things,' he explained.

'I will telephone. No need for giving money.'

'You must take it. I will give you a hundred rupees every day for seven days to let me know when someone comes.'

She beamed.

Having ended his story, CV gave his full attention to the scrambled eggs.

Emma had sat spellbound. She promised to check the drawer and wall every time she entered the office and to remember to start every message to Della with a comment on the heat.

'You did it all in only two hours,' she marvelled.

Maggie had joined them during his story. She now applauded, and so did his aunt.

'Ah, to be so appreciated!'

'I can't wait to work there now,' said Emma.

'Teddy agrees it's the last place someone would look for you. As Upul's out of uniform you'll look like office workers. Take one of the new phones. Don't enter the building unless Lakshmi tells you no one has been there since I left.'

Maggie said, 'Oh, my god, what swine did this?'

The *Island* had a front page headline, 'The Wrong Girl Dies'. Maggie started to read the account aloud:

> On Sunday morning a young foreign woman was murdered in Bambalapitiya as she slept. The police suspect a connection with the earlier murder of Englishwoman Dorothy Bell. This murder took place in the house of Emma van Eck, a close friend of Miss Bell's, who was at a party that night and had not returned yet. The assailant struck the victim as she slept and threw a pipe bomb into the room. She was killed instantly.
>
> The CID are working on the theory that Miss van Eck was the target of the bomb and the murder was a case

of mistaken identity, but they are not ruling out robbery as the motive as a computer is missing.

CV grabbed the phone. 'Jesus, Teddy, who the fuck talked to the press? Have you read the *Island* this morning?'

When he put it down he said wearily, 'Teddy says it has to be a leak from his department—someone who knows Emma is alive but doesn't know the body is Julia's. Only a few officers know that. Emma must stay in disguise.'

Upul had been listening. His mouth was grim.

CV said to him, 'The superintendent is sending a car. On your way to the office, Emma should lie down in the back until you're sure you're not being followed.'

'Would Michael have talked?' asked Maggie.

'No!' replied Emma emphatically. 'What about Ali?'

'Never,' said Maggie, but she called him immediately and confirmed that. 'He thought it was Emma who died. He's getting back to us.'

Upul shrugged at the idea of policemen talking to the press, 'Some reporters give money. Policemen are poor. Some take it.'

CV wondered if Maggie too might be in danger. She read his mind and said, 'Don't worry, I'll keep moving. I'm going to speak to the Chinese doctors this morning. I'll use the excuse that I'm getting clothes for Renuka's kids. But we can't leave Aunt Maud and Amily here alone, so we'll have to get someone to stay with them.'

But Maud would have none of it. 'We're old women. A killer of foreign girls won't kill us, and we never met Dorothy. Shantha is coming over, and she can bring her houseboy. But until we know Emma is safe, I wish she'd stay at home with me.'

Emma looked grateful when CV replied firmly, 'She's had too many shocks to hang around doing nothing. She'll be behind two locks and with Upul who has a gun. Phone every hour, Auntie, if they don't phone you. Maggie, take Joseph and the car, and look before you leap.'

'What am I to be looking for?' asked Maggie.

'Potholes. Emma, you don't have to work. Rest. Take a mat and cushions so you can sleep if you want to. I've postponed my meeting with Reggie till ten and am having lunch with Mahmoud at one.'

He asked Upul to speak with him privately and said, 'Stay in touch with Inspector Senaratne constantly.'

'Don't worry, sir.'

'Forget that *sir*.'

'Yes, sir.'

'What now?' asked Maggie.

'Get Jeff to be available about eleven—I have a job for the two of you. Are Reggie and you still an item in his mind?'

'He woke me this morning to suggest dinner. I said, 'What about lunch?' He said he's driving to Negombo for lunch and I could go with him. If you want me to go, I will.'

'No! The Negombo trip is a wild goose chase arranged by Ali.'

'I've been praying night and day,' said his aunt. 'It's not a coincidence that God is being helpful.'

'Ask Him to keep it up, Auntie. I'll be thanking Him personally every chance I get. Mag, even if Renuka's children are with you, don't stay in one place long. Do you have enough cash?'

'Enough to clothe a hundred children. Ali is being mysterious. Says about teatime he hopes to have something very very interesting for you.'

'Then we'll all meet here for tea. Look at the time! I'll barely make it to the Palace by ten. I'm seeing Bell before he leaves with Ali, and I want to poke around the Pettah before lunch. Come, let me give you the lowdown, Mag, on what to do after you've returned the kids to their mother.'

'May I listen?' asked Emma, 'or is becoming Chinese more important?'

'You know it is. You can play catch-up this evening.'

Meeting with Reginald Bell
CV skirted the hotel to the basement door. Just when it seemed that there would be no getting in, two men came through talking in English. A guard hurried towards them to declare the door as off limits, but CV intercepted him with twenty rupees.

He took the stairs to the lobby and saw Bell sitting on a couch watching the front door. He made a wide detour, came up from the opposite direction and said to the back of Bell's head, 'Good morning,'

'I didn't know you were here,' was the only greeting he got.

Bell did not stand or offer his hand but waved to a chair. It was a patronizing gesture so CV, used to corporate power games, pulled up a different chair. He said to a waiter who had joined them, 'Two fresh limes,' and to his employer, 'Is that okay?'

Bell said, 'What? Oh, yes!' and, 'I haven't tried the lime.' As CV made no effort to speak, he eventually continued, 'I want to know about Emma van Eck's murder. Do the police think it's connected to Dot's?'

'You haven't read the *Island* then?'

'No. Why?'

'There's a report on the front page. I was forbidden to tell you, but Emma is fine. A girlfriend who was in her bed was burnt to death. Teddy wanted to hold the story to protect Emma.'

'Another girl? Who?'

'I'll get the account.' He went to the front desk to borrow a copy of the *Island*. LL Perera came out of his office and said quietly: 'I'll be here most of the day. Everything all right?'

'I wish. Mr Bell didn't know Emma van Eck escaped last night. May I show him the paper?'

'Of course.'

As he walked back to Bell, he noticed the Englishman was about to spoon sugar into a glass of lime juice placed in front of CV's chair. As he preferred the drink semisweet tried, he to stop him, and their hands collided. The sugar went in all directions— some into CV's glass but more on the table and floor.

'I'm sorry,' he said. 'I prefer it without and didn't want to yell to stop you.'

Bell was not surprisingly irritated, and he began to wipe the table with a napkin. To make amends CV tried to spoon sugar into Bell's glass only to have it snatched away.

'I have already attended to my drink, thank you,' the Englishman snapped.

'Can we shelve this lime juice crisis?' CV said, knowing it had been his fault.

The other man began to laugh. 'A little sugar on the table and I behave as if the roof caved in. I apologize.'

He opened the *Island*, read the front page story, folded it and placed it beside him, then continued, 'I wish I'd known about Sri Lankan lime before.'

'Fresh lime! Otherwise you may get a fizzy drink.'

CV took a sip and tried not to make a face because his drink was too sour. He took another sip, abandoned the drink and said, 'The police are protecting Emma.'

'Where?'

'At the home of a friend.'

'Who was killed?'

'They're working on that. There was some rifling of Emma's possessions but only she will know exactly what was taken. I believe the expression is, "She's in shock".'

Bell lit a cigarette without replying. He seemed considerably put out by the news.

'Do you think this latest killing is connected to Dorothy's death?' CV asked.

'I'd expect some connection,' Bell said, but not immediately.
'So would I.'

A long pull on the cigarette, then, 'But I must ask that you remember you are working for me. Your job this week is to find how Dot died, why she was killed and who killed her—not why this other woman was killed unless there is an obvious connection. What's going to be your next step?'

'I think I'll poke around in the Pettah today. In fact, I'm already late. I'll give you a call later.'

'All right. I'll see you to your car,' Bell said.

'Thank you, but that's not necessary.'

'I'd like to.'

The remark seemed out of character, and CV now remembered Bundy's insistence that he was in danger and became more uneasy when the older man would not be put off. He found himself giving one lame reason after another why they should part company indoors—heard himself talking about phone calls he wanted to make. When Bell offered to wait until he had made them, he tried, 'I'm going to hang around for a bit. I wish you'd go on with your day, Mr Bell.'

'Make your calls!'

Reluctant to say, 'Will you get off my fucking back,' he continued to produce evasive lies.

Eventually Bell said, 'Is there some reason you don't want to walk out of the hotel with me?'

'Not really,' yet another lie.

'Then let's go.'

Help came as Perera appeared in the lobby. CV left Bell's side, bounded up to him to grasp the manager's hand and before the Englishman reached them said in Sinhala, 'Prevent him from following me.'

Bell sauntered up and took a stance beside them. Perera, with a cool that equalled the Englishman's, called to a passing waiter. In Sinhala he said, 'Fall over the white-haired man beside me to delay his departure.'

The waiter came forward smiling, slipped and crashed headlong into Bell, whom Perera caught as he fell, and CV fled for the door to the stairs, ran down them to the basement as if chased by demons and out of the building. By this time he had a slight headache. In the parking lot he considered with some embarrassment the possibility that he was becoming paranoid. However out of character Reggie Bell might have been in wanting to see him on his way, it was a friendly gesture. But it was also possible he had wanted them to be seen together by someone. True, they had sat together in the lobby, but the doormen made judgement calls on who to let in and out. The someone whom Bell wanted to see CV might not have been able to enter.

Well, better paranoid than dead! If Bell wanted to kill him he didn't have to make the job easy. He strolled on to the road being careful to look around without appearing furtive, flagged down a red three-wheeler and asked to be taken to the Pettah.

'Second Cross Street, but first go past the GOH.'

Mr Solomon

The Fort had been the major business centre of Colombo for generations until urban development had opened up greater Colombo and its suburbs. The harbour it had once protected with cannons, which are still in place, was no longer the most important crossroads in the Indian Ocean. During the day, the Fort's wide streets were lined with street merchants. Fashionable shoppers avoided them because the great old shops had gone or shrunk.

The huge Grand Oriental Hotel where Dorothy had had her last meal was across the road from the harbour. It was a legacy of Victorian England, and CV had been surprised that swingers like Michael and Dorothy had gone there. He did not know why he wanted to go past it or why he longed to spend the rest of the morning wandering around the Fort. Since leaving Bell, the question of who killed Dorothy Bell had almost ceased to interest him.

The Fort was overrun with trishaws, and for the first time he noticed that their drivers had a dress code. They wore button-fronted shirts and pants. It was as if a breed of kamikaze clerks had been set loose on the city.

After they had passed the GOH, they went north towards many industrial facilities. Then they circled to enter the Pettah at Main Street only to become enveloped in its claustrophobic chaos and forced to stop. The driver turned his head and laughed raucously, 'Better walking to Second Cross Street or taking one hour.'

CV paid him and continued on foot. He passed the cause of the main traffic block—a double-parked truck being relieved of huge bales wrapped in hessian. Drivers and loaders were screaming at each other, not in anger, but to be heard.

Those on foot had all the advantage, and CV went quickly past First Cross Street. Slowly a sense of disorientation was setting in, and he wished he had let the three-wheeler take him to his destination at its snail's pace. Traffic on Second Cross Street, which had been so eerie on Friday night, was also at a standstill. The exhaust fumes and blazing sun had become so debilitating that CV's limbs had turned to jelly.

He tried to concentrate on the store windows and the goods laid out on the sidewalks. Aluminium hardware, plastic bowls, and nylon ropes provided a psychedelic picture he might have enjoyed at another time. The dust made him cough. He wondered if he should get something to drink but decided to push on. Quite suddenly he knew he was not just tired but ill. He looked at his watch and was surprised to find it had taken him only four minutes to get from the three-wheeler to the step on which Dorothy's body had been found. It had seemed like thirty. He found a small metal plate which marked the building.

D.S. SOLOMON (PTE) LTD
PAPER CARDBOARD BAGS BOXES
WHOLESALE

The door was marked 'open', and he entered a room with paper products piled off the floor on every side. In its recesses three men were discussing an order for paper bags and, for no reason they were shouting. A silent youngster with the bright face of a college student was standing at a large table counting a stack of loose cardboard. He made a note on a sheet in front of him, smiled at CV, seemed about to speak then changed his mind when a man seated behind a counter snapped in Tamil, 'Pay attention to your work!'

The speaker was an old and fragile man, at least seventy, dressed in a kurta over a sarong. He came around the counter to where CV stood.

'How can I help you, sir?' he asked in educated English.

'I am looking for Mr Solomon.'

'I am Mr Solomon.'

CV looked around for somewhere to sit and settle the giddiness that coming indoors hadn't helped. He made an effort to hide his weariness. 'May we speak privately, sir, or I could take you out for a drink.'

Solomon's wire eyeglasses gave him the style of a bookkeeper. Behind them, faded brown eyes studied CV.

'I can't leave the shop now,' said the diminutive owner. 'We can have something to drink in my office. You look too hot.' To the youngster counting cardboard, he called, 'Bring two cold drinks.'

Inside his office he turned on the ceiling fan, took the chair behind the desk and invited CV to sit on the only other. As he did so, all his energy began draining away. The other man appeared not to notice, and they sat silently until the drinks arrived, bright orange and in tall glasses. CV reached out, grabbed one and drained it to the bottom, looked up in consternation and said, 'I'm sorry, I'm very thirsty. The heat! I don't feel well.'

Solomon said to the boy, 'Bring a glass of water quickly.'

'Thank you,' said CV. 'I'm giddy.'

'Bring a bottle of water, too,' the old man shouted. 'I must implore you not to walk outdoors in such weather again, sir.'

CV's voice was thick. 'Hot outside—probably dehydrated.' The symptoms were of dehydration but, even as he spoke, he began to suspect he'd been poisoned and recalled the lime juice incident at the hotel. When you are poisoned, he knew, you always know what food is the culprit—the one which comes to mind. He saw Bell's hand with the teaspoon of sugar over his glass and his quick move to stop it. That could have been why Bell had been eager to stay with CV. He remembered leaving his lime juice almost untouched. If a sip was doing this to him, what would he be feeling if he'd had a full dose of poison? And even as these thoughts crossed his mind, he wondered again if it was paranoia that was bringing them on.

'Carry an umbrella,' Solomon was saying, and he took one from a stand against the wall. 'Take this one. You can return it any time. Keep it until you have one of your own.'

'You're kind.'

One cure for any drug overdose is dilution. CV downed two glasses of water, poured himself a third, then a fourth. Mr Solomon came to his side and put a hand on his head. 'You don't seem feverish. You're cold—clammy. You must lie down.'

'No. No.' He knew he should keep moving and drink as much as he could. As he stood he felt the fog lifting from within. 'I thought my brain was leaving me. I'm better now.' He shook his head to be able to continue, stretched and paced the room. All the time he was thinking he had to get Mr Solomon's story.

He introduced himself at last and explained that he was looking for Dorothy Bell's killer. 'I am not happy having to ask your help, Mr Solomon, but I must. If you would patiently hear me out for five minutes without refusing what I ask, I'd appreciate it.'

He drank again.

The old man said, 'Your colour is better,' and smiled wryly. 'I had guessed why you are here, Mr vander Marten. Don't worry, I won't throw you out—at least until I'm sure you're well enough. Tell me what you want to know.'

CV repeated the story that Joseph had told him. 'I can understand that you feel you'd be endangering your own life if you told the police what you saw, but now there has been another death.' At last his voice did not waver. 'In return for my promise that the information you give me will be used only to look for her murderer, would you tell me what you saw?' He then switched to Tamil, 'I am not a foreigner, as you may have presumed. I am a Burgher, and my early schooling was in this country. Surely we can trust each other?'

Then, in English, he gave Solomon a brief outline of the situation as he knew it, ending, 'I am trusting you with information only a handful of people know.'

Solomon leaned his elbows on his desk with his hands twisted together. Overlapping yellowing teeth gnawed gently at his lower lip. He said slowly, 'What is my guarantee that you can keep your word? You say that the police have agreed that my name will not be revealed. The police in this country can't be trusted.'

'That's a problem, of course, with the police in any country. But Superintendent Senaratne of the CID is an unusually straight man and I trust him completely. But trust is not the only issue. This morning, for the first time, I have felt fear for my own life. I think about an hour ago someone tried to poison me. Yesterday a friend warned me that I am in danger. Abroad four men connected with Dorothy Bell's father have died in the way she was killed.'

'You mean there is someone stalking that family?'

'It looks that way.'

Solomon rose and shut the door. 'You should be a barrister. You are persuasive. Let us keep our voices down. I will deny everything if the police come to me. Others know what I have seen because we, in the Pettah, are like members of a club. But we don't trust strangers. Most of all we don't trust police promises any more than we trust our politicians.'

CV drank more water and waited. Eventually, the other began to speak. The story he told was much as Joseph had heard. Sometimes CV had to push.

'What time did you see the car stop outside?'

'At exactly 12.33 I decided to close up. I looked at my watch, thought my wife will be angry with me for being late again, turned the lights out and then heard a car on the road. I always wait till the road is clear before getting into my Toyota, for this is the Pettah, after all. But the car did not pass.'

'It stopped outside?'

'I will show you the spot before you leave. The road had not yet been swept that night and there was plastic and paper everywhere as usual. My own car was outside the door. The car that had arrived was going down the road the wrong way towards Olcott Street.'

'It's colour?'

'Dark blue, I think.'

'Like this?'

The room, like the main one, was filled with paper products. CV pointed to a book on a shelf.

'Darker. There was moonlight. It had been raining and the street was wet. There are not many street lamps in this section. Colours would have been distorted, but I looked at the car carefully wondering who would stop in this road at that time of night and drive in the wrong direction.'

'Someone who wanted to get away fast. If you are both facing the same direction, a faster car, like a police vehicle, will catch you. If the other car has to turn around, that buys you time.'

'I never thought of that! That car was also a Toyota, a Starlet.'

'You're sure?'

'I'm sure. I know Toyotas. Mine is a Corolla.'

'Tell me about the men.'

'One was quite tall and burly, shorter than you by only one or two inches. The other was thin. The big man wore dark trousers and a light shirt and sandals. A large ring was on his finger. They came to my step so I saw their clothes clearly. The thin man was about five foot three or four, and he wore an old shirt and dark shorts. Both wore very dark cloth bags on their heads with holes for their eyes and mouths.'

'Tell me more about those bags.'

'Big bags. Thick cloth with a speckled pattern. You can imagine how frightened I was. I thought they were coming to kill me for they came on to my step. If they touched the door, I was going out through the back of the shop. There is a space with a tap. If they set fire to the building with all this paper, I might be burnt to death unless I could get into another building. I thought I must turn the water on because it will protect me. I then wondered if they were going to steal my car or tyres. They were speaking to each other but I couldn't hear. I closed my eyes when they turned towards me. When I opened my eyes they were walking back to their car.'

'Was the ring the fat man wearing a wedding band?'

'A band?' He looked confused and then laughed. 'Oh, you mean a wedding ring. No, it was a signet ring.'

He took a large notepad from his desk and drew the shape of a ring. The top was rectangular with blunt corners. He drew an oval into it and blackened that. CV took the pad into his hand.

He was sure he had never seen that ring before—at least not recently on anyone's finger. He thought of Bundy who was a little shorter than him and burly. When they had gone swimming together, Budy had worn a simple gold band, but he had not been wearing even that ring either on Friday night or Saturday.

'You draw well. Could you the two men?'

Solomon tore off the sheet and with ease drew two men on the next page. The larger stood with his feet planted apart, toes pointing outward. The smaller man was extremely thin with straight legs, bare feet and broad toes. His T-shirt hung out over his shorts. The other's shirt was tucked inside his trousers and his stomach bulged over the waist band.

'Would you recognize the smaller man's lower legs?'

'Show me a thin-legged man and I might say to you, "He does not have the legs I saw." But I could not say of another's, "Yes those are the legs." There are many fellows here with legs like his.'

The rest of his story mirrored Joseph's and was irritatingly lacking in elaboration. Solomon admitted he was so frightened that sometimes he backed away from the hole even when he realized he could not be seen. His relief when he found the men had not come to break in or steal his tyres melted when he saw why they were there.

'When I looked again the small fellow was carrying something across his back like a sack. It appeared to be heavy and eventually I realized it was a woman. The big fellow slammed the boot shut and followed. The other brought her behind my Toyota and dropped her on to the step like a bag of dung. Then the bigger man did a gesture with his hand. Like this.'

The big man had fucked-off the dead girl!

'It was a terrible gesture—more so because I now realized she was dead,' Solomon said shaking his head with disgust. 'He walked away, then returned and bent down, took her face in his hand and turned it forward.' He acted out what he had seen, moving his own right hand as the big man's had moved. 'She was on her back with her legs apart, and her head had fallen to the side. He held her face in his hand and looked at it. Then he let it fall, rubbed his hand on his trousers, put that hand into his pocket and went to his car. He now seemed sad.

'So the big man had been ambivalent about killing Dorothy. I remember that the other gesture was vulgar, so touching her face gently was surprising. The big man drove the car away.

'It was about one now. I was surprised because it seemed that an hour had gone. I waited and a lorry passed, then I heard a car again. It too did not stop, and it was the same Toyota with the same two men. They had removed their hoods, but I could not see their faces as they were in the dark. As soon as they passed, I went down to my own car. When I was inside with the engine running I looked at the dead woman again—just a girl. I got out and rolled her body on to its side and placed her legs together. She looked asleep now. I prayed for her as I drove home.'

'Rigor mortis had not set in when you rearranged her?'

'No.'

'Both men were Lankans?'

'Their skin was dark. They carried themselves like Lankans.'

'How does a Lankan carry himself, Mr Solomon?'

'There are movements of hands, and they walked like Lankans—toes pointed outward.'

'And me? Do I move my hands and walk like a Lankan?'

'No!' he smiled.

CV knew he was very much better and allowed Solomon to show him to the bathroom where he splashed water on his face and immersed his arms to the elbows. There was nothing he could do about the way he looked. Before leaving he mentioned that he'd like to buy school supplies for Renuka's children and received a gift of eight exercise books. There was no one in the big room now but he could hear voices speaking in Tamil from the inner recesses. As they stood looking out of the front door Solomon pointed to where the other car had been parked. It was about ten yards away. He said, 'You see that Datsun? It was there.'

'You didn't see the licence plate?'

'I did not. I am observant. I think it may have been covered.'

Then he showed CV his peephole in the door—eye-level for him, chest-level for CV—and they went outside. It was easy to see why Solomon had not been spotted by Dorothy's killers. Even in daylight the hole was virtually invisible. Solomon advised him to walk to Olcott Mawatha before getting a taxi because there the traffic would have thinned and it would be quicker in the long run. 'And don't forget to use the umbrella. Monday is not a good day to come here, but telephone or come again when you wish and tell me how things work out. How are you feeling?'

'Better, I am sure it was my drink at the hotel. Fortunately I drank very little of it.'

'This country is going crazy.'

He thanked Solomon warmly, promised to contact him and fought the impulse to spend the rest of the day shopping for the kids. It was 12:45 and he was meeting Mahmoud for lunch at the Palace at one. He arrived at the front door of the hotel without mishap just as Maggie and Jeffrey also arrived. He didn't recognize her as she was wrapped in a *burka* and walked in the flapping garments with her legs wide apart. She bumped into him and said, 'Mind where you're going, you fucking Christian.'

He started and then recognizing her voice, murmured, 'You look yummy in that get-up. I'm lunching with Mahmoud upstairs. Join us as soon as you can but not looking like this. I want your take on him.'

Jeff had slowed down to hear what was being said and then continued on his way to the front desk without glancing back. Maggie plodded through to the lounge. CV hadn't wanted

Perera to know that she would be helping Jeff. He himself headed for the restroom to clean up.

Lunch with Mahmoud
Mahmoud was late which gave CV time to find a table and dial Teddy Senaratne on the mobile phone. He found Nora at home and she said, 'He's looking into that robbery on Fifth Lane. I'll get him to call you back.'

At that moment Mahmoud entered the dining room so CV said, 'Tell Teddy that I have a sketch of two guys who dumped Dorothy on Second Cross Street but not to phone as I'm tied up. I'll get back to you when I can.'

He rose to shake Mahmoud's hand and was surprised at its strength. Enormous Mo stood behind his master smiling obsequiously. He took a place facing CV at an adjoining table.

His employer exuded intelligence and authority. His face was long and lean and he had a two-part black beard—a dark tuft under the lower-lip and below it a carefully groomed goatee. His face was dominated by liquid light brown eyes, and the good humour that characterized his fellow-Muslim Ali. They had in common a laid back enjoyment in the present moment.

'Do we need him?' said CV nodding towards Mo as Mahmoud sat down. 'I'm uncomfortable being stared at.'

Mahmoud turned his head and spoke in Arabic, and Mo got to his feet at once and left the room. At the door he turned and gave CV a level look with no change of expression, which was unpleasant nonetheless.

'Odd guy. Looks as if he bites. If he waits outside, he may scare the guests.'

'He'll be in my suite,' shrugged Mahmoud. 'He's a habit I often wish I'd never acquired. When you see others walking about unprotected and unmolested, you realize the freedom you've lost.'

'He seems ferociously devoted to you.'

Mahmoud made a face. 'It is surprising how much ferocious devotion money inspires. He enjoys this job because his only talent—mindless violence—is being compensated. But, like most soldiers, he is required to stay in training for a battle—which seldom comes, and I sometimes wonder how good he really is, but at least he looks lethal enough.'

Mahmoud had a restless manner that made him seem younger than he was. He fidgeted. One hand moved to his face, then played with the table napkin, then moved to his glass and to the knife in his place setting, at the same time the other was also moving. He shifted his body in the seat like a child who was uncomfortable.

'Are you an athlete, Mr Mahmoud?' CV was reminded of Sri Lanka's famous cricketer Sanath Jayasuriya who had the same restless manner.

'I was. Very observant of you. Of course, I never had thoughts of professional sports, which annoyed the coaches. The only sports I do not enjoy are those connected with water. I own no yacht. I can swim but do not.'

After Emma's terror of Mahmoud, CV had been expecting someone brutish. Instead he had found an educated man with a relaxed manner and considerable personal charm. The Arabian *dishdasha* he wore suited him, emphasizing his aristocratic appearance. His expressive eyes and even teeth under those full curved lips Dorothy had liked to watch could also have belonged to an ageing movie star. CV suspected she had felt doubly betrayed because there had been some chemistry between them.

Mahmoud clicked his fingers at a waiter as he said, 'I have been hoping to speak to you after I learned that you were trying to find Dorothy's murderer. I was about to initiate a meeting so was delighted when you called. What would you like to drink? I'm a teetotaller, but I don't expect my guests to abstain.'

CV replied, 'I'd like an arrack and soda. Do order whatever

Murder in the Pettah

you prefer. You are my guest. It was my invitation.'

'Absolutely not. I would be embarrassed to take your money. I feel more comfortable if I am the host.'

'Even if I tell you it is Reginald Bell's money we'll be spending? I am in his employ.'

'Even if. Now let's get to the matter in hand. You want to know why I paid Dorothy to bare her little backside for me and why I am stalking Emma van Eck?'

His candour was startling, but it brought them to the point.

CV replied, 'I think we know the answer to both questions. You wanted sex and have the money to pay for it in the one case. In the other, man is the hunter and the chase is fun. I hope to persuade you not to continue it. Emma is extremely upset. The sight of you at Jimmy's party ruined her evening. What I primarily want to discuss is Dorothy outside your bed however. I am intrigued by a murder that has no suspects. From what I hear you could be one—the sinister mystery man in the wings—but I can't find your motive either.'

Mahmoud laughed easily. 'I've heard you don't beat about the bush. Good. We will be enjoying ourselves. We Arabs do look a bit sinister. Our beards and clothing are perfect for almost concealing evil intent. No, I did not kill Dorothy or want her dead. What do you know about my relationship with her?'

CV told him briefly what he had learned.

'You have the right story but the wrong slant,' said Mahmoud. 'Come—here are our drinks. I understand your need to speed up your investigation, but let us at least enjoy our meal like the gentlemen we were born.'

'But please keep the conversation on Dorothy. I have only four more days, Mr Mahmoud, to find out who killed her and why.'

The other man was studying him. His eyes were the only part of him that seemed capable of not moving. They did not wander around the room. CV suddenly wondered if Mahmoud thought his guest resembled a potato, and that made him smile.

The dining room had filled with businessmen. There were only two women, both in saris, and they sat together. The atmosphere was of a men's club. The men were talking with the animated attention that characterizes business acquaintances who are not friend.

Mahmoud said, 'I will tell you anything you want about Dorothy. I won't give you the positions, the number of times, the exact and considerable amount of money she made off me, but I will explain our relationship. I knew the moment I set eyes on her that she would eventually let me pay her for her company. I'm not a man who needs endless variety, but I like a woman, the right woman, in every port.' CV tried to look fascinated. 'These days of AIDS and other infections has made a single-sex companion much the best arrangement for a man like me. I like to fall asleep with a woman in my arms and wake to find her gone. A fifteen-year-old wife was provided for me when I was twenty-two by my father who has the same libido. He too was married to a suitable, circumcised woman selected by his father—a woman who did not expect fidelity, only that her children be the legitimate ones.'

'Why are you telling me these private matters?' asked CV.

'Because men love to hear such stories—women too—we all like to shudder. Christian priests, for example, rarely forget to ask about our circumcised women. How is it done? Why is it done? Does it make the woman more passionate or less? I tell them, it makes a woman hate men and that frees her husband. But what you want to know is how Dorothy became my whore when she was rich and intelligent. Come drink up. Another arrack?' He snapped his fingers and replenishments were brought at once.

'Initially, I was attracted to her body, of course. I do not like a lifeless or even small-breasted woman in my bed. She was neither. I began to enjoy her independence, her brazenness, her outrageous laughter when she'd won a point. She'd let you win a few battles even as she intended to win every war. She was a delightful companion. Even when she was bored she could amuse me. I eventually became so dependent on her company that I spent more and more time in Lanka just to be with her and I would even phone her from another woman's bed. I had not made a friend of a mistress before. Ours was the kind of friendship men usually have only with other men. I mourn her now.'

He spoke of feeling, but CV suspected he had forgotten how to feel. He spoke of mourning as if he could no longer mourn. Mahmoud could do without anyone or anything because his money had brought instant replacements for his needs all his life, but only by talking of his emotions could he pretend he too felt like other men.

'Money was something Dorothy demanded and I was glad to give, but she was not reluctant to indulge me, Mr vander Marten. Her fiancé Michael understood that when he sometimes came and performed with her for my pleasure. Those two were sublime together because they cut you out—acted as if you were not there. He is one of us—the non-monogamous who can take our carnal pleasures without guilt. It was a good time for all three of us. Four of us, really, if you count Mohideen. Dorothy and Michael got what they wanted: money. I got what I wanted: an alleviation from the chronic boredom that I suffer. Mohideen got what animals want and usually get: to relieve himself into another's body. I have no doubt he enjoyed it more because she was white and a Christian.'

'You expected her to be available to him and also your men friends?' The question was trite because he had guessed the response.

'Why not, if she was agreeable? She'd set her price and she

always got it.'

The arrogance and superficiality of the man had kept him blind to his own evil.

'You hit her.'

'Ah! No wonder Emma is so frightened of me. So Dorothy told her I slapped her sometimes! Let me tell you about my so-called violence. I do not touch alcohol because my religion forbids it. But I should not drink in any case. I have inherited the alcohol addict's gene. I was still a teenager when my father said to me, "Drink, and you will be the fool of all fools and any nondrinker will have power over you. Do without, and no man will be your master." I told that story to Dorothy, and that same evening she slipped some vodka into my Coca-Cola to see if it was true. I commented on the different taste and she explained it was a new cola. I could not stop and eventually took a belt to her. Of course, the next day she insisted I pay for her bruises and of course I did. After that she'd try to escape Mo's watchful eye and lace my drinks—for the money—always for the money. It happened four times.' He chuckled happily. 'Allah cannot blame me! I never take the first glass knowingly.'

'You say Dorothy got you to beat her so that she could make money from you?'

'Mo thought she was a masochist. All I know is there was nothing that girl liked as much as she liked money—yes, perhaps she was masochistic. Oh Mr vander Marten, lighten up, as they say in your country. Don't sit there scowling. Where is your sense of humour? Dorothy was an intelligent tart who'd found a john to her liking.'

'Mr Mahmoud, it is not uncommon for a bully to say his victim likes being abused. You raped her.' He could not resist saying, 'I think Dorothy slipped you drinks to remind herself that you were that fool of all fools and she had the power to demonstrate this. She did not need your handouts. She was successfully negotiating deals worth millions of dollars. I think she took your money and gave you her body because it was her only way to get even with a man she felt had violated her.'

Mahmoud showed no irritation at all. He laughed aloud. 'Every tart has her sad story. I was raped by the boys in my school, I am not punishing them now by selling my body to men. I can afford a hundred times more than what I gave her without missing it. We had a very pleasant arrangement that I wish I still had. That little Emma is frightened because she thinks I want her to be my mistress? Never! Unlike Dorothy, she is a lady. She has nothing to fear from me.'

Perhaps Maggie had been right, then. Emma would be safe with Mahmoud. CV felt confused.

The Arab handed back the menu to the waiter without looking at it and said, 'Bring caviar on ice, minted lamb chops, peas, mushrooms, mashed potatoes. No chunks of bread or rolls—Melba toast. Is that all right with you, Mr vander Marten?'

'Yes. Yes, that'll be fine,' he said but he had no appetite.

When the man was out of earshot, CV asked, 'And Emma, Mr Mahmoud?'

The Arab chuckled. 'Poor beauty! She misunderstood from the first. My second son Ahmed says the girls his mother introduces him to are spoilt, superficial and dull. I had him educated in England because he's inclined to be academic. He calls himself a socialist. A rich socialist is ridiculous, I tell him, but he says he cannot be responsible for his birth.

'Ahmed has always hoped for a love match. He deplores the relationship between his mother and myself. He's had three engagements to gold diggers who were pretending to have big hearts. I put a detective agency on to them and was always able to get a tape recording of the girl boasting about his wealth to her friends. One said that it didn't matter if Ahmed dumped her because the severance pay would be huge. All three times he confronted the girl, and all three times she responded that he was being unrealistic if he felt a woman could ignore such an exciting part of him as his wealth. I paid them off in cash and got a release for Ahmad—then had my money stolen back before they got home. If you want a woman to accept cash under the table, offer her double what she would get over it. If any had not threatened to sue Ahmed for breach of promise, they would have received a handsome severance, as one young woman had guessed rightly,' he chuckled at his triumph.

For all his outward amiability this man was obviously not one to cross. CV wondered if he realized that the more he talked, the more he showed himself as a man who could order an assassination.

Mahmoud leaned forward, fiddling with the silverware, his glass, the salt and pepper shaker. 'I saw Emma one evening when she was with Dorothy and on making inquiries realized she would make the right wife for my son. She has class, looks, intelligence and a big heart. She is healthy and has no boyfriend, lover or husband. At her age, she must want to settle down. Ahmed can help her realize her dreams—publish her book, give her a charity under her own name. Dorothy let me have a snapshot of her to send him, and he was charmed. Those eyes! That dimple! Even a lovely body. Then Dorothy died and apparently had not yet told Emma what I was proposing.'

'Is this nonsense on the level?' said CV with a mounting constriction around the chest. He wondered if Mahmoud had thought of involving Dorothy after her death. He could have got a snapshot of Emma from anyone. But then, CV reminded himself, he had not known Dorothy.

'All young people need help—a push.' Mahmoud pulled his wallet from the pocket of his *dishdasha* and removed a small photograph. 'This is my son. Would you show the picture to Emma when you meet her?'

CV examined it. Ahmed Mahmoud was handsome. His clean-shaven face had his father's large eyes, features and smile. To CV's sorrow Ahmed's was also a kind face.

'I'll show it to her,' he tried to sound unmoved. 'You want her to meet your son. That's the message?'

'Yes. He will not press her if she does not wish to marry him. First, I want to talk to her, to tell her about our family, and then if she agrees, we can set up a meeting.'

'I have other questions for you,' said CV putting the picture into his own wallet. He felt a blinding anger. 'In a photograph of you and Dorothy, she is wearing what looks like diamonds. Balasingham tells me she had a superb collection. Do you know where she kept it?'

'I gave that picture to her. That jewellery is mine. Yes, the necklace she was wearing is of diamonds. It was remade from one my mother owned. The other pieces are a bracelet and a pair of earrings. The set is for my daughter. There is a very fine craftsman in Colombo who makes jewellery for me. If you need a special piece I'll give you his name. Dorothy was not particularly interested in jewellery. She preferred money. But she wore it occasionally to please me, and as I knew her avariciousness I never let her out of my sight wearing pieces I owned. She had give it to Mo before leaving my suite or my car.'

'Did you pay for her in cash?'

'U.S. dollars.'

'Do you know what she did with the money? I mean, did she put it in a safe deposit box or hide it under the bed?'

'I believe she got it out of the country. There are couriers who do jobs like that.'

'Dorothy and you were rarely seen together in the hotel,' he said to Mahmoud.

'She didn't want anyone to know what she was up to.'

'Except Michael.'

'Yes,' and finally Mahmoud became thoughtful. 'You're

right. I suppose she never really trusted anyone else.'

'She trusted Emma, and from what Emma says, Dorothy would never have set her up with you.'

Again there was a pause before Mahmoud replied, 'I told you I don't want Emma for myself.'

'She may not have believed that.'

There was silence as they ate. The caviar had been served and they were now on the lamb chops. CV's usual huge appetite had shrunk. He ate little.

'The other men in that picture?' he asked at last.

'Not men who would kill Dorothy. I'll give you their names and you can contact them and set your mind at ease. We had a little fun together in my suite that evening, but they are businessmen who were here as my guests. One is the chairman of a television company at home, the other a toy manufacturer.'

'Dorothy took a percentage of your losses in the Casino Vegas. Did you know that?'

Mahmoud was at last astonished. He replied slowly, 'No! You are sure? Tell me!'

CV told him about Dorothy's deal with Bundy.

'My God, she was magnificent!' said Mahmoud gleefully and rubbed his hands together. He wiped his mouth with the napkin. 'How I miss her. One of a kind, Mr vander Marten, one of a kind.'

A dessert tray was at his elbow, but CV opted for coffee instead. Mahmoud chose a cheesecake covered with strawberry sauce, whipped cream and nuts. As the dish was placed before him, there was a stir at the other end of the dining room, and CV looked up to see Maggie in the doorway.

It was Maggie-the-famous in a short dress and high heels, her hair brushed out like a wild woman. She held herself mile-high as she talked to the head waiter, who nodded vigorously. She then smiled at him, turned and strode towards them. Attention followed her as word got around. Mahmoud got to his feet, and she gave him one of her other famous smiles—the cat-girl. She held her hand out and he took it, wiped his mouth with an elaborate gesture and kissed it.

'Sit down. Sit down,' she said huskily. 'Tip the waiter, CV darling, would you? I promised him you would if he'd keep people from asking for autographs.'

The waiter had already intercepted a young man with pen and paper in hand.

CV looked into the slanting eyes that said, 'Well done!'

She smiled back and asked, 'Have you guys decided to stick stilettos into each other's backs? You did not look happy when I came in.'

'We have got along marvellously,' said Mahmoud dropping his own voice to a purr. 'Now what would you like to eat or drink? How can I keep you at this table with me?'

CV said, 'Excuse me. Mr Mahmoud. She'll be all yours in a second. Mag, do you have fifteen spare minutes right now?'

'You bet. Jeff went home and wanted you to know nothing came of his visit.'

Mahmoud said, 'What is your secret, Mr vander Marten? Dorothy too talked of your attractions, which are not easy for another man to discern.'

'I have beautiful knees,' CV said. 'Mag, would you keep Mr Mahmoud company till I get back? I have to make a longish phone call.'

'Take your time,' she beamed, 'Mr Mahmoud, what is that luscious thing you're eating? I'd like one. I've recently discovered I can eat what I like because I'm naturally thin.'

Mohideen

The elevator door opened to let a waiter out, and CV rode to the fifth floor. Mahmoud's suite was number 515 and he found it easily. He knocked. The door was opened by Mo.

CV was just the right distance to kick him in the stomach. Mo was the taller, but there had been a sluggishness to his walk that suggested he was out of shape. CV had counted on a surprise attack to take him, and it did initially. A shorter kick and the Arab toppled as he rolled to protect himself. CV slammed the door shut behind him and hoped his own weight wouldn't slow him down. The surprise was gone and Mo bounced to his feet with a knife in his hand. CV hadn't expected a knife. He kicked at the hand that held it and saw it fly into the air. They hurled themselves at it and fell.

Mo got the knife again and brought it around in his right hand, but it hit the rug not his attacker, who used that moment to lean down and put his teeth into the Arab's wrist and hit him in the face. CV sensed rather than saw the blade in the rug and managed to get his left hand on to the hilt and toss it across the room under a settee. Mo tried to haul his bulk from the floor, which put him off balance again. Using his shoulder like a battering ram, CV came down on the Arab and pushed his head against the floor. He felt a child again for he fought from rage. He had Mo's arm in a hammer lock and heard him grunt as he tried to turn. Bending his arm backwards, CV told him to move to the bed, and they shuffled forward slowly, both on their knees.

When he at last released Mo, the man had both his arms and legs crossed behind him secured with cords from one of Mahmoud's robes. He shoved Mo on to his side and looked for the knife. It had a broad short blade. He used it to slice the fabric of Mo's *dishdasha*, rolled a piece into a wad and stuck it in his mouth, securing it with a strip like a bandage that he tied behind his head. The man was watching him with curiosity now but no fear. In the bathroom CV found a roll of bandaid in a drawer, cut a strip and pasted it across Mo's eyes.

CV then took the telephone off the table quietly and slipped it under the bed so it would not be where Mo expected. He didn't want the man putting a call to the front desk while he himself was in the hotel. Then he sat on the bed, exhausted. When he looked at his watch, he had been in the room sixteen minutes.

His anger gone, he surveyed his handiwork with distaste. As he straightened his own clothes and used Mahmoud's brush on his scant hair, he said wearily, 'I do this for Dorothy Bell. The next time you tie down a woman and rape her, remember when you lost to a fat, out-of-shape Christian. Tell your employer I don't buy his story of Dorothy Bell wanting to be raped. It is his sin. Your sin. She was just a young girl who had learned to deal with a world filled with men like him. I swear to God that if either of you killed her, you'll pay for it.'

There was blood on the sheets, and only then he saw it had come from a raw patch on the back of his own hand. He went into the bathroom and held his hand under the tap, then tied his handkerchief around his hand keeping pressure on the bandage to stop the bleeding and let himself out.

Maggie and Mahmoud were laughing merrily when he joined them and he said, 'Thanks Mag. All taken care of.'

She glanced at his hand as he put it under the table. Mahmoud was interested only in her. 'Your lovely cousin has refused to dine with me, Mr vander Marten. Will you persuade her that I am not an ogre?'

'Ah, but you are,' he said. 'We must leave you Mr Mahmoud. Duty calls. Thank you for a wonderful meal. Come Maggie.' Then he said to the Arab, 'I haven't asked what you were doing the night she was killed. Where did you go on Saturday night after you left Jimbo Rao's party?'

Mahmoud replied, 'Came here. When she died, I was asleep.'

'With Mo your only witness!'

The Arab nodded and only then said, 'You have hurt your hand.' As he had held out his own, CV had pulled away. The blood was still oozing through its rough bandage.

'A man ran into it.'

They locked eyes. Mahmoud's were troubled.

'Your umbrella sir,' said the waiter to CV.

'Umbrella? Oh yes, my umbrella.' It seemed a long time since Mr Solomon had lent it to him.

In the elevator he said to his cousin, 'Don't ask. I have to pull myself together. I'm a bit shaky.'

She looked at him tenderly and took his arm. 'It's all right. It's all right.'

He was disgusted to find he was near tears but they reached the basement without mishap. 'Do you mind waiting down here until I'm in control again?'

'What is it?' she asked. 'What happened? Tell me.'

'Later.'

'Now.'

'I don't think I can.'

She took his injured hand and pressed her own over the makeshift bandage, then untied and retied it. The bleeding had slowed but, within the graze, a large blood vessel had been punctured and she covered it with the handkerchief and pressed her thumb on it. 'Tell me,' she said, keeping the pressure on the wound. 'Tell me, so I can kill the person who did it.'

'Nothing like that. It's just . . .' and this time he put his head against the wall and wept. Her arms were around him and he felt her cheek against his shoulder. 'It's all right,' she kept saying.

Feeling foolish he told her he wept because of Ahmed's good looks and because of Mahmoud's plans for Emma. He showed her the picture. He wiped his eyes and laughed wryly. 'He says they're soul mates. No doubt about it they'll look spectacular at the wedding, if she'll just remember to hold her head up.'

'That rapist thinks your Emma is this gigolo's soul mate?' Maggie's slanting eyes flashed. She scowled at the picture. 'Oh my poor CV, what have we done to you? You really think this—this thing—is competition for you? For God's sake, he has blow-dried hair! Can you imagine Emma married to a man who blow-dries his hair every morning?'

His laugh had an edge in it. They clung to each other laughing. He held her away from him and said, 'Why doesn't your make-up run?'

'Because I'm wearing waterproof. Throw me into a swimming pool, and I'll come up perfect.'

They reached the parking lot arm in arm. Joseph was waiting.

'You get tired, and then you act crazy,' CV said. 'When he called them soul mates, you know what I did, Mag? I went upstairs and beat the shit out of Mo.'

'I've never known you to do something like that. Besides, he's bigger than you.'

'And stronger. And he had a knife. But I had anger—it gave me a short-distance advantage. I left him trussed like a Thanksgiving turkey. I told him I did it for Dorothy, but I did it for me, because I've lost Emma. If she marries Ahmed, she'll have the world. Sorry, Mag. I haven't even asked how you and Jeffrey fared.'

She said, 'Spare pickings but I got the *Anne of Green Gables* and the letter from Louise. Jeff was very quick. He could be a spy or a burglar.'

'Same thing. Mag, could you hold the rest till I get home? I want to speak to Frances Blue. When we meet Ali for tea—tell me then.'

'You trust Ali, don't you?'

'I like him. Do you trust Mahmoud?' he asked her.

'He has a kind of integrity. That kind of man keeps his word most of the time. If he killed someone, I think he'd pay to have it done. He wouldn't dirty his own fingers or suffer middle-class guilt afterwards. But he's a fool to think Emma is up for grabs. Are you all right?'

'Not entirely. I think I was poisoned this morning—or

nearly poisoned. I'll tell you about it later.'

'Poisoned?'

'Later.'

When they reached Frances' shop, he left Solomon's umbrella in the car.

Maggie said to him, 'Go in there and relax. Don't push it any more for today.'

In retrospect, he overdid that advice.

Frances Blue

Frances Blue's Life of the Party, a gift store on Thurston Road, had thrived because she had taste and a knack of putting objects together in a way that made you want to give them to friends. Her merchandise was a combination of the handicrafts of traditional Lankan artisans and experiments of the island's more eccentric ones.

The store had been a home and was set off from the street. Where there had once been garden frontage, there were several sidewalk stores with glass fronts. To reach her building, one had to walk down a brick path lined with decorated pillars and potted plants. The colourful pots on Michael's veranda had come from here. Others like them were stacked off the walkway. A multicoloured wooden door was opened by a smiling attendant in a pink shirt and orange sarong who greeted CV with palms pressed together.

'Please come in, sir,' he said. 'We have much to show you.'

CV asked for Frances Blue, but before the man could answer a corpulent woman in a flowery Kaftan separated herself from a group.

Frances had flaming hennaed hair frizzed around a face that exuded mischief. Michael had obviously not inherited his face or form from his mother, but his childlike smile beamed from her face. She approached in a mist of perfume with both hands outstretched. CV introduced himself and she squeezed his fingers. 'I'd have known you anywhere, my pet. I introduced your father to the pleasures of lovemaking, but I've heard it's too late to do the same for you. He was older than me, but I was the more experienced, of course.'

'Of course!' And he couldn't resist adding, 'Because you were born knowing about love.'

She gave a throaty chuckle. 'If he'd said that, I'd never have let him go, but he was a bit of a clumsy boy.'

Some foreigners had edged closer hoping to hear more about his father's clumsiness. She threw back her head and roared with laughter. 'Now, now, you naughty gossips, I'd better watch my tongue,' she said. 'Come with me, pet. You've come about Dorothy. Shantha told me to expect you.'

He followed the jiggling flowers on her hips into what he presumed would be an office but turned out to be a boudoir.

Frances asked him to close the door, and said, 'I feel like a nip, don't you?' He did.

Without asking what he wanted, she filled two tall glasses with ice and flooded them with a pink liquid from a jug, placed a chocolate in his mouth and the glass in his hand. She turned the key in the lock and returned to a long sofa covered with white cushions and patted the seat beside her. Amused and fascinated, he sat.

The store was a mass of colour, but here it was all white, brown and beige. She said, 'It's a lovely room, isn't it?

'I have never set out to change my environment to my taste, but when someone does it, I wonder why I don't. It is a lovely room.'

She covered his hand with her own, noticed the handkerchief around his injured hand, took his glass away and asked with honest concern, 'How did it happen?' She then leaned across him and placed her other hand on his crotch. He was reminded of Dorothy.

He told Frances the truth. 'I hit someone. I'm not proud of doing it. My hand has stopped bleeding now.'

'What did he do to deserve your anger?'

'A long time ago he raped a girl I knew... a girl you knew.'

The wound looked ugly. She turned his hand over and put his palm against her cheek then rose with a little difficulty from the deep seat and ambled off through an off-white curtain. She stuck her head around it and whispered, as gleefully as if she had found a diamond, 'I have absolutely everything you need, so we're in luck, pet. Usually I can't find a thing I want.' Her head disappeared. Whatever he had expected of Frances Blue, this was not it. Frances Blue was just an immense geisha girl.

She returned carrying a bowl of warm water, an open box containing the items she needed and a towel hanging over her arm, and placed the bowl in her lap. 'Soak that hand. For the oil to work the flesh must be warm. And talking about flesh, your shoulders and other bits and pieces are lovely. Dorothy told me about you, but not the half of it. She made you sound older—called you *mature*. So you hit a man who raped her! She'd have liked that.'

CV felt a bit foolish with his hand in this exuberant woman's lap although there was a ceramic bowl of warm water between it and her body.

He reached his other hand for his pink drink and commented, 'An outrageous colour. What is it?'

'A version of the strawberry daiquiri,' Frances said coyly. 'I call it pink fizz. The colour is for fun. The kick comes from white rum.'

She then placed a hand on his thigh and massaged it absentmindedly running her fingers along the muscle through the fabric of his pants. When she removed her hand, she took his from the warm water, and leaning across him again, placed the bowl on the table and began to pat his hand dry. Pouring oil into her palms, she began to massage it, not touching the raw patch.

Finally she poured oil directly from the bottle onto the raw area, expertly bandaged the hand and secured it with a pink safety pin.

'You won't believe it, but that hand will be almost healed by tomorrow.'

'I don't know how to thank you. It feels much better already; it was getting stiff.' He put the fingers of his bandaged hand out and touched her cheek. 'You're a very nice woman, Frances. I wasn't expecting that.'

'Am I nice enough to love for a few minutes?'

So that was why she'd locked the door!

'I'd like that. How much time do we have?'

A giggle, 'I'll need seven to ten minutes—you can have all you want.'

'Let's try for a record, Madame Geisha.'

Neither of them took off their clothes but somehow it didn't matter, and they laughed until their pleasure became too strong for laughter. At some point she said, 'You smell wonderful.' When he felt her convulsing under his body he let himself into his own orgasm, then held her close for a few minutes. At last he said softly, 'Madame Geisha, I have work to do and must go.'

She hooted, 'We came! You go! I stay!'

He kissed her.

As they began to pull their clothing straight, he said, 'Lucky Dad to have had his first time with you. My first was clumsy.'

She kissed him on the cheek. 'Why are you so young?'

He again kissed her lips. 'I know you've been the right woman at the right time for other men, Frances. Thank you for including me in that number because I needed you today, though I didn't know it when I walked through your door.'

'Silly boy. Now must I remind you that you came here to ask me some questions?'

He'd forgotten why he'd come to see her! So much for the cool-cat exit.

'I was about to walk out into the sunset with my head held high. I'd have had to turn around and come slinking back. Dorothy Bell! Tell me about her.'

Frances said, 'She was a nice girl. Yes, Dorothy was a very nice girl.'

'It's the first time I've heard her called *nice*. No other take on her? No guesses who killed her and why?'

'What good are guesses? She was a high-flying bird who got caught in the telegraph lines one night. You see them hanging there electrocuted, ugly in death. They were brightening the sky only yesterday. When Dorothy came into my shop, it was like turning a light on. Then, one day I saw her staring with blind eyes from the front page of the *Island*. Overnight she had become a blonde tourist with her mouth hanging open.'

'What was her downside?'

'That her happiness was always tainted because she expected her father to steal it away. In the end he did.'

'You think he killed her?'

'Or someone killed her for him. I loved her like a daughter, and she should have been my daughter.'

'If Reggie didn't kill her, who then?'

'Someone she turned her back on. She came to see me the weekend before she died, and we talked about Michael and herself, and we wept together.'

'Can you tell me what you talked about? What she said. What you said.'

'Help yourself to another drink and tot up my glass, pet. Another chocolate?' She was not touching him now. She sat with the kaftan barely covering her smooth plump knees looking frumpy, and he felt great affection for her. 'Michael won't tell you, so I must. If anyone speaks, it has to be me.'

He leaned back on the sofa and stretched his legs before him, saw his bloodstained blue handkerchief on the table and was about to put it in his pocket when Frances said, 'May I keep it? It has your initials on it.'

'A bloodstained blue handkerchief. What a gift for a lady! You make every moment special.'

'Oh, my dear.'

A moment ago they had had sex together—and there had been a kind of love—but now that part of what had driven him to want to hold this woman had been satisfied, and he knew it would not return. He understood why she wanted his handkerchief: there are few times between men and women when sex is right and perfect with no need of an encore. They had been lucky to have had such a time.

Frances was saying sadly, 'Now drink your pink fizz and I'll tell you what you don't know about Dorothy and Michael.'

The previous year when Michael had flown to England as a guest of Reginald Bell, they had spent the first two days sightseeing. In this environment Michael saw another side of the Englishman. His excellent memory made him a superior guide. He told Michael the history-book details that mean little until you are confronted with the visual reality of the past.

Bell also left him alone when he wanted to paint. In parks and squares Michael sketched the Londoners. He felt guilty that he was enjoying the company of the man who had caused Dorothy so much misery. He longed for her to arrive. On the third day, Bell told Michael they should have a talk. Michael expected a look-after-my-daughter lecture, after which he would let Reggie know that his incestuous relationship with Dorothy was not a secret. But Reggie had not wanted to speak of Dorothy. Instead, he took Michael for a walk through Hyde Park to talk about Frances.

'You see, Clive,' she said now, 'years ago I had an affair with Reggie. I thought I loved him. He thought he loved me. He was twenty-two. I was a teenager. He had plans for the future. I was dazzled, I got pregnant. Reggie was not pleased at first, but the same day began to rather like the idea of having a child. He said, "We'll get married." I was happy. That lasted about a week.

'Right away he began to think I'd bring him down. He'd say, "When we're in London, you won't be able to do that." I had to change because he would one day be mixing with couth people. I was full of myself and boys liked me and now this. This Englishman was telling me I'd have to wear suits and walk like this and talk like that—as if I was a pick-up. I took it for a while, then told him I didn't want him whining at me for the rest of my life.'

CV interrupted, 'They even look alike. I thought that the first time I saw Reggie. Of course! Michael is his son!'

'Yes,' said Frances. 'Yes, yes, yes, but that made Dorothy his half-sister.'

'Michael never guessed?'

'No. I never told him even after he met Dorothy. I wanted them to marry. But that day in London Reggie betrayed us all. He told Michael he was his father.'

'What did you ever see in Bell? He's an icicle.'

Frances looked into her drink as if it had the answers. 'I like danger. There was always something dangerous about him. He'd look at me with those eyes and I'd get a chill. He was beginning to make money and he was generous. He sent the cash to buy this property and then more to support myself and Michael for two years. He asked only that I never tell anyone who Michael's father was. I didn't want my child to have a reluctant father. So when Michael grew old enough to ask, I told him I had loved a man once but hadn't wanted to spend my life with him.'

'And he had no curiosity?'

'Not much.' She sipped her drink. 'He's not like other boy. He's content not knowing things. Reggie and I stayed in touch, you know. Even before Dorothy decided to live here, when he was in the island on business, he'd drop in, but I never let him see

Michael. Our law here gives the children to the father. Michael was all I had.'

'You must have been the love of Reggie's life. He's described as cold in his relationships with women, yet he kept coming back to you.'

'He didn't come because he loved me,' she shrugged ruefully. 'I hoped that at first. He came out of boredom. He has few friends here. I invited him to dinner twice before I realized he wasn't inviting me anywhere. After that it was just, "Hello, Reg, how's the wife and kid?" or, "Got a girlfriend yet?"'

'And his answer to those questions?'

'My, you're tenacious! He was non-committal.'

'Bell told Michael about his parentage—then what?' How differently Bell had explained that time in England!

Michael tried to get his mother on the phone to confirm Bell's story, but she was out of Colombo. A paternity test confirmed Reggie had spoken the truth. By now Dorothy had returned, and the sparks flew. She'd shouted, 'You can't claim Michael to bring me back. I grew up. I flew away.'

Later, she told Frances, Reggie had said when they were alone, 'You've become a bitch. You're standing in the way of my relationship with my son. Only because he wants you around do I put up with you.'

CV told Frances, 'My God, he's strange.'

On the plane to Sri Lanka, Michael and Dorothy decided not to part, but there had been much weeping until they got used to the situation.

'I told them, "You may not be able to have a church wedding, but I can find someone to marry you two. The problem is if Reggie talks there'll be a stigma on the children." I've never known Michael so angry. He loves children, and the idea of his father cutting that option from him hurt.'

When Dorothy went to India and was sterilized both Frances and Michael were appalled. She came back and said to them, 'I have put an end to the conversation.'

But now she was obsessed with getting even.

'Sometimes she would say that she and Michael had become closer than ever,' Frances told CV. 'At other times she said, something bad had happened that could never be undone.'

CV didn't know how much Emma had known of this. He asked Frances if he could tell her.

'Tell everyone.'

'Did you know about Mahmoud Mahmoud?' he asked.

'The man in the hotel? Michael told me that he was worried because Dor was doing stupid things for money. She wanted to be richer than Reggie so she could ruin him. She was also buying and selling too fast. But Michael thought she would calm down when she saw no one was chasing her, and she was beginning to.'

Frances did not know about Padmani's Blood or a blue sapphire. 'We never discussed money.'

'What then?'

'Men, of course,' and she laughed happily.

She unlocked the door and saw him out. She whispered, 'Don't tell your father he was a bit of a disappointment,' lifted her face up and he kissed her cheek. 'Because he was a quick-come, it doesn't mean he isn't a wonderful father.'

He shook his head. 'You are impossible! Wish me luck in finding Dorothy's killer,' he said.

'I do, my pet, of course I do.'

Ahmed

On his way home the sense of an afternoon enjoyed disappeared, and he cursed himself for what had happened with Frances. He realized he had promised to meet Ali Sharif at the house for tea and hadn't even called to say he'd be late.

He entered a house full of laughter, followed the sound and found Aunt Maud, Maggie, Emma and Ali in the drawing room. As he entered the laughter stopped.

'I see I've spoilt the fun,' he snapped.

'Not for a minute,' Maggie snapped back. 'We had tea without you. Some of us here did, however, worry that you had become the latest victim. Silly us.'

'All right. I'm sorry I fucked up. I'm a prime asshole.' He attempted a smile and went over to kiss his aunt. 'Apologies for being late, Auntie. Not a good day at the office.'

'We were so worried. You look terrible, darling boy,' she patted his cheek. 'Ali is staying for dinner, so why don't you lie down for a bit. I'll wake you.'

While he had been selfishly entertaining himself, they had been worrying about him. Made him feel just great.

Emma was curled in one corner of the sofa with Maggie's long feet on her lap. Her face was her own again, and she wore the blue dress which had become so charmingly transparent in the rain on Saturday. Now it was crisp and opaque and, as usual, she looked scrubbed. Ali, in a white knee-length kurta over loose white plants was also clean as a pin. Maggie and his aunt were also in white. He knew he looked dirty.

Ali said, 'Auntie is right. Get some sleep now. I have to take you out with me tonight, and you don't look as if you'll make it. I can't postpone this. Tomorrow'll be too late.'

'Too late for what?'

'To hear a story worth hearing,' Ali seemed pleased with himself.

'He won't tell us who you're to see or even where he's taking you,' said Maggie. 'Has some trouble understanding sexual equality and team spirit.'

He was too tired to guess what Ali could have come up with. 'My night is yours,' he eventually said. 'But I'm rummy, I'll have to nap first.'

But he didn't move. He just stared at his aunt in the low armchair she preferred as she threaded beads into a chain. What he wanted to do was look at Emma and couldn't.

'CV, are you all right?' Ali asked.

'What?' he jumped. 'It's—it's been that kind of day—too much at once.'

He finally glanced at her. He had felt her eyes on him, but she had not spoken, and he had not greeted her. Maggie was quick to fill the awkward moment. 'Will you go upstairs!'

He again said, 'It's been that kind of day.'

'Frances does that to you,' said Maud not missing a thing. 'She's a strange one.'

'But she was frank, and I'm more confused than ever.'

What the hell had he been thinking of when he had made love to her? Not her fault that she had sensed he'd been willing. What if the story got around Colombo? He wanted to ask Emma's forgiveness, but what he needed was a confessional not a test of the understanding of a woman. He didn't need a shrink to analyse his behaviour; he knew his anger at Mahmoud had been vented on Mo, and because that encounter had brought no release, it had developed into an anger at Emma because she was going to be faced with an offer she would be foolish to refuse. So he had reached for the nearest willing woman to punish Emma for her possible infidelity.

All this went through his mind in a blink, but he still could not force himself to speak to her or move. He wondered if Maggie had guessed what had happened because she came to him and picked up his injured hand. 'Whew, you've been sprayed with something expensive. Givenchy? And a new bandage on the warrior's hand! He's run into loving ministrations!'

He said, 'I sat on Frances lap so she could dress my wound.'

'What happened to your hand?' asked Emma, unable to keep silent any longer.

'Ran into something,' he replied. 'It's nothing much, but I like making a fuss.'

She followed him to the stairs, 'You're *not* all right,' she whispered. 'Everything's wrong. Did I do something to make you angry?'

'You? No,' he said too curtly. 'I made a fool of myself and am too tired to know how to undo it.'

'But we all make fools of ourselves. That doesn't explain why you aren't talking to *me*.'

'What we're doing now is called talking.' He smiled and her dimple responded.

'Go on, then. Go sleep it off. You're the one we're all leaning on. You've got the right to be nasty sometimes.'

Upstairs he looked in the mirror. His thinning hair was standing on end, his face was red and his clothes a mess. There was blood on his shirt and pants. His eyes were missing the energy he was accustomed to seeing there. The man in the mirror was too tired even to shower. He turned on the fan, flung himself on the bed and lay on his back with his head on the cool pillows. With his eyes closed he felt a little better. Then he heard someone enter the room, thought it was his aunt and smiled. He opened his eyes, saw Emma and shut them again.

'It's you!'

'Yes, Maggie told me about you getting poisoned and about Ahmed, Mahmoud's son, so before you fall asleep I wanted to see the picture of him. If he's to be my future husband, I should know what he looks like.'

He didn't answer, and she continued, 'Maggie says Mahmoud gave you a snap for me and that his son is rich and handsome.'

'It's in my wallet.'

'And where is that?'

'It's on the dressing table, for God's sake.'

She brought the wallet to the bed and through half-closed eyes he watched the long eyelashes veil her thoughts as she searched its compartments. She found the picture and studied it. 'Maggie's right. Ahmed is very handsome. Don't you think so?'

'Adorable. And rich. Kind too. He is ready to publish your

book and fund any charities you favour. It will be a marriage made in heaven. Mahmoud says you are soul mates.'

She was pressing her lips together. 'Della is looking for a man, so perhaps she would like him? I wouldn't be comfortable with that hair.'

He said, 'So Maggie's been working on you?'

'Working?'

'His blow-dried hair.'

'No, actually, she didn't mention it. How do you feel about blow-dried hair?'

'I feel you should take your fucking Arab, marry him and tell him you want his hair some other way. I don't want to talk about him. I want to sleep.'

'Goodness, you're grumpy when you're tired. Do you mind if I lie down?'

She didn't wait for an answer but stretched out with her back to him. He put his arms around her and said into her hair, 'I'm sorry.'

'Sorry enough to wash Frances' scent off you?'

He turned her on to her back and looked into her eyes, which were gentle. 'I've done a number of things today that in retrospect were not wise, but it was because of you. You torture me. For making me suffer, can't you put up with some very pleasant perfume for a few minutes?'

'Only if you promise you won't come down smelling of it—of her. I've missed you today while you've been crashing around. I'll lie here until you fall asleep.'

He turned on his side and held her gently. Before he drifted off he heard her say, 'I wish I knew how to seduce a man.'

'Oh, you do!' he murmured. 'But don't seduce me now, sweetheart. I'm so fucking tired.'

When he woke he looked at his watch. More than an hour had passed. Emma was sitting at his desk typing on her computer. He wanted to go to her but decided to take a much-needed shower first. When he came out, she and the computer were gone, so he followed them downstairs.

Evening Update
Maud's Story
What he would have liked to do was to get back into bed and sleep to sogginess. What he had to do was go downstairs and give the appearance of being in charge. He'd at least washed off Frances' perfume, or so he hoped, but the shirt he tossed into the laundry basket reeked of it.

'Ali is still being secretive about where you're going,' Maggie said raising her voice. 'I've offered him my body if he'll share the secret. It has been rejected.'

CV said, 'I'm sorry to hear it, Mag. That must be a first.'

Ali had moved to a chair near them. He said, 'We should leave the house at eleven. But first, Miss vander Marten, Maggie and Emma want to unload what they've learned today.'

'Let's start that now. Anything new, Auntie Maud?'

'Not about Dorothy. But a lot about Ali. I've been asking my friends about him—because what did we know after all except what he told us?' She spoke as if he were not there.

Ali's genial manner changed.

'You checked him out, Aunt Maud?' Maggie said quickly. 'Why didn't I think of that?'

Ali did not laugh. CV had no intention of stopping his aunt from telling her story, but it was awkward now that the happy mood had gone so abruptly.

'My friend Gertie knows the Perella family,' Aunt Maud continued blithely. 'Ali married Rose Perella when he was twenty-three. She was one of the perilly Perellas from Bandarawella; they can't seem to make it past thirty without going to pieces. Jay Perella used to breed scorpions and West Highland terriers. His wife was a Claudine vander Smagt, which is how I know about him. One of the lawyer Perellas died of syphilis during the war because he wouldn't take penicillin and his offspring were the worse for it. Gertie says Rose went mad suddenly, like her Aunt Gloria, who hung a cat when she was a girl, and also her cousin Tom. Tom was normal and then suddenly there he was dressed in Muscovy duck feathers chasing the cook around the kitchen with a bread knife. Rose killed their baby when Ali was in Europe. He put her in a home for people like herself in Switzerland. As long as she's there, she doesn't have to stand trial.' She turned her attention to her ginger beer.

Ali's black eyes were steely. He looked at the glass in his hand as if with distaste. Maggie did nothing, but Emma, who was sitting on the floor showed no awkwardness whatever about the revelation.

'What a sad story!' she said, and her eyes were flooded with tears. 'Poor Ali and even poorer Rose. Imagine how she feels.'

CV said, 'Jesus, Emma, give the guy a break!'

'What? Oh, *yes*, I'm so *sorry*, Ali,' she was twisting her hands and added, 'Murder and bombs have become such ordinary things that I think I'm going crazy. I was horrible to say that. It must have been much worse for you—much worse.'

Ali looked at her distracted. Then he smiled at her, and she smiled back.

Maud continued, 'It's much better to know what people say than to pretend they're not saying anything. Ali, we've only just met you, and you know how some Burghers are about Muslims.'

'Aunt Maud, what else did you find out about Ali?' asked Maggie. Then she reached out for her glass, and CV for the first time noticed she was wearing a gold bracelet patterned with flowers with petals of red and white stones.

She saw him looking at it and waved her arm, 'Ali gave it to me today—rubies and diamonds. Do you like it?'

'Of course,' he replied cautiously.

Now there was a different awkwardness. She looked at her

bracelet, and Ali looked at her. CV looked from one to the other.

His aunt said, 'Ali, you mustn't give expensive jewellery to someone you've just met.' Then she thought it over and added, 'Or underclothes.'

Maggie hooted, and Ali laughed wide at last. 'But I haven't just met your niece, Auntie. I've been living with her for five years. By the way, how do Burghers feel about Muslims?'

'That they're not like us. In my first *A Is for Apple* book, it said, "T is Tamby, not to be trusted." Yes, it did.' Tamby is a derogatory local term for Muslim. Ali and Maggie began to laugh helplessly.

'And that's it on Ali the Infidel?' asked CV frowning at his aunt, but Maud couldn't be silenced.

'A little more. Gertie says since his divorce he's been a love-em and leave-em man.'

'He leaves them!' Maggie groaned.

Emma put her hand in front of her mouth and giggled.

Ali shook his head in amused disbelief. 'Gertie is wrong.'

CV couldn't resist, 'Rumour has it that there was one Desireé Johnson.'

'Desireé Johnson! She was in college with me. That was before I met Rose. Where did you hear about Desireé?'

'Della, my friend in Chicago, gave out an Internet alert on everyone connected with Dorothy, including you. Next thing she had Desireé on line saying you play polo and she wants another chukka.'

'A gentleman should always oblige a lady,' said Maggie.

'No, I am not going to chukka with Desireé, Miss vander Marten, because I am currently pursuing, as you may be aware, another woman. And, Auntie, if you have anything else to share about me, it should be now. I don't think I could stand more of my Tamby life in dribs and drabs.'

The old lady looked at him seriously over her glasses. 'I know you must feel I've been poking around behind your back. I know you aren't a murderer, but Maggie is very dear to me and has no father here to make inquiries on her behalf. I also heard lots of lovely things about you—how kind you have been in building a home for refugee children and how you look after everyone in your family and pay for Rose's hospital even though you're divorced.'

'What home for refugee children?' asked Maggie and Emma together.

'It's a very small contribution. The Tigers turned the Muslims out of Jaffna—gave them a few hours to get out with no belongings except a change of clothes. Many lost their lives and mosques were blown up. Those who could came south, and those of us who can have helped. My family runs a part-home part-school on property we were neglecting. Orphans are cared for, and we try to get them adopted into Muslim families—here and abroad.'

'And I'm so useless! While I've been writing rubbish, you've been doing all that!' Emma wailed. 'Can your school use someone like me? I could teach English or history.'

'The next time I go there, why don't you come with me?'

She said, 'Oh, I'd love it. I really would.'

'Now that we have no choice but to accept Ali into our fold,' CV said, 'let's move on. What other stones, no pun intended, were turned today?'

Emma's Story
Emma had a folder beside her that she now opened. 'A talk with Della this afternoon was worth it, and my friend Queenie de Soyza has something.'

'What did Della have to say?'

'She asked me to tell you that Helen has flu and is on sick leave, but Della sent the earlier report by fax—it's in a plastic bag in your room. The scariest news is that Peter Yarrow found his father's address book, and it had a Louise Lawrence in it. Charles Yarrow drew a line through *Lawrence* and put in *Hammer* and a new phone number. Louise is alive, married and has two children. Della phoned Louise too, but she was grumpy because she woke her up. She said she didn't know Dor had been looking for her, and she was sad to hear she died.'

'She hasn't seen Dorothy as an adult?'

'She saw her outside Reggie's flat last year. They couldn't talk much as Dor had an appointment. I think it's peculiar that Louise was cross when Della woke her. If someone woke me with news of a friend I hadn't heard of for a while, I wouldn't have been.'

'No one would,' Ali said.

'Which means?'

'Which means Louise is lying,' Maggie said. 'Dorothy looks for Louise, treasures her only letter from Louise, saves money for Louise, calls herself Louise and plans to set up a trust for Louise. Then, she met Louise and brushed her off because she had another appointment? Why is Louise lying?'

'Perhaps it wasn't a happy meeting. But would she then come to Sri Lanka and kill Dorothy?' CV asked.

'She didn't. Della accused her of killing Dorothy. That did it. She came to life and produced an alibi.'

Dinner was ready, and they were on their way to the dining room when Emma stopped them in the hall. 'I nearly forgot,' she said, 'Queenie, who is a girl who hangs out at Michael's, says Dorothy was like a circus performer who throws knives. She had that skinny knife I told you about. She once kept throwing it at a tree at Michael's and never missed. Then, Queenie tried and the knife went backwards and nearly hit Michael. She tried again and missed the tree. Dor stuck a temple flower in the bark and said, "I'll bet you a hundred rupees I can hit that flower." Queenie said, "I'll bet you a thousand you can't if you take five steps backwards first." And Dor did and hit the flower dead centre. She used such great force that she had to shake the knife loose.'

'Well, Dorothy didn't throw a knife into her own back,' said CV.

'It's getting overwhelming,' said Maud.

They were standing in a circle in the hall and heard a screech from the dining room. Amily appeared with a ladle in one hand and a towel in the other.

Maggie stuck out her tongue at her. 'What a grump you're becoming.'

'You don't have to cook for people who don't eat.'

Maud took Ali's arm. 'You must sit beside me because you've been such a sport.'

Inside they discovered why Amily had been upset by their dawdling. In honour of their guest the table had been laid with the finest china, glassware, silver and white damask table linen. The napkins had been folded into open lotuses.

Maggie said, 'You can be as grumpy as you like, Amily, this is the most beautiful table I have seen.'

But CV's thoughts were still with that knife. 'Did Dor tell Queenie who taught her to throw it?'

'No. But when Dor was killed, Queenie wondered if someone used her own knife to kill her.'

'Did she tell the police?'

'She was going to one of these days if they didn't bring it up themselves.'

Maggie's Story
All the time Maggie had been looking at the bracelet on her arm as if it was a bandage, but when she caught Ali's eyes her face always softened.

'It's your turn,' CV said to distract her. 'Recount your idle day, Mag.'

She started, 'After you left, I had a phone call from Julia's father. He wanted to know if they should come this week and have her cremated. I said she would want to be remembered as she was—she hadn't chosen one life over the other, she lived both. So next week we're going to do it and send the ashes back to them, and they will have a lovely funeral there. She'll have twice as many prayers. If anyone feels I did wrong, there's time to undo it.'

Ali said, 'Yes, undo it. Loneliness is worse than horror. Looking at a burnt corpse won't cause someone to kill himself but loneliness will. They'll be less lonely here than in Duluth.' Of them all, only he had lost a child.

'I'll phone after dinner,' Maggie said. 'I'll tell them we must have them—we want them.'

'That's what they need to hear.'

Maggie continued, 'After buying clothes for the kids, the rest of my morning was spent raiding Reggie's room with Jeffrey. Perera got the staff off that floor, and when I went up, Jeff was already inside. You were right, CV. She thought nothing of putting down a thousand or more dollars for a dress or a suit. She also had garments that must have cost fifty rupees.'

'We'd get those in Wellawatte,' said Emma. 'They were her favourites.'

'I stole six of her books for you. If he notices, he'll think the roomcleaner took them for her kids. Louise's letter is still in the *Anne of Green Gables*. Saw the diaphragm—she probably just hadn't got around to throwing it away. Reggie doesn't leave his personal stuff around. Nothing in his pockets. I think he must use a safe or keep his treasures in the car.'

'No knife?'

'No knife. No passport. No address book. Then I joined you and Mahmoud in the dining room, and Jeffrey went home. He's going to lend me a purdah outfit to impress Ali's parents so they'll think, "What a nice woman he's picked up this time, not like that bitch Desireé who was always sitting on a horse." When you were upstairs, Mahmoud invited me to dinner any day I was free but put no hand on my knee. Not on my thigh either. He offered me no cash for favours. No pretty things. No trips to Lalaland.'

'Why doesn't he want *you* to marry his son?' said Emma. 'You're so beautiful and smart.'

'Only an idiot would want me to marry his son,' she said suddenly harsh.

Ali caught CV's eye and frowned.

'Are you through with feeling sorry for yourself, Mag?' her cousin asked.

'I am. I came home and went to sleep.' But some thought had upset her.

'I had better tell you about my own lunch with Bell,' Ali said quickly as if to calm her down. 'It was not entirely fruitless because he bought a pink sapphire. He did not admit to killing his daughter. He did not speak of her once except to say he didn't think you'd find her killer. I loyally said nor did I.'

'Did he speak of me?' asked Maggie.

Their eyes locked, 'He tried to.'

CV's Story

'And so to me?' asked CV quickly. 'Bad day and good day. Too much happened too quickly. I can't remember getting this close to the edge since Mummy threw away my teddy bear that time she found a rat had produced babies in it.'

'You cried for hours,' his aunt recalled.

He then told them about his meeting with Bell and his sudden fear that the Englishman might have planted someone outside the hotel to identify him for later assassination.

'You may have saved your life,' said his aunt.

'I do wonder. Perera helped me get out of the hotel without

leaving my chagrin all over the lobby. Then I realized I was really ill . . .' He told them about his suspicions that Bell had poisoned him.

Aunt Maud said briskly, 'Tell us about your lunch with the Arabian millionaire.'

'First there was Mr Solomon of Second Cross Street.'

He showed them the drawings of the two men and the ring. Only Ali showed more interest in the ring than the men. 'I've never seen this ring,' he said. 'Not in a collection, not on a finger. Is that a stone set into it? The small oval?'

'He thought it was a dark stone. He says he has the proportion exact.'

Ali explained, 'The ring is so awkward that it must have been designed by an amateur. Even mass-produced rings are better designed than this. I'll need a copy of the drawing. Someone in our business might recognize it.'

Emma began to put the sketches into her folder. 'I'll make copies for everyone.'

But Ali said, 'May I? I want to show the drawing to a friend tonight. I'll have copies ready by tomorrow morning.'

'The fat guy could be Bundy,' said CV, and Emma nodded. 'But the only ring I've seen on him is a wedding ring, though the other night he wasn't wearing it. To go on with my sad tale, even after I left Solomon, I didn't feel a hundred per cent.

'I crawled away with my tail between my legs and decided to visit Frances Blue, whose perfume knocked you all out. She came up with the story of all stories,' and he told them about Reginald Bell being Michael's father.

There was a long and appalled silence until Emma said, 'No wonder she cried so much after she came back from England. She never told me. How strong she was.'

'Poor Frances too! A son but no grandchildren. What a pity she doesn't like me. I should go over, but she'll probably shut the door in my face,' said his aunt.

'She's harmless,' CV told her. 'Do go, Auntie.'

Maggie said, 'We think of Reggie as the monster, but what about Dorothy's mother? What a pair! And what about me? I called Dor a tart.'

'She could have been one,' said Ali. 'That doesn't make her tragedy less.'

'Mahmoud showed no compassion for Dorothy,' CV told him.

He was thinking about Dorothy's options and wished that she had taken advantage of her friends more. He did not tell them Michael had sometimes joined her in Mahmoud's suite.

He said, 'But what does Reggie being Michael's father have to do with Dorothy's death?'

'Or Julia's?' asked Ali.

Aunt Maud said, 'When something doesn't make sense to me it's usually because I've believed a whopper.'

The Drive with Ali

As CV and Ali left Colombo, a million stars shone from the ink blue of space. There was the buzz of night creatures, the scent of flowers that bloom only at night. Three flying foxes crossed the sky. A less fortunate companion's twisted body hung from a power line.

'There's Dorothy,' said CV pointing and repeated how Frances had described her vitality and grace in life so abruptly converted into grotesque stillness.

'I've not met Frances Blue. Does she live up to her reputation?'

'I wasn't expecting to like her, but I did. That was a shocking story about the relationship between Dorothy and Michael.'

'Shocking, but it's hardly new for siblings to be romantically drawn to each other.'

CV's thoughts moved to Louise, to whom Dorothy had

been so ferociously devoted and who had been attending to her own life without bothering to find out what had happened to her tormented charge. 'We should find out more about Louise. Teddy's the one to do it.'

'Perhaps she should be on Emma's list of suspects, which did not, did you notice, mention the second murder.'

'She's blocking on that.'

'Then let her block. When my child died, I needed to block.'

'A terrible time for you.'

'Oh yes.'

They were in Borella, a cluttered business section with an ugly metal overpass, but an area that CV was fond of because it had changed little since his childhood. The air conditioning in the car made him sleepy. Ali said, 'We could sing Christmas carols to keep you awake. That's an Islamic joke.'

'Don't laugh at the one true way, Mr Muslim. When you go to heaven you'll need my recommendation to get in.'

'Time for serious talk. We're going to meet a businessman who lives in Singapore and is coming into Colombo tonight just to meet you. His name is Li Chen Wee and is a friend of my father. Uncle—I call him Uncle—knew Dorothy. He hadn't heard of her death. I broke the news yesterday. His plane comes in about midnight, so we're going to wait for him at the Carlton Ran.' The Carlton was a hotel about a mile south of the airport.

'Mr Li leaves Lanka early tomorrow morning. I have promised that you will use what he tells you with discretion, that is, not involve him. As far as Uncle's concerned, a young woman he thought of as one of his family has died, and he will only talk to you because he wants to find out who did it.'

'You're talking in riddles. He considered her one of his family?'

'Yes, and Uncle says Dorothy was alive after eleven the night she was killed.'

'Was he the man she went to meet at the Oberoi?'

Jeanne Cambrai

'No. They met in the Fort.'

'She seems to have been living a dozen lives.'

'Which has always been the problem,' said Ali. 'She was a smart girl but did not understand her limitations. If any of us had sensed she was in danger, we could have saved her. Uncle is not surprised at all that she was killed. He's angry. He described her as, "A little girl so addicted to living dangerously that those who loved her didn't hear her last cries." I too didn't hear her cries. I was deaf and I was blind.'

'You trust this Li?'

'My father does. I have no reason not to. I don't know Uncle well, but his reputation as a businessman is impeccable. His family is much like my own. They have been in the gem business for generations, and some members are active, while others prefer to live off their inheritance. He has his black sheep, but none with a reputation for killing women, he says.'

His expression changed to a frown. 'When your aunt came out with the story of Rose, my own black sheep, I felt helpless. Did you have any idea how angry I was?'

'Perhaps, but Aunt Maud is without malice, and now she's old she no longer bothers with tact—actually she was never very tactful. She thinks nothing of revealing our own family weaknesses to strangers. Actually, she spoke out of foresight. She told Maggie what you would have had to tell her sooner or later.'

'We don't like to know we're gossiped about.'

'No.'

Ali eventually said, 'This week I fell in love and got enmeshed in two murders because my girl has a cousin she says she would give her life for and wants to help him solve the crimes.'

'Tell her cousin more about Mr Li.'

'We talk gems when we meet. Today there are many of us with old hands in the game but many more newcomers—some only with greed.'

306

'If Dorothy didn't go to the Oberoi, Michael made that story up.'

'I don't know.'

'And Li doesn't want it known that he saw her. Where does that leave me?'

'With a problem.' Ali said. 'He says she was boisterously alive when he left her and she was not alone. When you talk with him, you will understand how deeply he is mourning her. Only because my father and I both begged has he agreed to let you question him. I am afraid I must have your assurance that his name will not be passed to Superintendent Senaratne—or Mr Bell. You may tell Maggie.'

'Even if what he says enables me to tie up the investigation? How do I tell Bell and Teddy, "Here's your killer, but I can't tell you how I know?"'

Ali did not answer.

'Well, you've got your promise.' He knew, as did Ali, he would have to accept Li's terms.

They were at the hotel, and the turn to the airport was ahead. Ali left his car at the front door and gave the keys to the doorman. Inside he wrote a message at the front desk for Mr Li Chen Wee to tell him that Ali Sharif had arrived.

The bar was off the dining room. They ordered beer.

'Perhaps I should tell you more about Uncle,' Ali said. 'Until the night Dorothy died, he owned Padmani's Blood. He's owned it for thirty years. He bought it from a Hong Kong Chinese who felt the curse was bringing him bad luck. Uncle is not superstitious about the stone, but once he had it his wife began to blame every misfortune on it. So he told her he had sold it but put it in his safe. He thought he would give it to one of his grandchildren, if there was one who would be able to dismiss future misfortune as accidents that happen to everyone.

'When Dorothy asked me to help her find Padmani, my father phoned every friend in the business and that included

Uncle. Only when my father told Li the name of the woman who wanted to buy it—Dorothy Bell—did he admit he had it.'

CV said, 'You're not making this up?'

'I'm not. My father told me that he had found the owner of Padmani's Blood, and he was willing to negotiate with Dorothy. It put me in a dilemma because I have always felt that if the stone was found, it should be returned to Sri Lanka.

'When I told her we had found the owner, I did not divulge his name. I just said someone would contact her, as Uncle had asked. She called up three days later and told me arrangements were being made for her to speak to the owner. She was charming and apologized for doing something I didn't approve of. She even came up to Kandy and we went out and had a few drinks together and . . . if you knew Dorothy, you'd understand why the evening turned into three delightful but exhausting days.'

'And she bought the stone from your Chinese Uncle?'

Ali put his hand up and said, 'No more! Uncle must tell you the story himself. I knew that the sale had gone through because my father told me it had. Two months ago Dorothy and Uncle both asked me to act as a negotiator and to be present when the stone was to change hands again. I refused. I've had much bad luck without Padmani's Blood. If I had had anything to do with the stone, sooner or later Padmani would have been accused of bringing on my wife's madness and my daughter's death. I didn't want that kind of superstition hounding me in the future.'

CV didn't believe in curses. He believed that when millions of dollars were at stake, there were people who would murder to get it.

Li Chen Wee

Li Chen Wee did not fulfil CV's expectations of a Chinese businessman. He bounded into the bar with a night-owl hoot and a cowboy confidence. His iron-grey hair was tousled, and his white suit was crumpled. Under it he wore a conspicuously bright black, blue and white striped shirt. CV had not been expecting him in a Mao jacket but someone shorter, thinner and more modest of manner.

Li was about sixty, five feet eleven inches and overweight. Later, CV would realize that it was only his personality that was mercurial. His face was identical to the reclining Galvihara Buddha at Polonnaruwa. The stone Buddha had a face that could transfix you with its spiritual intensity, and Li's full, curved lips, straight nose and mystic lidless eyes could appear as profound. When on the go, as now, there was nothing of the mystic about him.

He dropped a white plastic carrier bag on to a table and bellowed in a sonorous English public school voice, 'Ali! What a handsome bugger you have become, you old rascal. Come and give your uncle a hug.'

Ali was enveloped and kissed on both cheeks. He put his arms around the older man, pulled away, then chuckled when Li grabbed him for another bear hug. 'Kissing a man with a beard is a delightful novelty to us Chinese,' Li declared. 'But, my dear boy, you were more handsome without. Only a wispy chin should be covered.'

He turned on CV, who became aware that the fingers that grasped his were strong and smooth, 'Ah, vander Marten! I am delighted to meet you because I hear you have found a woman for this lonely fellow and are moving those lazy Lankans into the computer age.'

CV replied, 'No way—they are already there. And as for Maggie, I can't even take credit for that. But I'm enjoying seeing the two moths caught in each other's flame.'

'A poet!' Li's laugh resounded, 'I am here to talk of death with a poet? Ali insists I tell you my secrets and has promised you will forget where you heard them. But first the presentations! We Chinese must give humbly on arrival, and as I had time at the airport, I bought my miserable offerings there.' He had switched to heavily accented Chinese-English. 'Honourable sons will join honourable father for a swim!' Then he was back with his Oxford voice, 'An old man like me needs to exercise between flights—bloody jet lag becomes bloody worse each year.' Another big laugh as he pulled three pairs of bathing shorts in different colours out of the bag: green, blue and red. All were decorated with coconut trees and the word *Singapore* on the right thigh.

'Poor Ali,' said Li to CV as he held each out for inspection. 'He's still slender, so he will look as if he's wearing the queen's knickers—I expected him to have put on weight. He politely described you as of similar size to me. What a diplomat! We have the extra-large. There was also a jumbo for later days, so do not despair. Which colour?'

'I'm going to look splendid,' CV said grabbing the red pair. 'I've always been much too cautious in my choice of swim clothes.'

'How did you know blue was my favourite colour, Uncle?' asked Ali holding his to his waist and wriggling his hips Hawaiian style and received a punch in the arm.

Li then placed an arm around his shoulders. 'Love agrees with you. My room is on the second floor. We'll change up there.'

It was against the hotel rules to use the pool so late at night, but Li had apparently pulled strings because when they came down in their trunks, there was no protest. He stopped at the front desk and requested coffee to be sent up in an hour and breakfast at 5.30 a.m. because a car would be calling for him at six.

The pool was outdoors but still at midday temperature. Ali did not test it but dived in. CV stood with Li and watched him knife through the water.

'You'd never guess he's several years older than me.'

'You don't fool me,' Li replied. 'Those buttocks are solid, those shoulders are like a bull's. Of course the women must ask that you be supported by a crane.'

'Is that why I can't get one into bed?'

'Don't lie to an old man.'

CV's muscled buttocks and powerful shoulders did not help him in the water for the other men easily outdistanced him. Ali swam as efficiently as a porpoise but Li was not far behind. CV's breast stroke which stood him well on long distances was no match for their freestyle, and he was eventually lapped. After about twenty minutes, Li shouted, 'Enough, boys, out! The old man is tired.'

He was obviously used to calling the shots.

CV climbed out wishing he could stay there longer. He still didn't feel a hundred per cent. As he towelled off, he saw the moon reflected a perfect circle into the water that, he realized with irritation, meant they were nearing a Poya Day—Sri Lankans do not work when there is a full moon.

'When is Poya?' he asked Ali.

'Tomorrow.'

'Shit. Shops closed and an exodus out of Colombo!'

'You need the rest. Take the day off.'

'For £1,000 plus a day Bell deserves more than sleep from me. I'll rest next week when my price drops to zero.'

Suddenly he lost his sense of cheer. Less than two weeks ago Dorothy Bell had died, and he recalled Michael's painting of her, which now seemed more real than she had ever been to him.

Li had noticed the change and said, 'You are sad?'

'It comes over me from time to time that Dorothy did not have to end up dead on a Pettah street!'

'No she did not. Let us go upstairs and weep together.'

'You knew her well?'

'Oh, yes.'

In the bedroom they opted to wear their underwear, leave

the windows open and turn on the fan so they could enjoy the fresh air. There was a knock on the door. It was the waiter with coffee and sandwiches.

When the door was closed, Li presented his green bathing suit to CV. 'I'm not going on to London carrying a bag of wet skivvies, my dear chap. You must take them. I'd say give them to a friend, but there are not too many of our size around.'

'As Colombo doesn't cater to fat men who love Hawaiian prints, the extra pair will be most welcome, sir.'

Ali and the Chinese were seated against the pillows on the beds and CV opted for a chair. It was time.

'Mr Li . . .'

'Uncle. Ali always calls me Uncle.'

'Uncle, tell me about Dorothy.'

'I loved her. She called me her Chinese Daddy,' he said, and gloom descended. 'When you find her killer, first drive your own splinters under his nails then send him to me. I will finish the job.'

'Unfortunately, I don't know who he is. Please tell me about her last evening.'

'What do you know?'

'It has been confirmed that she had dinner with Michael, who says she then took a three-wheeler to the Oberoi Hotel. At about midnight her dead body was thrown on to a step in the Pettah by two men wearing bags over their heads. They didn't know they were watched by a shop owner who thought they were hoodlums about to steal his car tyres. They left. He left. At 2.30 two soldiers on patrol found her. Others may have seen her body but the Pettah people are secretive, and no one admits to it.

'Ali now says she never went to the Oberoi because you met her in the Fort. That should make you one of the last people to see her alive. He says she was not alone when you left her.'

Li sat easily in the lotus position. 'She was not. What I have to tell you is hard for me to say, so I must ask you to let me talk uninterrupted.' He sat with eyes half-closed for a few moments and, without opening them fully, continued, 'I did not kill Dorothy. I am sure you want to hear me say it. To understand why she was so important to me, I must tell you how I came to know her, and to do that I must go back six years.'

Li and Dorothy Bell
Six years before Dorothy Bell died, Li Chen Wee, his son Joe, pregnant daughter-in-law Mei and four-year-old grandson Sammi were vacationing in the south of France with the child's English nanny Anna Butler. Li did not mention where they had taken their holiday, the name of their hotel or the time of the year. CV sensed the omissions were no accident.

One afternoon the father and son ran into an acquaintance playing golf, and Joe had phoned Mei to say they would be late. After tea, she, Sammi and Anna were in the lobby where the little boy started playing at the fountain and Mei became immersed in a magazine.

She suddenly became aware of a creaking from above and wondered if they were about to experience an earthquake. Without further warning, a section of the first floor with an indoor balcony fell. The upper floor began to collapse, and people in the lobby began to scream. Mei shouted to Anna to grab her son even as she saw her do so, but as more sections of the roof came down, she herself didn't know in which direction to run. A beam fell. A block of plaster shattered, and she saw people being trapped under marble and concrete. A woman was crushed before her eyes.

Mei feared for her unborn child even as she wanted to get to her boy. She could see Anna running with him in her arms, but they were unable to cross the spreading debris. Mei ran towards them only to see Anna and the child disappear behind an avalanche of wood, concrete and plaster. She had a clear path to the front door and now ran in that direction stopping strangers, screaming to them that her child had been buried and she needed help. But they had their own troubles. Mei was convinced both Sammi and his nanny had been killed.

She found herself outside without remembering going through the door. It was dusk. She was now weeping hysterically and crashed into a girl who shouted in English, 'What's happening?' Mei grabbed her and kept screaming that the hotel was collapsing, her boy was inside and she wasn't sure if he was dead, and she didn't know how to get him out and she was carrying another child.

The girl was blonde, about nineteen or twenty, and in blue shorts. She looked at Mei's stomach and shaking the young mother, she shouted, 'Stop yelling! Tell me where he is!'

Mei tried to explain: 'At the fountain. His nanny is Anna. She's English.'

'What is he wearing? How old is he? What is his name?'

'Red shirt. Blue trousers. Four years. Sammi.' Mei clung to this girl. 'Help me, please!'

'And Anna? What is she wearing?'

'Orange frock. Brown sandals. Brown hair. Help us.'

Just then someone came running out of the hotel and knocked her off her feet again. This time she twisted her ankle and screamed in pain.

'Get away from here,' said the blonde girl. 'Or you'll lose the baby. I'm going in.' And she was gone.

The panic continued but men were now trying to prevent people entering the hotel, and others came out carrying bodies—not all seemed alive. They'd put them down, turn round and go inside again. Mei saw a man strong-arm the blonde girl when she ignored his command to keep away from the door. The girl brought her foot up, and kicked him in the crotch. He curled over and yelled something at her, but she did not turn or stop. She was through the big doors before anyone else could touch her.

'My poor daughter-in-law is a bit of a ninny, but she's

good-hearted,' Li told CV and Ali. 'She had never seen a girl like that, she says, fearless like a warrior—but she also knew she may have sent her to her death. She wanted to follow but decided not to because her ankle hurt and she was pregnant. Finally, she climbed into a circular flower bed in front of the building, knelt on wet earth among the flowers and prayed.'

Then, she did not know how long afterward, the blonde girl was beside her with Sammi and Anna. She was kneeling beside Mei, and saying, 'Now just lie there. Lie quietly, everything's all right.'

Mei now looked at her closely for the first time and couldn't believe the blonde was grinning! Laughing aloud, she then sat on the stone edging around the flower bed and announced, 'I need a drink.'

Mei said, 'Stay here. I will bring you one. But first your name please.' The girl laughed and said, 'The drink was a joke. My name is Dorothy Bell. Look after Sammi. I hope he has a nice Daddy, too. Good luck with the baby,' and she stood up and left them without a backward glance.

Sammi was crying again, and as Mei comforted him she watched Dorothy move away so fast that she knew she could not follow. It had confused her that the girl did not give them another glance. She wondered if she had had an encounter with an angel.

'And shortly afterwards, for the first time, I heard the name Dorothy Bell,' said Li. 'She was only seventeen that day, but she looked older. He paused then continued, 'We decided not to leave until we found her. Mei hobbled on her sprained ankle, and we looked in the hospitals, hotels and guest houses. Joe searched too with no luck.'

He was silent, and CV got him a Coke. There were chocolate bars in the refrigerator. He opened one, and Li took a piece absently. Ali refused, so CV ate the rest. He opened a beer for Ali who was now also sitting on the bed cross-legged like Li, who seemed to have fallen asleep. When he opened his eyes CV saw they were filled with tears.

'She's dead. I was not able to save her. I should not have left her that evening when I did.

'What? Yes!' Li broke himself from his daze and continued, 'Mei and I were having lunch the next day after searching all morning. We had a window table. Suddenly she stood up, pointed out of the window and began to shout, "Dorothy Bell! Dorothy Bell!" She ran out, and when I got there. the two girls were laughing and embracing.

'Mei introduced us, and it shocked me because I realized I had seen Dorothy before. A man came up and took her arm. I had seen her with him at a casino. She introduced him as Roland Guerre.

'When I had seen them earlier he was playing roulette, and I kept staring at her. There was something about Dorothy that made men look. "That girl is too young to be with that man," I had thought. She seemed disinterested in the game, but when he spoke to her, she would smile. What a terrible smile! When she smiled at him, she became his slut. He was that kind of man.'

'What kind?'

'Smooth. Practiced. City slicker. I did not think Dorothy was his wife or even his daughter. Their relationship was explained by that smile. And now here they were, and I did not care if she was a tart. I only knew that I owed her a debt that could never be paid.'

'How's Sammi?' she asked.

'Alive, because of you,' said Mei.

Li kissed her then on both cheeks and invited her to join them—not just for a meal or a drink—but for life. He ignored Guerre. He told her his family's resources were at her disposal. When Guerre realized the Asian had money, his attitude changed. He asked them to lunch. Li refused. Guerre said to her, 'We're going, Dorothy. This restaurant has nothing I want to eat.'

She replied, 'You're going, Roland. I'm staying. I've just had a better offer. So you can fuck off.'

Li chuckled as he recalled her then—seventeen years old, so brave, so vulgar when she wished.

He took her with them to their hotel and put her in a room next to their suite only to find that when they went to pay her bill on leaving two days later, that she'd settled it herself. She had explained Roland Guerre casually as a necessary evil in her life, but she had been reluctant to discuss why exactly he was there. Li had pressed and finally she had said, 'My father pays my bills. But you have to take money to be able to get away from men like my father. When it's their money, Daddy and Roland expect their own way.'

Mr Li had told her that he had seen Roland with her at the casino.

'And you guessed what was going on?' Her lips had curled disarmingly, and her eyes had twinkled. 'I'm afraid I'm not a very nice girl, Mr Li. Not so bad really, because all I'm doing is collecting a little nest egg. It's from men like Roland and my father that I am filling my treasure chest.' She added casually, 'I steal from them.'

He had begged her not to be so foolish—begged to be allowed to provide her nest egg himself. She had taken his hand. 'Look, I don't have many real friends. Don't pay me off, Chinese Daddy, please.'

'That was the first time she called me *Daddy*. After that it was never Mr Li again.' Li Chen Wee put his head in his hands and wept.

It was nearly three. Time had passed rapidly. Li now lay back against the pillow and became an elderly man with grey hair and a fantastic Buddha face and eyes swollen with tears.

'You are tired,' CV said.

'We are all tired,' said Li. His white jacket was hanging

across the back of a chair, and he rose and took out a small metal box from the breast pocket. 'I'm not a person who enjoys drugs, but we're going to need something to keep awake. I do not intend to sleep tonight—I'll make up for it in the plane. But I have to tell you the rest of my story.'

CV and Ali didn't argue. They washed the white pill down with beer and waited for the effects to set in.

Dorothy Finds Padmani's Blood

'Three attractive men in their underpants in bed together and heterosexuals all. What a waste.'

Li was doing knee bends and patted his flat stomach. 'You should have seen me before I lost my flab to the knife eight years ago.'

'You had your stomach removed?'

'I did,' said the Chinese now panting through sit-ups. He stopped exercising and began to towel himself off. 'Dorothy and Juli'as murderer must be stopped. Never think a killer won't try again. Some people kill only once. Two-time killers continue. How do I know that?'

'How?'

'Because the first time I ordered a man killed, I agonized over the decision. Now I make it like that!' and he snapped his fingers, 'The order is given. The deed is done. The wife and children receive their compensation. I believe the law takes care of us very well. If it cannot, we have the right to interfere. Don't drop this investigation when your week is up. I'll be grateful for the honour of paying your price to continue. Find him and one way or another he will be brought to justice.' Li did not smile.

'Uncle,' CV said to get back on track, 'did Michael Blue know of your relationship with Dorothy?'

'Yes, but we haven't met. She was devoted to him. The year she met him she gave me a birthday present of a painting he did of her. It became a treasure immediately. Michael and I have spoken on the phone at least a dozen times. How is he handling her death?'

'Devastated, but he's kind of spiritual and has that comfort. And Emma—have you met her?'

'No. I will invite them to visit me as soon as I get back. Dorothy could be secretive, so Emma may not have heard my name. She never told me she had brothers or that her mother was alive. Ali told me about them when I asked if there was anything I could do for her family. She once said to me—she said something like, "Daddy, I'd make a terrible mother. I wouldn't know how to be strong. I'd spoil my children, and they'd grow up unhappy. You should see Emma with children—she's so confident that she scolds them. She doesn't have to be soft." She seldom talked about her own childhood and never mentioned her father without disgust. Dorothy already had enough money to support Michael and herself for the rest of their lives, but not enough to ruin her father if the opportunity came. She wanted to take him down. I tried to dissuade her. I said a vendetta can destroy your life. Prophetic?'

Ali told him about Mahmoud's statement that Dorothy was helping to set up Emma with Ahmed.

'Ridiculous! Dorothy wanted to protect Emma from men. I never heard, "If only Emma had a boyfriend."'

'Can you help us on why Emma may have become a target?' CV asked.

'To suppress information,' suggested the older man. 'Now Dorothy is dead, Emma might have her secrets—knowledge that can take someone down.'

'Did you know Dorothy's father made her his mistress when she was thirteen?'

Li's eyes squeezed closed. When he opened them they had become opaque.

'She never told me. I knew there had to be something in her past—something that was twisting her, making her—what is the word? . . . There had to be a reason for her corruption. It had not happened overnight I knew, there had to have been a build up to cause such rage. You have entrusted me with the missing piece.'

'There is more.' CV told Li about Dorothy and Michael's shared parenthood. 'She decided to stay with him, although it meant she could not have children herself. She didn't seem to have considered having them by anyone else.'

He glanced at Ali who lay with his eyes closed.

Li had returned to the lotus position. One elbow was on his knee and he leaned on his fist. 'So that's why she was so sad when we talked about children. I could have helped her if I had known. I once offered to set up a trust that would have given her an income of at least half a million a year for life. My gem business is an inherited sideline. I have made my real fortune in commodities and property. She refused. Flatly refused. She could not take money from those she loved, and she had come to love us. Money was a weapon to her.'

CV couldn't resist telling Li that Bell had hedged at paying £10,000 for his services. 'He agreed if only to put a good face on it. If he had not patronized me, I would have helped him without charge, of course. I thought it might as well cost the bastard. Dorothy decided the same thing. When did she learn you had Padmani's Blood?'

He couldn't take his eyes of Li. The man fascinated him. His large body had almost female breasts. He had parchment-coloured soles and plump toes which were turned upwards. His Buddha's face could change from contemplation to anger to grief or amusement without appearing to move a muscle.

'At first, it never entered my head to tell Dorothy though she would have kept my secret. I heard stories from gem merchants that she was an agent for Mr Bell, but she never approached me with any offer. So imagine my amusement when I heard from Akbar Sharif that Dorothy Bell was looking for Padmani's Blood. I thought Akbar knew I owned it and was pulling my leg.

"Who wants it?" I asked. He said, "Dorothy Bell." I called her and said I knew where the stone was and asked her to come to Singapore to meet its owner.'

She had been excited. 'Will he sell?' She had bubbled with questions. Li had teased, 'Patience! Patience!'

Dorothy stayed at his home because he told her he had invited the gem's owner to lunch. She spent the morning in a salon and returned with her hair in a French knot. She was Dorothy Bell the businesswoman. Thirty minutes before lunch she changed into a pink silk suit and went into the garden room to wait.

'"What a performance," I told her. "Just to talk to an old Chinese gentleman." She kissed my cheek and said, "When you're twenty-three, Daddy, and have to talk millions, you can't look twenty-three."'

Li had arranged that his family be absent and to make the surprise complete worked in his office at home until exactly one. Eventually, he led her by the hand to the dining room where the table was elaborately set for two. She had said, 'Aren't you going to eat with us?'

He said, 'I am,' pulled out a chair for her and took the other seat.

'The English usually reach for their napkins as they sit down—and ours had been folded to resemble swans. Lying on the back of Dorothy's swan, between its wings, was Padmani's Blood. She remarked on the beauty of the swan and moved to unfold hers, and only then was the light above turned on. The star shone with such brilliance that she gave a cry. It even took my breath away. Her expression was wondrous.'

Dorothy had taken it gently into the palm of her hand. 'Daddy,' she said, 'Oh, Daddy! Look at it! Oh, it's enormous. Oh, it is so beautiful. Oh, Daddy, who owns it?'

'A girl owns it,' Li had replied and signalled to the houseboy to start serving the meal. 'A girl called Dorothy Bell. It is my gift to you. I have been its owner for many years and it is time to pass it on.'

They had then had an argument, which Li had lost. She would not accept the stone. She refused saying that she wanted her father to buy it from him.

'Then sell it to him and the money will be all yours!' Li replied. 'Give up chasing for a dollar here a dollar there. It will buy you your freedom from him and other men forever. Michael and you can live out your lives doing whatever you want to do. There will be no more looking for a sale.'

She had replied, 'No. Because, Daddy, I have to do it my way. I'll make my money, don't you worry. But I want *him* to buy it from *you*.' She'd relished the words. 'Oh, the irony of it! I want him to take on him all the bad luck that comes with it and to release you from it.'

'That's a superstition!'

'My mind tells me it is, but my heart hopes it will curse him, so ask a fair price. He is not expecting a bargain. Imagine what he would have to pay at an auction; with that history it is much more than just so many carats. He has someone ready to take it off his hands. Ask enough to take care of my cut.'

At last he had thought he had found a way to repay her for saving his grandson. She told him Sammi's laughter and Anna's smile had been her reward. Eventually they set a price of $13,000,000. He told her to take the stone to Sri Lanka with her.

'No, it's too dangerous. My father will suspect I have it, and it will be stolen from me.'

'Wait a minute,' said CV. 'The night before she died, her hotel room had been turned upside down. Perhaps it was a search, not a fight or lovemaking.'

Ali said, 'Would Bell kill to steal?'

Li said, 'He didn't have to. He bought the stone.'

She had wanted the money transferred into Li's account in a blink, saying, 'He's a master at delay.'

CV said, 'Thirteen million at even six per cent would give him an extra $2,000 a day.'

She had also wanted the sale to be carried out without her father knowing Li's name.

'But surely you had to give him proof of your ownership of Padmani?'

'It was owned by one of my companies.'

Li had taken the stone to Colombo. 'I left my bodyguard at Bandaranayake Airport because I was met by a friend who had his own as well as a chauffeur. We were driven very slowly to the Fort, arrived twenty minutes early, used the time to drive around, deplore the grubbiness, admire the new buildings and be nostalgic about the old shops. With one minute to spare we drove down the street where we were to meet the Bells. My friend and I got out of the car and crossed the road. Our bodyguard positioned himself outside it with the chauffeur remaining at the wheel. Both men were instructed to apprehend anyone who left the building before we did.'

The Sale

Li had been reciting his story as if into the air, but now he spoke directly to CV.

CV listened carefully.

'The front door was unlocked, and we saw the stairs in front of us. I had been instructed to go up and take the door on the left. I was ahead, my friend behind.'

'What time was this?' CV had been asked not to interrupt, but details such as time were important.

'It was exactly 11 p.m.'

'Who was the friend who accompanied you?'

'He wishes to be anonymous. Ali knows him. I wanted

someone who spoke English, Sinhala and Tamil. He said he would do the job himself. He has a permit to carry a gun.

'Such precautions are standard. Mr Bell would not negotiate in Singapore without someone who spoke more than one Chinese dialect. Dorothy would sometimes take someone I recommended when she was dealing with a Chinese.'

'You entered the room.'

'Wait a minute. I was the first to enter the building. There was a light—a dim bulb hanging at the end of a wire. There were doors to either side, and the stairs, as I said, were ahead. As I was about to go up the stairs, I heard the door to the right of me click—it was not the sound of a key turning—more,' he reached beside him where he had placed the room key, and clicked it on the table. 'The sound was something like that but not so loud.'

'A sharp sound,' CV said.

'Exactly.'

'I stopped and looked at the door. A brass lock was set into it, and there was no key on our side. As the sound was not repeated I went on upstairs.

'The other door—on the left?'

'It was a simple hasp-and-clasp job with a padlock,' he described it with his fingers.

'Only you heard the click?'

'No. I turned to my friend and nodded towards the door. He took out his automatic pistol, put it in his trouser pocket and kept his hand on it. We continued cautiously.

'My friend had a mobile phone in his other hand. I carried only a briefcase of folded newspapers in case someone wanted something to grab. Padmani was not in it—it was strapped to my body. I could feel it under my elbow at my waist. You must understand there is no law against the transportation of gems to and from Sri Lanka, and I had not declared the stone when I came in.' He was silent for a moment. 'I did not do so partly because of the gem's controversial nature. Ali feels it is the property of this country. I do not. I didn't want some customs official saying to me, "That's ours."' He became silent.

'You were uneasy,' CV prodded.

Li opened his eyes. 'Yes, definitely. I was quite shocked a the sort of building Dorothy had chosen for the exchange. It was inappropriate. It was shabby. An office, a home, this hotel would have been appropriate. It had crossed my mind that I should leave. I did not because I was dealing with Dorothy. It also crossed my mind that what I had heard was a rat—it was that type of place. Of course, a rat would have continued to run around. There was just that one click then dead silence.

'I braced myself to enter the room at the top. Dorothy had told me that door too would be unlocked. My friend moved past me and entered first. I saw there had been no need for concern. Dorothy was there by the window, and she smiled at me warmly.

'She did not say my name, just introduced a man sitting at a table to me as Mr Reginald Bell. He said, "It was good of you to come."'

'What did you think of Bell, your first impression?'

'A Wall Street cowboy—the shining white hair, very distinctive that white hair. I had expected Dorothy's father to be a different kind of man.'

'We all had that experience,' said Ali who had been silent. 'I expected a earthy north-country entrepreneur—not someone so lacquered, so veneered.'

'Veneered!' Li grunted. 'That was it exactly. She was not veneered; she was always clean, fresh and alive. I think *modern* is the word I would apply to her.'

Clean? Fresh? She'd put on different but consistent fronts for her different audiences.

'What was she wearing?'

'Red blouse. White billowing trousers. She looked beautiful that night. She was not a classically beautiful woman, but she could make you forget that.'

Yes, indeed.

'Her eyes were dancing, and her blonde hair was shimmering—it hung down her back so simply. She was triumph. She was mischief. Next to her vibrancy the rest of us seemed ready for the mortuary. There was one other in the room. He was not introduced and stood beside Bell, so I presumed him to be a bodyguard—a short brown fellow in a T-shirt and long trousers. Big on the shoulder, strong buttocks, strong arms. Not a servant, but no master either. A freelance thug, I'd guess.'

'Local?'

'My friend spoke to him in Sinhala, and the man looked as if he understood. My friend told me later he had said, "If you try any tricks I will kill you. I have this house surrounded and I carry a gun."

'Dorothy said, "No more Sinhala, gentlemen. It leaves us at a disadvantage." My friend apologized.'

'Was the upstairs room in better shape than the bottom floor?'

'No. It was unspeakably shabby also. It was dark outside, but there were no curtains on the open window which overlooked the red brick wall of another building a few feet away. Two bare bulbs were hanging. There were chairs. The table was plastic topped. My friend went to the window, looked outside and then at me. He had guessed my mind. I had no intention of taking a thousand-carat star ruby out in front of an open window. There was some cloth—a shabby tablecloth it turned out—dark brown—folded on one shelf, there was also a mat rolled up against a wall. He shook out both. He began to put the brown cloth across the window, and Bell's bodyguard helped him, standing on a chair to tuck it into the curtain rod. It was then I became aware of the boy's strength. His thigh muscles pressed against the cloth of his trousers. His waist was narrow. Thick neck. He had huge biceps.

'Mr Bell suggested to Dorothy that we close the window and

she said, "Okay, but you'll regret it. The fan doesn't work, so there'll be no fresh air." She looked at me, and I indicated that the window could stay open.

'You see, boys, I trusted Dorothy. I knew she would never set me up. That never entered my head. I still do not know why she chose such an awful place to meet in and intended to ask her about that one day. I knew nothing of her father except that she hated him. I didn't know how to assess him or his man. Still I was uneasy about giving this white-haired white man that stone. Now I know I was right to be uneasy for Ali has told me about the missing emerald in America. It was as if Dorothy and I were playing roles in a comedy. She was directing, I was a player, but the other actors were unknown factors.

'Let me move on. The tablecloth was arranged over the window so not even a lizard clinging to the brick wall could see into the room. At one moment when Mr Bell's attention became distracted, Dorothy winked at me. I winked back.

'Finally, all was ready. I sat down, opened my shirt, unzipped my body pack and took the leather bag out of it. I opened it and pushed it across the table. Bell came forward and reacted predictably—his chin fell to his knees. It was not the first time I have seen a man fall in love with a gem. For a moment his face looked as lovesick as a boy's. He took the star in his hand and turned it over and around.

'Dorothy said, "What do you think—is it worth $13,000,000? Its weight is 99.92."'

'Ali says that would be egg sized.'

'A small egg that is flattened on one side—but that gives no idea of the impact. A precious stone half an inch in diameter can take your breath away. Imagine one the size of a small egg, the colour of blood, with a perfect star that comes from its depths and crosses the surface edge to edge.'

'Colossal and spectacular?'

'Gargantuan and humbling!'

He stretched out his legs and lay back against the pillows. CV moved to give him more room and then rose to get himself a glass of water. He poured one for Li. Ali did not open his eyes but lay there almost smiling. He said, 'I wish I'd seen that stone, Uncle. What a story to tell one's grandchildren!'

'With an ending that should have been happy. Mr Bell tried to hide his enthusiasm, but, as they say, you cannot hide a man in love or an Englishman sitting on a camel. At that moment he was both.

'He had a scale in his briefcase and weighed Padmani. He examined her through an eyepiece and looked at the papers I had brought confirming my ownership. Then, still without a word to me he picked up his cell phone, dialled many numbers and said, "Belladonna. Three blind mice." We waited in silence for ten minutes, and then he nodded to me. I dialled on my friend's phone and said to my banker, "The star is here." He replied in our code, "Thirteen, three ago." It had taken only three minutes to effect the transfer of $13,000,000 from Bell's account to mine.'

'Uncle, you're sure he said *Belladonna*?'

'Yes. Is it significant?'

'I don't know.' He told Li about Vincent Belli, alias Horace Belladonna, dying as Dorothy had. 'I'd say it's a coincidence, but Ali says there are no coincidences.'

'At least very few. Horace Belladonna! Don't let me leave without writing down that name.'

'He died in Milan. But please go on with your story.'

'It is ended. Bell replaced the stone in its bag. I left. I had not spoken except into the phone since entering the room. I shook his hand, kissed Dorothy's cheek and left. She went to the door, put her arms around my neck and whispered, "Thank you, Daddy." Those were her last words to me. Now I had no concern about the door downstairs. I had Bell's money. Padmani was with her new owner. It was not my problem to protect her. Outside, my friend's bodyguard said no one had left or entered the building.'

'So whoever was downstairs was still there.'

'And went upstairs to steal the stone. There must have been a confrontation. Bell and his bodyguard fled. Dorothy was killed. I never realized she was in danger. We drove straight to the airport and, during the drive, my friend and I couldn't help laughing at the melodrama. The seedy building, the silent transaction, the blonde with dancing blue eyes. He was very taken with her and asked if I thought she would go out with him. I told him she was engaged to Michael Blue. We stopped at a hotel and had a bite to eat. There was a plane leaving for Amsterdam in the early hours, and there were seats to spare in the first class. The bodyguard who had come with me went back to Singapore. I have brought our ticket counterfoils and boarding passes, so you can confirm our flights. It all happened exactly as I said.'

'I have no doubt of it.'

There was a long silence. CV broke it.

'And you never tried to contact Dorothy?'

'Of course I did. I phoned her from the plane to her hotel and was told she hadn't come in. I phoned the next day and got the same reply. They did not say she was dead. I phoned Michael's number, and some French fool told me she'd gone away. I was surprised she hadn't left a message for me in Singapore. Eventually, Ali called me with the news. I phoned my friend who had been in that room with me and asked him why he had not let me know. He had presumed I would have heard immediately. It was, after all, only a few days ago.'

'So much for Reggie's alibi. Uncle, if you were to go into a room to steal a ruby, wouldn't you go for one of the men, not the girl? She was stabbed in the back. You describe Bell's bodyguard as a very strong man. A bodyguard doesn't run.'

'He could have been in on it.'

'How was she going to get her cut?'

'It was transferred within minutes from my account to hers. It raises the value of her estate considerably.'

'CV wants Mr Bell to have killed her,' said Ali opening his eyes. 'But do you know a man who will stick a knife in his daughter, Uncle?' He got up and went to the chair on which he'd left his clothes and began fumbling with his shirt. He came back with a folded paper and handed it to Li.

'Have you seen that ring? One of the men who left her in the Pettah was wearing it.'

Li looked at the drawing, carefully. 'I didn't see it that night. I am sure of that. I may have seen one like it somewhere, but it has left no impression. It is not a particularly pleasing design. A little awkward, don't you agree?'

'Very awkward. Which is why I think you would remember it.'

'You're right. I would have noticed it. I haven't seen that ring.'

CV said, 'You don't remember anything more about Bell's bodyguard?'

'About your age. Curly black hair combed to one side with oil, as if to straighten it. Unnatural muscle. He is a body-builder or a man who lifts weights.'

Ali said, 'One of the men who dumped Dorothy's body was a tall heavy man who was wearing that ring. The other was thin but strong enough to carry her on his back from the trunk of a car to the other side of the road.' He handed Li the other sketch while CV told him Solomon's story. 'Could this man have been Bell's bodyguard? The man who did that drawing particularly remarked on his thin strong legs.'

'No. The legs I saw had thighs as thick as a waist. This man is a stick.'

Ali said, 'I think you're right, Uncle. These two men were hiding downstairs, killed her and left her in the Pettah.'

While they waited for breakfast they went over what they knew. They did not hide anything from Li but he showed little interest in Bundy, the Arabs or Dorothy's casino antics.

At some point he said, 'What you boys are forgetting is that Mr Bell is not a stranger to this country. He must have some friends—even enemies. He knew Ali. He knows he is too unusual looking to be forgotten easily. He wouldn't take a taxi going back and forth from the airport if he didn't want to be remembered. Someone, perhaps that bodyguard, would do the ferrying.'

'Which was why no one in the airport saw him! I described him as being alone. Uncle, you haven't given us the Fort address where you saw Dorothy for the last time.'

'Deliberately. My friend's chauffeur and bodyguard know he was there that evening but did not know who Dorothy was. They did not see her and have not connected us to her. If they did, we'd be answering police questions at the very least.'

It now seemed that Michael had held not just an important piece of the jigsaw puzzle but perhaps all the missing pieces. Yet if he had killed Dorothy, why would he involve others in disposing of her body? Michael was not known to be in debt. His paintings were selling. With Dorothy alive he would have been as wealthy as if he inherited from her—and she was getting richer, it seemed from all accounts, almost by the day.

If Michael had not killed her and did not know who had, why had he not exposed Bell's lie—his alibi? Was it because he could not implicate his father? Had the invention of a meeting at the Oberoi been his invention or hers? Perhaps she had kept the sale a secret from him—circled the Fort in a three-wheeler and had it drop her off at the side street.

He put those thoughts aside and said, 'Just after Mr Bell asked me to take on this job, he phoned a number in Singapore.' He took out his pen, tore a sheet from his notebook, and wrote down the number and handed it to Li. 'Was he calling you? The number has been disconnected. On Friday a man answered twice, Chinese by the voice, but it could have been another Asian. I said I was calling for Bell, and he hung up on me.'

Li studied the number and said, 'I don't have your memory for figures—you wrote that down without having to look it up. I cannot even tell you if the number is one of mine; there are so many. But there is a possible explanation: Two of my friends know I owned Padmani's Blood. I had to tell someone because if I had died owning it, it would become an important holding for my heirs, and I couldn't risk one of my family finding it because some can't tell a ruby from a conch shell. I told both friends I was selling it to Bell. Remember, Bell did not know who I was. He could have seen my photograph somewhere, but I think we all know that one fat Chinese looks much like another to an Englishman. I hoped he'd think I had been sent as an emissary, and Dorothy agreed to imply that, which is why I think he didn't speak to me—he was too grand to talk to a peon.'

'The friends who know you owned the stone are Chinese?'

'Yes, from Singapore. The day after I sold it, the nephew of one, who had had business transactions with the Bells previously, got a call from him. Bell said he wanted to talk about a gem known as Padmani's Blood. The nephew hung up saying he could not talk more at that moment.

'He had presumed Padmani's existence to be a myth and phoned his uncle to find out more about it and learned that it did exist. He told him about the call. He thought Bell wanted to sell or buy it. His uncle told him he had taken a pledge to an old friend not to discuss Padmani's Blood and asked his nephew, as a favour, to do the same. When Bell phoned that evening the nephew told him he preferred not to discuss the ruby because of the curse. Bell became persistent, and the nephew hung up. He then refused to take any calls from Bell. I am not sure of the details, but my friend knew I'd be interested and called me in Germany. I told him Bell might be trying to get another evaluation of its worth before selling it.'

CV made a face. 'So I did the wrong thing by giving his name when I phoned. Would you check for me if that is the nephew's number?' He also wrote *Vincent Belli/Horace Belladonna* on the same sheet.

Li's wallet was on the table beside him, and he glanced at the paper, folded it and slipped it inside.

'If it isn't, would you get someone to check who had that number.'

'I had intended to do that.'

The phone rang to remind Li that a taxi would be at the front door in thirty minutes, and almost immediately a waiter entered with their breakfast. In the east the sky had begun to brighten. Another day had come too soon.

Ali wanted to drive Li to the airport but he refused, saying, 'It might not be wise for me to be seen getting out of your car.'

CV said, 'Not true that one Chinese looks like another. I've never seen one who looked like you.'

'When I get home I shrink to a skinny little chap with wire glasses.'

As they stood in the lobby, CV thanked him for having gone the extra yard. Li shook his head, 'I won't rest comfortably until I know how this turns out.' Then he said with a mischievous smile, 'You haven't asked if I know where Dorothy kept her money. The bulk of her fortune she left with me. When you find an heir I approve of, I will release the funds. As they are not in her name and only two others know the details, they will be untraceable. If I don't approve of her heir, a charity will benefit.'

'If she dies intestate, Reggie and her mother will inherit—he says.'

'They will not. Nor will I release any of her fortune to some ex-nanny in England. Her brothers will be taken care of.'

It was time for him to go, and CV wished it wasn't. He tried to think of other questions he should have asked. 'Uncle,' he found himself saying, 'every path I go down turns out to be a cul de sac. What am I doing wrong?'

The words came from Li as quickly as if he had rehearsed them, 'Your enemy has been watching you. You set traps. He avoids them. He can plan his own traps and, because you do not know who he is, you are falling into them. Go back to the time when you were not after him—when you did not know you were going to be his adversary. He may have been careless then.' He smiled and said, 'My advice is not given free. I also have a favour to ask.'

'Ask it, and it's yours.'

'When you have found the killer of Dorothy, explain to me why you think he is guilty. If I agree with your conclusion, I will take care of him.'

CV didn't know what to say.

Li continued smoothly, 'You boys look exhausted—remember no one can think clearly without sleep. I have told the management you will be using my room. Those pills I gave you were placebos. I took the only stimulant in the box. I've found I can keep my friends alert if they think they're medicated.'

They went down the steps to a Peugeot, and Ali hugged Li. CV opened the back door for him and put out his hand, but it was pushed aside, and he too received a bear hug. Before he closed the door CV said, 'I'll see you again in happier times.'

'Keep that promise.'

He stepped back, but the Chinese was laughing and beckoning. He approached the car with Ali, and Li said, 'There were only two heterosexuals in bed upstairs in their underpants.' The window was rolled up again. The car drew away, and a laughing face enjoyed their astonishment.

'Not a simple man!' said CV. 'I had noticed he never mentioned his wife. I presumed he was a widower. I feel sorry for the man who killed Dorothy.'

'You're going to do what he asked?'

'I can't answer that. I come from a different way of thinking. The law must be followed.'

'When you were pissing, Uncle told me you'd have made the perfect husband for Dorothy.'

'No way. I'm a romantic. One guy to one woman. I think I'd have enjoyed her friendship, though.'

'I think he meant you were temperamentally similar. You are not as puritanical as you make out. You'd have understood her pain, and after a few more years of being in love with a bisexual promiscuous half-brother, she might have wanted more. I don't think Michael and Dorothy would have been able to stay together.'

'I'm not sure.' CV added, 'That Peugeot was no taxi.'

Chapter VIII

Tuesday

CV Oversleeps

A waiter was moving a trolley into the room that was now flooded with sunlight and fresh air. Ali was reading a newspaper by the open French windows. He looked up and said, 'It's time to rise if we are to get back to Colombo. I've been pretending to be your nanny, but tiptoeing around is never easy for me.'

CV sat up feeling adrift, peered at his watch and started complaining, 'I left a morning call for ten and its twelve-thirty! I've lost half a day.'

'I cancelled the wake-up call. I've had a swim. Room service has provided disposable razors and toothbrushes. Relax, baba. Nanny Ali was worried. You needed to sleep.'

'Nanny Ali has lost his fucking mind.'

He shaved, showered and when he re-entered the room Ali was again turning pages. He said, 'Our white-women murders are no longer front-page news. Tourism is on the mend. The LTTE blew up a truck by accident. *Wisden* has declared Sanath Jayasuriya the number one batsman in the world.'

'You and Mag will be well matched—you can chirp together like happy little robins at dawn. Odd that no one has phoned.'

'I turned your phone off.'

CV wanted to yell at him but said, 'I suppose I should thank

Murder in the Pettah

you because I feel a lot better, but there are only three days remaining, and I've lost time I needed.'

'You're forgetting Uncle Li has invited you to stay on the job at his expense. Say the word, I'll let him know.'

As he poured himself coffee, however, CV relaxed. 'I shouldn't be complaining because I asked for the Friday deadline, but if I stay on it won't be on someone else's dollar. When Emma's place blew up, it became my war. Interesting that our Chinese uncle didn't ask my price. Did Maggie tell you how Reggie and I played poker face and he blinked first.'

'She did. Yet there's a side to him I like—the businessman. He makes up his mind on the spot. When he was in Kandy, he sent me a very generous but somewhat inappropriate gift to be distributed among the needy. He has his good side.'

With considerable relish CV told him who had sent the gifts.

'Did Maggie want to have tea with me, or was she just punishing him for the insult?' Ali was much amused.

'Who would want to have tea with you?'

Ali threw the paper at him again and then switched on the phone, but CV decided to make his calls later. Li's story about Dorothy's last night had changed everything but solved nothing. He just had four more suspects.

'Any chance Li could be playing games with us?' he asked.

'Same chance Mohamed was a Christian.'

'I can't take anyone on trust.'

'You can trust Uncle.'

'All right then, so that it lets off his companion, or does it? The bodyguard is a new suspect, and whoever was downstairs is another. Can Li's friend be persuaded to tell me which building they met in?'

'I can ask. But I think he won't. For the muscled guy we can put the word out at the gyms. Body-builders might know him.'

'A job for Mag. Beautiful-body confronted by beautiful-body creates a bond. Aren't you going to join me, or do I have to eat all this alone?'

Ali had ordered ginger chicken, omelettes, prawns on toast, vegetables, roast potatoes and coffee. There were hot Danishes under a cover and desserts on the lower tray.

Ali took a plate from the trolley. He said, 'I don't like Maggie being so involved.'

'She's trained in martial arts.' CV shrugged. 'Her only weakness is that she'll never have the nerve to put someone out. No killer instinct.'

In sudden anger Ali tossed a cushion across the room. 'You treat her as a robot for your use. You let her wander around Colombo without a guard,' his voice had become shrill. 'She could become the third victim.' His good mood soured, he returned to his chair.

'You on the other hand do have killer instinct. When you flicked that paper, I saw it,' CV felt rather pleased that Ali was irritated. He had that nasty habit of appearing above it all. 'Mag's a tough broad. A moving target is harder to hit than a stationary one—you should know that—football and rugger. Julia was helpless because she was asleep.'

No answer.

'Of course, I could order Mag never to leave the house except in a grey Mercedes 280 driven by a long-nosed Muslim jeweller.'

The rolled newspaper hit him on the head.

'Bowling or polo?' CV continued, pleased with himself, and he saw Ali smile again. 'I think I could live in a hotel indefinitely. I like surprise meals ordered by my grumpy nanny.'

'Nanny only ordered food that is good for you, Master Clive. No pudding unless you eat everything on your plate.' Ali's irritation was gone.

The phone rang. It was Teddy saying, 'Where the hell are you? I've been calling all morning. Nora told me you had drawings of the murderers, and you've been out of touch for twenty-four hours.'

'I know and I apologize, but yesterday was hell and ended in an all-night talk session that has produced new suspects. Then a well-meaning friend turned my phone off to keep me sane and let me get some sleep because yesterday morning I was poisoned.'

He saw no point in mentioning his hand injury but stretched his right hand as he talked; it was still taped and still sore.

Teddy said more evenly, 'I wish I'd thought of that... I hope you're not serious.'

'God's truth.'

'Where, what, et cetera?'

'Palace Hotel. Lime juice. Probably Bell.'

'He poisoned you?'

'He was there. I can't think of a motive for the waiter.'

'You're all right now?'

'Yes. I got drawings by an eyewitness artist who won't speak to the police. Since then, much much more. Do you have time today for show-and-tell?'

'I'd say this morning, but it's already afternoon.'

'Four at the Galle Face? I'm hoping Mag can get Bell there for a swim a little later. He wants a daily meeting. Will you be seeing her?'

'No, but I'll phone in and set it up at the hotel so you and I won't run into him. Where are those sketches now?'

'About to be photocopied. Teddy, I'm sorry about the silence, but the new info takes the whole damned thing in a different direction.'

'Then let's meet right away. What are you doing now?'

'Eating lunch. Even four will be pushing it because we're an hour out of Colombo. Would you do me a favour and check with Scotland Yard on a Louise Hammer in Watford, Hertfordshire. Hammer was Dorothy's nanny, the one her father fired and said died in an accident. She was Lawrence once. Emma can fill you in on what we know. You saw Louise's name in the notes for Dorothy's will.'

'You should be a policeman, CV. I have developed some respect for you—grudging respect. Who is with you? You said, "*We're* out of Colombo".'

'The friend who kidnapped me.'

'Female?'

'Male, I've decided to come out of the closet. For God's sake, Teddy, stop talking nonsense.'

'I don't think it is nonsense for you to disappear for twenty-four hours.'

'It wasn't as if I was at a party—and my absence has paid dividends.'

'I'll see you at four, then.'

CV put down the phone and then helped himself to more ginger chicken. 'Teddy says I should be a policeman. Can you imagine having to dig into other people's lives every day? I would have no stomach for it. Try this chicken? It's good.'

But Ali was pressing phone buttons and held the receiver away from his ear to protect it from Amily's squawk. 'Amily, is Maggie there? It's Mr Sharif.'

More squawking.

'Thank you.' Then after a moment's silence, he said, 'Yes, he is. I am too. How are you?'

CV leaned over and shouted into the mouthpiece, 'Hi Mag. Bring the ransom in a brown paper bag,' and went back to his food.

As he listened, Ali said, 'I take cold showers and meditate... Teddy and CV are planning a swimming date for you with Mr Bell. I'd like to see you before that—about three... no, clothed. We should be back in Colombo in an hour... No, I'm not being devious.'

When he put the phone down, he said, 'I am playing hard to get.'

'If you're a eunuch, you can confide in me, Ali.'

'Sometimes, I wish. I just don't want to get sidetracked into an affair until she stops playing games, because I'm not playing games. I've decided to stop giving her jewellery. I'm expecting a long future for us.'

CV wiped his mouth and began to look for his belongings. 'You can't commit yourself to a permanent relationship after two days.'

'Well, that's what I've done. It was the same with Rose. The first day I saw her, I wanted to marry her. When her madness took over and the woman I loved disappeared, I kept thinking she would be there again one morning and we'd be as we were. Eventually the sane woman disappeared permanently. Do you want to marry Emma?'

He began to stuff his bathing suits into their white bag. 'Emma is easy to idealize, but I don't want her to be less free. It seems we could be tolerant of each other.'

'Did you ever think you were in love with *her*?'

'*Her*? Oh, Maggie? It often seemed it would have solved everything. Once, between her first and second marriages, we went to bed together in our underwear—we couldn't even get naked. Eventually, we laughed ourselves on to the floor. Maggie and I are twin souls, not mates. Christ, we've even fallen in love on the same Saturday this time. That's some coincidence.'

'There are no coincidences—it's Allah's way of drawing our attention to his desires and our mistakes.'

Before leaving the hotel, they had photocopies made of Solomon's sketches and tried to pay for their lunch only to find that Li had asked for all their bills to be put on his credit card.

Mahmoud Skips

They got away before two. There was much traffic on the road, but air conditioning protected them from the dusty unbreathable path to Colombo. There was much to do.

First he had to make peace with Mahmoud; the way they had parted gnawed at him. He got the Palace on the phone, but when he tried to leave a message, Nihal explained that Mr Mahmoud and Mr Mohideen were no longer there.

'They checked out? They've gone to another hotel?'

'No, Mr vander Marten. Mr Perera wants you to know that they are taking a 4 p.m. Gulf Air flight to Saudi Arabia. They left for the airport. He called, but your phone is turned off.'

'Jesus,' he said to Ali after relaying the message, 'we may have passed them on the road.'

CV got through to Nora to inform Teddy and added, 'I'll call the airport myself and try to stop them.'

When he hung up, Ali said, 'Look in the glove compartment and you'll find my address book—there are airline numbers there. Shall we turn around?'

'If we have to go to the airport, my whole afternoon is lost. The plane doesn't leave for two hours, so let's pull up and see if I can reach Mahmoud by phone. If I can't, and Nora can't reach Teddy, we'll go get him.'

Ali brought the Mercedes to rest under a shade tree while CV asked a courteous Gulf Air female employee how to contact a passenger bound for Saudi at four.

'That must be the flight at 1605 to Bahrain, sir. The passengers are checking in now. I'll give you the Gulf counter. If he's not there, ask to have him paged.'

'Thank you. Write this down. The man's name is Mahmoud. M-A-H-M-O-U-D. He is travelling with a Mr Mohideen. M-O-H-I-D-E-E-N. If they don't cancel their own reservations, Superintendent Senaratne of the CID will be contacting you to stop them from leaving the country. Now put me through to the Gulf counter.'

Another friendly voice, this one male, said, 'I think the

gentlemen you want are approaching the first-class counter, sir. They have just left customs.'

Moments later Mahmoud's voice said, 'Yes?'

'CV vander Marten here, Mr Mahmoud. Why are you leaving the country when you have been told not to by the CID?

'I will not speak to you, CV. You violated my hospitality.'

'Just listen a minute and don't hang up on me you son of a bitch,' shouted CV, and Ali leaned over and took the phone out of his hand.

He began to speak in Arabic. CV had never heard a Sri Lankan speak the language and had had no inkling that Ali was fluent in it. He did not raise his voice, and the rolling words were smooth and chilly. Ali listened a while then spoke again. The only words CV recognized were 'Dorothy Bell' and his own name. Finally, Ali passed the phone to CV. He could hear Mahmoud saying something in Arabic then the dial tone returned.

Ali said, 'He'll cancel his flight.'

He started the engine, and in a moment the car was once again heading for Colombo. CV hurriedly called Nora, explained that Mahmoud would be returning and asked Ali how he made the Arab change his mind.

'His excuse for leaving is that his business here is over, and as you insulted him, he sees no reason to help you. I told him that he had insulted Islam by his behaviour to Dorothy, who was a friend of mine. Fortunately, he had heard of our family and understands I can make him look a rascal in the eyes of his own people.'

When Ali pulled rank, he certainly knew how to do it, which meant he wouldn't let Maggie call all the shots. It might work—that union—it just might. 'When did you learn Arabic?' CV asked.

'My father thought I'd make a scholar, but my love of athletics gave me no interest in academics. All of his children had

Arabic lessons because he wanted us to understand our prayers. But it wasn't until I went to Egypt that I began to converse in the language. It seemed one day I was searching for words, the next I wasn't. Now I keep up by reading.'

'Comes in useful, I can see.'

'Not for the first time.'

CV said, 'Will I see you again today?'

'This evening? When we've attended to our chores, we can touch base.'

'You like our American idioms?'

'I like the US of A, period.'

Emma in Crisis

Every time he approached Bundy's office he was offended that it had been allowed to emerge and, like Soong's utilitarian and temporary shoeboxes, turn a city once famed for its elegance into a dry dock.

A white Nissan van was parked inside the gates. There were lights behind the office's curtains. He knocked and, when there was no response, panicked and banged with his fist.

'Emma, it's Clive!'

A key turned and then another, the door opened, and Emma threw herself into his arms. For a brief moment her Nellie Soong disguise confused him. But there was no mistaking the voice.

'It's you! I thought it was him again.'

He held her, lifted her off her feet, stepped inside and shoved the door close behind them with his foot. Behind her Ranjan was facing him with his revolver steady in both hands. The black eyes stared without emotion into his, and then the gun went back into its holster. The policeman moved around to lock the door. He said, 'I am glad to see you, sir.'

'What happened?' CV asked over Emma's head.

'Mr Balasingham came to the door, and we did not open it. After that he has telephoned very much.' Ranjan used an interesting mixture of English and Sinhala. 'The first time Miss Emma answered, and because she thought it was Miss Della from America, she said, "Hi, sport, what's cooking?"'

'Oh, Clive, I'm so sorry. I just picked up the phone and said that because Della sent me a fax starting, "Hi, sport, get your ass on line." Now Bundy probably knows I'm here.'

'What else did you say—on the phone?'

'I said in my Chinese voice, "Sorry, sir, thought you were Dr Hoong," and handed the phone to Ranjan, who said we were working for you and had instructions not to open the door to anyone except the police. After that Ranjan answered the phone instead of me, and Bundy kept calling for you.'

'What you both did was exactly right. What did he want?'

'He left no message, sir.'

She said, 'He's bonkers because he couldn't get in with his key. I was so frightened I didn't know whether to talk to him or not.'

'I'll call him. What time did he come here?'

'About ten, then he phoned about ten minutes later. He called at eleven, at twelve and again at one. Almost on the hour each time. Your phone isn't working.'

'Ali turned it off to let me sleep, and that's caused problems. On the plus side, I feel alive today. Whatever it was that poisoned me yesterday is finally out of my system.'

'Oh, I'm so glad. I thought you were dead.'

'No way, my angel, no way.'

The Chinese girl blushed. She had pulled away, and he began to look around. An email from Della was on the computer screen. He opened the desk drawer to assure himself that there was no tape recorder there and then looked behind the computer, which was also as he had left it the previous morning. Then he called the Casino Vegas, asked for Bundy and got Dravi, who sounded troubled. He said they had not seen Mr Balasingham since Monday.

'Would you give me his number at home? I've been away from Colombo and have a message to contact him.'

'Mrs Balasingham has been calling me, sir, because she hasn't seen him either. When was the message left, sir?'

He hoped Dravi wouldn't notice the pause as he wondered whether to tell the truth and decided not to. 'It could have been yesterday.'

The man explained, 'I've phoned the Colombo hospitals, but he's not there. Mr Balasingham has had some heart trouble in the past, so there could have been an accident.'

'Where is his BMW?'

'At home. Mrs Balasingham says yesterday he went to the gate after lunch and said that someone was going to pick him up at one-thirty. She thinks she heard a car stop.'

'If you hear from him,' CV said, 'tell him I'm back.'

He said to Emma, 'If the kettle's working, let's have a cup of tea. I need to think.'

'I'll make it.'

'Let Ranjan do it. Do policemen learn how to make tea from tea bags Ranjan?'

The young man looked confused.

He repeated the question in Sinhala and got a smile. 'Yes, sir.'

He pulled a chair up for himself, turned Emma's around so she was facing him and took her hands in his. This was the Emma who had been so frightened of Mahmoud.

'Honey,' he said, 'we have two choices. One is to get you home with Aunt Maud where you can be spoilt a little—the other is not. Which is it to be?'

'Yes. No. I don't know,' she said slow and plaintive. 'I feel better now you're here. It was just that Julia died instead of me and her parents are miserable. I don't want mine to lose me.'

Ranjan was back and asked, 'Tin kirri?'

'Yes. But first I want you to hear this,' and he told them a brief version of Dorothy's last night. 'I want you to think about this seriously, Em. Why hasn't Michael told us that Dorothy was with her father that last evening?'

She said with a tremor in her voice now, 'I don't know. But I did see him at the Red Fox. I'll talk to him if you like.'

'No, not you. If Reggie wasn't confident Michael would back him up, he would not have denied seeing her. They are relying on each other. What I am wondering is if they ganged up on her.'

She held on to his hands. 'They must have, mustn't they? No! I can't believe Michael would hurt anyone, and she wasn't anyone. She was Dor.'

'If he was in the Fort with Jimbo, they could have killed her together, given her body to someone else to dispose of and made it to the Mount in time. But what did Michael gain?'

'Perhaps they had a fight.'

'And he killed her?'

'No.'

'Perhaps that three-wheeler driver did see Michael in the Fort alone. He could have been in the house while the sale was taking place. He and Jimbo could both have been there. What do you know about Jimbo?'

She said, 'Drugs—chewing, swallowing, snorting, smoking all the time. Good-hearted but unreliable. Michael has started to see what effect they have had on his work and mind but has never been completely free of them. Jimbo's whole life is where to get them and how. Jimbo went bonkers when he heard Dor was dead. He was bashing his head against things. Frances brought a doctor, who gave him an injection.'

'And Michael?'

'He was numb. Tears came down his face, and he put his head in his hands. Mostly he just wandered about. Jeffrey was crying a lot too, but he watched over Michael all the time. I wouldn't have left Michael for a minute if it hadn't been for Jeffrey. Michael was so gone that I thought he might kill himself.'

'Sir,' said Ranjan, 'if Mr Bell bought Padmani's Blood, where did he put it?' He was right. Where exactly was the stone?

'He's never mentioned that he has it, Ranjan, and he's good at making precious stones disappear. Belladonna!' he said suddenly. 'Reggie gave a code name Belladonna to his banker. Em, did you ever hear Dorothy or Michael say the word Belladonna?'

'They could have.'

The kettle was choking, and Ranjan left them.

While he was away, Emma leant over and kissed CV's cheek. He caught her head with his hands so he could kiss her lips. She touched his cheek with her palms, rose quicky, followed Ranjan and returned with two mugs of tea.

'Who does Ali think did it?' Emma asked as she handed him one.

'He hasn't speculated, but he's helping. He's more interested in Maggie than who killed Dorothy. What about you calling it a day and getting home?'

'I think I'll stay in case any messages come in. I'll go back just before it is Steven's time to take over. I feel better now you've asked Bundy to phone you. If he calls here, we'll give him your new mobile number.'

He called the Casino Vegas and once again got Dravi.

'It's vander Marten again,' he said. 'When did you last hear from Bundy?'

'Yesterday afternoon, sir. About four he dropped in and said he'd see me later.'

'Call me if you hear anything.'

He phoned Michael and got Jeff, who told him Michael had flu. 'Yesterday evening he went out and came back almost unconscious. He's a little better.'

Almost unconscious seemed an excessive description of flu. 'If I came over, could we talk? It's really important, Jeff.'

'He's been asleep two hours. When he wakes, I'll call you.'

'Do that. Thank you for the job on Reggie's room, even though there was nothing there. Only three more days!'

'Michael was going to talk to Mr Bell yesterday, but then he got ill at the Palace.'

'At the Palace! What time?'

'Evening.'

'He saw Bell?'

Jeff hesitated. 'I don't know, Clive. I should have asked him. He said he got food poisoning, so that's how I treated it, but the doctor says there's a virus with the same symptoms.'

'See you later then, Jeff.'

He sat silent until Emma said, 'What is it?'

'Yesterday I spent a few minutes with Bell and got ill. Later, Michael went to see him and got ill.'

'You mean you were both poisoned?'

'If we were, what then?'

He got up to leave and said, 'I'm worried about Bundy. He may be in trouble.'

She said wryly, 'He's in a lot of trouble if he killed Dor and Julia.'

'But then why turn to me? I'm meeting Senaratne at the Galle Face. If Bundy phones, tell him I'll be there till six or longer—maybe at the pool. Give him my mobile number. Then I'll go back to the house. Don't open the door till you're ready to go home. What's that email from Del?'

He walked to the computer and read:

Me again, virgin woman, calling from the land of the free. Got the headmistress of Dor—she practically fucked me on the phone. 'The girl was impossible, my dear, and when I met her father, I was not surprised— but this is off the record, my dear. I've never heard from them after we asked him to remove her.' Next item: Dor's mom has turned herself in again—not for murder but booze—spoke to her new ex-husband, who has an IQ of 43. How did he get to be an orthopaedic surgeon? Eventually got Marie at a rehab centre in the Netherlands—surprise of all surprises—Reginald himself is paying for her to go dry again. She is having remorse over losing her only daughter. Is that late or what? Take care of that Perry Mason balloon, won't you? I'm thinking of doing my vacation out there. Was the offer genuine? Over and out. Della Street née Marsh.

He was smiling as he read, and Emma said, 'She's awfully nice. Why did you leave her?'

'We brought out the worst in each other. Ask her about my faults—she saw a lot of them.' He said softly as Ranjan took the cups away, 'I only think about one woman now.'

The Asian face beamed.

Before he left, he went over to the front house and knocked on the kitchen door. Lakshmi eventually opened it and said in English, 'I am ironing upstairs. You are drinking tea?'

'No, thanks.' He handed her Rs 200 and said, 'For today and tomorrow. Did you see Mr Balasingham when he was here?'

'Yes, he asking why typist isn't opening door. I say all women in Colombo are frightened of bombs now. He ask if I see you. I say, last time yesterday morning. You are angry as man making bad with his computer.'

'And?'

She switched to Sinhala, 'He said, you are his good friend.'

'How did he look, Lakshmi?'

'Very bad. He needed to put on washed clothes. *Poosma!*' She sniffed under her arms.

'Did he come in his blue BMW?'

'No, he came in kangaroo cab.'

'If you see him, Lakshmi, tell him I'd like to speak to him.'

'Yes. Doing,' she said in English.

Before he left the grounds he looked around and could see no one watching. Even so he walked two blocks north quickly, turned down the first four three-wheelers, and it took him only five minutes to get to the Galle Face Hotel at 3.50 p.m. in the fifth.

Teddy and CV Make a Deal

Teddy was pacing the red carpet and looked so impressive in full dress uniform that two of the hotel employees were giving him the celebrity treatment. They circled protectively, which was not easy given the superintendent's habit of lurching rather than walking and turning on a four-step. One of his own men and two other hotel employees hovered in the distance.

When CV reached him, Teddy said, 'These men think I'm a film star.'

'You look one. That's some get-up you're in.'

'I come from official business, that of assuring a new ambassador that we're a benign lot. Uniforms give the impression you have nothing to do but attend parades and receive medals. Come, the manager has given us a room on the first floor.'

The moment they entered the room Teddy grabbed Solomon's drawings.

CV ordered roast beef sandwiches and left a message at the reception desk for Maggie to tell her where they were. He started to describe her to the desk clerk as 'very tall and thin'. He replied, 'No need to describe Maggie vander Marten, sir. I see her every day. My son has a picture of her in his bedroom.'

The Galle Face was famous for its vast rooms. The policeman settled himself at a table near the big windows with a view of the Fort, including the Celinko Building, which had been brought down by a suicide bomber in a truck. He showed no interest in the view but spent time looking at the pictures and then said wearily, 'I don't have a clue who they are, and I've never seen that ring. What else have you got?'

'You've heard that Michael Blue was Dorothy's half brother?'

'Steven told me. What a tragedy for those two. I phoned your aunt in case Steven had misunderstood. There's something else?'

'I know how Dorothy really spent her last evening.'

Teddy then listened to the story of the sale of Padmani's Blood with his brows moving so rapidly at times that he seemed wound up to twitch. He said at the end, 'Michael has obstructed justice. Why did he make up that Oberoi story? It's a very serious matter.'

'What we know now,' CV continued quickly, 'is that Reggie probably has the ruby but says it is lost—could be another insurance scam though that's unlikely because he hasn't reported it missing to you. Will you confront him?'

'Not yet, and I can't afford the men to put a full-time watch on him. He's not a murder suspect, and he's not in need of protection. Tell me about the building again. I need to know where it is so we can search it.'

CV repeated every word he had learned about it. 'Bell wouldn't have left the stone there.'

'But someone could have left bloodstains and the murder weapon. Signs of a struggle.'

CV began to talk about a plan that was growing in his mind—he wanted to get all the suspects together to talk about the case.

Teddy's reply was, 'Those sort of confrontations usually backfire, but I can't stop you from going ahead. If you bring them together of their own free will, I'll be there. You must promise nothing you do will be illegal.'

'That's the point. I need you because I have to bring the

investigation to a head legally, even if I have to admit later I have been doing things the law might take a different view of.'

'You've been breaking the law?'

'Minimally for expediency—the equivalent of jumping a gate marked "Do not enter". This is my rationale: as the murderer thinks I'm quitting on Friday, he will expect my last-ditch effort to be geared to Friday. A social melée on Thursday thus becomes of less interest, and we may learn something.'

Li had given him the idea when he had said he should stop showing the killer his hand.

He continued, 'Reggie will return to England after Friday. I'll bet he's already booked his flight now he's done his fatherly thing. You won't be able to hold Mahmoud either. Once the foreigners start going home, it is going to be harder to crack this case. Let's hear what they have to say in a head-on.'

'So?'

'So, on the surface I'll be the same old bumblebee telling what I have learned to the neighbours. In reality, I'll keep my own counsel. You'll be my confidant because I need your mind, your expertise, the doors you can open. But I can't confide in you if you have to pass every word on to the whole fucking police force. I'm saying hold it till Saturday when the case will be all yours again and I'll be there for you doing much the same as I'm doing now, but without the pressure.'

Teddy didn't answer. He got out of his chair and went to the window.

'Can a policeman keep such secrets?' CV pressed. 'Is it allowed?'

Teddy did not reply, but CV had seen the Sri Lankan headshake which meant yes.

'Thank you.'

He went to the door to let the waiters in with their food and asked that the tea be poured for them. As soon as they were alone again they began to eat.

'Now what's this about someone poisoning you yesterday?' the superintendent asked.

He described what happened. 'I'm going to see Michael tonight. He obviously had a much larger dose of whatever it was than I did. He's bed bound.'

'Why did he choose yesterday to see Mr Bell?'

'I don't know.'

Teddy said, 'It is unusual to kill five times by one method and then switch to another. I presume the men died by the same hand that killed Dorothy but not Julia. I need the dates on the killings in England and Italy. Where did you say you got the information?'

'I didn't.'

'From another fool frightened of the police?'

'No, behind a "Do not enter" sign I ignored.'

'How good is your source?'

'The best, and remember it provided four knifed men before I mentioned how Dorothy died.'

'Why did he not kill Julia Ware the same way? The bomb is a Lankan speciality. I bet you wouldn't even think of it as a weapon—you've been abroad too long. In America bombs are the products of lonely maniacs, but they are a daily occurrence here—so casually handled that sometimes they explode prematurely and blow up the person who is carrying them. A Lankan killed Julia.'

CV now lay on a bed on top of the coverlet. 'A hired killer? One hired killer for the first five who wasn't available for the sixth?'

'Possible. And I see a motive. There was none till now. When it comes to murder for financial gain one person may kill for a $13,000,000 treasure and another for a seventy-carat sapphire, but in both cases we are looking for someone who will take a life for an object. But this motive was covered up by Mr Bell, Michael and who knows how many others. Why? If Mr Bell is our man, why did he risk a local assassin to kill Emma and then sprinkle poison on Michael and you? He didn't need a noisy bomb if he had poison. Poison Dorothy in a resthouse, poison Emma on a beach at a pinic because the evidence would be destroyed. It is possible we have three killers here—each with a different interest. The poisoner is only after you and Michael Blue. Who are you threatening?'

'I'm a general threat. Anyone with something to hide would want me out of the way. But Michael is not.' He got up and began to walk around the room.

Teddy said, 'Michael could have faked that poisoning to take attention off himself.'

'As I faked mine?'

'Don't be touchy. Criminals do it—set themselves up as the victims.'

'Have another cup of tea so I can drop poison into your cup.'

'Wish you hadn't said that,' and Teddy slurped noisily.

Then he told CV he had got Louise Hammer on the phone. She had been in England at the time of both killings and could prove it. 'Scotland Yard will be checking her alibis, but I think she is speaking the truth on that. She told me she gave up on the Bells a long time ago and had no idea that the child Dorothy had been so devoted to her. She said that whole family had seemed a lost cause.'

'Does she have ideas on who killed Dorothy?'

'Says no. But Dorothy was always a wild one, and she's not surprised she died young.'

'Yet, Emma says Dorothy became a wild one only after her favourite nanny left. What do you think of Louise Hammer?'

'I think she's a liar who is not very intelligent, and if Dorothy ever put her in an old will, she'll try to collect now.

Might have a case—Dorothy may have cut her out because she believed she was dead. But being a foolish greedy liar doesn't make Louise a murderess. She must have known the child was devoted to her—as her Christmas card proves. Her words were "Dorothy, Mr Bell and Marie were all lost causes." I don't believe she thought ten-year-old Dorothy was a lost cause. I asked her if she had sex with Mr Bell or if he had made sexual overtures. She said, "He never looked at me—I was just the nanny."'

'Sounds as if she wanted to be looked at—as if she had a crush on him, or his money. Maybe she played mother to Dorothy hoping he'd marry her.'

'We think alike. And after she left she kept hoping. She could have helped him with the nude shots, then suggested she had something on him, and he fired her.'

'Dorothy's will is important. Do you know who has it?' CV asked.

'No, but the rich don't usually die intestate these days. Mr Bell says she never discussed one with him but that she made one when she was eighteen. He gave me the name of his own lawyer, an English solicitor G.J. Welles with an office in Knightsbridge. I phoned Welles, who has handled Bell's legal affairs for twenty years or more. Dorothy telephoned him four years ago to ask about English inheritance laws. He told her to come and see him, but she never did. He sent her a bill for the phone consultation, which she ignored and eventually Bell paid.'

'Welles charges for saying "Come and see me?"'

The room phone rang, and CV was asked if he would take a call from Miss vander Marten. Maggie said she was going down to the pool, where Reggie would join her at about six. 'I've brought your suit and a towel.'

'I'll need the towel, but I've two new bathing suits.'

'Don't hang up. The bank called. Reggie's cheque is in.'

'When he arrives, act as if you don't know that.'

Before they parted CV wondered if he should tell Teddy about Bundy's disappearance. He decided not to, if only because words spoken could not be unspoken.

A Swim

Maggie was swimming freestyle up and down the pool, and so was a blonde man with the power and concentration of a Popov. Not unexpectedly, he got much less attention, although her briefly clad body was barely visible in the salt water and her braided dark hair was mostly submerged as she streaked along. Both seemed oblivious of the stares of those who sat on their pallets ignoring a stupendous display from the ocean behind them.

The roof turret of the Indian embassy next door overlooked the pool. Two guards were watching Maggie with a sniggering jerking of their hips. CV stared at them until they became uneasy and pretended to be looking out to sea.

He whistled and she swam to the edge and shouted, 'Come in, the water's lovely.'

'You've made quite a stir.'

She blinked rapidly. 'Someone must have heard I'm trying out a new eyeliner. Has it run?'

He bent down and studied her eyes. 'No.'

He headed for the changing room amazed that she was so used to an audience that she could function as if it wasn't there. If she'd seen the thrusting hips of the Indian guards she would probably have waved. He returned in his new red swim trunks, and went over to where Maggie's beach bag, straw hat and pink towel lay on a blue plastic mattress. A black and white towel and his old blue shorts were on a separate pallet. He shoved his wallet under her hat then dived in from the side, making an enormous splash. When he came up, Maggie was alongside. The buoyancy of the salt water made staying on the surface effortless.

He shouted, 'Need to talk.' They went to the middle of the

pool where they could not be overheard. He explained he wanted her to separate Reginald Bell from his travellers' cheques. 'You told me he cashed one at the Queen's and made a note of it. I don't need the cheques themselves. I need to look at the register where he made that note.'

'Why?'

'To see if he cashed one at the airport. He's a conspicuous-looking man, so I can't understand why no one remembers him. Teddy too wasn't able to turn up the taxi driver who drove him to the Palace, and I'm curious how Reggie happened to have rupees on hand for the taxi. Of course, he may have currencies of all kinds put aside for his visits, but you can't get hold of Sri Lankan rupees out of this country. If a bank teller remembers him, he might also remember if he was alone. If a friend was there to meet him, why didn't he say so?'

'I don't see how I can get to his money belt unless I let him fuck me again, and that's out.' She made a happy comic face. 'My boyfriend wouldn't like it.'

'Or your cousin. But we have to get that list, Mag. Just now I threw my wallet on to the seat and covered it with your hat. I couldn't leave it inside because there are no lockers or attendants in the changing room. Reggie will have to do the same, and you may get a chance to look through his body belt. You're sure that's where the register is?'

'Where it was in Kandy. He had a wallet too and some loose change in his pocket. At the Queen's he unbuttoned his shirt, unzipped the money belt, took the cheques out and signed one. The pack is joined at the perforated end, and while the cashier was counting the cash, Reggie turned it over and wrote on the back.'

'That's terrifically observant. If you can get the money belt into your hands, write down what's on that back sheet—where he got his rupees.'

'He tries not to let the belt out of his sight. He put it into a drawer in the hotel room, and when he came out of the loo, the motherfucker took it out and looked through it as if he suspected me of stealing.'

'Do you have a pen?'

'In my red bag.'

'Keep it handy with something to write on. If the chance comes, take it. Also note what else he carries in that belt. I am specifically looking for Padmani. She's the size of a small egg, I hear.'

'You think Reggie has her? I suppose she is a her.'

'That's also what I hear—of course she's a her.'

'Where did he get her?'

'I'll tell you later. She was last seen in a chamois leather bag.'

She said, 'Before you puff along, tell me where you got those trunks? It is a fashion fact, cousin, that one should never surround the broadest part of one's anatomy with strong prints or psychedelic colours. You've done both.'

'Uncle Li gave me two pairs—the other is green. In future, all my swim suits will make a statement.'

'Who is Uncle Li?'

'Forget you heard the name. I'll tell you later.'

She swam away turning in the water like an eel, and he followed flopping like a dog. After a few laps they climbed out because Reginald Bell was signing in. CV placed a pallet for Reggie between their own and began to cover himself with sunblock lotion. The Englishman had gone directly to the changing rooms, and when he joined them, he was in brief khaki shorts that emphasized his bronze tan, now heavily oiled.

'Hello, you two. I saw you in the water. Maggie has brought her fan club. Up in the foyer I heard someone say she was here.' He then said to CV, 'Is your phone connected? I tried to get you this morning.' He spread his towel over the middle pallet, put a khaki money belt only a shade lighter than his shorts on it and lay down.

'Sorry about the phone. I was poisoned yesterday, then sabotaged by a friend who thought I looked sickly, so I slept past midday. I'm grateful now, but when I woke I was not.'

Maggie had her pink pen in her hand, and she dropped it beside her next to her pink notebook. She said, 'Reggie, I wish you'd tell CV where to buy his swim togs. You have a gift of looking properly put together.'

'I get a compliment from the lady! Thank you. Is the poison story true?' he spoke to CV but looked only at Maggie.

'Oh, yes. I think someone spiked my lime juice at the hotel. Did you?'

Maggie was tightening her stomach muscles and wriggling her toes.

'No more jokes of that kind,' Bell said lazily and turned on to his stomach. Then he turned his head to CV and said, 'You didn't really think I drugged you?'

'As you were the only one there, I did wonder.'

Bell seemed amused, 'Must have been something you ate, though I've never been ill at the Palace. I recommended it to Dot because of its excellent kitchen. Anything new on her?'

'Not enough though I've been following leads. I've heard many nice things: She was brave. She was kind. She was loyal. She had the gift of making people care about her. If you'd like to swim, I feel ready for a few more laps and then we can talk.'

Bell was silent a moment, then said, 'I won't be going in. I think I'm getting a cold.'

'The water is warm, and there's nothing like salt water to clear the sinuses.'

'I'll take my cure from the side. It is a luxury to be able to lie outdoors with an overcast sky and be covered with spray from the surf. There are sides to the life here that are extremely pleasant.'

CV guessed then that the other couldn't swim—or perhaps didn't swim well enough to want to be seen doing so by Maggie.

He toyed with the idea of picking him up and dropping him into the deep end to give Maggie a chance to look in the money belt; he himself could then become a hero by saving Bell. Then, seeing the conditioning of the Englishman, he realized he might lose in such a confrontation.

Instead he said, 'Shall I bring you up to date now, Mr Bell?'

'Yes, please do.'

He sat up. 'What I found, after I left you yesterday, is that two men left Dorothy's body in the Pettah. They took her there in the trunk of a dark Toyota Starlet. This means she died elsewhere.'

With this information, the golden body jackknifed, and Maggie turned on to her side to watch. Bell was facing CV, and she jerked her pen vertically at his back in the same manner as the hooded man was reported to have given Dorothy a final vulgar salute. CV wondered what the staring tourists thought of her now. Probably felt privileged to have witnessed the action.

'Who were the men?' Bell was asking.

'I don't know, but someone made a drawing of them.'

'Where is the drawing?'

'In the changing room.' He lay back. He'd thrown his fish the bait. He continued, 'I can't bring it out here as I've had a feeling that I'm being followed and don't want anyone to know I've got it.'

And the fish went for it: 'Then let's go in.'

'Mr Bell, please sit down. The drawing won't run away.'

'Tell me where it is and I'll—no! I can't be found rifling through your belongings. Kindly come with me.'

CV rose slowly and ambled off after his employer. When he reached the door he glanced back and saw Maggie sitting up watching them. He went inside and shut the door. They had the room to themselves, and as slowly as he could, he looked for the waterproof plastic packet he had slipped inside Li's white duty-free bag that was hanging under his clothes on a peg. He removed a sketch of the two men, took his time examining it, then handed it to Bell.

'But their heads are covered!'

'I think we will agree innocent men don't cover their heads.'

Bell studied the drawing intently. Eventually he said, 'I thought we had something concrete at last, but no one could make an identification from this.'

'And the witness who saw them refuses to talk to the police.'

'Damn!' If Bell felt any relief he didn't show it.

'My feeling! But we now know she didn't die in the Pettah.'

Bell said, 'May I keep this?'

'Of course. The witness also made a drawing of a ring he says the big man was wearing—an unusual ring.'

That stopped Bell's movement to the door. 'What ring?'

At the moment the door opened and a blond youth slammed in and headed towards the toilet leaving the door wide open behind him. CV could not see Maggie from where they stood but made no movement to the door. He moved so that to face him Bell would have his back to to the door when he faced him, and he gave Bell a photocopy of the second drawing.

'What else do you have in that bag?'

'A second swim suit in case this one is stolen.'

Bell looked inside. 'What possessed you to buy them? The one you're wearing makes you look double your size.'

'It's important we big men not be ashamed of our bodies.'

Bell, obviously amused, went back to studying the ring.

'Have you seen it?' CV wondered if Maggie had had enough time to look in the money belt. He could think of no further way to prolong the conversation.

Bell said, 'No.' Without taking his eyes from the drawing he said slowly, 'I can't say that for sure. I may have seen it. It's not an unusual ring.'

CV, working on a delay, pointed, 'That's a dark stone set into the top. I suppose we should get back to Maggie.'

'I want a copy of this sketch too.'

'Of course, and show them both around.' CV took it from him again. 'Actually, the ring is not that ordinary. The place where the band joins the top is unusual.'

'It doesn't look unusual to me.'

'Nor me, but a gem man says it is.'

'No name again?'

'I am sure he won't mind you having his name, but I'd have to ask him. Poor pickings, but I thought you'd want to know about the drawings,' CV said

'Not poor. This is a real step forward.'

'Thank you.'

CV took his clothes off the peg to gain a few seconds, hung the white bag back where it had been and replaced his clothes on the peg one item at a time. 'Let's get out of here.'

Maggie lay immobile with her straw hat across her face. When they reached her, he again began to spread her sunblock lotion over his skin to give him a chance to watch Bell without appearing too curious. She said, 'I hope you two weren't doing what you had enough time to do from the age it took you. Your phone rang, CV. I answered it, and the caller hung up. Who'd do that?'

'Beats me. Did the fans cluster around to touch the body?'

'No, because I told the pool men when I arrived that if no one came near me today, they'd get a big tip.'

Bell had stretched out again, and she said, 'What do you think of the drawings, Reggie? Do you know those men?'

'How could I? None of my friends wear bags over their heads. I haven't seen that ring either.' He said to CV, 'How did you find the person who made the sketches?'

'He found me.' He had rehearsed this lie in anticipation of the question.

'Did he want cash for his story?'

'No. But if he had, he'd have got it.' That put him in the right mood to ask, 'Would you mind a personal question? When we were at Bentota, I noticed one of your front teeth seemed a fraction different from the others. Again today when the light hit it, one seemed a different colour. I know this is quite uncalled for, but do you have a capped right front incisor?'

'Damned dentist!'

Maggie sat up and said, 'Let me see?' Bell bared his teeth for her. 'They look a perfect match to me,' she said and lay down again. 'Reggie, don't worry about CV—he's got eyes like a cat's.'

'I'm *very* annoyed,' said Bell. 'I paid for the cap to be undetectable.'

CV said hastily, 'Sorry, I shouldn't have said anything. It is just that I have a front tooth my dentist says should be capped while the root is still there. Do you have to keep replacing them?'

'They're as rugged as the real thing. You pay dentists a fortune, and they can't even produce a tooth that matches the others.'

'How did you lose it?'

Bell then laughed. 'Someone hit me.'

'Did you hit him back?'

'I did.'

'Well done.'

'No. He got a bruise, and I lost a tooth.'

So Charles Yarrow had told his son Peter the truth when he'd said he'd knocked Bell's front tooth out.

The phone rang, 'Yes?'

A man's voice said softly, 'Don't say my name if you're not alone.'

'Hold on,' he walked away from the others to the wall, turned to protect the phone from the sea spray and said equally softly, 'I'm alone now.'

'You know who I am?' asked Bundy.

'Yes, of course, where are you? Your wife is worried and so

is Dravi. So am I. Sorry my Chinese assistant got so scared when you came by.'

'Did you change the lock?'

'Yes, of course. Did you bug the room?'

'Of course not. I wasn't expecting my key not to fit. I'm in trouble. Very bad trouble. Do me a favour, will you, Clive? For old times' sake?'

'If I can.'

'Listen carefully, man, because I can't talk for long. Please go see Millie, and tell her I have to go away for a long time. If you tell anyone else, Clive, I'm dead. I didn't kill Dorothy Bell, that other girl or anyone else, but I'm going to be saddled with their murders. Tell Millie I may not be able to contact her before I leave.'

'Okay, but how long will you be gone—days?'

'Months. Even longer. Clive, please get out of Sri Lanka yourself before it's too late for you too.'

'You know I can't. Who is the threat?'

'You're safer not knowing.'

'Let's get together—no one need know. I have to talk to you.'

'There's no time.'

'What about the casino . . .?' He wanted to keep Bundy on the line, hoping for some clue to his whereabouts. His voice had a slight echo but there were no other sounds.

'I have partners who'll run it. Tell Millie to behave like a widow—unhappy and not to tell the children I'm alive. When it's safe, I'll get messages to her.'

'Where's the house?'

Bundy gave him the address and said, 'Goodbye, Clive. Thank you.'

CV said quickly, 'Bundy, do you know where Bell has put a ruby called Padmani's Blood?'

A silence. Then, 'No, I didn't know he had it. Dorothy asked me about it. Keep away from that stone. It brings bad luck,' he said and hung up.

CV held the phone to his ear, pretended to listen while he thought of a story to tell Bell, then returned to say, 'I have to go. Millie, Bundy's wife, says he's disappeared. He hasn't been seen since yesterday.'

Maggie sat up and said, 'Oh God. Hope he's not dead too. I'll come with you.'

'No,' he didn't want Bell to be able to follow him.

'I'm paying you to find my daughter's killer, not to look for Balasingham,' said Bell.

'Then you don't think he's running because he killed her—you'd rule him out?'

Bell saw his mistake, 'That wasn't what I meant.'

'I told his wife I'd come over. She needs a friend, and I may get some clue to his whereabouts.'

'What else did she say?'

'Just wanted to know if I had heard from him. Look Mr Bell, I feel that every time we meet I'm too brusque. There's nothing personal—it's how I work.'

Bell was lighting another cigarette and even smiled. 'I understand.'

'Take the car and send Joseph back for me,' said his cousin.

'Thanks, Mag. I promised the desk clerk you'd give him your autograph for his son.'

Bell said to her, 'Maggie doesn't need a car. I'll take her home.'

CV thought it better not to argue with him.

He dressed quickly. Before leaving the hotel, he phoned the swimming pool from the office and asked to speak to Maggie. 'I just ran into Charlie Soysa, and he'll collect you in about an hour and take you home.'

She said, 'That will be fine. I don't know why I forgot.'

He heard Bell say behind her, 'Is everything all right?'

Without hanging up, she replied so that CV could hear, 'It's Mr Soysa reminding me that I am to be photographed with him in an hour.'

Millie Balasingham

In spite of his friendship with Bundy, CV had seen Millie Balasingham only once, but he knew of her Sinhala family, which had produced generation after generation of successful names in cricket, tennis, swimming, track and golf. Bundy had told him his wife had inherited their athleticism, and the only time CV had seen her, he had noticed that she had long limbs and carried herself as if she was on the sidelines waiting for her turn to compete. In the States she would have seemed just another woman who put health before cuteness. In Sri Lanka she stood out.

From her veranda Millie stared blindly from reddened eyes in a face of sorrow. Because she didn't look huggable, she seemed the more tragic. A barefoot girl of about ten wearing denim shorts and a T-shirt and two grim older women in saris stood behind her.

CV introduced himself, then said, 'Mrs Balasingham—Millie—I must talk to you.'

'I can't talk to anyone now,' she said, as if he was the cause of her misery. When he didn't move, she snapped, 'Another time, man. Don't you understand?'

'I understand that you want me to leave, but I have to talk to you before I do.'

In exasperation she rolled her eyes from behind their swollen lids. 'Then say whatever it is quickly.' Over her shoulder she said in Sinhala, 'These whites think they can push us around.' Only the child smiled.

'Alone!' he persisted.

'I have said I cannot. I have troubles. What did you say your name was?'

He repeated it.

'Oh . . . you are that vander Marten who is looking into Dorothy Bell's death.'

'Yes I am.'

'Well, I know nothing about her except that she was a tart. Now, I must go.'

She was without shoes and in slacks and shirt that left her midriff bare. The house stretched deep behind her. He could see into its recesses and beyond to a bright outdoors where people were moving. There was movement in the house too. Two small boys peered at him from a doorway, and he heard voices behind them—shrill, loud but friendly. If he hadn't seen Millie's face or known Bundy was missing, he would have thought he had interrupted a party.

'Millie, listen,' he said softly, 'I know why you are upset. I am not here to ask questions but to tell you something.'

She looked at him with curiosity for the first time. He kept his expression neutral knowing that six other pairs of eyes were watching.

She said over her shoulder in Sinhala, 'He wants to speak to me,' and the *he* she used was a contemptuous word only used for inferiors. She had called him a lout. To him in English, she said, 'We can talk in the garden.' She strode to the centre of the lawn, turned and said wearily, 'Well what is it? In a minute the ants will find my feet.'

To prevent that from happening she moved from one foot to the other. He led the way to the driveway. As they walked, he said quietly, 'Bundy phoned. He is in trouble—danger—and is going away—perhaps for a long time. He wants you to continue to act as if you haven't heard from him.'

She turned so her back was to the house. He could see the others still watching them.

'Where is he?' she whispered.

'I don't know.' He repeated Bundy's words as accurately as

he could. 'He'll have to get in touch with me again to see if I've spoken to you. His absence seems to be connected to Dorothy's and Julia's deaths.'

She became thoughtful.

'No!' he said sharply, 'You're acting relieved. Stay angry. Cry if you can. Tell your family I came to talk about Dorothy. Continue to call me a *godiya*.'

Startled eyes met his and he smiled. 'And don't try Tamil. I haven't forgotten that either.'

'Oh, I am so sorry. I thought you were . . . no, there was no excuse. Bundy says I behave like a street woman when I get angry. Why did he phone you? Why not me?'

'I think because I wouldn't scream with joy at his voice.'

She bit her lip to keep from smiling. 'Thanks to God, he's alive.'

'He's one of my suspects in these killings,' he continued. 'I'm torn between our long friendship and the fact that he seems to have set me up for a fall.'

He took the two drawings from his pocket and unfolded them. 'You'll see that one of these men who left Dorothy Bell in the Pettah could be Bundy. Don't worry. No one could positively identify him from that sketch. That man was wearing this ring,' he said as he handed her the second sheet and watched her reaction.

Millie's face froze. She stared at the drawing, rearranged her thoughts and expression clumsily, then hissed, 'It isn't Bundy's ring, if that's what you're saying.'

'That may be true, but he's told me about his . . . his kleptomania.'

Her expression now soured. 'What has that to do with it?'

'Everything. It's the only way the man in the drawing can be positively identified.'

'No,' she said not quickly enough. 'I thought . . . at first . . . I had seen it somewhere, but the one I'm thinking of, which isn't

Bundy's either, is more round on top—much more.' She was a terrible liar, and her tongue practically knotted as she forced it to do her bidding. She did not raise her eyes to his.

'Millie,' he pleaded, 'I am sticking my neck out by not telling the police that I know Bundy is alive. Can't you stick your neck out a little for me? If he is innocent of these killings, the more I know, the less I'm likely to get him into trouble.'

She pressed her lips together, obviously thinking about what he said and meanwhile looked at the veranda and gave a wave that was more like a flag salute.

He continued, 'Bundy has warned me twice that I am in danger in continuing this investigation, although it was he who got me into it in the first place. I'm guessing he was set up and moved Dorothy's body so he would not be accused.'

'Bundy couldn't kill a fly,' she said very gently. 'I'm the tough one in this family, not him. He told me about you. In school you were just a bag of muscle, and yet you've done something with your life. Then day before yesterday he said to me, "I always thought Clive was a fool, but I was the fool to think it." Bundy told me about Dorothy Bell and her Arab lover. She was rich but couldn't resist prostitution. We're born-again Christians, Clive. We live by the teaching of Jesus Christ. We don't believe that people like Dorothy Bell are following the Bible's teaching. People like her corrupt the whole world.'

She stopped abruptly. He said, 'So Bundy's kleptomania must have troubled you both deeply—a sin against the Seventh Commandment.'

'Yes, of course it did,' she seemed grateful that he understood, whereas he had said it because he was angry that they had condemned Dorothy without understanding. 'It is a sickness, and we will overcome it by our prayers. God gives everyone weaknesses, and as long as you try to overcome yours, you'll be saved. Bundy says it is as if he has a devil on his back. He sometimes doesn't even know what he's taken. I give it all back.'

'He took my sunglasses and wore them openly. Did you return those to me?' He didn't want her to rationalize Bundy's stealing too much.

She looked at him stricken. 'I never knew he took your sunglasses. Are you missing anything else? I have a drawer where I keep the things I don't remember either of us buying.'

He said gently as he put his hand on her arm, 'I'm sorry. I don't like to hear Dorothy Bell slanged by people who know nothing about her. No, I am missing nothing more. Bundy probably kept my glasses in his BMW, so you never saw them.'

'If I had, I would have asked him where he got them, and if he hadn't bought them, I'd have tried to find out whose they were. I promise.'

'Whom did you return that ring to?'

'I . . .' she was almost caught. 'I told you I have never seen that ring.'

'Millie,' he said, 'you've got to trust me. Bundy does.'

She thought about that and glanced back at the veranda. So did he. There were now seven women and one man watching them. The child had gone.

'We should have gone somewhere else to talk,' she grumbled.

He didn't remind her the garden had been her choice.

She said, 'Bundy did have that ring. I found it on our dressing table one morning. It belongs to a friend of ours, and I gave it back to him. He is not a murderer either.'

'Is he one of the men in the sketch?'

Her eyes filled with tears. 'No, I swear on the Bible that neither is him.'

'Will you give me his name?'

'How can I?'

'Who is the thin man in the drawing?'

'Don't ask me that.'

He liked Millie Balasingham.

'Millie, here are my phone numbers.' He wrote them down. 'The trouble with murder is that when someone kills twice, he'll do it again. Murder is against the Fifth Commandment.'

She looked at him without expression and then gave him her hand. 'I hope you're not mocking me.'

'I am not. But I believe it is possible to preach Christianity yet ignore its precepts when it becomes self-serving,' and he turned and left her.

As long as Millie needed him to contact Bundy, he knew she would talk with him. Bundy was the fat man who, wearing a stolen ring, had helped put Dorothy's body in the Pettah. The ring's owner, for one, could identify him. Even if Bundy did not kill her, someone could have blackmailed him into helping with the second murder.

Meechi

CV brought Joseph up to date on Bundy's absence. 'Ask around to see if anyone knows where he is, Joseph. Do you know him?'

'Only his face, sir. I went into Casino Vegas on Sunday—I am looking to see if I know either him or Mister Dravi. I have not seen them before.'

CV then told him Li's story.

'Who owns the Cedric Brougham?' the chauffeur asked.

'I don't know. It's Mr Sharif's friend, but he can't tell me the name.'

'If you send Sharif Master to that friend's house, I will follow him and see who it is.'

'We can't do that. I accepted the Chinese Master's terms in exchange for his story. They both want to be kept out of it.'

'But that driver will be already talking to his friends, so why not to me?' Joseph had the persistence of a pit bull terrier. 'We have only two more days, Master Clive.'

'Three! Joseph, what about the bodyguard Mr Bell took with him?' He described the man. 'Any suggestions of where we can look for him?'

The old man replied, 'I have seen such a man, sir. He was outside the Chinese doctors' house this morning when Miss Maggie went in.'

It would be luck indeed if it was the same man—but do you get that lucky? He had forgotten that Maggie had gone to see Soong—he was forgetting too much. 'Tell me about Muscles.'

'Muscles! That's a good name! He asked me if I had seen Mr Balasingham.'

'Jesus! Stop the car. I want to talk to you about this before we get home. Why didn't you tell me?'

'I was going to, sir,' Joseph replied stoically as he turned into Havelock Road. 'But it wasn't as important as what you were telling me.'

They were outside the Police Park. On the other side of the metal railings, horses were being schooled in parade formations. It was a magnificent sight—something to watch another time.

'Joseph,' CV said, trying to show no impatience, 'if the man outside Soong's is the one who was with Mr Bell, it's very important.'

'I know, sir.'

CV gave up. 'Tell me everything that happened.'

'I drove Maggie Missie to Soong Doctor's at nine o'clock and parked on the road. Then the Muscles came and said he was looking for Mr Balasingham, where was he? "There is a casino master of that name," I said, "but I do not know him." He asked me why there is a policeman at the Soong gate every day. I said there had been a bomb. 'I asked him why he wanted Mr Balasingham—why not look in his casino? He said Mr Balasingham was not in his casino. I asked, "Who do you work for?" He said, "You would not know the name." When Maggie Missie came out we went to see Michael Master, but he was out, so we came home.'

'Your Muscles may not be the same one. There are many

short strong men, and Balasingham is a common name.' CV leaned back in the seat.

Joseph said, 'In that lane I have a sister-in-law of a niece who comes in to do the washing and ironing for Mrs Modder every day. I can ask her to keep a lookout for Muscles.'

'Will she chatter?'

'All girls chatter.'

'Joseph, isn't there someone who doesn't chatter—someone to find out about Muscles quietly? We have to be careful, Joseph. People have been killed.'

'My friend has a bicycle shop. It is Poya, so his shop will be closed, but he lives there.'

'Let's go talk to him now.'

Joseph drove down to Thimbirigasaya Junction on the same road, turned left and stopped outside a cycle repair shop. While Joseph went to find his friend, CV lay with his eyes closed. He eventually heard the car door open and simultaneously a tapping at his own window. A skinny youth outside gave him a wide smile.

Joseph said, 'The boy is my friend's son Meechi, sir. He is sixteen and has a friend who will go to that road with him. If there are two boys on bicycles, no one will think anything.'

CV said to Meechi in Sinhala, 'You will say you are there taking notes on how policemen act for your school work. Take a pencil and a book and write a lot in it.'

Meechi beamed.

CV passed him two hundred rupees. 'I will pay by the hour, but don't make anything up. You will get the same money if you find nothing. The money I give you now is for expenses only.'

Meechi's eyes sparkled. 'I will find everything.'

'Now tell me what you are going to do,' CV said.

'I am going to play cricket outside the Chinese doctors' house and ask about the police and what they are doing when there are bombs. If there is a short man with big muscles and Vaseline on his hair, I will follow him.'

'That's excellent. But take no risks. He may be a very dangerous man.'

The boy laughed gaily. CV knew he would have loved such a job when he was a teenager. It was a bit late, but perhaps that's what he should have done long before this—brought in teenage boys to stake out all the suspects.

Money Talks

Before he reached the front door, Amily came out. Knowing her deafness, he yelled, 'Everything all right?'

'Why not?' she yelled back. 'Lady has gone out to do scrapbook.'

He hurried inside and shouted, 'Maggie! Where is Auntie?'

She shouted back, 'At Shantha's.' He found her in the back drawing room, and she said, 'Some reason we have to yell? I insisted Aunt Maud go. She needed to get out.'

'I suppose it's all right.'

'Of course it is. Shantha came herself to pick her up. Perera called, there's nothing wrong with the lime juice—he drank a glass from the same batch himself. They squeeze the limes in the morning and keep it refrigerated till it runs out.'

'Then it was the sugar.'

'He said the sugar is usually thrown out because guests put wet spoons in the sugar bowls. The Palace is trying to avoid those dreadful little packets and, worse, the sugar-liquid served elsewhere.'

'I don't like it when someone implies I've imagined something that happened.'

'You thought he was going to say, "Yes, we poisoned you." Come to the front room. I have something to show you.' The something was a finely polished wooden box. He lifted the lid off. There was an envelope inside.

'The box is the wrap,' she said. 'The letter is the present. Isn't it a lovely box?'

'Don't tell me Reggie sprang for something this stunning?'

'Reggie! Why would I take a present from that rat? On the other hand, why not? Ali was here this afternoon and he asked me if he could have the bracelet back. I was annoyed and said, "Go ahead, take the damned thing. I hate it anyway."'

'You actually said that?'

'Yes, I'm so ashamed. I was even ashamed when I said it, but you know how he is—wouldn't rise—just smiled away. I wanted to smack him. He said, "Stop pouting." He said there are some women who are just too beautiful for jewellery. I'm not puffing—he really said that, but of course he's in love and has a tongue like syrup, which I distrust. He said he'd replace the bracelet with something else, and I thought, "Oh shit, now I get a necklace." But he came in a little while ago with this box that was his grandmother's. It is for his letters to me, and the first one is inside. It's a poem. Pure slop, but he wrote it himself.'

'I can't read it?'

'No, it's so yukky, it's private. I'm so happy.'

He kissed her cheek.

'It's a very beautiful box, Mag, and you deserve a beautiful box with a bad love poem.'

'Why won't he sleep with me? Did he say?'

'You know the answer. We men can't stand being loved for our bodies. We're not objects, we have minds. Now, make me happy, and tell me where Emma's body is?'

'Upstairs.' Maggie was looking at the box, then at him, 'Before you go, why haven't you asked me about Reggie's traveller's cheques?'

'My visit to Emma is postponed.' Since the poisoning, his memory had flattened.

She pulled out her notebook, 'He has a bunch of £500 and £100 cheques from Thomas Cook. He's written each number at the back of the booklet: one list for the 500s and one for the 100s, so when he cashes one, he just has to add the date, where he cashed it, how much he got in local currency. He must have arrived with a new batch because he cashed the first one on the eleventh, the day he arrived here.'

Maggie had written:

500 Hongkong Shanghai. Rs 47,000 11th April
500 Palace. 46,400 13th
500 Queen's. 47,500 19th
100 Thomas Cook. 5,600 11th

'To save time I wrote the rupees to the nearest hundred. On the eleventh, he cashed two cheques: one for five and one for one hundred pounds. The last one was at the Queen's Hotel on Saturday the nineteenth, when he was with me in Kandy.'

'The fifty-six hundred can't be rupees.'

'They were all rupees.'

'Then the amount is wrong.'

'No. I was careful.'

'He wouldn't suddenly take fifty-six rupees to the pound instead of ninety-four—and Thomas Cook doesn't chisel.'

Then he had an idea. His aunt had several *Asiaweeks* that listed the major world currencies against each other. He looked through the stack; the newest was three months old, and it listed the Indian rupee at fifty-five against the British pound and the Sri Lankan rupee at ninety-two to the pound.

'If Bell's flight came in from India that evening, he changed a hundred pounds into Indian rupees there.' He continued wearily, 'But here's another problem: How did he cash £500 into Sri Lankan rupees on the eleventh at the Hong Kong Shanghai Bank, which doesn't have a branch at the airport? He says he arrived in Colombo around 6 p.m., which is after the Hong Kong Shanghai Bank in Colombo would have closed.'

'That's right.'

'But,' he said thoughtfully, 'it is only forty-five minutes by air from here to Kerala. If Reggie was already here on the eleventh morning, he could have cashed £500 at the HSBC in town for lunch, drinks, gifts, whatever left Colombo for India, cashed £100 there and returned here at 6 p.m.'

'That's idiotic.'

'Or he sent a £500 traveller's cheque to someone here who coincidentally cashed it at the HSBC the day Bell arrived from India, where he had cashed a £100 cheque. In which case why not write that person's name on his record? Why the name of a bank? Probably some simple explanation, but I don't see it.'

'The South Indian travelling is a bit farfetched too. Flying in and out, and in, would have shown on his passport and be in the police report. Does it matter?'

'It bugs me like an itch when figures are off. The entry stamps on a passport only show the date of entry—not the time. Maybe the police were just checking to see whether he arrived when he said he did and missed a previous entry and departure. But at least we have one explanation for why he didn't get money at the airport here. He already had Sri Lankan rupees.' He shook his head. 'If he entered Colombo twice on the eleventh, wouldn't he have said so?'

'Wait a minute! We know he travels under aliases, at least the CIA says he does. What if he used an alias?' As she spoke she continued to stroke her new box as if it was a cat.

He said, 'Identities have to be backed by passports when travelling. Did he have a second passport in that money belt?'

'Definitely not. There was a stack of thousand-rupee notes held with a rubber band, an English passport, two credit cards, and the traveller's cheques.'

'No airline ticket?'

'No.'

'No Indian rupees? No sterling? When you travel, you pick

up all kinds of notes and coins. Where does he keep that stuff? In a pocket? In his shoes? In his coat lining?'

'Where do you?'

'In the nearest drawer. If I was in a hotel room, I'd put it out of sight—like in a shoe.'

She said, 'Me, too. When we were in his room, Jeffrey searched everything. He's a professional room searcher because he has a Californian burglar friend who taught him how to do it. They met in jail when Jeff sold a policeman a couple of joints and got pinned. You should see him search—he starts from one end of the room, and when he's reached the other, there are no secrets. He's even looked at the soles of shoes and tasted the toothpaste. If a passport was in that room, he'd have found it. He didn't find any money either. None. He even thumbed through the hotel's Bible and looked in her diaphragm box, for God's sake.'

'Then Reggie's tickets and foreign cash are either in that Camary or someone is holding them for him. Perera says he doesn't use the hotel safe. Also, I think you should have told me that Jeff's a trained burglar, Mag. Stuff like that is important.'

'He isn't a burglar. I didn't become a tart just because a tart I met told me about all kinds of kinky sex that I've sometimes used.'

'I had no idea! I thought men liked you because you're tall.'

He went upstairs leaving her fondling her wooden box in the front drawing room. Steven was seated on a chair in the hallway outside CV's room. The door was open, but the curtain was drawn across it.

CV was expecting Emma to be working on her laptop, but she was lying curled on his high bed with a book beside her. She'd taken off her Chinese wig and contacts, but the eye make-up was still on. When she saw him, she got on to her knees and reached out, and he took her in his arms. As they kissed, she rolled her body against his apparently untroubled that only a curtain separated them from a police officer. He pulled away first because he couldn't forget that.

'Seeing you on my bed was a wonderful surprise, but is there a reason you're not in your own room?'

'I feel safer here.'

'That's good to hear.'

'Maggie says you've made a rule that we are to keep our personal feelings buried until we've found out who killed Dorothy.' She was still kneeling on the bed with her arms locked around his neck.

'Then I've broken my own rule.'

'I am just aching from personal feelings,' she said. 'I wasn't expecting love to hurt so much.'

'Nor me, but we do have to keep our thoughts on Dorothy because day after tomorrow I want this thing tied up.'

'Is it possible?'

'If the final pieces will just fall into place. I still don't have a motive.'

He was about to tell her about the traveller's cheques when Maggie barged in.

They turned towards her, Emma still kneeling against him with one arm around his neck.

'I've thought of how Reggie could have got to India and back,' Maggie said. 'He used another passport and washed his hair with a dark rinse. Without that white hair he'd be unrecognizable. Or he wore a wig or a cap or a hat. He wore dark glasses. Cheap clothes. Polyester! Jeff made a joke about the one polyester suit and the one pair of cheap shoes among the good stuff—said you never can get the bourgeois out of the bourgeois. That was why Reggie didn't cash traveller's cheques at the airport—he couldn't. If he used his real passport, he wouldn't match the picture in it. If he used the false one, he'd have had the wrong name on the cheques.'

'That's so beautifully interlocked I want it to be true,' he told her.

They gave Emma a quick explanation of what Maggie was talking about.

'You're so clever, Maggie,' said Emma. 'And as you showed me, disguise is all in the walk. Why was he travelling on a false passport? And why was he here on Friday?'

Maggie began to walk like a cowboy. 'It's just a guess because we don't have the slightest idea. We don't know when he came here and if and why he had to leave the country and come back the same day.'

'We still don't have the whys.'

'No we don't,' she said. 'But at least we have a possible modus operandi.'

'Wow, Maggie, Latin already!'

He didn't tell her that by using those words she had just dropped an important missing piece into place.

CV told them about hiring Meechie and his friend to look for Muscles. 'What happened at Soong's this morning, Mag?'

She made a face. 'I got a cup of green tea and a fish roll. She has something more substantial for Emma but wouldn't tell me what. She doesn't like me, so I think she's a bitch. After all, I don't dislike her because she looks like a Mao reject. Why should she mind if I was born symmetrical?'

Emma was eating papadams, mindlessly putting one after the other into her mouth and said, 'It isn't that Soong doesn't like you, Mag. You scare people because you're so unusual.'

'Well, I'm not going to look like a toad just for her peace of mind.'

'I'll take you there tomorrow,' CV said hastily to Emma. 'Maybe Dorothy left you some poison with instructions how to feed it to her father.'

Emma told them that Della had talked again to Marie on the phone. This time Marie dropped a real bomb and said she once believed that Reggie was not Dor's father.

'Come again?' said CV.

Even Maggie looked shocked. 'Michael is his child? Dorothy was not? Della is making these stories up.'

'Not her,' said Emma plaintively. 'Though Marie might be.'

According to Marie, Dorothy had strongly resembled the man she had been seeing before she married Reggie. They all four had blue eyes, but Dorothy's were round and darker blue like this man's. She had his smile. Her mouth was like his—a little up on the right side. Even as a baby she'd had his mannerisms.

When Marie was married to Reggie, she had begun to think he was sterile and that he had only married her guessing she was pregnant. Two years after Dorothy was born, he had suggested adopting a child, but then had started nagging her about her drinking, and they decided to break up. Soon after her second marriage, she got pregnant with the twins.

Della asked Marie if Reggie had driven her to drink, and Marie had responded, 'I'm an alcoholic, and that's no one's fault. That's what I've had to learn.'

Emma said, 'Della thinks Marie and Reggie could both be sub-fertile. Two sub-fertile people may be unable to have children together but be able with other partners. Reggie made Frances pregnant, and Dor too.'

Marie said Dorothy and Bell had a paternity test at Childers' Lab, and it confirmed she was his daughter, so her suspicions had been incorrect. She had herself given its name to Dorothy when she had called to ask if she had known that Reggie had a son in Sri Lanka. She had not.

'Della is amazing,' said Maggie. 'She moves like lightning.'

'She's Clive's amazing ex-girlfriend.'

'Ex. Remember the ex,' he said.

Maggie was doing her stretching exercises on the floor now, and she straightened up to say, 'I've begun to feel everything is a lie—that Dorothy is alive—the police cooked up the story of her death—Julia is alive—Reggie is in love with Mahmoud—Michael and Jeffrey are brothers.'

Emma was obviously sick of the conversation, but he continued, 'Julia's murder, Teddy feels, was done by a Lankan. I can't see Mo leaping the wall and blowing up a girl. People our size stand out, particularly if we speak only Arabic and broken English.'

'We'd better go while CV is still a little bit coherent,' said Maggie standing. 'Em, he's not usually as boring as this. He just doesn't like being outsmarted.'

'Neither, I think, did Dorothy,' said CV.

A Visit to Michael

'Question. Can Uncle Li describe a male body with accuracy? Answer, if he likes to fuck one, he probably can.'

Maggie was paying the taxi driver and said over her shoulder, 'What are you mumbling about now?'

'I'm talking in my sleep.'

The road outside Michael Blue's home, even this late in the evening, had men standing, leaning, squatting and smoking by his gate. Hanging out stag was something Sri Lankan men did a lot.

CV asked her to look at the shortest man in a checked sarong leaning against the concrete gatepost, a cheroot somehow clinging to his upper lip and front tooth.

'A bodybuilder?'

She shook her head. 'I'd guess a swimmer.'

They entered the house unannounced, stepping carefully over three men asleep on the veranda with fireflies above them. There was a burning mosquito coil in one corner. By these dismal lights CV tried to study the bodies. None looked capable of lifting a small suitcase, let alone gym weights.

Maggie said, 'Your interest in the male torso is becoming obsessive.'

Jeff heard their voices and called, 'We're in here.'

They found a door beyond the studio that led to Michael's bedroom—a simple white cell with a single overhead electric light covered by a white paper shade, a low cot with white sheets, a reed mat. The table was small and white and had a glass of water on it. The chair was low, and its cane seat was sagging. CV was reminded of the unexpectedly muted hideaway of Michael's gaudy mother. This hideaway was monkish.

Sweetie had barked as they entered and was now under the bed growling with fervour. Jeff said wearily, 'One's been throwing tantrums because he can't smoke, and the other has been snapping at shadows.'

'Jeff,' Maggie told him, 'try to get some sleep tonight or you'll collapse.'

'She's right,' CV said, 'you've begun to look like seaweed. Can't one of those guys out on the veranda sit by Michael for a bit?' To his surprise, while Jeff didn't reply, the little dog recognized his voice and emerged with a yelp to nuzzle his legs. He picked her up, and she licked his face.

Jeff said sourly, 'Yes, you are attractive to women.' CV was not quite sure if he was being funny.

On the bed Michael was curled on his side with his back to them apparently undisturbed by the noise of their presence. Maggie leaned over him and placed her hand on his forehead; his body swung around and his fingers grabbed her wrist. He dragged her across him shouting, 'Now I've got you, you tart!'

She fell across him laughing, then clambered up on to her knees to straddle his body, pulled his pillow from under his head and began to hit him with it, chanting with every blow, 'Liar! Liar!' and continued in the same rhythm. 'She didn't go to the Oberoi. The police are coming to get you.'

CV had intended to ease into that particular conversation but it was too late.

'So our Jimbo talked!' Michael had dragged her down on to

him and locked his arms behind her so he now spoke into her hair. 'I told him he wouldn't be able to keep his mouth shut.' He might have been discussing the weather.

'It wasn't Jimbo,' CV said putting Sweetie on the bed with them. 'It was Dorothy's friend, a Chinese. Michael, may I presume you're not dying?'

'I was almost dead yesterday and almost dying this morning. Now I am almost well but unnaturally empty, because if it tastes or smells good I can't have it. I'd kiss Daddy Bell for an arrack right now. Mum brought a bottle of brandy when she heard I was dying, but Jeff told her I was only allowed soup, so she's taken it away. It was Daddy Li who ratted?'

'What really happened that evening, Michael? I have to know.' CV looked around for somewhere to sit, and Maggie patted the bed beside her.

There was a pause. Finally Michael said, 'I promised Dor I'd stay mum about that evening, so I can't.' He reached under the bed, pulled out a basket that contained a hairbrush, began to brush his long hair, secured it with an elastic band handed to him by Jeff and then moved on to the mat beside Jeff.

'But you were there?' CV persisted.

'I was thereabouts.'

'Thereabouts! Screw you, Michael. You know exactly what went on. Dorothy, Reggie Bell, Li Chen Wee and two other men met in a building down a side street in the Fort and Padmani's Blood changed hands. Bell was in Colombo that morning, went to Trivandrum, then returned for the meeting in Colombo. Did you know all this?'

'I didn't know he went to India. I knew he arrived on Thursday. Why did he go to India?'

So Bell had arrived on Thursday not Friday, thought CV.

'I wish I knew. Did you see him on Thursday as well as on Friday?'

Michael avoided having to reply by saying he had to use the

can, and Jeff used his absence to pour anisette into tiny glasses for the visitors. When Michael returned he sat next to Maggie on the bed and began to kiss her cheek and then her shoulder.

'Michael, darling,' she said gently, making no movement to stop him, 'tell CV what happened.'

He stopped touching her and said wearily, 'I promised Dor so I can't.' He then said quietly, 'I need a smoke. Clive, I understand your being pissed, but she was not your life, your breath, your heart. You see her as a puzzle that must be solved. I see her as my lost life.'

CV also wished he could smoke. There were times when he needed a cigarette to ease the moment—the distraction tobacco had provided for him once. He sipped at his anisette, but its pungency was wrong for his mood. Then he said, 'Even if I don't believe you killed Dorothy, you've lied so much it's going to look bad for you—and for Reggie who has lied too. You can't do that to the CID and expect them to shrug it off. I didn't know Dorothy, but would she want you accused of murder to keep a promise to her—particularly now she's dead?'

Michael was standing. 'Reggie came to Colombo on Thursday. Daddy Li came on Friday evening.'

'But you're missing the point. I don't need your confirmation of facts I know,' he glanced at Maggie, who was also sipping her anisette as if with distaste. Jeff had offered her a joint when they had arrived, and she had refused. Now she began taking one out of her Benson and Hedges box absently, put it to her lips, passed him one and lit hers from his match. CV realized he should have let her come alone. She was a chameleon who could become their kind of person. He could not.

Michael settled on the chair, pulled his heels up and hitched his sarong between his legs village style. He did not look like his father at that moment. He looked so classically gypsy he was unreal. He certainly did not look like a man who might find himself facing a murder rap or feared one. For one horrifying moment CV imagined he saw Dorothy entering the room, climbing into Michael's lap and laying her head against him. He shook himself out of his fantasy and felt a pricking at his eyes.

'Michael, I need the name of the street where the meeting was held.'

Silence. Then Michael said, 'Why did Daddy Li talk? There was no need. I wouldn't have told anyone he was here.'

'He wants to find Dorothy's murderer to punish him.'

'And because I don't, you think I killed her?' A sudden groan escaped his throat, and the laughter was gone from Michael Blue. 'I killed Dor!' Tears flowed. He sat down and put his head into his hands. CV put a hand out to Maggie to prevent her from going to him. Jeff hadn't moved. It seemed he wasn't even listening. He was folded in the lotus position on the floor beside Michael. His eyes were open, but his face still as a statue.

Eventually, Michael stretched out a hand, picked up Sweetie and placed her on his lap and began to stroke her. He brushed his eyes with the back of one hand and said, 'Jeff, I have to have a cigarette.'

'Mendis said no cigarettes, no drugs, no liquor—only bland food and tea for three days.'

'Fuck Dr Mendis!'

'You fuck him.' Jeff's accent made the word *fock*.

'Poor Dr Mendis. What would that long-lipped wife say if I focked her husband?' He did not bring up the cigarettes again.

CV said, 'At least tell me what *you* did that evening.'

'After dinner I walked to the meeting place and looked through the house to make certain no one else was there. I left her inside and waited on the other side of the gate. I saw Reggie and a short man go in. A little while later a big Chinese fellow I thought must be Daddy Li came by car and entered the building with a man I recognized. They came out talking and smiling. Dorothy waved to me from the window. That meant it was all right, and I must go. So I went to the end of Hospital Street, cut across to

Chatham Street where Jimbo was waiting on his BMW, and we went to the Red Fox.'

'Jimbo stood on Chatham Street with a BMW bike in the middle of the night?'

'They know him at the casino and restaurant there. He talked to the security guard until I arrived.'

'And the guard conveniently forgot seeing you?'

'It's possible he didn't. I went to the clock tower. Jimbo was watching it. Next thing, he was there.'

'You recognized Li's friend!'

'It was Ralph Wijewardene, a bank man. I know him.'

CV picked up his phone, called his aunt's home and Steven answered. He asked for Joseph and said, 'The Chinese man's friend is Mr Ralph Wijewardene. Michael says he is a bank man. Auntie knows some Wijewardenes in Horton Place. Ask her to find out from them where this one lives. If you can find his driver, ask him about the night Bell Missie died.' He said to Michael, 'Li says only Reggie and his bodyguard were with Dorothy when he left. So they had to be with her when you left. Do you think she was going back to the hotel with her father?'

'She would never have left that place with him. The sale was her sign-off. She was to be finished with him from that night. She had a mobile phone with her and was going to call for a taxi to bring her down to the Red Fox. She said she'd be all right . . . . oh it's useless. Of course I shouldn't have left her, but I didn't know she was going to be killed.' He was rocking his body back and forth.

'Obviously neither you nor Li thought she was in danger.' He thought of words to comfort Michael and came up with, 'The wrong person always feels guilty when there's a crime. If someone steals from you, you think "I was careless." If it's rape, "I asked for it." Dorothy was murdered because someone murdered her, not because you weren't there.'

'I told her not to wait for the taxi alone, and she said, "Of course, I won't." I think they must have had a fight and he went off and left her in the building alone. I thought the taxi driver came in and killed her, or when she was on her way to the Mount the driver killed her. But I've phoned the taxi companies; none say they got a call that night from Hospital Street.'

'Would she have taken a trishaw?'

'Not if there was an alternative. The family types go home at night and leave the streets to the drunks.'

'Li said he heard someone downstairs behind a door. He took it for granted that it was someone who came with Bell. Mr Wijewardene got his handgun out. That gun lets them both off the hook, because why use a knife if you're carrying a gun?'

'I didn't see anyone downstairs. Anyway, you can rule Daddy Li out. He loved Dor because she saved his grandson's life. He tried to give her Padmani's Blood. She wouldn't take it. She was right. If you save a life, you cannot be paid as if it was a job. You give the person another chance at life as a gift.'

'Ali vouches for Li too, and he had no motive. He has his money. Oh God, it's such a mess. I have to believe someone, and I like that man.'

'And you believe me because you like me,' Michael said.

'Tell me what happened when you got to the Red Fox. The parking jockey lied about the time you arrived. I hope you didn't give him money to do that.'

'I didn't even have to say, "Come on, tell a lie for me." Clive, you know how it is? You can arrive at 11.20 and an hour later say, "When I came in, it was 10.43," and the doorman, the parking man, the receptionist are all going to say, "That's right, it was 10.43." It happened like that. I went to the Taprobane and told the waiter a time when Dor and I arrived and left and he said, "Yes, that's right." But he hadn't been paying attention. Lankans don't bother with exact times. My bad luck was that the only three-wheeler driver in the country with a watch that works happened to be driving in the Fort that night. He saw me and remembered the time.' Michael looked at Maggie and said, 'Beautiful creature, don't you understand?'

She made a sound like a cat in pain. 'Oh, Michael, I don't know what I understand. Someone is out there killing people, and CV's working day and night to stop him. Someone tried to kill CV yesterday—poison him at the Palace. You've been wonderful the way you've held up, but he needs your help now.'

'At the hotel! Clive, you didn't tell me you were poisoned at the *hotel*!'

'I told you it was poisoning, not flu,' said Jeff.

Both men listened attentively as CV described his sudden illness after leaving the Palace, and Michael said, 'Why did Daddy, the swine, try to poison you and then me? He needs you to find out who killed her. I'm his son. He probably even wants to fuck me—he likes to fuck his babas. Yesterday, I decided it was time we had a talk about what he did to her—what he didn't do. He loved Dor. When they were together, he stared at her. When she wasn't there, he talked about her. He couldn't even look at her picture without his eyes dilating, and not only his eyes. He needed me because if I said, "Forgive Reggie", she would have. I was his only key to another fuck of his chosen one, and he had no pride about offering me the world to make that happen. I understood. There was a time I too thought love was possession, so I had compassion that he wanted to possess her. But you can't possess anything—try it and the joy has gone. I went to the Palace yesterday because I thought we should talk about that last evening, and I was going to ask him what happened after I left. I wanted to ask him why he left her in the Fort alone so late at night. I wanted to tell him I too felt guilty for leaving her there.'

'You are too kind to him. The guy has the morals of a *polanga*,' said CV.

'Perhaps. But you don't kill the person who is holding you together—making your life sing—because when she's dead, there's a void.'

'Were you the person downstairs behind the door?'

He frowned. 'No. I told you I was outside the building on a side path in the little garden. I didn't know there was someone inside. We'd searched the building. I am sure there was no one there when I left her.'

'Anyone saw you?'

'I don't think so. I could see out through the cracks in the gate. I saw one man outside and one inside Ralph Wijewardene's car.'

'The car was a Mercedes?'

'It was a Brougham.'

So this time Michael wasn't lying. He had stopped rocking and was as still as Jeff. He said carefully, 'I didn't know there was going to be someone downstairs waiting to kill her.'

'Bell's bodyguard was a short, powerful Sri Lankan. Mr Li said he had the body of a weightlifter.'

Michael asked him to repeat that, then said, 'Jeff!'

The Frenchman was still smoking his joint, and he looked up when he heard his name. Once again CV got the impression he hadn't been listening to the conversation, and he said, 'What, Michael?'

'The man who came to the gate today asking questions about me—the one you called a pocket-sized Adonis—the bodybuilder?' Michael said gently. 'Please draw that man for me, Jeff.'

Jeffrey was focused now and his fine-boned face turned predatory. 'What a beauty he was. Pecs so. Biceps so.' He used his hands on his own chest and arms to show the other's bulk.

'Draw him!'

The Frenchman got on to his feet and wandered out.

'Jeff went out this morning to see why Sweetie was barking

Jeanne Cambrai

and came back drooling about a man who was looking for me. A fellow who hangs around told Jeff the same man had been asking about me yesterday, too.'

'Tell me exactly what happened to you at the Palace yesterday,' CV asked.

The mood had not changed, but the artist was no longer detached. It was as if he had at last moved to their side. The initial shock had worn off, and he wanted to point a finger. He spoke of his visit to the hotel with animation, his concentration no longer slipping away.

At about one o'clock he had phoned the Palace and left a message for Bell that he would be coming over that evening at seven. His van was still at the repair shop, so he went by taxi. He arrived a few minutes late, went to the desk, asked for Bell's room and was given a message that he was to order himself a drink and wait in the lobby. Michael was regretting the whole idea by now and wanted to go home but decided to sit it out.

There was the usual floor show of dancing girls so he ordered a beer and watched them. He wasn't sure how long after—it seemed just five minutes that he became aware that a waiter was asking him if he'd like another beer. He looked at his watch and realized more than half an hour had passed. He wondered if he had dozed off with his eyes open, if such a thing was possible, for there had been no sense of time passed and the girls were still dancing. He decided to call Bell's room again.

Michael tried to tell the waiter he had to make a phone call and found he could not articulate properly. He got to his feet and the room began swaying. He managed to get to the front desk, mumbled that he wanted a taxi and left a message for Bell that he had taken ill. While he waited, he leaned against the desk and someone asked if he had a friend they could call to come and get him. His next memory was of Jeff and the houseboy carrying him into the house. Jeff, Michael believed, then saved his life. He forced him to put his fingers down his throat and vomit, made him drink warm tea and vomit that, and continue until his vomit began to look clear. Then he made him drink weak tea—cup after cup. He and the houseboy walked Michael up and down until the doctor arrived.

When Dr Mendis arrived, he found Michael lucid enough to refuse to be taken to hospital. Because his temperature was not high, the doctor recommended fluids and Panadol and left saying he'd be over again in the morning. By then Michael was getting better and was diagnosed as probably having contracted a one-day stomach virus.

'No tests?'

'Dr Mendis suggested I have a blood test and wanted to take samples from every orifice, but I decided to let it go. Do you know a poison that makes all extremities feel like putty?'

'I don't know anything about poisons, but you're describing how I felt—obviously to a much lesser degree. Reggie was with me, so I thought he did it, but you say he wasn't near you.'

'I don't remember anyone except a waiter.'

'Perera—the assistant manager?'

'No!'

CV said, 'Why would a waiter want to kill us, frighten us or slow us down? We'd better find out if we were the only ones who got ill. We may not have been targets at all.'

Maggie said, 'I'm going to ask Mahmoud.' She phoned the hotel, and the Arab was not in his room. He was paged and found with friends at the bar.

'Mr Mahmoud, this is Maggie vander Marten. We met on Monday. Please, Mr Mahmoud, I need your help.' When she hung up, Mahmoud had agreed to find out if there had been any other cases of poisoning in the hotel.

She said, 'He wants to get home to Saudi and said he would help us any way he can if you'd just keep your hands off Mohideen. He's realized that you stopped him from getting into trouble with the CID and is grateful. Says Mo is joining a gym now. He was pretty embarrassed that he couldn't get a flabby like you down.'

'Thanks, Mag.'

Jeff was back with a chalk drawing. None of them recognized the man he had drawn, but he did fit Li's description. This was a man with immense shoulders for his size and bulging arms. His lower body was hidden by a sarong, but you got the feeling of a small waist and big legs. His hair was of medium length and arranged into waves. Most bodybuilders wear their hair short, and it gave this man an odd look. It would also make him easy to spot. CV borrowed the sketch to show Joseph and Teddy.

'Keep it,' Jeff said.

CV said, 'Roll it carefully. Later I'm going to have it framed.'

Secrets and Lies

Michael looked tired, so CV and Maggie switched places with him, and he lay down. Another time it would have been tactful to leave, but there was one thing more.

'Jeff.'

Exhaustion showed in every line of Jeff's face and body. CV suspected he had not slept at all the night before, and of course Michael had not made the easiest of patients.

'Jeff, I need your help,' CV persisted.

The light eyes focused but the reply was a wary, 'Haven't I always given it?'

'I'm afraid that's why I'm asking again.'

Jeff found that amusing and said more brightly, 'Of course I will help you.'

'I want you to get into Mr Bell's hotel room again.'

'I can't without Perera's help.'

'Of course, so let's ask him.'

However, when they phoned, they found Perera was off duty.

'I can't wait,' CV told Jeff.

'The new locks are difficult.' Jeff, sounding particularly French added. 'When is it, M'sieur, I would have to break and enter?'

'Tonight or early tomorrow. And it would be a complete search again.'

Jeff shrugged. 'It would have to be morning. We don't know what time he goes to bed. Mr Bell has breakfast every morning between seven and eight, and that's when his room is cleaned—because he likes his bed made before he returns. The cleaners have a supervisor to make sure they don't steal the drinks from the refrigerators and look in the suitcases, so it is not just one person I will have to distract.'

'Where did you find out about the cleaners?' Maggie asked. 'Not when you were with me.'

'I asked questions that morning.' He was amused at their surprise, 'Burglars should know if they are likely to be surprised.'

'Well, obviously you can't just hang around waiting for Bell's door to be left open. And what if he eats later tomorrow morning? What if he's spending the night out of Colombo and shows up while you're in the room?' CV said. 'Anyway, how do you find out if he's in the room without asking at the front desk?'

'If he picks up the phone, he is there. If I am in the room next door, I can wait till he leaves then try to open his door or climb through the window. He is room 411, and 409 is on one side and 413 on the other. Many tourists cancelled since that hotel bomb, so one of those rooms could be empty. The Palace is four-star hotel, so we'll have to find a hundred dollars or more.'

To everyone's surprise Michael, who was trying to tug Maggie into his bed, said, 'I got a cheque today. I'll pay for the room.'

'Your father's money will,' CV reminded him. 'We'll do it,

Jeff. I can let you have two hundred dollars, but someone else must make the booking. As Perera isn't there, you better go incognito.'

Maggie said, 'Reggie won't recognize Jeff—he didn't go to Dor's funeral service.'

'He may have seen us together. What about Jimbo?' Michael had given up teasing Maggie. 'I'll ask Jimbo to book the room.'

'He was at the funeral party.'

'He can phone in the booking. There are lots of Indian Raos. Daddy won't connect J. Rao with our Jimbo.'

Maggie reached for the phone. She said, 'Mahmoud might book the room for us.' When she put the phone down, she said, He's thrilled we asked. He's going to send Mo to check on the room numbers and will get one next to Reggie's if he has to pay a thousand to turf another guest out. Mo will let Jeff in tonight at eleven-thirty exactly. Knock on the basement door four times so he'll know it's you.'

Jeff's lean face was now alive with mischief. 'And what am I to look for?'

'Passports, airline ticket stubs, a huge star ruby, a wig, the murder weapon, a signed confession. Anything that seems relevant. Don't remove anything. Do you have a camera? Photos would be best.'

Michael said, 'Jeff take your Pentax. It has a good lens and will put the date on the picture. There's some of Dor's 400ASA Kodacolor around. We can get one-hour processing on the film tomorrow.'

He said after Jeff left them, 'What makes you think Daddy has Padmani's Blood in his room?'

'He has to have it somewhere, and he doesn't use the hotel safe. He doesn't have that many options here. He's in a foreign country.'

'What's new about Julia?' Jeff asked later.

'Nothing more. You know something, don't you?' The usually silent Jeff hadn't asked a question for no reason.

'The police know she was doing it with someone that night.'

'Is there evidence?'

'There was semen evidence though she had condoms in her backpack.'

CV said, 'Teddy and I are supposed to be sharing information, and though I find myself hiding things from him, I'm really irritated he didn't tell me this. I bet Teddy thinks it could have been me! That when Emma was asleep, I realized Julia would be alone and went down for a little fun and took a bomb in case things went wrong. I wish I could remember what she looked like.'

Jeff said, 'I'll give you an alibi if you like. I'll say I saw you in the Fort,' and he smiled.

Before going home CV and Maggie drove by Jimbo's. The lights were out, and CV had the taxi stop a few yards down the road. He then walked back to the gate alone and found the security guard asleep sitting upright on a chair. He had to shout to waken him, and the man jumped with a groggy puppet energy.

'Good evening, sir.'

'Good evening. I hear Mr Rao went out at eight o'clock this evening,' CV said in Sinhala.

'What, sir? he cupped his hand to his ear.

CV repeated the remark loudly.

'Yes, sir.'

'Mr Rao went out with Mr Blue?'

'Yes, sir.'

'What time?'

'Eight o'clock, sir.'

'They'll be coming back at eleven o'clock?'

'Yes, sir.'

CV rejoined Maggie and told her of the conversation.

'So that's how Michael got his alibi. That guard always says *yes*. He was probably asleep all evening and didn't know what happened. When Jimbo told him a story, he said he remembered. I think security guards are hired from a pool of honest old guys whose minds are in the never-never.'

'Do you think I'd make a good security guard? I say yes too.'

'I think you have to be short. I've never seen a security guard as tall as you.'

Voices on Tape

CV and Maggie reached their aunt's without saying another word.

The security guard was inside the gate on a chair in the one-chair-width house Maud had had built for him. There was also a bench, which he often slept on but never used it unless all members of the family were at home. Now his eyes were open, but CV had to clap his hands to bring life to them. The old man recognized him and shouted, 'Good evening, sir,' with exploding relief.

'My aunt came in at ten o'clock?'

'Yes, sir.'

'And Mr Sharif at 10.30?'

'Yes, sir.'

'Miss Emma is sleeping?'

'Yes, sir.'

'Good night, Security.'

'A week ago I'd have laughed,' Maggie said as they walked up the drive.

To her further irritation, Ali had called and left a message with Emma that he had to go to Kandy because his father had broken a finger.

'If someone breaks a finger, why does every member of the

family have to show up?' she complained. 'For the first few days I think how lovely it is to be back in such a caring society. It's really a sick dependent one.'

Emma told them smugly, 'Steven did such a clever thing. He tried the cassette CV found in the Panasonic, and there are voices on it.'

'Whose?' he asked as excitement caused through his body.

'Neither of us recognize them, but the men are talking about putting a microphone in the office!'

'It was just good luck,' Steven tried to sound modest. 'If anyone had spoken after the machine was set, sir, those voices would have been erased.'

'It's too much to hope we have a confession?'

'It is too much.'

They stood around the machine, and Steven turned it on. After several seconds of background sounds, a man said in English, 'Move that. It's going to fall.' There was a pause, and then the same voice said, 'Are you sure this microphone is powerful enough?'

'Well done, Steven,' CV said.

Someone with a local accent and phlegm in his throat, coughed and replied, 'It picks up sound from twelve feet. We can get another, but we won't need one.'

'Get it. Don't take chances. Isn't even one shop open today?'

'It's Poya. Nothing is open,' he said and cleared his throat again.

'Hotels and shops owned by Muslims don't close on Poya. Can't you borrow another mike? What if they go to the window and talk facing out? Only the American's voice will be heard.'

'He has a loud voice?'

'A clear voice.'

'The recorder is twelve feet away now, and I've been taping us so you can hear for yourself. I'm going to play it back.'

Several seconds' silence followed and then they heard children talking and giggling. CV fast-forwarded in spurts, but the rest of the tape was taken up by sounds from a children's party. There was only one adult voice—a woman who suddenly howled, 'I'm going to give you a slap next time you do that.'

Maggie said, 'Such incredible good luck that they rewound without erasing.'

'And luck that Steven was on the ball. I wasn't. We'd better break the tab so that the voices can't be erased accidentally.'

'I have done that, sir.'

CV replayed the first part of the tape again then tried the other side, which was blank.

'I don't know the voices, but Superintendent Senaratne may,' Steven was saying after they listened a third time.

But CV thought he had recognized one, and if he was right, he had been making a serious error of judgement all along. He said nothing.

'Who is it?' Emma grabbed his arm. 'You know who it is, don't you?'

'I know this eliminates a lot of people.'

'It's eliminated everyone I know. Maggie?'

'The first voice sounds a bit familiar. I love it that he doesn't want to take risks and then uses an old tape!'

Hospital Street

It was eleven when CV went to the kitchen and came back with sandwiches and meat cutlets that Amily had left in the refrigerator. Maggie had poured him a brandy and was drinking one herself.

'Got to keep awake. I'll pass, Mag.'

When he had first started the investigation, he had realized the importance of keeping a meticulous record so no detail would be forgotten and had asked Emma to do that job. But after the assault on her home he had not mentioned it again. He needed such a record now. He didn't like Steven picking up on something he had missed. Other important details could have been overlooked.

The doorbell announced the arrival of Teddy like an out-of-control twister—his feet knotted at every step. He was followed by Joseph, and they both almost collided with CV and Emma, who had hurried into the hall. Teddy said, 'I have news.'

CV put his undrunk brandy into Teddy's hand. 'You can tell any story, but Steven will cap it with his.'

The terrier eyebrows wriggled.

'I've found the building.' Teddy stuffed a sandwich into his mouth, literally smacked his lips and ran his tongue across them, 'Nothing like a meat sandwich to pick you up.' He swallowed and sipped the brandy. 'Ah!'

'The building where they met?'

'Yes, in the Fort.'

Was it coming together at last?

'How?' Maggie asked.

Teddy suddenly calmed down and pushed away the plate he had almost emptied. 'At first we didn't believe the trishaw driver who said Michael was in the Fort that night, but we did take a report, so I knew where to get him. He says Michael was on York Street at the entrance to Hospital Street. Hospital Street is so short you can see from one end to the other even if you're on York Street. And you know why I know Hospital Street so well? We have a police depot in the old Dutch hospital it was named after.'

He looked around. CV placed another plate of sandwiches near him and refilled his brandy glass.

'In Hospital Street there is one building that matched your description, and it is almost opposite the police building! The next thing I'll hear is that Dorothy was murdered by one of our officers!' Apparently, the idea was very amusing to him, and he said with pleasure, 'I myself may be accused of it!' He beamed and took another sandwich.

'And the owner of that building has disappeared! He is Bundula Balasingham. Tamil father, Sinhala mother, what can you expect? He's disappeared. He is a fat man. He sometimes wears rings. Dorothy Bell was left in the Pettah by a fat man wearing a ring!'

Maggie said brightly, 'Goodness! Bundy killed her?'

Teddy looked at her, his head tipped on to one side. 'He has no alibi for that night.'

She said testily, 'No one has.'

When Teddy heard about the old security guards asleep on the job his mouth twitched. 'I hope you don't expect me to arrest old men who are lucky to be able to earn a few rupees.'

'Oh Teddy, you can be so sweet,' said Maggie.

'While you were idle, Teddy,' CV poured himself a brandy and put his feet up, 'Steven was not.'

He made the policeman tell his boss what he had found, and they played him the tape. 'And neither of those men is Bundy,' CV said flatly. 'The office is his, but there isn't even a mention of him. No, "Bundy thinks" or "Mr Balasingham says".'

'It doesn't let him off because someone didn't talk about him. Who are the men? Someone will recognize them. That woman at the party and the children, none of their voices are familiar to me.' He smiled at Steven.

CV then told him about their visit to Michael and showed him Jeff's drawing in pastel.

Teddy scowled. 'Again, I don't know the man. I'll keep this.'

'I'm going to frame the drawing, so treat it with care. I'll need a copy or two.'

'I don't know how to treat drawings with care. I'll return the original and colour copies by morning. Fournier has even given us the colour of this man's sarong—that may be useful. I must ask my witnesses to draw the suspects in future. I'll also make a copy of that tape for you. But I'll have to take the recorder, mike and the original tape—they're evidence. I suppose you've destroyed the fingerprints.'

'Jesus! Fingerprints! I thought of voice-print but never once of fingerprints. I'm sorry Teddy.'

'We'll check anyway. As for the alleged poisoning, Mr Bell can't be considered a suspect just because you got ill and he didn't. You didn't see a doctor, and even if it was possible for him to add something to your drink, how did he know he'd have the opportunity? In Michael's case, he wasn't there, and a doctor diagnosed flu. But I'll check it out.'

CV didn't tell Teddy about his plan to have Jeff break into Bell's room but said that Mahmoud had promised to help them.

'That kind of man is reliable,' said Teddy, reminding CV of Maggie's assessment of the Arab. 'Aristocrats act as if they are above the law, but they need the police to keep them safe in their ivory towers. They butter us up. Think you'll find the murderer by Friday? I don't.'

'Looks that way, but how many matches have been turned around from two sets down and match point? Let's go,' said CV.

'Go where?'

'To Hospital Street.'

Emma said, 'Do I have to be left at home again?'

'No,' said Teddy, 'because you'll be protected by this country's finest.'

They left Steven to watch the house, and in the car Teddy said, 'Steven seems ready for a promotion. He's a thinker.'

'Yeah. He said to himself, "What if there's something on it?" And once he knew there was, he broke the tab to prevent the evidence getting accidentally erased.'

'Most of my men would have accidentally erased it the first time they played it.'

The atmospheric congestion of the day had dissolved and had been replaced by a warm tropical evening. In particular, the Fort was a surprise: its streets were clean.

Hospital Street is a flag-stoned two-block alley lit by an occasional street lamp. The old hospital, now a police depot was soon to be reclaimed by historians as a national treasure. An emaciated old man in a loincloth was seated against a wall. Teddy asked him if he knew about a woman murdered in that street about a week ago.

'Someone is killing lies. No one comes here at night except those like me.'

He stayed on the covered walk on the main road when it rained, he said. It had rained, they knew, the night Dorothy had been killed, so he had not even been on Hospital Street.

The hospital stretched the full length of the second south block. It was a one-storey building with a wide veranda and solid polished wood posts holding up the tiled roof. The north side and half of the south of Hospital Street formed an impenetrable facade, and if there were people behind, it there was no way to tell.

Teddy stopped in front of a building with two doors. The wall was soft brick covered with the cheapest local building material—a lime-based stucco called *chunam*, which had been used to front most of the other buildings. A notable exception was the building adjoining Bundy's, which was being stripped so the original brick showed through.

'You see,' said Teddy, 'there is no exposed brick anywhere else, and the man who brought Padmani's Blood here said the window faced a red brick building.' But as he had no proof that the building had anything to do with the crime, Teddy said he had no authority to break in. 'Luckily Mrs Balasingham is cooperating. She'll have the keys for me tomorrow morning.'

'When did you speak to her?'

'Two hours ago.'

CV was glad he'd got to Millie first and suspected she had delayed handing over the keys in case Bundy was hiding inside.

CV leaned against the second door and then borrowed the flashlight to examine it. He had felt it shift under his weight. It was not a simple garden door with vertical panels but solid and roughly carved into rectangles. On the right was a large keyhole. He shook the door, but there was no movement, then placed his hand where he had leaned and there was. That section had play to it, which meant that the door had been made from more than one piece of wood. The pattern of the rectangles reminded him of a magic box his parents had given him when he was eight. To open it, he'd had to shift a panel diagonally and upwards. This released a second panel that slid to one side and revealed a drawer. He tried that same principle now, and sure enough a six-inch strip moved diagonally upwards to the left and then directly upwards, which allowed a lower panel to slide to one side The largest panel now moved back on a hinge that was invisible from the street. He was now standing before a gap of about two feet by three. A key probably opened the whole door, but if you wanted to slip in or out, all you needed was the knowledge of how a magic box is built.

Teddy and the policemen were impressed, if not quite as much as Emma. Maggie crowed, 'Oh CV, if we could just bottle whatever it is you have.'

One by one they climbed through the opening and stepped on to a walkway edged by a few neglected plants.

Bundy's was a two-floor building that had seemed small from the street but, like Mr Solomon's warehouse, was unexpectedly deep. Three large glass-paned upstairs windows were without curtains or bars. All were protected by curved iron spikes like those used to prevent spectators from climbing in with the dangerous animals at a zoo. Li had spoken of being in a room with only one window, which meant there was at least one other room upstairs. The brick wall he had seen was the next building.

Teddy said, 'Touch nothing, step carefully and let's get out of here.'

'Michael and Dorothy searched the building, but the front door was left unlocked for Uncle,' CV told them. 'We know no one entered after he arrived because the two men in the car were watching. Someone would have had to get in before that.' He demonstrated: 'Michael said he looked through this door, which he called a gate. From it I can see the other side of the road but not much of this side. By staying on this side of the road someone could have got into the building unseen by Michael.'

Maggie asked, 'Before Uncle arrived?'

'Right. He might not have even known Michael was watching,' Teddy said.

'And if Dorothy was leaning out of that window waving to Michael,' CV added, 'wouldn't she have been in the bent position the autopsy said she was in when knifed?'

Emma began to shout, 'Stop it! I can't stand it any more! Just stop it!'

Maggie folded her arms around the younger girl, and CV touched her hair. He took a last look at the building and followed the others to the car. When he passed the old man, he got a smile and gave him his smaller paper notes. The smile disappeared, and the man pressed the palms of his hands together in thanks.

After Emma went to bed, Maggie stayed downstairs. 'You and I—we nearly fucked up today, didn't we?' she said. 'Why don't you want Emma to know whose voice it is?'

'Because if we don't move carefully, one of us might follow Dorothy and Julia. This is the closest we've got to knowing who the enemy is. Emma's been through too much in the last few days—she may get edgy and give the game away.'

'You don't trust Steven?'

'I do, but he has a boss to report to. Teddy didn't tell me about Julia's condoms, so I'm sulking.'

She said, 'I can tell you about my condoms if you like. You can take them to bed with you.'

'No, thank you, but I do appreciate the offer. I have three—which should hold me for an hour or two.'

'Mine have feathers.'

'Feathers? Do women like them with feathers?'

'No, but men think they do. I'm going to bed featherless and I'm going to take a pill to sleep. You want help in that direction?'

'Nah.'

Chapter IX

Wednesday

Early Morning Phone Calls
CV slept fitfully and woke at 8 to a now familiar sense of there being not enough time.

Then the phone rang. He picked it up and Bundy said, 'Thank you for talking to Millie. I've called to say goodbye. Are you alone?'

'Yes, and you can't leave because you're in the clear, Busnd. I need you.'

Maggie had walked into the room, so he put his finger across his lips.

'The police know Dorothy Bell died in my building.'

'I know, and that lets you out.'

'Out? I can't prove I found her dead. There's a drawing of me. There's a ring.'

'True, but we're looking for the person who killed her not who toted her to the Pettah. You've everything to gain and nothing to lose by staying. I'm setting something up, and I want you there. You didn't do this Bundy—you don't have to tell me that—you have no motive, and you're not psychotic. You're telling me all of a sudden that you know which two ribs to put a knife through to reach the heart?'

Bundy made a sound that was either a choking laugh or a sob.

'Four others have been killed the same way in Europe.'
'Oh my God!'
CV took the mobile phone into the bathroom.
'The police!' Bundy was saying. 'I know those fellows. They want a culprit, and I am the one they'll choose.'
'Senaratne is not trying to pin the murders on just anyone who is involved. He wants the right guy.'
'What's that noise?'
'I'm pissing.'
Bundy could still laugh. 'I'm frightened for my life, and you're making wee-wee.'
'Best feeling in the world if you leave out two or three. Can I trust you now?'
'You always could. Millie says I can't say no to anyone. Mr Bell said, "Find me an investigator," and I got you because I thought you'd get the money and forgive me for trying to take yours. I didn't know you'd move so fast.'
'Did Bell kill her?'
'Why would he? He says he didn't. The next day, after her body was found, I went to him and told him I'd found her body and moved it. He seemed to understand. I asked if there was anything I could do. He asked who I thought did it. I said I didn't know because that building could have been filled with people for all I knew. The front door was open when I arrived and everyone was gone and there she was dead on the floor. I had a boy with me to clean the room. I don't use that building, but we put out rat poison and sweep the floors from time to time.

'I told Mr Bell that occasionally Michael rented the building for friends. I didn't tell him he rented it for army and LTTE deserters and Tamil refugees. You know I'm half Tamil. About a year ago I heard Michael was looking for a place to hide four LTTE deserters for a few days. I offered the building through a third party, and they stayed a couple of months. I didn't ask questions. If they had turned themselves, in they would have been tortured. I don't know where they went from my place. I looked the other way.'

'You put up Tiger deserters in a building opposite one used by the police?'

'That was the beauty of it. This time Dorothy told me she needed a building for a private meeting. I didn't know what she was up to—probably dishonest or she'd have used a hotel. I said yes.'

'Did Bell or anyone else ask you to kill or find a killer for Emma or Julia?'

'No.'

'Where are you now, Bundy? I want you to be here tomorrow.'

'My flight leaves tomorrow. I can't Clive. If you saw Bell's eyes when he threatened me, you'd go too.'

'He threatened you?'

'He threatened us both, you and me.'

'What time is your flight?'

Bundy hesitated, 'Evening.'

'You won't need it, but if it makes you happy, keep the booking, and I promise I'll help you get on it if things go wrong.'

Bundy said, 'I'm sorry, Clive. I'm very sorry.'

'I know, you old bastard. I'm sorry too. Insensitive. That's what my old girlfriend called me. I fucked up with you because I was too insensitive to guess what was going on. Keep your word and call me again today, and I'll tell you why I want you with me tomorrow. Call me about three.'

He hung up. It was 8.30.

While they had been talking, he had been shaving. Now he had a quick shower, but before he had time to towel himself, the phone rang again.

This time a laughing voice said, 'This is your secretary Mr Li from Singapore, I have the information you needed, sir.'

'Uncle!'

'The phone number you gave me is my friend's son's. He says that Mr Bell had called him several times about two weeks ago to talk about Padmani. He wanted to know who has her. Eventually he disconnected his phone.'

'But you said you left Padmani with Bell.'

'He told him I stole it back.'

'My God!'

'No, just Uncle Li.'

CV laughed too, though he didn't feel like laughing. 'Just Bell's word that the stone is missing?'

'Yes, so it may not be. He may be playing a game with his insurance company. How is the investigation?'

'Loads of information, but none on who killed her or why. I'm going on an idea you gave me. Trying to come from behind.'

'Protect yours.'

'I will. Uncle, where are you?'

'Is that important?'

'Yes, because I want to ask you to lunch tomorrow.'

'Where?'

'Here.'

'I'm in Paris.'

'There's probably a direct flight into Colombo. All the suspects will be there, so you should be too.'

Li was laughing when he hung up.

He called back immediately. 'Forgot to tell you. Horace Belladonna became Vincent Belli legally, but the rest of his family remain Belladonna. When he died, he didn't even have an overdue parking ticket—no police records on him at all. He was twenty-four, in college in Belfast, studying interracial problems. He died during his holidays.'

For the first time in several days CV was not starting the new day only to feel it was almost over. He wondered if Bell had lost Padmani. If so, why did he not report the theft? Was it because that would place him with Dorothy near the time of her death? But if the great ruby had been stolen from him, he still had no reason to kill her.

He went downstairs still wearing a sarong to find both Emma and Maggie similarly dressed. Upul was in slacks and found their family morning attire very amusing. CV kissed his aunt. She said, 'Emma says you've solved the crime.'

'Just had a phone call. I am afraid it's unsolved again, Auntie.'

'I had a call from a boy called Jeffrey this morning. Very oo-la-la Frenchified like they used to be. Said to tell you he was in place and Mo is with him.'

'He's going to do a little thieving for me.'

'Be careful. It's not like the old days when we could call your grandfather and he'd get the police to blink the other way.'

'Too late for careful. My fat neck is in the noose.'

She looked at him with concern, and he grinned.

'Don't tease me with words like noose,' she said. 'I'm very old, and I might have a heart attack.'

Amily had made an enormous English breakfast.

Maggie pointed to a vase of large pink roses. 'Ali sent them. What do you think?'

'I think he loves you,' said Emma.

'Red means passion. Pink means he's gay,' he said.

'Oh, don't spoil it. You know he loves her.'

'Send the damned things back, Mag. Tell him you want diamonds.'

'You shouldn't tease her.' Emma continued frowning at him. 'She loves him so much it hurts in her stomach and chest.'

'I also love someone so much it hurts in my stomach and chest.'

She said, 'Is that person in America?'

'No.'

Maggie said, 'Talk about the weather, children. You can behave like animals on Saturday.'

Later they settled down in the study where his aunt had left her ever-growing scrapbook. As CV looked through, he found pictures from his childhood and one of his grandfather's wedding. He told them his plan for the following day. 'Auntie Maud, isn't it time for your birthday?' he asked.

'Not for seven months, darling boy. Remember you sent me a silk dressing gown in November?'

'We have to celebrate it twice this year so that Maggie can give a luncheon party at the Palace Hotel tomorrow. As it's your birthday, you must choose the menu.'

'Lobster,' she said at once. 'Not a chopped-up thermador but in its shell with melted butter.'

'There it is, Mag! And include all Auntie's other favourites. I'm going to use Dorothy's Chinese Daddy's advice and try to surprise our murderer. Invite all the suspects. I had better hopes for this party an hour ago, but we can still clear the air, talk about the case and get all the opinions out in the open.'

Emma said, 'Julia's parents are coming tomorrow morning. I'm going to the airport to meet them at seven. They're going to stay here. We're going to clean out the old nursery.'

'I'm glad,' he said, though he was not. 'Honey, they can't come to the lunch. I want to keep attention on Dorothy's death, not Julia's.'

She didn't look pleased, but Maggie nodded and began her list: 'Reggie, Michael, Jeff, Mahmoud, Frances, Teddy, us, Soong and Hoong and Ali. That makes thirteen—a bad number.'

'Add Mr Perera, who's been dying to meet you. I hope to get Bundy and his wife, Millie, and don't forget Nora. That's fifteen.'

'I thought Bundy's disappeared.'

'I'm hoping that he will reappear spontaneously like the swallows.'

'What a lovely party,' said his aunt. 'I'd like little mushrooms and chocolate ice cream with whipped cream on top.'

'What about asking Renuka, Joseph, Amily and the policemen who've been helping?' said Emma.

'It has to be an English-speaking event, or we'll need interpreters. Later we'll have a bigger shindig—a real party—one without murderers and with balloons.'

'And an elephant for rides,' said his aunt.

'And a cobra man.'

'Steven speaks good English,' Emma persisted.

'We can't ask one policeman without the others.'

The phone rang, and Jeff was on the line. He said, 'I didn't find the ruby, but I found two thin long knives. Identical. I took photos of them. He also has two English passports under Charles Smithe and Harold Belladonna. He travels very much and uses different passports in the same country. I photographed the pages. He came from India on the tenth and went back on his Belladonna passport on the eleventh. I found the package taped under the table with the drawers—but it was not there when I came before with Maggie. He has a wig, coloured contact lenses and a false moustache—I've taken pictures of all. It's a brown wig, cute with short curls. I found no hair dye but a bottle of brown hairspray.'

'Thank you. Just when it seems he's squeaky clear, you come up with all of this. So he's been using the name Belladonna! And what about the Charles—one of the men who died was Charles. What do you want as a reward? You have done a great job.'

'I want Michael to stop crying.'

'Stay with him. Don't let him do anything foolish. Tomorrow my Aunt Maud wants you both to come to the Palace for lunch at twelve-thirty—a birthday celebration with a little something I'm cooking up. This is important, Jeff. If Michael moves prematurely, we're lost.'

Jeff replied in his silky French-English, 'I'll chain his leg to the bed if I have to.'

CV phoned Mahmoud at the hotel. 'Mr Mahmoud, you have given me a huge leap forward by helping Jeff. I thank you.'

There was a chuckle.

'I'll settle that hotel bill the next time I see you, but if you prefer, I could send someone round now.'

'I've told you, CV, I like paying bills. Besides you've introduced me to young Jeffrey. What a charming lad.'

CV said, 'Sir! Are you trying to upset me?'

'Yes. I am.'

'Hold on, Mr Mahmoud. My cousin wants to book you for a party she's giving tomorrow.' He handed Maggie the phone.

Maud was saying to Emma who was rubbing her swollen feet. 'Do you think I should be eighty-two again tomorrow or eight-three?'

'I think you should be a ninety-nine. Then everyone will ask you what you do to look so young, and you can say, "I run around the cricket grounds every morning," and older people will start taking exercise.'

They beamed at each other.

Maggie was off the phone and said, 'He's coming and has promised to leave Mo upstairs, if you promise not to visit him there. He says that Perera and the other staff deny that anyone has complained of illness after drinking at the hotel. But they would, wouldn't they?'

'The person to ask would be the housekeeper and whoever would provide stomach medication.'

'Mahmoud thought of that. He complained to Perera of feeling dizzy. A female appeared pronto and said the usual problems she has to deal with are with diarrhoea and flu. In strictest confidence she told him that someone died of a heart attack at the hotel last month. Doesn't seem connected to Dorothy—it was an elderly guy from New Zealand who'd already had bypass surgery.'

'I wonder if our sheikh paid for the info.'

'I imagine she just gushed it out. He can be charming.'

When they disbanded it was 9.45. Soong had wanted to see them at ten.

Soong

Emma went to Soong's looking Chinese. She had become so familiar with the disguise that she now showed no discomfort with it. Before they left, CV phoned Della and left a message on her machine: 'We're giving a luncheon party tomorrow for suspects and sleuths. Visas can be obtained at the airport.'

She called back before he reached the front door. 'You fucker,' she said, 'why didn't you tell me about this party before?'

'It's a last minute thing.'

'You've nailed the guy? You lose our bet, right?'

'No, you've lost. It's because I don't have a murderer that I'm shaking the trees.'

'So you and Emma can walk off into the sunset dick in hand, or should I say hands?'

'Your bad taste has broken what used to be a thread of decency. Call you later.' He disconnected realizing Della's capacity for irritating him was intact.

On the dusty road outside Soong's, Meechi and a lookalike were wobbling around on their bikes playing polo with cricket bats. CV waved. They waved. The doctor was standing at her gate waiting for them, and Maggie greeted her formally then stalked off saying she would visit Renuka's kids.

Soong was not a good-looking woman but had the smooth skin and even features of her race. She had made no effort to capitalize on her slightly exotic look and wore an ill-fitting white dress with a grey panel. She made no comment on Emma's change of appearance except to nod. She greeted CV also with a nod and led them past the little concrete house, which was still blackened and scarred. The doors and windows with the broken glass had been removed. Emma turned her head from the sight.

The doctor's house was surprisingly comfortable inside. The floor was covered with mats woven from dyed palm fronds, and they were invited to sit on cushioned seats. The walls were stark white with several Chinese silk scrolls depicting rural scenes.

Soong made small talk about the rain, which was unseasonal, and the war, which was being mismanaged. CV looked for polite rejoinders not knowing if he should broach why they were there. It was only when she asked how Emma was and when she would be able to collect the package Dorothy had left for her that he realized she hadn't seen through Emma's disguise.

'I'm very well, thank you, Dr Soong,' Emma said giggling. 'What a cold welcome!'

'It is you, no kidding?' Soong's laughter was high and shrill but her expression tender, and there was much embracing. 'I could not give Dorothy's will to anyone else because I promised her. How have your eyes and hair become black?'

So Dorothy had left her will with Soong! What an excellent choice. She was the last person Reggie would think of.

'Contact lenses and spray,' Emma was saying.

The two women had begun to bring each other up to date; apparently they kept no secrets from each other. When Emma asked about Muscles, Soong said she was well aware that a man who fitted the nickname had been asking questions, but she was sure he was not their bomber and was adamant in that view.

'When men are as strong as him, they do not set bombs to kill women,' Soong said firmly. 'A strong man can break a girl's neck—he does not need a bomb.' She suddenly turned to CV. 'You! If you had to kill a woman, would you choose a bomb?'

'Well no, but he may have found the loss of Julia incidental.'

'Why the bomb, then?'

'To cover his other mischief.'

'You talk nonsense. The bomb is a political statement. As for that boy, he wouldn't show his face for ten miles if he'd left a bomb here. He is in no fear of the police because still he comes.'

He had underestimated this woman. He should have talked to her earlier.

She waved a finger at him as if he was a school kid. 'Julia was not a girl who drank until she was unconscious, not like Emma's friend Valerie who vomited at the gate. Renuka said Julia came here about midnight and she was not drunk. She had a headache. Renuka gave her two Panadols with a glass of water, although I do not approve of pain killers.'

'What do you think happened that night, Soong?' Emma asked.

CV, wondering what Maggie was up to, was standing at the windows. She was playing kick-a-tin with the children, and he saw the tin fly.

He turned back to Soong who was saying, 'I think Julia was asleep and the lights were out when a man came in. He knew Emma was out and came to steal. Julia woke, and they were both surprised. To calm her fears, he asked for Emma and made an excuse for being there. He looked respectable, so Julia thought he was Emma's friend. The police say Julia carried condoms in her backpack. I think she was lonely and hoping to meet a nice man, so she encouraged this one. When he could, he knocked her out. He'd brought a small bomb as a warning to Emma and afterwards would have followed that up with a letter to tell her what he wanted. But his plans went wrong. He now had to kill Julia, who could identify him.'

Emma nodded vigorously. 'Julia had taken classes in self-defence. She'd have fought.'

'That's an impressive theory, Dr Soong,' CV said thoughtfully. 'They say most rapes and attacks on women come from men they know. Julia may even have known the man. But if she had sex with him, perhaps he left evidence.'

'We don't know what she did or what he did or if he put on a condom when he did it, but the police seem to know something,' Soong said pursing her lips. 'They have been asking many questions about the men she knew and their habits.'

'Their habits?'

'Their sexual habits.'

So Teddy had indeed been keeping his own counsel.

'Do you think the intruder could have been Mr Bell? He is apparently very attractive to women,' he said to Soong.

'Mr Bell did not climb my wall with a bomb in his hand. I have thought much about this. I think it was a local fellow who could speak in Sinhala and make an explanation if he was seen. A bomb is not an Englishman's weapon.'

Teddy had come to the same conclusion.

Soong rose, went to the door and clapped her hands—a signal for Renuka to bring tea and rice cakes.

As they sipped their tea, she brought Dorothy's documents to Emma. There were three envelopes marked *Emma*, *Last Will* and *Documents*.

Because her eyes had filled with tears, Emma handed the first to CV and asked him to read it aloud. He said, 'It's marked PRIVATE AND CONFIDENTIAL—big and clear. Read it later. It would have been what she wanted.'

She blew her nose and sat staring at the sheets of paper then handed them to him again saying, 'Please.'

Dr Soong got up and began to leave the room, but Emma

called her back. 'Oh, Soong, if Dor trusted you to give these to me, you should know what they say.'

The five pages she had given him consisted of two handwritten letters dated the eleventh of the previous month—exactly one month to the day before she died. He read the first aloud:

> Sweet Emma—I have become rather rich because Chinese Daddy has been looking after my money. I hope you don't mind but I've made you my executor. Take this letter to him. He will pay for your flight because you'll have to go to Singapore.
>
> My will is in the other envelope. No one except Michael and Chinese Daddy need know you have it—and if there is a need, he will provide a lawyer . . . It would be better if you pretended ignorance or Reggie might make trouble. Another thing, he mustn't know that Daddy Li exists.

She'd added Li's address and contact numbers. CV read silently and then said, 'It's too personal for me to go on. I have no stomach for it.'

'Please, Clive.'

Emma was holding her knees, and her face was turned away. Soong was paying close attention. He decided to get it over:

> Emma, you are my best friend. You have been like a sister. I may have told you by the time you read this that Reginald Bell isn't my father. He changed the records. I didn't have to be sterilized. What a joke. All along he knew it wasn't incest—it was his creepy idea of love. Louise told me. She isn't dead. She's married and has two children. Last time I was in London, I was coming

out of the flat, and I saw her on the street waving at me.
I was so happy she was alive. Angry at Reggie for lying.
We went back inside because I wanted to catch up on
the missing years.

'I told you,' Emma said softly. 'She would never have put any appointment ahead of Louise.'

She said that when she was my nanny and I was asleep
and he was away, she'd poke around the flat. She'd
read his letters and looked at his things. One day she
found a blood test report with a letter that said
Dorothy Marie Bell could not be the child of Reginald
Bell. So I was only six months old when he knew.
Another evening she found some pictures of me naked.
Louise had a fight with him about the pictures, which
seemed kinky, and he threw her out.

But when she told me everything, I began to hate
Louise. She knew where I lived. She knew it all. Charlie
Yarrow told her what he saw. Now she has children. I
never will. I just didn't want to see her again, so I said, 'I
don't like you any more, Louise. You must go.'

I'll probably rewrite this letter lots of times. I wonder
if you will ever read it.
Love,
Dorothy

The second letter was to Li and read:

Dear Chinese Daddy Li,
Please put my money in a trust for Michael and Emma
as you and I discussed. Please continue to invest it for
them.

> I am putting Emma in control with you because Michael is such a loop that he'll probably give it to a toy boy or some crazy cause.
>
> Carlo and Mark should get something—I don't know what. Emma will know.
>
> I have made a list of my friends. Some will prefer cash and others a bit of me.

There followed a list of twenty-six names among which were Dr Soong and her husband Hoong, Renuka and the children, Jeff, Li himself and members of his family. She had not included Reggie, her mother or Louise.

'Thank you Daddy Li,' the letter ended, 'for your letting me be your daughter. I love you too. Dorothy.' Underneath she had signed and also printed her full name, Dorothy Marie Bell, and written the date.

Both letters had been notarized by a Mr IT de Saram.

Dorothy's last will left all her movable and immovable property to Michael, 'except what I have deeded separately to Emma van Eck for distribution according to my wishes.' The document package contained her insurance policies and other papers, and a list of them was attached. One item was a letter from Childers' Laboratory saying that the report she had sent to them had been tampered with and that they were enclosing the correct report of the same day. The correct report confirmed that DNA testing had shown Reggie could not be Dorothy's father.

Also intriguing were three sheets stapled together. One was a handwritten love letter from a Vincent asking Dorothy to marry him. The second was a report from a London private investigator, Tilden Morse, who confirmed Vincent Belli had died in Milan from a knife wound in the back. The third was a covering letter from Morse stating, 'Mr Reginald Bell was in Milan the day before Mr Belli was killed—he paid for lunch in a

Milan restaurant with his Visa credit card. I have found no evidence that he was in Milan the next day. I am unable to find out where he was. Six days later, as you will see from my report, he flew into Gatwick from Paris, and he later gave a deposition admitting he had met Mr Belli in Milan and had a brief conversation.'

CV said, 'He must have got out of Italy using one of those false passports.'

Interlude
Their little party was silent as they trailed out of Dr Soong's compound. CV handed Maggie the three envelopes, and she put them into her large purse. Emma's tears were gone, but her face was grim.

Renuka's children lined up at the gate to bid them goodbye, and the eldest girl Peggy prostrated herself in front of Maggie, kissed her hands and placed them on her feet.

'I wish they wouldn't do that,' she growled.

Emma said softly, 'It is their culture.'

Joseph told CV with some irritation that Meechi and his friend had disappeared. He had turned away to light a cigarette, and the next second he saw them pedalling away up the road.

'Something frightened them?'

'They just went.'

So they drove to Bundy's office where Lakshmi waved from her doorway as they entered. He went over to speak with her, and she told him with obvious delight that she had something to report. A man had tried the door, but he was no one she recognized.

The day creaked on as plans for the luncheon the following day became more elaborate. Teddy thought the whole scheme was doomed to failure and didn't hesitate to say so. 'Criminals think they're innocent. They don't jump up and say, "I did it",' he said sourly. But he agreed to attend and bring Nora only because he hadn't eaten lobster for two years.

Maggie told him he was getting the disposition of a lobster himself. 'I'm treating the drinks. Good champagne. The best of the best,' she said.

'I won't miss it then,' said the superintendent and twitched his eyebrows.

Michael was totally supportive of the party, if not for the right reasons: 'If I'm going to be arrested or get a knife in my back, I'd prefer friends to be looking on.'

Jeff, who'd had a full night's sleep, said he was coming for the food. 'We never have grand meals.'

CV would have liked to tell him that Michael was going to be able to afford the grandest of meals in the future but decided it wasn't his business.

Bell also accepted gracefully when Maggie phoned, but then he called CV to say, 'You promised me sixteen hours a day on the job. Postpone this party till next week.'

'A prior commitment, as it's Aunt Maud's birthday. Shouldn't take long. I wish I could hold it down to sixteen hours—it has been running much more.'

'Who are the other guests?'

'Friends and acquaintances. It's a no-no here to ask questions like that. Oh yes, do you eat shellfish? We're having lobster and will order something else if you don't.'

'I am particularly fond of it.'

'We're opening the Dom Pengnan at twelve-thirty. We'll sit down at one.'

Just before dinner Joseph came to the door and asked to speak to him.

Muscles
Ralph Wijewardene's chauffeur Colman had talked to Joseph

about the evening Dorothy died. He still did not know that she or Michael had been in Hospital Street that evening.

'I know Colman, sir,' Joseph told CV. 'We were drivers together at the American embassy before I had my heart attack and he got diabetes.'

'I didn't know you had a heart condition, Joseph. Are you sure you should be working?'

'My heart is in no trouble, sir. I had a heart attack because I wanted to take the job with Maud Lady. My father worked for her father the great man. Colman got diabetes there because of a family tie with the Wijewardenes.'

'Colman is a kind of mustard,' CV couldn't help saying.

'His father got the name from a yellow tin.'

'And what else did Colman say?'

He had confirmed Li's story. He had driven Mr Wijewardene to the airport to pick up a Chinese who had, on the return journey, given Colman Rs 1,000—demonstrating he was both rich and generous. A fellow employee, Guneya, the bodyguard, had been in the car on both journeys. Wijewardene and Li were inside about fifteen or twenty minutes during which time no cars and no people came down Hospital Street. Joseph commented, 'No one wants to see why a big car with guards is there at night.'

Colman had seen Mr Li once since then. He was sent to the airport to meet him alone in Mr Wijewardene's Peugeot. He came off the plane without luggage and went to the Carlton Raj for a meeting with Mr Sharif and a foreign gentleman. Colman had seen them when they had said goodbye to Mr Li next morning, but they had not accompanied him to the airport.

So that was Colman driving the Peugeot!

Joseph became more excited telling his other piece of news. Meechi and his friend had seen Muscles, which was why they had suddenly disappeared that morning. He had come into the lane while Joseph was lighting his cigarette, saw the Magnette, turned and left hurriedly. The boys followed. Muscles took a bus on the Galle Road and as the traffic was slow they had been able to keep up on their bikes. He got down at Bagatelle Road and made his way to Michael's. There was no one outside, so he waited for twenty minutes during which time the boys bought ice creams from a passing vendor. He did not seem suspicious, nor did he seem to recognize them from outside Soong's—supposedly he'd had eyes only for Joseph. Meechi got tired of waiting and got into a conversation with Muscles. They were still carrying their cricket bats, and he asked if he would throw balls for them.

To their delight, he said he should be leaving and asked if one of them would give him a ride home. Meechi's bike had the stronger crossbar and Muscles rode with the boy sitting in front of him. He took them to a big apartment building about a mile away, thanked them, gave them thirty rupees and went inside. They asked questions about him on the street and were told his name was Raja and that he worked for a man who lived in one of the apartments.

When Joseph told him the name of Muscles's employer, CV said, 'We've got to confirm that. Can you go there yourself and make inquiries without being conspicuous?'

'When, sir?'

'I know you've been running errands for us all day, but this is urgent.'

'I'll go at once.'

'Take a taxi. Auntie's Magnette is too easy to recognize.'

CV did not tell Maggie and Emma what Joseph had told him.

He phoned Ali and said, 'Has Maggie told you we're giving a lunch tomorrow?'

'I'd better stay away.'

'You must be there. The pink roses were a hit, and she's inseparable from the box. You have to give me tips because poor

Emma hasn't had as much as a shoe flower from me. Can't believe there will be a time when I'll be free to pursue that girl.'

'You think there will be such a time?'

'Will things improve? Yes. Will things deteriorate? Yes. Now, what was the question?'

'I forgot. Good night!'

'Good night.'

Seating

Perera vetoed CV's choice of a large round table for lunch because he didn't have a one to seat fifteen. Instead four long tables would be set in a square so they guests could still be facing each other. He was obviously pleased to have been invited.

Maggie had to work with the seating because there were so many volatile relationships. Emma told CV smugly, 'Even I'm making a fuss. I won't sit next to Mr Bell, Mr Mahmoud or Frances.'

Frances!

'I phoned Frances,' Maggie said. 'She'd prefer to sit next to you CV but has agreed to be next to Reggie. Nora hasn't met him, so she'll be on his left.'

He said, 'Bundy can't be next to Teddy because he expects to be arrested—or Reggie.'

She said, 'Or Michael, Jeff or Emma because he left Dorothy in the Pettah.' She consulted her plan. 'I've put Bundy between you and Frances.'

'Let me see.'

	Teddy	Aunt Maud	CV	
Perera				Bundy
Millie				Frances
Ali Sharif				Reggie
Emma				Nora
	Michael	Maggie	Mahmoud	Jeff

He studied the plan and said, 'It's good—amend that—it's great. Of course, Perera will be disappointed he's not nearer you.'

'Tough! He touched my famous butt while we discussed the menu, so I'm not pleased with him.'

'Touched or pinched?'

'Stroked.'

'Cruder than I thought. Ali won't be pleased that Mahmoud is next to you.'

She grinned. 'That's why he is.'

'Women can be nasty.'

'Jeff may not want to be next to Mahmoud but having Nora on his right will protect him. I actually put Mahmoud beside me not to make Ali jealous but because I enjoy the cultured old pervert.'

His aunt also approved the seating. 'What a clever girl you are, Maggie. It's got sugar and spice for everyone.'

CV said, 'We've all lied about something. It's time for us all to be faced with our lies. The killer, he or she, will be there, remember.'

'She?' asked Maggie. 'All of a sudden a she? Which she? Aunt Maud, Emma or me?'

'Nora, Nora killed Dorothy because . . .'

'Because Teddy needs an exciting case,' said Emma and surprised them.

Chapter X

Thursday

Gloria and Fred Ware
Gloria and Fred Ware carried their mourning for their daughter with dignity rather than reserve. They were both younger than CV had expected and dark blonde, pink-skinned and freckled.

Fred was in management, he told CV after they shook hands, and Gloria was a hospital supervisor. He followed that saying that they were grateful for the interest he had shown because they were both very angry that not enough fuss was being made over their daughter's death by either their embassy or the Sri Lankan police.

CV replied, 'But you'll find there are several of us working full time to find out who killed Julia and also Dorothy Bell, who was the first victim.'

'We'll help,' said the Wares together.

'Thank you. The crimes were needless and sickening. Superintendent Senaratne, who has been investigating both cases, is particularly troubled over Julia, whom he thinks was killed by a Sri Lankan.'

He had driven the MG to the airport alone, he told them, because Senaratne had vetoed Emma's coming. The Wares nodded grimly.

Gloria said, 'What a terrible country this is.' It was no time to point out that murder is terrible anywhere, and the United

States was no stranger to it. She began to weep on the way to Colombo but talked about her daughter and asked questions. He had nothing to add above what they already knew. He then told them about the lunch and apologized for their not being able to attend. 'You should be there, but if the focus of attention is on you, it will be easier for the murderer to avoid that spot.'

They weren't happy about it, so he changed the subject. 'I think that the death of one's child must be terrible. You'll meet a friend of ours, Ali Sharif, who lost his daughter before she was a year old. That was five years ago. He still can't talk about it.'

Fred suddenly said, 'You're right about us not going to your lunch meeting. Julia's weeping parents would not be a help.'

At Bliss, the arrival of the Wares provided a distraction, but everyone was unnaturally formal and on edge. CV took Maggie into the back drawing room. 'Do me a favour, Mag. Call Michael, and ask him if Dorothy told him about Vincent Belli wanting to marry her.'

'Emma did, and Dor did. How could I have forgotten to tell you about it? Jeff came over to tell us yesterday. Dor and Vinny met in England when they were students, got engaged and went off together around Europe. In Milan, Bell caught up with them and confronted them at some cheap place where they were staying. Dorothy had the flu, it so happened. Reggie accused Vinny of being after his money, and as Vinny hadn't known about it, he was furious. But she was a minor and knew her father could have Vinny arrested, so she agreed to return to England with him if she could spend a last night with Vinny. Reggie agreed. That evening Vinny suggested he go and get some takeout for supper. He didn't return.'

'Tell me the rest while I dress,' he said, leading the way upstairs.

She finished the story sitting on his bed. 'Dor was very upset but couldn't go looking for Vinny because she was feverish and full of cold pills. She fell asleep. In the morning her father picked her up and took her to Spain and then England, and naturally she didn't tell him that her fiancé had got cold feet and decided to drop her, which is what she thought when Vinny wasn't there in the morning. Weeks later, in England, she found he had been killed that night and was convinced her father had done it. He denied it, of course.'

'Michael believes this story?'

'Jeff didn't say.'

'Do you?'

'Murders sound like fairy stories to me. You think they can't happen to people you know,' she replied.

'What's worrying you?'

'When Ali finds out what I'm really like, maybe he won't come back one day.'

'What are you really like?' he took her arm and shoved her to the door.

'I'm a bitch. If I do something bitchy, will he come back?'

'If he likes bitchy women.'

'Don't you laugh at me!'

'All right. You're not bitchy. He's a lucky guy. If he is mean to you, I'll bash him.'

Poor Maggie had never loved before, he realized and hugged her. 'Go on down and be charming for me. I'm going to think. Try to keep anyone from talking to me for an hour or so.'

Champagne

The time had come. Even his aunt looked nervous. For the first time in several days, Emma was leaving the house as herself, and she wore a bright print dress he had not seen before.

They left the house in two cars after Teddy and Nora showed up just before twelve.

Emma and Maggie travelled with Teddy in the police car and Nora, CV and their aunt in the Magnette with Joseph at the wheel. They found two policemen waiting for them outside the hotel and several more inside. A lounge with sofas and armchairs had been reserved for the prelunch get-together. CV joined his aunt on one of the white and gold sofas and said, 'Watch the lime juice, Auntie. Last time I was here, it nearly killed me.' Perera heard him.

'Mr vander Marten, you know we don't poison our guests,' he said indignantly.

'Darling boy is teasing,' said Maud graciously. But darling boy was not.

After the manager moved away, CV reminded her they had brought a champagne bottle filled with aerated lemonade, 'Go ahead and drink what you want, Auntie. Emma, Mag and I have decided to go it sober in secret.'

'Oh, you poor children! Never mind. You can have champagne this evening. It's my birthday.'

Perera couldn't take his eyes off Maggie, who was wearing one of her outrageous dishevelled hairstyles and white platform shoes that made her seem over seven feet tall. Between the hair and the shoes was a tailored blue dress. He followed her to the dining room and, while she distributed the place cards, plied her with toast circles covered with oysters, truffles and caviar. She tasted them and made appreciative noises. It was turning into the kind of ooh-and-aah party he hated and CV wished the guests would arrive. He eventually went to find Teddy who was talking to four of his uniformed policemen. He asked one of them to look after his briefcase.

When he returned, the first bottle of Dom Perignon had been opened, and at exactly 12.35 Bundy and Millie Balasingham arrived bearing a gift-wrapped package. They somewhat nervously skirted Teddy to greet CV, who hurried them over to his aunt.

She said, 'It is so kind of you to have brought me a present. Some of the champagne is only lemonade so be sure you get a glass of the real thing.'

'Lemonade?' asked Bundy of CV.

'For the vegetarians.'

Bundy laughed. Millie did not now, nor did she when her husband said to Teddy, 'CV has promised you won't arrest me for the crime I did not commit until after I've had lunch.'

'Did you have to disappear like that?' was the reply.

'I'm alive, aren't I?'

When Frances arrived, she kissed CV on the mouth and managed to leave perfume on him. She shook hands with all the others.

Maggie said, 'Don't act so innocent, Frances Blue. I recognize that Givenchy. He's come in smelling of it before.'

Frances fluttered her false eyelashes. 'Men love it. Don't you feel too high on those shoes?'

'Men love them.'

'Are you Emma?' asked Frances, changing her target.

'Yes. You must be so proud to have a son like Michael.'

Jeff floated in wearing a sheer white kurta and white pants, but before CV had time to greet him, he whispered that Michael had disappeared.

'Shit.'

'He was dressing, went out and didn't come back. Do you want me to go and look for him?'

'No, but I'd like to wring his neck. We'll wing it without him.' He had warned the others that such meetings never went smoothly. The first blip had shown, as always, from an unexpected direction.

Mahmoud strode across the room, and his manner suggested he was the guest of honour. At Aunt Maud's chair he bowed low to kiss her hand and congratulate her on her birthday, and he told her a small something from him had been delivered to her home.

'No, no,' she protested, now on her second glass of champagne, 'because it's really not my birthday.'

'Oh, I'm so glad. You must tell me when the real one comes so I can send you the mate.'

'Is it a dog?'

'It's a chair.' Then he looked around and saw that Maggie, Emma, Nora and Millie were standing around CV and raised his voice, 'Your nephew continues to amaze me, Miss vander Marten. How quickly he collects a harem. We other buggers have to put up with his dregs.'

CV sensed an insult to Dorothy but decided not to respond. 'Glad you could come, Mr Mahmoud.'

'Ah, Beauty!' continued Mahmoud, gazing at Emma and holding her hand. 'You see I am not the ogre you suspected? Did CV show you the picture of Ahmed?'

Emma nodded gravely. 'He did, Mr Mahmoud, and I'm sorry I misjudged you. Ahmed is very good looking, but he's not my type.'

Reginald Bell arrived, went around working the room and introducing himself.

'I am so glad you could come. My mother wishes she could be here,' CV said as they grasped hands.

Bell was taken aback, then chuckled. 'You and I must get to know each other better. I'm beginning to like you.'

Ali's arrival also made a stir, if only because not everyone knew him. He kissed Aunt Maud, opened her hand and slipped a small box into it. 'Happy birthday.'

'But . . .' she protested, and he touched her lips with his finger. 'I know. But this is something I want you to have.'

He then kissed Maggie carefully on each cheek, and she said, 'You'd better say how nice I look because I got dolled up all ladylike for you.'

Reggie looked at her. She looked at Ali, who said, 'Come to think of it, you do look rather nice.'

The Portrait

Seeing the empty place beside Maggie, his aunt whispered, 'Who's missing?'

'Michael,' he whispered back, and, as he said the word, the door opened and there Michael was. He certainly knew how to make an entrance.

He was dressed from waist to ankle like his father—stylish pale grey slacks. But his chest was almost covered by a long loose embroidered vest, and around his neck was the necklace with huge medallions, the one he had worn at Dorothy's memorial service. His long dark hair was hanging to his shoulders, and his brown skin was glowing.

CV once again thought, 'Gypsy!' He glanced at Michael's mother—another gypsy. He could imagine her telling fortunes out of the back of a covered wagon.

Michael carried a large flat package wrapped in brown paper and propped it against a wall; then he made his way to Maggie and they embraced. They were so decorative together that CV was surprised no one gasped. He rose and Michael came around the table and embraced him too. Then he leaned down and kissed Aunt Maud and said, 'Happy birthday, Auntie. I have a present for you.' He reclaimed his package, tore off the paper and then placed it on the table so she could see it.

'Oh my dear,' she said. 'It's Dorothy! Thank you so much.'

She asked CV to show it to everyone, and Mr Perera suggested that they prop it on a table by the wall so it could be in view during the meal. Dorothy was wearing a halter-neck and the half grin that was so much part of her. Emma began weeping, and Ali, who was visibly moved, began to comfort her. Then CV noticed Reggie was about to faint; he was swaying in his chair. Before he could move to help, Frances caught the Englishman's arm and shook it, and Nora handed him a glass of water. Reggie recovered but remained pale and somewhat disoriented until slowly his colour returned.

Mahmoud was staring at the picture with astonishment. He caught CV's eye and mouthed, 'It's good!' Bundy, beside CV, had his elbow on the table and his head in his hands. Of the others there who had known her, Jeff had obviously seen it before, and Perera was unmoved.

Michael stood before his work as if he was facing the actual girl he had loved, and they were smiling at each other. Then he turned and went around the table greeting everyone by name, kissed his mother warmly on the cheek, even shook hands with his father. When he sat down, he said something to Emma. She kissed her fingers and placed them on his cheek.

The soup was served.

Champagne glasses were refilled.

The meal began.

Showdown

The meal was over, and the time had come for the rehearsed part of the show, which they had gone over again and again that morning: keep cool, remember your lines.

Maggie had led the women to the restrooms saying, 'There's more to come.' CV suggested the men do the same trek. Now everyone was back. She caught his eye, he nodded, and she raised her voice, 'I've asked for coffee to be served here.'

'Good idea,' he agreed also on cue. 'Because there are a few things I have to talk about before we go home. Are you all right, Auntie? How about a more comfortable chair?'

'I'm as right as rain,' she assured him and, forgetting her rehearsed dialogue, added, 'Teddy has been telling me about a murder in Negombo last month. What an exciting life he leads.' She was supposed to say, 'What do you want to talk about?'

Emma piped up, 'What do you want to talk about, Clive?'

Aunt Maud beamed, 'Oh, thank you Emma. I was supposed to say that.'

'Well, I'm glad someone did because I want to talk about

Dorothy.' His group had all been instructed not to stare at Bell, though his aunt had obviously forgotten that too. Fortunately, she was not the only one the champagne had relaxed, and the mood was genial.

He waited until the waiters brought the coffee, by which time the chatter had started again, and he used that time to collect his valise. He cleared a space in front of him and took out his folders and the Panasonic tape recorder he had found in the office. There was an unused cassette in the recorder now, and he stacked three others beside the machine. The cassette at the bottom of the pile was a copy of the one he had found. He finally nodded to Teddy.

The superintendent then explained that from now on, unless he gave his permission, no waiter would enter the room, and no one already inside it could leave except with a member of the police—even to the toilet. He nodded at the man at the door who opened it. Two policemen and one policewoman entered and moved to the south wall, where they stood side by side.

Mr Perera stood up and said pleasantly but firmly, 'I am afraid the Palace Hotel cannot be used for an unscheduled meeting such as this, even if you are present, Superintendent Senaratne. The management has given permission for a birthday lunch only. This meeting must therefore be transferred somewhere else.'

Teddy had a clipboard beside him, and he placed it before Perera. 'You'll see that Mr vander Marten has booked this room until four o'clock, and my department has been authorized to control the security. Your chairman has given us his blessing, and so has your manager.'

Perera looked at it and frowned. 'Why wasn't I notified?'

Teddy replied, 'At my request, none of the guests was.' He then snapped, 'Let's get started, or we'll be here all day.'

But Perera would not be rushed. 'I must tell my staff I won't be available for two hours.'

'I have done so. Now I must ask that all mobile phones be turned off, because if one rings while Mr vander Marten is talking, I will confiscate it.'

Perera sat down and kept his cool by suggesting that the coffee and teapots be left on the table.

'A good idea,' said Senaratne.

'What is going on, Clive?' asked Bundy under his breath.

'A butting of horns to establish who's king of the forest.'

From across the table Millie glared at him. He ignored her, removed his mobile phone from the valise, made a show of turning it off and placed it in front of him. Bundy and Frances were also carrying mobile units and did the same. Frances seemed to be enjoying herself and said loudly, 'How very very! How cloak and dagger! When I saw who all were here, I guessed there'd be fun.'

The mood in the room had, not unexpectedly, changed after the Perera-Senaratne confrontation. Reggie was questioning Nora in an undertone, and she kept glancing at her husband for help, but he gave her none. His dark eyes moved slowly over the faces before him. Maggie and Michael held hands and smoked. Mahmoud was murmuring to Jeff, who seemed happy with the turn of events. He was not talking, but he was smiling. Ali leaned back with one arm across the back of Emma's chair. She was biting her lower lip.

Bundy suddenly whispered fiercely, 'You promised to stand by me, Clive.'

He whispered back, 'Will you relax.' Then, lowering his voice further, he said, 'Actually, an anxious expression from you would be helpful.' Bundy kept the one he already had.

CV reached forward, turned on the recorder and explained that he was doing so because he did not want his words misquoted later. He remained seated, raised his voice and spoke slowly. 'If anyone cannot hear me or would like me to repeat something, please say so at once. Otherwise, I'd prefer to say my bit without interruption.

'My name is Clive vander Marten, and today is Thursday April the 24th—that's just for the tape. You all know that last Friday I accepted an assignment from Mr Reginald Bell to try and find Dorothy Bell's murderer. That assignment runs out tomorrow. I thought we should get together before then to share what we know. This luncheon has provided me with such an opportunity. Please relax. This isn't an inquisition but an effort to hasten to the end of a situation that has already destroyed two women and to prevent the death of others.

'Why would anyone would want to kill Dorothy Bell? It is a simplification to say she was a brilliant young woman of unusual physical and mental courage. Many of you loved her. Many of you had also learned not to underestimate her. But she was also a troubled girl who rashly took on dangerous opponents. Her willingness to confront those who wronged her, of taking it to the edge, caused her death.

'It does seem that whoever killed or ordered the death of Dorothy and also Julia Ware must be here among us. I have talked at length with each of you about the case. Please do not all be offended if I say that it became obvious to me from the first that some of you have been lying—so much so that I got on better examining your lies than your truths.

'Let me give you an example. Both Michael Blue and I were at different times on Monday drugged in this hotel. In my case it happened in the morning while I was talking to Mr Bell. I barely touched my doctored drink and got off lightly. Michael was not so lucky. While drinking a beer as he was waiting to talk to Mr Bell that evening, he became seriously ill. In both cases we had appointments, so certain members of the staff knew we were coming.

'As no other guests in the hotel complained of similar symptoms on Monday, I have to presume our poisoning was deliberate. Yet Teddy has not been able to find anyone who will admit to even knowing about it. Obviously there is a cover-up, which led to some conclusions.

'First, the person who poisoned us is capable of poisoning others.

'Second, someone specifically wanted Michael and me out of action either permanently or temporarily on Monday.

'Third, as it was Dorothy's death that had brought Michael and me together, the poisoner is involved in it.

'Fourth, a liar on one matter can be expected to have lied on others.'

He looked around. They were intrigued. 'You see my point? It was from the untruths that I found a place to start.

'My dilemma was that none of you appeared to have a reason to have wanted Dorothy or Emma or Julia dead. However, as I started asking questions I began to find . . .' he looked through his notes, 'that nine of you had relationships with Dorothy that were far more complicated than at first appeared.'

He picked up the recorder to be sure that the tape was turning. Then he looked around. As he had hoped, they still seemed relaxed. One coffee jug was in front of Frances, and he asked Bundy to fill his cup from it. He wanted a short breather to give them time to think over what they had heard.

He then said, 'The nine I spoke of are, first, Mr Mahmoud whom Dorothy charged to have sex with her; Bundy, from whom she demanded and got ten per cent of Mr Mahmoud's casino losses; Ali, who put her in touch with the owner of a star ruby known as Padmani's Blood but regretted doing so because he feels it belongs to the people of Sri Lanka. Then there's Mr Perera who has been Mr Bell's business associate in a variety of matters that affected Dorothy; Michael and Emma are her heirs; Jeffrey lives with Michael and thus also benefits indirectly from his inheritance; and Frances who, if Dorothy had married Michael, would have had no grandchildren.'

'What rubbish,' Frances said.

'Bear with me,' he told her. 'But as you've spoken, let's deal with the grandchildren question first. It is an important one to the background of this crime and makes Mr Bell the ninth person on my shortlist.

'Dorothy and Michael were engaged and naturally presumed they would have children together one day. Then, last year, Mr Bell broke the news to them that they were both his children because he and Frances had once had an affair. She had never revealed the fact to Michael because Mr Bell had told her he would deny paternity if she did. When he started claiming paternity, she felt betrayed. Even after Dorothy and Michael became engaged, Frances had not divulged the truth because she's a romantic. She didn't care what the law was. She put their happiness first.

'It is illegal in many countries to marry a half-sister or half-brother. The rationale is that the children from such unions are more likely to be mentally unstable and develop genetic problems. So when Mr Bell told Michael and Dorothy he'd prevent their marriage, he knew he'd win. But a ray of hope came to them. Dorothy spoke to her mother, who is divorced from Mr Bell. She told Dorothy that Mr Bell was probably not her father.'

CV went on to tell them that Dorothy had a DNA test that confirmed she was related to Reginald Bell. 'Dorothy decided she'd had enough of the discussion. Michael was her world. She had her tubes tied and told only Frances, Michael and Emma what she had done.

'I tell you these things to show you the extent of the anger that had come to boil within Dorothy. It was not easy for her to cut herself from the hope of motherhood. But what she felt then was nothing like the anger she felt when a woman called Louise Lawrence told her Mr Bell had known from when she was six months old that he could not be her father. She confronted Childers' Laboratory, which had done both tests, and discovered the report she had received from them had been tampered with, and she had been sterilized unnecessarily.'

Everyone began to speak at once.

An enraged Frances began hitting Bell with her open hand and shouting. 'You son of a bitch! You swine,' she went on and on and yelled anything she could think of.

Bell caught her blows midair and began to shout back that she mustn't believe what she was hearing.

'Shhh,' some of the others started saying, but Frances wouldn't be silenced. 'Why did you tell her she was yours? Why? Why? Why?' She was now on her feet and looking for something to hit him with.

'Frances,' said CV. 'Please!'

She turned on him. 'What do you know about women? You didn't watch Dorothy cry. How she cried! And it was unnecessary!'

'Mum, stop yelling,' said Michael. 'I've known the truth for some time.'

She stopped, looked at him and said, 'Oh, my poor son,' and sat down heavily. She was shaking and red-faced.

Bell said, 'Superintendent Senaratne, I refuse to sit through this.'

Teddy ignored him.

CV continued, 'Mr Bell is right. We must speak one at a time, and this is still my time. We have seen Frances's reaction. Imagine Dorothy's and Michael's. She had suffered much from Reginald Bell all her life. This final straw took her into a dangerous mood.'

He then described her childhood: first, the deprivation of affection and then finding she was Bell's sex toy; her beginning to stockpile money that would one day buy her freedom from him; her plans to ruin him.

Bell had taken a toothpick from a small holder on the table and was picking his teeth. Whatever new reaction CV had expected from him, this was not it. The icy calm that had melted under Frances's anger was astonishingly back in place, as if it had never left. All but Emma were paying close attention. She had her fingers in her ears.

CV said, 'Before going further, I want to tell you all about some people I would have liked to be here today because they have also played a part in the drama of Dorothy's life and death.

'First are two medical doctors: Emma's landlords. It was on their property that Julia was killed. It was to Dr Soong that Dorothy entrusted her will and a package of documents that includes proof of her parentage.'

Reggie's eyes had narrowed.

'Also missing is Della Marsh from Chicago, without whom I would not have been able to tie up this investigation so quickly or at all. Through the Internet she found people connected to Dorothy—her mother, her headmistress, her nanny—people who knew of the relationship between Dorothy and her father from the time it started going wrong.

'Even before I took on this assignment, Della had provided me with information on Mr Bell.' CV suddenly laughed aloud. 'I'd become curious about him at the memorial service he hosted.' Reggie's light blue eyes were now watching him. 'So even before I was offered the case, I had learned from Della that four other associates of Mr Bell had died exactly as Dorothy had—from being stabbed in the back: a single thrust which had penetrated their hearts. That's some coincidence!'

'She was my daughter, not my associate,' said Reggie loudly.

'I have shown she was not.'

'Bravo!' Michael shouted and clapped his hands above his head. He laughed but with hysteria, and Maggie began whispering to him. The rest of the guests had turned into statues.

It was obviously time to speed up. 'These stories, however, show only that Dorothy had a motive for wanting Mr Bell dead. But there was still no motive for him or anyone else to want to kill her.'

Bell lit a cigarette.

Frances said to him, 'She should have killed you.'

'No, Mum,' said Michael. 'Stop that. You're getting boring.'

'And there we may still all be but, fortunately, Ali Sharif then went that extra yard. He persuaded a man, whom I shall call Uncle, to come to Colombo and tell me a story that has provided a very strong motive for someone to kill Dorothy.

'On April 11th, Uncle flew into Colombo bringing with him Padmani's Blood. The secrecy around the transaction is understandable. It is a humungous star ruby. It weighs nearly a thousand carats. Its colour is pigeon's blood. Its star is perfectly centred. Dorothy herself called it a stone to die for.

'The autopsy places Dorothy's death somewhere between 11.30 p.m. and 2 a.m. that night. At 11 p.m., in the presence of Dorothy and two Sri Lankan bodyguards, Uncle handed Padmani's Blood to Reginald Bell, and through an electronic transfer he received in return $13,000,000.'

He looked at the Englishman, and he thought this must be how it is to come face to face in the jungle with a leopard that had begun to pick off children in a nearby village.

Then suddenly the predator disappeared. What was left was an elegant silver-haired man—a little amused, a little patronizing, a little weary—and it was CV who was breathing hard. He reminded himself he was surrounded by friends.

CV cleared his throat and looked at his notes. 'Uncle had his money. Mr Bell had the stone. At 11.20 p.m. Uncle and his bodyguard left Mr Bell alone with Dorothy. At 11.55 p.m. her body was placed on a step in Second Cross Street. At about 2 a.m. it was found by two soldiers driving by in a jeep. The medical report states she had been struck behind the ear but died from a knife plunged in her back and that she had been crawling away from her assailant.

'Exactly a week later—Friday, April 18th—Mr Bell hired me to find Dorothy's killer. On Saturday night Julia Ware was struck on the side of the head. While she was unconscious, a man ejaculated into her mouth. At 2.27 p.m. someone threw a pipe bomb through her window and killed her. On Sunday Bundy warned me that I might be next in line. On Monday I found my phone calls and computer activities were being monitored. That day someone poisoned Michael and me, and Bundy went into hiding in fear of his own life.

'These are facts that can be authenticated. Each one must fit into a single scenario.'

He looked around and smiled ruefully knowing it was now or never for the plunge.

'I am going to give you the only scenario that fits all these facts. It places the lies in the mouths of the liars who, with the possible exception of Michael, did so to protect themselves and get away, quite literally, with murder. It's a story that starts the day before Dorothy died. On that day, Mr Bell flew into Sri Lanka under the name Harry Belladonna.'

Reggie's smile was gone. 'What is this? Am I being framed?'

'There are others in this room, Mr Bell,' said Teddy smoothly, 'who must be feeling as uncomfortable as you. I now ask all of you to stay in your seats and keep your hands on the table. No, Miss vander Marten, you are the exception. You may keep your hands on your lap.'

'Thank you, Teddy,' said Maud.

Showdown-2

CV picked up his notes again,

'Brown-haired Harry Belladonna travelling economy class

arrived in Colombo at 6 p.m. on Thursday, April 10th from India. He left Colombo for south India at 6 a.m. on Friday the eleventh.

'White-haired Reginald Bell travelling first class from Trivandrum arrived in Colombo twelve hours later—6 p.m. on Friday. His daughter was murdered that night.

'Mr Bell, or Belladonna if you prefer, could not have escaped detection without an associate—someone who has not come forward even in light of Dorothy's murder.'

He glanced at Bell, who was shaking his head.

'There is proof of the existence of the associate because Mr Bell lists his traveller's cheques. When he cashes one, he notes the date and place he cashed the cheque and the rate he received. That list is in his body belt right now.

'On Friday Mr Bell converted £500 into Sri Lankan rupees at the Hong Kong Shanghai Bank—an apparent impossibility. He was not here during banking hours.

'There had to be someone who did the transaction for him—gave him the cash and deposited the cheque into his or her own account. Mr Bell did not write down that associate's name for the same reason he did not mention him to the police. He wanted their relationship to remain secret. Instead he wrote HSBC.

'Why the secrecy? Why also was Mr Bell travelling on an illegal passport? Why was the return trip to Trivandrum even necessary? He could have come on the tenth and stayed on.

'The answers are that Mr Bell wanted to leave no evidence that he had been here because he planned to steal Padmani's Blood, and he thought there was an excellent chance Dorothy already had the stone. If she had the stone, it was an incredible chance for Mr Bell to make more than ten million untraceable dollars.

'Ali tells me some collectors display their treasures only to a few trusted friends. Mr Bell lined up such a buyer, maybe more than one, who would buy Padmani for a special price on the understanding that there would be no proof of sale. If he could not steal Padmani, he planned to return to his original plan, re-enter Colombo on Friday, buy the stone and sell it for a good profit.'

He made a strategic pause and sipped from his water glass. Maggie gave a small smile. Emma too was listening intently.

'That was the plan. What actually happened on the tenth night was that Mr Bell, in his Harry Belladonna outfit, was driven by his accomplice to this hotel, got into Dorothy's room and started looking for Padmani. Dorothy walked in. There was a fight. Mr Perera confirms that the room was in a mess the following morning. Lamp broken. Liquor spilled. Sheets on the floor.

'Dorothy was a strong young woman, but Mr Bell is in remarkable condition for his age. In any physical confrontation she might put up a fight, but he would win. He probably tied her up while he completed the search. I believe he then raped her, for the maid says the sheets were bloody. It was not unusual for Mr Bell to rape her. He had been doing it for years. Satisfied that the stone was not there, he then left and once again, as had happened since she was a teenager, Dorothy was left powerless to complain.

'In Trivandrum he cashed a £100 travellers' cheque at a Thomas Cook office, so we know he was there. He returned to Colombo looking like the man we see here and was again met by his accomplice. He did not expect Dorothy to meet him as he told the police and me. There was no tout—no taxi ride.'

Bell said icily, 'I will take you to court for this, vander Marten.'

'No, you won't,' said Michael Blue. 'Clive's got the general gist. Dor was in her room that Thursday evening. Reggie called from the lobby to say he'd taken an earlier plane. He suggested he come up for a drink, and she let him in. She was at the fridge when he came up behind her and pinned her arms. He tied them, put her on the bed and tied her feet. He then searched the room, she said, like a mad man—threw things around—but of course Padmani's Blood was not there. I phoned while he was at it, but she couldn't answer, so I left a message at the desk for her to call me when she came in. There was rape—all that. She got to my house at three and told me what he'd done.'

CV said in astonishment. 'Thank you, Michael. Was Mr Bell in disguise when she let him in?'

'She didn't recognize him at first—he said, "How do you like my new look?" The brown wig fell off when he was doing his thing. He put it on again before he left. She didn't tell me there was blood, but then she wouldn't have.'

There was a rasping from the throat of Millie Balasingham—no one else made a sound. CV touched his aunt's head because she was mopping her eyes. Bell was smiling slightly. There was nothing to do but press on.

'The sale of Padmani's Blood was the first time that Dorothy was going to be the middleman between Mr Bell and a client of her own on a substantial deal. He didn't know that Dorothy could have pocketed the whole enchilada—that the owner had already offered her Padmani's Blood as a gift.'

He stopped speaking abruptly for the missing piece had fallen into place right, as it were, out of his own mouth. He wanted to laugh to tell them about it, even as he knew he must not.

Bell was saying. 'No one would give away a thousand-carat ruby.'

'On Monday, Uncle, the recent owner of Padmani's Blood told me he did. She refused to accept it. When she was seventeen, she had saved the life of Uncle's grandson, and he had been trying to reward her ever since. But, as most of us here know, Dorothy never took a penny from those she got kindness from—even as she mercilessly, ruthlessly milked those who hurt her—a revengeful flaw in her nature that, in the end, killed her. Didn't it Mr Bell?'

He caught Mahmoud's eye, and the other man had the grace to look troubled. He knew that Bundy must be doing a lot of reassessing of Dorothy too for turning his own offer down.

Bell said, 'You've all been taken in! Do you think I gave you £10,000 to find Dot's murderer thinking I could be faced with this kind of debacle. False passports! Disguises! Rape! Theft!'

'No more interruptions,' said Teddy. 'Go on Clive.'

So he told them about Dorothy's last evening—the dinner with Michael, the walk down to Bundy's building, the arrival of Bell and then Uncle, the telephone calls in code and how Padmani finally changed hands.

'Dorothy was now alone with Mr Bell, and she signalled to Michael who was outside that the sale had gone through and that he should leave. However, she had not forgiven Mr Bell for wanting to steal Padmani's Blood or for that final attack on her body. She knew it was his chance to bring her back under his protection—his control. Mr Bell knew nothing of Uncle's affection for Dorothy. He thought that faced with a $13,000,000 loss, she would have asked him for help. He would have agreed on his own terms.

'That's what I meant when I said I'd seen the star! She decided to pay him back in kind—to take the star ruby from him—to put him in the same position as he had tried to put her the previous evening. It was the reason she had chosen a remote building for the sale. It would have been almost impossible to pull the same scam some place else, like in a hotel.

'There she was alone with Mr Bell, and Dorothy threw Padmani's Blood out of the window.' He stopped a moment to choose his words carefully. 'In anger Mr Bell ran his knife into her back, and the ruby has not been seen since.

'One minute Mr Bell was the owner of one of the most beautiful gems in the world, and in the next he was a man with a

$13,000,000 loss that could bankrupt him. But he killed her, because in that moment he realized she was free of him at last. He was an expert with a knife, so he made a thrust she would not recover from, and he left her there. You said to me, Michael, that your father would never have killed Dorothy because he loved her, because without her, there would be nothing. But I bet it was, "Now she'll always be mine," and that even now he feels he has taken her from you. She is his.'

The sadness in the room was like a fog. Faces that had been tranquil minutes ago were now twisted, and it was as if ten years had passed and aged them all. Jeffrey's thin face was like a death mask. Maggie had become angular as a stick insect. Emma was hunched. Millie bovine. Mahmoud decadent. He wondered if Bundy was still smiling, but his face was turned away. The two who had not changed were Michael and his father. Their faces had frozen.

Michael cleared his throat. 'Bundy arrived to lock up, found Dorothy's body and panicked. Fearing that he would be implicated, he just wanted to get rid of it and took it to the Pettah. Isn't that right, Bundy?'

Bundy said, 'I didn't know anything about a ruby. That morning Dorothy called and asked me if she could borrow my building from ten-thirty to about eleven-thirty that night. I told her the last time I let Michael have the key he'd lost it, and I'd had to have the lock changed. So I said I'd leave the door unlocked from ten-thirty. I was at home till eleven forty-five and then drove to the Fort with one of the houseboys. We found her lying there dead. I thought Michael or one of his friends had killed her. We took her body into the Pettah, then we returned and washed the blood from the floor.

'The next morning Mr Bell phoned and asked me about a seventy-carat cornflower blue sapphire I had spoken of to Dorothy. He said she'd been found dead in the Pettah and that he was finding it difficult to sit around idle. Perhaps looking at that

Murder in the Pettah

gem would distract him. I was feeling very bad about what I'd done and decided to tell him about it. I went to the hotel and confessed everything. I thought he'd turn me in and was prepared for that. He did not even get angry. He told me to leave things as they were—it was not important who moved her body but who had killed her.'

Bundy still managed to smile. His soft hands played with his empty champagne glass and then pushed it away.

'I didn't know he'd been in the building, but he took it for granted that I did. He said he'd left her waiting for a taxi. She'd insisted that he leave. He said, "She must have been killed by the taxi driver." Then he said that if I told anyone he had been there, he'd say he'd left her with me alive. I was shocked at how it had turned around—now suddenly I was to be accused of murder.

'Later in the week, I went to tell him that an Indian had bought the sapphire. He said he'd be leaving as soon as the police had dropped the case. I said, "Before you go perhaps you should get someone to find out who did it." I thought, if it were my child I would want to know.' Bundy struck the table with his fist. 'I'm sorry, Clive.'

'But Mr Bell hired me, hoping I'd learn the whereabouts—or should I say the thereabouts?—of Padmani not his daughter's killer. As the police had not connected him with Dorothy's death, he thought I too would not. He just wanted the stone.

'But I already knew that there had been others around him killed the same way, and so I was always open to the idea that he had killed his daughter. That made no sense on one level, but from the first he had told me many many lies. I also didn't see how he could have done it without a Lankan accomplice.

'Until yesterday I presumed that person was Bundy, though to my knowledge, he's never demonstrated a streak of violence. His wife Millie's vehemence on that subject was impressive. She said she would be more capable of murder than he. So I thought Bundy only got rid of Dorothy's body and probably arranged for someone else to handle the bomb. Hold on, I'm going to put another tape into this machine so we don't run out suddenly.'

He did it slowly—again to give them time to think.

'We were talking about Bundy,' he said at last. 'I thought Mr Bell had some hold on Bundy, and I wasn't sure how tough that hold was—what Bundy would be prepared to do to protect his family and his family's name. It was Bundy who had lent me an office for my investigation, and when I checked it before moving in, I found everything we did there was being recorded elsewhere through a network setup.'

CV took the recorder into his hand now, the tape moved steadily. 'Everything anyone said in Bundy's office room was also to be recorded on this little voice-activated Panasonic.' He held it up. 'It picks up voices at twelve feet. Imagine that. American voices come across best.'

A glance around the room showed him he'd finally hit his target.

'Bundy knows my business is computers. Jerry-rigging a computer the way it was done seemed to me much like sprinkling curry powder in a kitchen and expecting a chef not to smell it. If he'd bugged the room, he'd have got an expert to set up something that didn't have *alert* written all over it.'

Millie now smiled at him.

Bundy said, 'Mr Bell borrowed my keys on Friday night before you saw the room because he wanted to see for himself what equipment you would be using. As he was paying your bills, I didn't even think of refusing.'

'Then he—or his accomplice—must have had the keys copied, and they got someone else to mess with the computer and put a tape recorder into the drawer. I smelt the curry powder and had a big break. CID officer Steven Ranasinghe noticed that an old tape had been used in the voice-activated recorder, and as I had turned it off when I found it, if there had been voices on it, they would not have been erased.' CV pulled out that duplicate tape from under the stack.

He said, 'On this tape, Mr Perera, we heard you talking loud and clear about bugging the office. Only then did I know you were the accomplice.'

'No!' Perera frowned.

'A voice match can be made. After finding Mr Bell's accomplice everything fell into place. You were downstairs in Bundy's building while the sale of Padmani was taking place. It was your employee Raja who acted as Mr Bell's bodyguard. It was you who masterminded the plot that ended in the killing of Julia—you killed her yourself—not because you thought she was Emma, but because she was an eyewitness to your presence in Emma's house as you looked for Padmani's Blood. It was you who couldn't resist performing a final despicable action—but one that should place you on the scene for the inside of her mouth was not burnt. The bomb, as Dr Soong guessed, was to have warned Emma. Later you would have found a way to tell her "Get me that ruby, or I'll kill you—I've demonstrated how easily I can." You warned Mr Bell we were going to search his room, which is why we didn't find the knife, his other passports—anything that could incriminate him the first time.

'You were looking for Padmani's Blood for yourself by now. When Julia died, Mr Bell was genuinely surprised. You were much clumsier than he would have allowed you to be. He wisely sat back and gave me nothing to work with. You couldn't sit still—the poisoning—sending Raja to hang around once we'd cut off your access to the office. Raja has admitted he told you where you could get a bomb made. On your instructions, he followed Emma and me all Saturday evening with a mobile phone so you could stop your search and blow up the place if she headed home.'

Perera said, 'Superintendent Senaratne, that boy Raja is fanciful. He will say anything.'

But CV was on a roll. 'The second time we searched Mr Bell's room, we got lucky. We called to get your cooperation again, but you were out. So Jeff went in and photographed the three passports, the brown wig, the two identical knives—Reggie's murder weapon and Dorothy's, which he had denied finding. Jeff found the address book she carried in her purse. Photos of what he found are in this envelope, and while we've been here, that room has been searched by the police. It will be your account at the Hong Kong Bank into which the travellers' cheque was paid, Mr Perera. It's been a long so-called friendship, hasn't it? Matched sociopaths—my opinion, of course.'

He looked at his notes. 'I think that ties it up.'

Reggie's Story

There was silence as no one knew what to do, but before CV could speak again, Bell began. He was sitting back and did not sound troubled. He said in a measured, even kindly, voice.

'This fiasco has gone on long enough. It is true I killed my daughter, Dorothy, and I have no doubt someone will be able to prove that. The knife I used is upstairs, as you say, CV. But it was not mine I used, but hers. You are right too that I have known, almost from the time of her birth, that I was not her biological father. She was my daughter in every other sense—I brought her up. Her mother didn't want a full-time child and eventually didn't want her at all. But what you don't know is that while I adored my daughter, yes, I will call her my daughter, she was not the angel you describe. She fooled you all. I was the only one she couldn't fool, and as the years passed, that began to enrage her, and she was a dangerous girl to enrage.

'It is true too that I intercepted—changed—the DNA findings from Childers'. I did it because I didn't want her destroying you, Michael. I knew what she would do to you—not just turn you against me—that was only part of it. She would make you a part of her own ugly inner life. One day you'd find yourself in jail or dead, and it would be too late to know it was her hand that did it. I didn't want you to marry an apple that was rotten to the very core.

'CV talks as if I abandoned you, Michael, but Frances will tell you it was she who turned me down. We weren't right for each other, but for a while we had a wonderful time, and out of it came you. Isn't that true, Frances? We decided together that I would get out of your life, but I gave you enough—more than I could afford then—to see you through a few years. You've often told me I acted well, Frances. You used the money to start your business—it supported you both.'

Her ravaged face looked at him in consternation.

'Wasn't it you who kept Michael from me?' he persisted. 'Did I not ask to see him? Did you not refuse?'

'I didn't want you to take him away.'

'I did not intend to take him away.'

Michael Blue was staring at Bell, and it was difficult to guess with what emotion. CV had not expected Bell to admit to the killing of Dorothy or to discuss his role as father to both children. He tried to see into the mind of the person speaking the words.

Bell continued evenly, 'Dorothy and I were both experts with a knife. We had learned how to throw knives from my father the way other children learn to throw darts or play snooker. My father was so skilled that I would put my hand against a wall with the fingers open and he would throw his knife between two fingers and never miss. He showed us how to kill a man with one knife thrust, how to kill a wild animal if it attacks, how to hit a swinging rope. I never thought I would use a knife to kill, but it gave me confidence to know I could protect myself, and so I carried the knife he gave me sometimes. Dot did the same.

'I did not kill those four men. She did. First Yarrow, who

had worked for us. I thought it was a coincidence that a man I knew should have died the way my father had demonstrated on a skeleton—how a knife thrust into the left side of the body should go through the heart. Then there was Crewel. I confronted Dorothy. She did not deny it. She said I should be grateful because both men had been heard talking in a bar about us. I think she had told Charles Yarrow stories when he worked for me; she certainly told them to her mother. But when she heard Yarrow was repeating them, she decided he was dangerous. She said to me, "I don't mind your going to prison, but what will happen to me?" Dot killed Iglesias—she admitted to that one too; he had upset her by preferring another woman. She killed Vincent Belli because he was unfaithful to her. She told me that laughing. She said our names were so similar it had been like killing me.'

'Why, then, did you use his name?' CV asked.

'I didn't know, until some months after he died, that Belladonna had been the name of his family. I chose Belladonna because a woman friend once called me that. She called me Belladonna—night killer—I think as a compliment. You can see how things get twisted.' He smiled very slightly.

No one else did.

'Why the false passports?'

'Because you can't go into a hotel without showing identification. But it was nothing to do with Dorothy.

'I had begun to see the real evil in Dorothy much earlier. She started lying before she was three. She'd say, "Daddy smacked me," to get sympathy. Much later there were the stories of rape, which Michael believed. When her mother remarried, Dot was a teenager and decided to live with her. She had blossomed but by now was accusing others of rape too. When she came home, she told me her stepfather raped her. She told them similar stories about me.

'One morning, when she was thirteen, I woke to find her in

my bed, her hands on my genitals. I was half asleep and woke from a dream that her action had caused. I am not proud that I didn't throw her out. I even rationalized later that, as she was not related to me, there was no incest, and she looked seventeen or eighteen at that time. It never happened again, but she never let me forget it. Knowing that she had roused me sexually gave her a sense of power over me. I did not know what to do. I suggested therapy. She refused to go. I am afraid I just gave up and hoped she would fall in love, marry and settle down. Instead she went hunting for rich men. She'd find one, milk him and then move to another.'

He sat back in his chair and shook his head ruefully. Then he looked around—meeting every eye. He still did not show the emotion one would have expected from this horror tale.

CV took a sip from his coffee cup and found the dregs were cold. He cleared his throat. 'Are you through, Mr Bell?'

'No. There is much more, for there was her death,' Bell continued. 'I had been covering up for her and that continued until the day she died. I arrived in Colombo on Thursday as I had an appointment in Trivandrum the next day—one not related to Padmani's Blood, as you thought. I met a woman friend. Mr Perera drove me to the hotel from the airport, and I told him I had a meeting the following evening in Colombo and would prefer others not to know I was already here. Dorothy was expecting me, I went to her room, and she let me in. She was pleasant and hospitable. She ordered something to eat. We drank together. I had to be at the airport at 3 a.m. to take the six o'clock plane. She offered to take me there. I told her Mr Perera was doing it, said goodbye and, "See you in the evening." If something ugly happened in that room, it happened after I left it. She probably cut herself—put the blood on the sheets, made it look as if we'd had a fight. She'd done it before.'

'I don't believe you!' shouted Emma.

'Em,' said CV, 'we must let him tell his story. He listened to mine.'

She looked at him in horror. No one else spoke. Emma began to scream at them. 'Don't listen to him,' she moaned. 'It isn't true. She wasn't like that. How can you listen to him, Clive? Tell him to stop! She wasn't like that at all. Dot would never have killed anyone. Tell them Michael! Tell them Michael!'

But CV's eyes did not move from Bell now. Michael too seemed frozen.

'Oh, she deceived everyone,' Bell was saying. 'She charmed you all—every person she met.'

'I'm not going to listen to you one more moment. If you don't stop him, Clive, I'll never talk to you again. Never!'

Emma rose from her seat tentatively as if hoping to be stopped, but still CV did not move and did not look at her. She ran to the door, found it locked and started pounding on it. Teddy rose, looked back at CV who nodded, then spoke through the door to the policeman outside. The door was opened, and Emma was gone.

Bell said to CV, 'So you believe me! It isn't nice, but it's true. Dot was a tramp.'

'She seemed a bit loose the first time I saw her,' CV said and thought of her as she had left him, without looking back. 'It was that way she had of leading you on.'

'Yes. That way of laughing at you! One minute you'd kiss her feet if it would make her happy, the next she'd kick you in the mouth.'

'You didn't see her again that night?'

'Not that night. I went to Kerala.'

'And Mr Perera?'

'It is true that LL Perera has been my associate. But our business was never murder. I returned to Colombo, and on Friday night the sale went as planned. Mr Perera's man left the room. I had intended to talk to Dor and suggest now that things

Murder in the Pettah

were working between us why not continue that way—an ordinary father-and-daughter relationship. But she had Padmani's Blood in her hand, and she began to laugh and tease that I would never see it again. I asked her to give it to me. Then without warning she threw it out of the window. She said, "You'll never have it now." But when she turned back, she was a frightening sight, and she had her knife in her hand. She came at me, and I am not quite sure what happened except I was now protecting my life—I knew my daughter was going to kill me, and I anticipated the move, caught her wrist and wrenched the knife away. She went for it, and I tried to keep it from her, then she suddenly fell, and I saw I had plunged the knife in her back. Only then I realized I had killed her. I had instinctively done what my father had taught me to do to protect myself. She was dying. I sat beside her and held her hand until she died—as I stood up Mr Perera and his boy Raja came in.

'I was in shock and told LL what had happened. He suggested we look for the stone. I suppose I agreed. I hadn't taken in her death yet. I was relieved to be alive. We didn't find the ruby outside and weren't sure what to do. So we left. We talked about what we should do, and he—I agreed, I am afraid—suggested that we not tell the police—it seemed that there was nothing to gain by telling them. I was letting him think for me. I said I wanted a burial for my daughter. He suggested we have it at sea. But when he sent someone to pick up Dorothy's body, it was gone. He came to my room before dawn and told me that.

'You are right, CV, I wanted you to find that stone. Thirteen million is a lot to lose and, although I insured Padmani's Blood from the moment of sale, I obviously did not want an inquiry.

'I decided I would have to hire someone to see what happened to it and asked Mr Balasingham for an investigator. He came up with your name. I didn't tell him I was looking for Padmani's Blood, because if the wrong person got to it, I realized

I might never see it again. I did not know that he had decided to get to it first.

'I remembered you from the funeral service, and of course Maggie made quite an impression on me that day. I intended telling you about the loss of the stone, but it became obvious you would never have taken a job just to find it, so I emphasized it was Dot's killer I was looking for. You, Maggie and your aunt seemed intrigued by the murder.

'I did not commit a murder. I defended myself. There was nothing whatever to connect me with the room that night except Mr Perera, who I knew would not talk if the price was right. Balasingham believed a thief had killed Dot. Michael had distanced himself from me and had made up some story about her going to the Oberoi—I think to take suspicion off himself. Superintendent Senaratne also seemed convinced Dot had been killed by a stranger. I did not know the man who sold me the stone. I was sure he would not say he had been there. He had his money. As the man who accompanied him had not come forward. I didn't worry.' He sighed.

'But why did you need Emma dead? Did you think she had Padmani?' CV asked him.

Reggie's eyes were looking directly into his and suddenly became as flat and empty as a dead man's. He said with bare movement to his lips. 'She took Padmani's Blood from me and threw it out of the window. I should have killed her little friend—another tart—Emma, who took it, but I didn't. She came on to me, you know, that Emma. She came on to me in my hotel room. She touched me with her hands. I said to her, "Dot, why did you do that?"'

CV did not know which girl he was talking about now.

'She turned to look at me, and I saw her smile—how she liked to mock me. She turned her back, and leaned down and waved because she'd won. She always thought she'd win. But she couldn't win against me. I'm her father. I had my knife in my hand, and I threw it.'

Michael moved so fast that they were all caught by surprise. He was on the table and running across it as china and glass spilled their contents in every direction and silverware fell to the floor.

The reaction of three ageing athletes, Mahmoud, Ali and CV, was instinctive, and they all rolled over the table in front of them. The policemen had pulled their guns and were also moving forward. It was, however, Millie Balasingham who got there first. She reached Michael and saved his life by pulling a leg from under him. He crashed head first towards the floor, and Ali was somehow there to break the fall. Then, without so much as an interruption in the flow of her run, Millie threw herself across the table on to Reginald Bell with such speed that he fell backwards across his chair. When the others reached them, Mahmoud had the knife, and she had her foot on the hand Bell had used to kill his daughter.

'Jesus, Bundy,' CV heard his voice say. 'What a woman!'

'He threatened to kill my husband,' Millie turned on them and screamed. 'He wanted Bundy to die for his own dirty crimes,' she looked around as if looking for someone else to take on. Bundy went slowly to her and put his arm around her, and she flung hers around him. 'As if you haven't had enough troubles,' she told him stroking his head as though he were a child she'd just saved from drowning. 'So many troubles. I could have lost you.'

'Shhh,' Bundy replied, 'it's over.'

After the Storm

Reginald Bell and LL Perera were arrested and taken away. It had all been done quickly and quietly like the sweeping aside of a couple of dead rats. Teddy stayed. The others were trying to act as if nothing had happened. CV couldn't help wondering how Dorothy would have reacted. He looked at her picture still on the table and winked, but it didn't wink back.

Maud was strolling around looking at the landscapes on the wall. CV went to her, 'You all right, Auntie?'

'Yes, dear, wasn't it exciting? I wonder where these paintings have come from. I think I've seen them all before.'

'They do have that effect.'

'You're such a clever boy to have solved the murders.'

He put his arm around her. 'And I'm passing the rumour I did it all alone too.'

She said, 'Did I help at all?'

'You surely did. Do you remember saying that someone must be telling a whopper?'

'No.'

'Well you did, and it changed my focus. After that I started looking for whoppers.'

'Where's Emma?' she took his arm.

He led her to her chair. 'I don't know. One of Teddy's men is with her. Would you like Joseph to take you home now?'

Teddy joined them and took him into the other room. 'I didn't think you could pull it off, but you have good instincts.'

'I've lost my girl, and you talk about good instincts?'

'Nora says you haven't, and Nora is never wrong on women.'

'I had to stay,' CV said needing to be forgiven. 'He was beginning to crack.'

'I had begun to wonder if we had all been wrong and if Dorothy had really been a split personality. Only when he started calling Emma a tart did I know you had been right all along. You were always so sure. Why?'

'He was guilty of so much that he had to be guilty of the whole thing.'

'How is it that a man like you was so taken with a Dorothy Bell?'

'I admire her for being there when needed and not whining when things went wrong. No matter what happened or how others perceived her, she'd examined all her options, her very limited options, and she'd made her choices. How cleanly she made those choices too. She was not going to hang her head. That was why powerful men like Uncle were mesmerized. She made them feel they too could be incorruptible. I better shut up. I need to settle down. Will Bell get off?'

'The wealthy often do. Raja is our chief witness. What happens if he says we tortured a story out of him? Perera will have a good lawyer and someone will try to arrange that Raja washes up in the surf one day. So I will keep Raja alive to eventually accuse me of brutality.

'Mr Bell has broken civil laws, so we'll probably send him to England to face those charges if he gets off here: the forged passport—possibly some income tax evasion. Then there are those other murders. He won't walk free from them all but he may from some.'

'Shit.'

'As you say. I've been caught flat-footed all along—too busy to deal with any of my cases properly. I'm going to have to change that.'

'Upgrade your team.'

'I like your American expressions.'

His aunt had fallen asleep in her chair at the table, and the others sat down again, moving so they could be closer to each other.

'I'll speed it up,' he said. 'Thank you for coming here today. You know now that it is not my aunt's birthday, and she has asked that I thank you for your kind gifts. Please take them home and enjoy them yourselves. Now for the questions. It may not be easy for us to meet like this again—all at once—so let's tie up loose ends.'

'Is Mr Bell insane? asked Millie.

'In my opinion. His madness revolves around his sexuality— as opposed to general brutish behaviour. Such men have a long history of minor offences before they begin to kill. They find themselves becoming impotent and blame the women. I'm speaking from memory of articles I've read. It will be interesting to hear the professional opinions.'

Maggie said, 'Funny that he pulled a knife in broad daylight when we thought he only does it at night.'

'This time he really was defending himself,' Teddy said.

'Did you believe his story?' his wife asked. 'Even for a second, did you?'

'I did. Clive didn't.'

'Because I knew, if it was me, I'd have a good story waiting. I didn't know what he'd cook up, but he'd had time for two weeks to have cooked up something plausible. He'll have time to tighten that story to take care of the details he couldn't explain today.'

Maggie said, 'Reggie didn't choose the name Belladonna because some woman called him that. That's male fantasy. Women say things like, "You have nice shoulders", or "That never happened to me with another man".'

Ali asked, 'Is that what you say?'

'If you'll come off your high horse, you'll find out.'

'Does anyone think Mr Perera did not kill Julia?' asked Teddy.

No one replied.

'How did you get into Bell's room without a key?' the superintendent asked Jeff.

'I knocked at the door, and Monsieur Bell invited me in. He showed me around and invited me to take the pictures of his knives, passports and wigs.' Jeff's eyes slid over to Mo who had joined them and was bowing his solemn argement. 'Mohideen was a witness.'

'Meeting's over,' said Teddy. 'Before I arrest a few more of you.'

CV woke his aunt and helped her to her feet. Mahmoud shook their hands and said, 'You give such wonderful birthday parties, Miss vander Marten, let's have another before I leave on Saturday?'

'May I bring Julia's parents? They're my guests.'

'You may bring the world, but we will go to another hotel. Beauty was magnificent. What grandchildren I would have had!'

Maggie said she would be going back with Ali and kissed CV's cheek. 'Don't you worry,' she told him.

'I couldn't help Emma,' he said. 'I couldn't let him go.'

'I know.'

As they waited for Joseph in the Magnette, Jeff brought the painting of Dorothy to CV and said, 'Michael wants you to have this.'

Not Going Home

Aunt Maud fell asleep in the car. When they reached the house, they helped her to the door and handed her over to Amily.

'When Auntie wakes, tell her I don't know when I'll be back. Please tell Mr and Mrs Ware I'll see them as soon as I can,' he said.

'Where are you going?' Amily scowled at him with intensity.

'I don't know.'

He asked Joseph to drop him in Hospital Street.

It seemed a long time since he had meandered in the Fort—and he first went down for a daylight view of the building in which Dorothy had been killed. There were people around now, and each had something to sell him. 'Not today. Not today,' he said. He had a sense of making a pilgrimage to Dorothy and stood outside the building—reluctant to turn away.

To his surprise, the front door opened, and Bundy and Millie came out. They were as surprised to see him.

Bundy chuckled. 'Too late. Padmani's Blood isn't here. We've looked.'

'I guessed she wouldn't be.'

'Then why are you here?'

'Because this is where I should be. If you'd found the stone, would you have given it back to Bell?'

'She's part of our heritage,' Millie said. 'Ali Sharif asked us to look for her because she mustn't leave the country again—she was stolen from here in the first place.'

'There's a thought! What about the curse? You don't think we have enough troubles without a dangerous stone like that setting off more bombs?'

'You're always laughing at me,' she pouted.

'With you. May I go inside?'

'Why?'

Bundy said, 'Millie, give the man what he wants. He saved my life.'

Upstairs he leaned out of the window as Dorothy had done. and then spun around quickly.

Bundy said, 'I did the same. I was looking out and then remembered she hadn't expected a knife in her back.'

CV leaned out again and imagined he was Dorothy waving to Michael who, in the dark, she may not have been able to see except as a shadow. A peek to see he was there, then, if the stone wasn't still on the table, she would have asked Bell if she could see it one last time. She took it in her hand and tossed it out. Michael caught it and was away, and she began laughing. Michael—the least materialistic of men—the least violent—had unknowingly left her laughing with a knife in her back.

Perhaps she didn't realize what had happened immediately. Then she tried to save herself and crawled away. Reggie karate-chopped her behind the ear and gave her the bruise. Perhaps he just couldn't watch those eyes he loved lose their sparkle, but she twisted around. Those blue eyes would have been on his as long as she could focus them. Even if she hadn't had the strength to speak, he heard her voice in his mind: 'You've lost me forever.'

Damn you, Dorothy.

Millie was beside him now, and she said, 'Come on, Clive, it's no good. You can't undo what's done.' He felt Bundy's arm across his shoulders.

He said without shame at his tears, 'Let's get out of here.'

Before they left the building, he once again looked out of the window on to the narrow path lined by plants pale from lack of sunlight and waiting for rain to revive them.

Outside he said, 'I need to keep moving. If you'd like to join me, I think I'll move towards the GOH. How about tea there?'

Millie strode ahead, and they ambled after her. Their childhood memories of the Fort included going to Millers and Cargills with their mothers and being bought potato toffee to keep them quiet. In Millers, Bundy bought potato toffee, pumpkin preserve and devilled cashew nuts from a girl surrounded by bottles, bags and boxes of the stuff.

CV thought of Emma. 'I envy you both,' he said.

Millie said, 'Emma needs a good slap.'

'No, she's had a terrible time.'

'Anyone can be nice when she's not having a terrible time. She needs a good slap.'

After tea they offered to drop him off at home and Millie went back to get their car. When he saw it his stomach churned for it was in this dark blue Toyota Starlet that Dorothy's body had been driven to the Pettah.

'I'm going to see the man who saw you leave her on Second Cross Street,' he told Bundy. 'I promised I'd tell him who did it, and I think I'll do that now. Why don't you come along?

'Did he watch the whole thing that night?'
'Yes.'
'You're right. I must come.' Bundy came right to the point with Mr Solomon. 'I am not proud of what I did that night. I am sorry there was a witness to know how badly I behaved.'

'Why did you hate Dorothy Bell?' He was sensitive enough not to mention the gesture Mr Solomon had so graphically described.

Bundy replied simply, 'I misjudged her.'

'Now you have said that, I am happier. But tell me, sir, do you always carry a bag with holes to put over your head?'

'Those awful bags. I started to choke. Millie had removable covers on the front seats. So we took those off, cut them short and made holes in them and hung the rest over the licence plates.'

Millie said, 'And the next day he told me that someone had stolen my seat covers! I had an alarm clock in the glove compartment and tools under the front seat and I said, "What kind of a thief steals seat covers and leaves tools and clocks? This country is going mad."'

'When did you know it was Bundy who found Dorothy's body?' CV asked her after that revelation.

'When you showed me that drawing. But I knew he hadn't killed her. He'd been very depressed recently, but I didn't connect him with Dorothy Bell. I thought he'd lost money.'

When they left Mr Solomon's, CV considered his options and went to Michael's.

Their meeting was almost a duplicate of the first time they had spoken. Michael was coming up the road just as CV arrived, and Sweetie yelped from behind the gate. When he drew close, the younger man put his arm around CV's shoulder. All signs of his numbness at the hotel just a couple of hours ago had gone, and he said, 'Welcome to my humble abode, honourable brother.'

Michael and CV Commune

There were no sleeping bodies, and CV couldn't resist saying, 'Something is missing underfoot.'

Michael said, 'Even Jeff is missing underfoot. Being alone didn't help, so I went down to the sea. That didn't help either. When I saw you, I was relieved.'

'I too need company. Do you have beer?'

He wandered off and returned with two open bottles. CV was already stretched out on a long chair under the fan.

He wanted to rejoice that the case was over, that against the odds he pulled it off, cracked through to Reggie's core of madness.

'If Emma hadn't made that scene, it may not have happened,' he said. 'We might be muddling along like yesterday. When she jumped to Dorothy's defence and I didn't respond, he thought I was on his side—believing him—not believing her. It had become just us two. Which is why he forgot about you. Which is why he forgot to watch you.'

'Oh yes.'

'Michael, what did you do with Padmani's Blood?' CV asked. 'That is, what will you do with her now?'

'When did you know I had her?'

'At lunch when I said I saw the star. Suddenly, I saw there was one way she could make him choke on his own vomit. She could steal back the star. Her revenge would become ecstasy, and there was only one person she'd trust with it—you.'

'I never could say no to her. It was so easy to say yes to each other, so we did it every time. It came right into my hand, and I blew her a kiss and lost her. If you want it, take it.'

'No.'

'Frightened of the curse?'

'Not at all.'

'Well, then break the ball and take it. It is very beautiful. I have never seen a more beautiful inanimate thing.'

He got to his feet and beckoned. 'I could hardly call up Daddy Li and ask what temperature a star ruby could take because I wanted to bake one inside clay—so the piece is still unfired.' He stood above the life-sized terracotta of his dog with her hindquarters raised, her front paws on either side of a ball for which Bell had given $13,000,000 and Dorothy's life.

CV said, 'Let Sweetie play with her toy a little longer.'

Michael stroked the clay. 'You're right. What's the hurry?'

They walked into the darkened garden, and he said, 'Stay the night. You don't have to go back. You can have Jeff's bed, and he can sleep with me. Will you rest with us for a few hours?'

'I'd like to.'

'Somebody left a bag of grass. Will you smoke with me?'

'I will.'

Chapter XI

Friday

Emma
Early Friday morning he woke to darkness and silence, realized he was in Jeff's bed and fell asleep again. This was the first day in a week that he hadn't reason to look at the time. The next time he woke, it was light, and there were voices. It was nine o'clock, and he began to listen to a conversation that was going on between Michael and Emma.

Emma!

She said, 'I don't believe you.'

Michael replied, 'There's no point in asking me questions and then saying you don't believe me.'

It was a Michael CV hadn't heard before. There was a harshness to the usually indolent voice.

Emma said, 'You lie when you feel like it, and I think you're lying now. We're all worried about him. I just want to know if he's all right.'

They were talking about him. He liked that.

'I just want to say I'm sorry.'

'Go home and look in the mirror and you'll feel better.'

She screamed, 'Stop saying things like that! If only he'd given me a chance to say sorry yesterday.'

Michael said, 'He's to blame again?'

CV knotted the sarong Michael had lent him and went to

the bathroom—this was too interesting to listen to with a full bladder. When he came out they were still talking about him, so he settled down to enjoy himself.

M: 'Clive practically licks your feet, and what has that got him? You walked out on him, Em, because you like to control others by showing them up as less saintly than yourself. Now you're sulking because you can't control me. You're so sweet and you pout and you cry. Clive's a big fool who'll make a nice rug at your feet. Leave him now when you've shown him what life with you will be like—and that's hell. Don't patch things up, because it will be patching up for the rest of your lives. Could you manage a whole month without once having to say, "I'm so sorry, Clive," and hearing, "No problem, Emma". Eventually, one of you will forget to say "I'm so sorry" or "No problem," and you'll break up. So why not break up now?'

E: 'I won't be like that.'

M: 'You were nasty to Maggie the first time you met her. How did she treat you? She was kind. Who were you to make a judgement on her? You're so spoilt.'

E: 'Clive gets angry too. He gets grumpy.'

M: 'And when he gets grumpy, he gives you an ultimatum and walks out?'

E: 'How could you all sit there and listen to Reggie saying that Dor was a murderess? You should have defended her. All of you just left me to do it. I was the only friend she had.'

M: 'It hurt her, Em, to have a knife put into her back—through her heart. How helpless she was as her life slipped away. And I was not there. She should have died in my arms, but she died at the feet of a man she hated. I was not there. Clive is not like us, you and me, he's like Dor. Daddy Li phoned me this morning and he said, "That CV is a male Dorothy. Do you see it, Michael?" I said, yes.'

Emma spoke so softly that CV had to press his head against the wall to hear her. 'It is true—what you said. I do think I'm

God's gift to the world. She never did, and he doesn't. I suppose I didn't love him enough to just be there for him yesterday. But I love him now.'

CV moved to the window, wishing now he hadn't heard any of it. He looked glumly across Michael's modest garden—at its trees and its bushes and its flowers moving in the sea breeze. At the gate, Joseph stood talking with the hangers-on whom Michael accepted around him. Then he saw Joseph stand aside and a man in uniform speak to him. Another policeman began to open the gate, and Teddy Senaratne leaned out of the back window of a black car that was being driven through.

Still bare except for the sarong, CV ran into the studio where Emma and Michael were talking, and he shouted, 'Teddy's here. We've got to get rid of it.' He looked around looking for the sculpture of Sweetie with the ball, but it was gone from its stand. It had been replaced by a block of clay. Sweetie herself began to leap at him yapping and whining, and he pushed her away. He yelled, 'Michael, move it! Move!'

Emma was saying, 'I didn't know you were here. Michael didn't tell me. Where were you? I . . .'

He ignored her and said to Michael, 'Where is it?'

Even as he spoke, he heard the car's tyres on the sand of the path outside.

Michael in his favourite chair hadn't moved. He shouted, 'Sit down, Clivo, it's all right.' When CV stopped mid-yell, he continued, 'I thought Auntie Maud might like my little model of Sweetie, so Joseph and Jeff have put it in the Magnette's trunk. Emma will take it home with her.'

Emma said, 'I'm so sorry, Clive . . . I . . .'

He took her wrist and led her on to the veranda where they nearly collided with Teddy and two policemen. 'Em, if you're ill, you're ill,' he said sternly. 'For God's sake go back to the house and take one of those pills women take. And tell Auntie I'll be there for lunch. Hi, Teddy, I drank too much last night and passed out.'

When they were out of earshot, he said tersely, 'Em. Take that sculpture of Sweetie, and hide it.' He pushed her out of the gate and strode back in. He was in time to hear Teddy completing his orders to his men to search the premises.

Michael still hadn't moved. He said, 'Emma'll be all right, Clive. Jeff is making you scrambled eggs. You'd better eat a lot, or you'll hurt his feelings. He says he had to take the money for the eggs out of your wallet, but he'll pay you back. I told him to cash Padmani's Blood, but he said he's lost the damned thing. Will you put that wet yellow cloth over the block of clay for me.'

'Jesus,' CV said, 'I thought the investigation was over. How are you Teddy?'

The policemen were going through the room, moving pictures, moving sculptures—all with great care.

Teddy said, 'I should have come the minute I realized Michael was standing outside the window and must have caught it. That's why you came here yesterday, isn't it? If I hadn't been so busy getting statements I'd have been here first. Why don't you tell Michael to give me the ruby? We're going to find it, and if he gives it to me now, I'll see there are no charges against him.'

'Tell him I don't have it, Clive.'

'You two must start talking directly to each other. He doesn't have it, Teddy.'

'We'll find it,' the policeman stopped midsentence. 'Did Emma take it with her?'

CV said, 'Teddy, Emma was wearing a dress the size of a handkerchief. She had rubber thongs on her feet. She had no bag. Where do you think she was carrying a ruby the size of an egg? I hope you don't think Michael would stoop to placing it where a doctor would have to remove it, and do you seriously think she'd allow such an assault on her person?'

'Something has been changed in this room. What is it?'

'New painting and three to a stack where there were four,' replied Michael.

At that moment, Sweetie decided to join Teddy and waddled down the steps.

He shouted: 'Where's the dog statue? The ball!'

'Ouch!' CV said softly.

The policeman hurried back tripping on the top step. 'Where's that statue of your dog, the one you made the day after Dorothy died?' he shouted at Michael.

'Shhh, or I'll get a headache. Statue? I reserve that term for dead saints. Sweetie doesn't qualify for a statue yet. I did a sculpture called *Sweetie with the Ball* and one called *Sweetie on her Back*. The one on her back is in the kitchen.'

'The ball!'

Michael went to the block of clay and uncovered it: 'Teddy, Michelangelo said that in every block of marble there is a figure waiting. In this block of clay is a *Sweetie with a Ball*. Sometimes I destroy a piece, reclaim the clay and then remake it.'

'Break it!'

Michael picked up a heavy knife on a stand and handed it to Teddy. 'Help yourself—it's fun slicing soft clay. Better than taking Valium.'

Teddy sliced the clay carefully. He finally placed the knife down. One of his policemen looked into the room, and he called him over. 'If you see clay like this, cut it up. The ruby may be inside. Put all the sculpture pieces in this house together in one place.'

'Yes, sir.'

'Where do you do the firing, Michael?'

'In Panadura. Also a place on the Ratnapura Road for the higher temperatures.'

'I'll need a list of what they have of yours.'

'They have nothing. You can see from the kiln charts Jeffrey keeps.'

'I'll need the addresses.'
'He has those too, or I could take you there.'
'What was Emma doing here?'
Michael said, 'She came to apologize to Clive.'
'Where did she go?' Teddy asked.
'Home,' said CV.
'Whose?'
CV said, 'Did she tell you, Michael?'
'No.'
'Nor me.'

Teddy shouted to one of his officers, 'Go to Miss vander Marten's house immediately. Don't let anyone near her car. Get everyone in the house into one room until I come. I'll send more men. Send one to Dr Soong's, and see if Miss van Eck is there.'

'Yes sir.'

'I don't think you broke up that sculpture, Michael, I think Padmani is still hidden in the cricket ball. You sent it out of here in the Magnette. Well, it won't go far.'

Teddy Gives Up

Teddy insisted on Jeff accompanying them to Bliss. He showed his displeasure by travelling alone with this chauffeur while they, all wearing shirts over sarongs, crammed into a narrow three-wheeler seat behind an old Tamil driver. They were in a giddy mood.

CV declared, 'How do I explain to him why a dog sculpture is in the upstairs toilet that drips, or is under Auntie's pillow, which doesn't? Can I be put in jail if I haven't seen the thing I stole?'

Michael made a noise like a rooster.

'His men will think you're one of those Red Cross buggers who've been running guns to the terrorists, and you'll be hung like a parrot.'

'If we were in the States,' CV told Michael, 'we'd call a

lawyer who'd say it's going to cost the police millions if they defile your valuable sculpture. Sweetie and her toy would have to be X-rayed. We could try that. As it's Sri Lanka, the X-ray machine will break down, which will give Aunt Maud a chance to crack the cricket ball and swallow the stone. Why do I suspect Emma has no talent for hiding rare gems?'

They arrived at his aunt's house still light-headed. There was no one to greet them at the gate or the door, which was opened by a policeman who told them sternly everyone, including the Wares, was in the front drawing room. There they found the family drinking leftover Dom Perignon while the household staff and a policeman watched with more ennui than envy.

'Good morning, darling boy,' called his aunt who was swinging to and fro energetically in a rocking chair he hadn't seen before. 'You must have some champagne. Emma says you fell asleep at Michael's. I'm sitting in Mr Mahmoud's birthday present. On my real birthday he's going to send me the pair. What shall I do with two old English rockers?'

'One's an upstairs rocker and the other a downstairs rocker,' he said kissing her. 'Teddy is here to land a grand theft charge on us.'

'What did you steal, darling boy?' Aunt Maud tried to bring her downstairs rocker to a standstill, and there was a collision as everyone tried to help.

'Nothing. He's picking on me,' CV told her.

There was an artificial gaiety as if they were bad actors in a bad sitcom. Ali and Maggie even sat holding hands. She caught CV's eye and winked, and he took that to mean that Ali was no longer playing hard to get.

The talk continued to sounds of policemen searching. CV avoided looking at Emma but finally caught her eye and gave a sheepish grin. To his surprise, she came up and said under her voice, 'I have a message for you.'

'I hope it's that you love me.'

'Yes. And one from Meechi's father.'

He put his hand over hers.

'Meechi's father says he is so glad he could help.'

He said carefully, 'Come again.'

Joseph was standing near Amily, and they went over to them. 'Meechi?' he asked the driver.

'He is a guard now.'

So Joseph had left the Sweetie sculpture at the cycle repair shop!

CV said to Michael, 'Fireworks are appropriate. Another glass of champagne, Mr Blue,' and he filled his glass. 'A toast to absent canines.'

'To absent canines!' shouted Jeff who hadn't missed a thing, and the Americans joined in looking confused.

Teddy had entered the room and stood at the door glaring. Michael said to him, 'We're toasting our friends, Teddy, and that includes you. You can search this house. You can X-ray our bodies. You can dig up the flower beds. What you're not going to do is find Padmani's Blood.'

Startled, Ali looked at them. 'What made you think it was here, Teddy?'

'Michael has it. Dorothy threw it to him. I'll find it. You can't hide a valuable stone like that forever.'

Maud said, 'You've been looking for that terrible ruby here, Teddy? I wouldn't have it on the premises. It has brought everyone bad luck. Look what it did to Dorothy and Julia.' Then she pursed her lips. 'I hope you're not like your grandfather, Teddy, always up the wrong spout. And if your men open the girls' drawers upstairs, I'll be angry.'

'As a matter of fact, I have never liked men opening my drawers even downstairs,' said Maggie and lifted her skirt.

'Maggie dear,' said her aunt, 'you must be careful when you dance. I can see your knickers.'

Gloria said, 'Fred, as I said before, I can see why Julia was so happy here.'

The End of the Story

Two weeks after his pretrial, Reginald Bell was washed up on a beach south of Colombo. He had been mutilated before dying, and a knife very similar to his own had been driven into his back. LL Perera also was never convicted of his part in both murders. He was poisoned while in prison. It was never discovered who was behind either killing.

Two main loose ends were easy to tie up. Reginald Bell's buyer for Padmani's Blood had been waiting for him in India. If he had been able to steal it from Dorothy, Reggie would have left Sri Lanka, delivered the stone when he was in Kerala on Friday morning and not returned. His use of 'Belladonna' as a name on the forged passport he sometimes travelled on was also understandable now because Dorothy had once loved a boy who had had that name. Reggie killed him and used the name himself—in his twisted mind, to become loved by her.

Dorothy Bell's death had brought certain lives together, and those people continued to feel her influence. They accepted the friendships that had emerged as their destiny.

Julia Ware did not just fade away either, though CV was to say to Michael that he had been considerably embarrassed that, having been shown an enormous quantity of snapshots by her parents after they were glued into Aunt Maud's scrapbook, he did not even remember her face.

Barely a year after their daughter's death the Wares leased a bungalow upcountry in Bandarawella and called it Bliss Junior. This was to bring much happiness to Maud. Attended by the Wares, Amily, Joseph and a large picnic basket, she shuttled in her Magnette between the two cities. In Bandarawella, Maud developed the garden she had always dreamed of—with gladioli, violets, dahlias and other flowers that could not handle the unrelenting heat of the lowlands. The dirt, grime and exhaust fumes of crowded Colombo was not always easy to return to, but, after two weeks, Gloria always started to miss her bridge and Fred got restless wondering if Bliss Junior was developing termites or fungus, and they'd move back.

By dying, Julia had thus changed her parents' lives for the better, and through them, Maud vander Marten's. From that first drive back from the airport CV had liked them, and it comforted him that his aunt would have such people around her for the rest of her life. Julia had left a fine legacy.

As for Maggie and Ali, there was the expected stir in the media when she bowed out of the fashion world. It wasn't an earth-shattering stir for, as she observed wryly, 'There's always a new face coming up, isn't there?'

There was one memory of Maggie in Sri Lanka that was to remain with CV. When he was depressed in the years to come, he would close his eyes and bring it to mind knowing that when he opened them he'd be smiling. Emma and he had gone down to Bentota on their second-last weekend before he returned to the States with her. Aunt Maud had been too tired to join them, and the Wares had decided to stay with her. It was to prove yet another holiday in which they checked out of a hotel soon after they checked in. Ali had phoned to say he wanted to take them on a very special trip.

Forty minutes later they were headed north in his Mercedes, and he was in an unusually lively mood. He told them they were going to one of his family properties where Maggie was waiting for them.

'I sense a reason for this particular day, for this particular trip,' CV said.

'Yes, of course, there is. Yesterday I saw something, and I wanted to show it to you both before you leave.'

The timing of their arrival was important, he told them, as they began climbing into the hills. 'We have to be there at four.'

CV said, 'Before we get there, Mr Sharif, what have you done with Padmani's Blood?'

Michael had once again tried to give CV the ruby saying that Dorothy would want him to have it. He didn't have to think to reply, 'I don't want the hassle.' Michael said he didn't want the hassle either. Emma too refused.

When Uncle Li heard there were no takers, he laughed noisily but refused to take it back. 'I'm not going to even sell it and give the money to the poor. I never want to touch it again.'

So Michael offered it to Ali, who said without hesitation, 'Thank you, I am honoured that you would entrust it to me. I'll take care of it.'

He now replied, 'My family has had a discussion, and it has been decided that very soon a very large star ruby will be found in a private gem mine, and it will be about the same weight as the unlucky Padmani's Blood, which is now in Iran, we have been told on the best authority. This one will be called the Crimson Star of Sri Lanka, and it will be placed on display where every Lankan may visit it but where our politicians and thieves will not be able to sticky-finger it away again.' He sounded very pleased with himself as he continued, 'A famous astrologer will provide a legend for the Crimson Star. All who see it will find much good luck coming to their households. If it is ever stolen, terrible things will happen to the thieves.'

'Wow. And who will know the truth?'

'No one.'

'Thank you for making me one of those.'

Emma said from the back seat, 'Thank you for me too.'

They were off the main road and had entered a tea estate

with a river down in a ravine on the left. At an open gate a man greeted Ali in Tamil, 'You are here.'

'I am here,' Ali replied.

The Mercedes took the hill easily and came to a stop around another turn. Ali led the way through the tea bushes and thin shade trees and stopped when they were standing on the verge of a hill where, on another slope, they saw a many-storeyed building like a hotel with two tennis courts, a big lawn and a house off to one side.

Ali said, 'That's the school for Muslim refugees I told you about. At 4 p.m. something happens. It's 4 p.m. now.'

Between them and the buildings was a slope covered with tea bushes except for a levelled clearing. On to it came Maggie dancing to a music they couldn't hear. She was in tights the colour of her brown body, which made her seem sexless—extra-terrestrial. Her head was covered by a red and yellow peaked cap.

She was moving like a bird: her long limbs lifting and falling, both awkward and graceful. Her arms began flapping.

Emma said, 'She's a stork. She's become a stork.'

'Today she is a stork,' said Ali. 'Tomorrow, who knows? And here come her chicks.'

Behind her, down the path stepped children, fourteen in all, copying her movements. They too were dressed in tights but theirs were off-white. Their tiny legs took careful reaching steps and the smaller ones got knotted, and they brought one another down but scrambled up as they moved into a circle—all slowly flapping, stepping and stretching.

CV said, 'I'm glad you brought us.'

Ali said of his wife, 'So beautiful, so strange, so kind and I cannot believe it—so mine. All of what you see around us is hers now. At last she understands I have no demands, no expectations. I want her with me doing whatever she wants to do. With my father's permission, I gave her the school. We'll continue to fund it through the foundation, but she will decide on the staff, the curriculum, the bed linen, the food.'

He turned to look at her again.

'But for how long?' he asked. 'How long will it take her to get bored with it?'

'Shit, Ali, she's always wanted lots and lots of children,' her cousin said. 'No way will old Maggo get bored with a kid. It's too late, man. Looks like you've got her pinned for life.'

At that moment Maggie turned and saw them. She shaded her eyes against the evening sun. Then she waved and must have been smiling her wide famous smile. Fourteen small hands shaded their eyes in an identical movement and fourteen hands waved. Then she turned, became an elephant and led the way around the circle one arm twisting before her as a trunk. Fourteen small elephants followed her, and round and round they went.

'It seems you're going to have a school with a strong emphasis on the arts,' said Maggie's cousin. 'But don't let them grow up computer illiterate.'

'Let's drive up to the house,' Ali said.